Remember Friend

Remember Friend

ELIZABETH WESTCOTT

KDP PUBLISHING

First published in the UK by Elizabeth Westcott/KDP 2018

A CIP catalogue for this book is available from the British Library

ISBN 978-1-7901363-8-4

9781790136384

Cover photography by Jenny Greaves

PROLOGUE

In November there were gladioli in the garden, tall and strong, as he had been.

There were scabious, too, she noticed, in the shade of the old lavender hedge, edged with brown and struggling to survive against the odds. They reminded her of Felix. It had all begun with his death.

Or had it...? There were graves to which she could take the flowers quite easily – even appropriately – and one where the first frost of winter would shudder the blooms overnight into a macabre adornment for the whining truth of its carved inscription. A tiny revenge!

She left the flowers where they were, on that crisp November day, as she passed by.

Chapter I

TRAVELLING HOPEFULLY

A few months after their arrival at Amsworth in 1955, Ruth was born, and once established in this chattering market town with its thriving local industries, obliging tradesmen and energetic citizens, Amelia quickly learnt all there was to know of her dual role as 'vicar's wife' and 'new mum'. Things happened at Amsworth. Never again was life to bubble with such vigorous activity. Nine years younger than her husband, Adam, Amelia, at twenty four, was full of idealism and enthusiasm. She threw herself into everything. A clergyman's wife, she decided, needed many attributes. Some she possessed, others she lacked, but by the end of her apprenticeship she was a reliable caterer (high-rise blocks of sandwiches and 'Martello Tower' heaps of sponge cakes), handy at tapestry (an 'inspiration' to hassock renovators), dexterous at lampshades (both with and without fringes and a popular selling line if made by the vicar's wife), better at flower arranging than the Guild ladies (thanks to a Constance Spry handbook and a garden wilderness of unlikely foliage), and a dab hand at jumble sales, Caledonian markets, harvest suppers, parish parties, and missionary 'do's' of all kinds.

And Sunday after Sunday, regularly processed like a train chugging through suburban stations, 'the Reverend Ellis and his wife' travelled the church year. Amelia was now doing the gardening, too, since Adam had less and less time for it and she accommodated the various church festivals with appropriate flowers – Advent chrysanthemums, Christmas berries, Easter lilies. She endeavoured to become a sort of extra-sensory social worker, but the hot line to the Almighty with which she and Adam were credited was not a very reliable source of accuracy about parishioner indispositions: folk were easily affronted when not visited and it was difficult to make excuses for God's lack of interest! Inevitably the rectory became a centre of babycare. It housed a successive trail of crèches and nursery groups. Sebastian arrived three years after Ruth and 'Mel' as she became known had a total of seven years of tolerating other peoples' childrens' messes. She endeavoured to glow with hearty, haphazard, happiness as she ploughed through the rusks and rosehip to her next good deed. But inwardly she fumed at the casual way in which parishioners used the vicarage – 'tied cottage' it might be, but this was no licence for 'little darlings' to puke or pee unchecked on wise old rugs. Mel cared just as tenderly for her floor coverings as the young wives with their bright mottled fitted carpets. Availability meant vulnerability but she could not complain, and although Adam agreed with her privately, his main concern was spiritual wellbeing: he did not actually call parishioners his 'flock' but was happy to accommodate their bovine ways!

The one non-parish activity which Mel tried to indulge was her physiotherapy for which she had trained, but barely practised, when love and marriage intervened. Captivated by the debonair young curate whom she met at a drinks party at the home of her eccentric aunt Hester, she had known almost instantly that this man with his brilliant intellect, memory as accurate as a calculator, and blessed with huge dynamic energy, was the one for her and fortunately they met at a time when Adam was ready for marriage. The courtship was swift and Mel duly introduced to Adam's parents. His father, George Ellis, was a prosperous funeral director who had doubtless nursed the hope that his only son would join the family business, instead of choosing to become 'one more idle Church of England parson'. His mother, Mary Ellis, was a quiet, self-effacing, woman of gentle, equable, temperament who appeared content with a life of devotion to her dominating husband and brilliant only child. Sadly she died suddenly a year after the wedding – a loss keenly felt by Mel who had no affinity with her father-in -law. Her own parents, who regarded themselves as upper middle class, described him as 'That unctuous, unitarian undertaker' and although they respected Adam they were secretly of the opinion that Mel was marrying beneath her. So Mel's attempts to have a part-time career of her own were fraught with problems and had to be abandoned during the Amsworth years but she hoped to remedy this once the children were older, depending, of course, where Adam's ministry took him as he climbed the ecclesiastical ladder. Meanwhile Adam and she were a team; his ideals were hers and so, unashamedly, were his ambitions.

When the time came for them to leave Amsworth it was on a bleak mid-December day in weather conditions which might have eased their departure. But the austere grey pall of the sky emphasised the granite tones of the church and lent them the stark intensity of a Buffet drawing with every line and angle etching grooves on their memories. Adam, vulnerable now that the removals van had trundled away, was biting his lower lip in an effort to conceal his emotion. They were leaving, finally, and dying a little in the process. Offers of help for this last day had been eschewed. The Parish was quiet after a lingering fortnight of ritual presentations and farewells. It was a shock to realise how much it hurt. The whole operation would inevitably mean the severance of friendships. How could they hold fast? Adam and Mel were moving a hundred and sixty miles south to new commitments and alliances and had to accommodate a metaphorical hardening of skin over this painful amputation, which was now almost complete.

The children fidgeted impatiently by the bulging old Morris. Mel banged the front door of the vicarage for the last time, plaster showering into the porch, predictably, as she did so. With unnatural concern she scuffed it away down the three awkward steps. What hell they had been with the pram!

'Time, Mel,' murmured Adam, extending his hand sympathetically, despite being blinded by his own tears as he turned, choking, towards St Mary's.

'Don't you have a text for this moment?' whispered Mel.

Tightening his grip he replied:-

'O sweeter than the marriage feast – is that appropriate?'

'Sorry, I don't follow darling.'

'Coleridge. 'O sweeter than the marriage feast, 'tis sweeter far to me, to walk together to the kirk with a goodly company. To walk together to the kirk, and all together pray: old men and babes and loving friends, and youths and maidens gay'...'

Adam's voice steadied as the poem took over but only momentarily. The sight of both parents sobbing was the cue for Ruth and Sebastian to join them, shocked into a screaming duet. Such a thing had never happened before – Mummy and Daddy did not cry even when they hurt themselves. Adam, capitalising on the diversion was quick to scoop up Sebastian together with fistfuls of precious wooden train which no one had been allowed to pack.

'Come on, little chap, big blows' he encouraged, hugging Sebastian and simultaneously brushing away his own tears. 'Big blows! Listen to Daddy's!' and with a handkerchief which looked like a car cleaning rag he blew with such force that his nose began to bleed.

Pandemonium reigned. The screams of the children redoubled, for they were now genuinely frightened, as Mel ransacked the packed car for something with which to stem the flow. She yelled 'don't cry' at the children and eventually unearthed a towel. Ruth, pale and hiccoughing, crept over to the comfort of the creaky garden swing and watched anxiously as Mel tried to mop up the blood which was now pouring down the path. Sebastian, curiously reassured by Adam's muttering about 'rivers of blood' and 'the Red Sea' crouched down and pushed his tiny engine through the crimson puddles, fascinated by the bright sticky tracks which it left on the cold paving stones. It was quite a haemorrhage but had the surprising effect of raising their spirits and they finally drove away singing 'Good bye bloody Amsworth' to the 'Tipperary' tune at the tops of their voices. Later, Adam and Mel were to wonder who heard them as they steered away from 'Church Lane' and waved a final 'Goodbye' to the ungainly heap of house which had been home. Paint-parched, yet proud, it mustered an opaque neo-whiteness for them as it rested beneath a blanket sky and awaited its next incumbent.

Adam's new appointment was to Bishop's Chaplain. Accommodation in The Close comprised number twelve, a narrow town house, pinched self-consciously between wide Georgian dwellings like a tatty paperback amongst tooled leather volumes. Conservationists and schedule-makers sucked their teeth at this nineteenth century blunder, affronted until they were past it and into the sanctuary of the 'pure Queen Anne' end of the street. From day one, and to atone for any other shortcomings, Mel was to ensure that her windows, which were at least 'sash-type', were always cleaner, and the door brasses more shiny, than anywhere else in The Close.

Above them, in Flat 12A, assistant deacons came and went, politely sharing (but never cleaning) the hallway which led from the front door to a dismal back staircase and their upper territory. Feet, fixtures and fittings vibrated above, and beds, too! One sexually energetic deacon and wife forced Adam and Mel to swap bedrooms with Ruth after Adam had wryly remarked that 'Air on a Bed Spring' was not conducive to bedtime reading, or prayer, and moreover a deterrent to any local bed tunes, too! Initially, seven-year-old Ruth could not understand why they had squeezed the wide double bed into her room and shunted her neat divan into the vacuum of the master bedroom. The excuse was that they could not hear the telephone from their room! 'And look, darling,' Mel cajoled, 'at all that lovely floor space for your dolls and doll's house.'

The randy ordinand and wife outgrew their quarters and left after twenty months, with a toddler daughter and new twin sons. It was a relief, and worth the cost of a smart extension phone, when Mel was able to coax Ruth back into her former surroundings. A bonus, too, that 12A was rarely inhabited again during the Ellis tenure.

The steep, carved, magnificence of the cathedral dominated 'The Close'. An apologetic fortress, it was a building for which Mel found it hard to feel empathy; its very existence was a mocking reminder of tireless vision and energy beside which her terms of reference began to pale. She resented the sheer stone hulk and it screened her from the sun in their walled strip of garden. For the following five long years she pined for parochial Amsworth, as much for its home spun crafts and amateur oratorios as for the friendly curving hills, calm highways, and caring friends. She disguised her true feelings, hiding them from Adam, and feigning a sophistication and enthusiasm which did not come naturally. Metaphorically she cut her wisdom teeth on the upmarket accessories of the wealthy worshipping widows, registering (but ignoring) any disdainful glances from those in the fashionable matins congregation who deplored her fidgeting children, shabby handbag, and hatless head.

Somehow she won through, largely due to the enormous amount of entertaining which she undertook for Alastair Ridley, the bishop. His official housekeeper was his sister, Florence, but she seemed to spend most of her time either in hospital or convalescence and as soon as Sebastian was old enough to join his sister at school Mel was available. Undoubtedly Florence was miserably afflicted. However, one never knew the exact medical details and when Adam tried to discover them, in order to assuage Mel's curiosity, Alastair rebuffed him with a curt 'sewage complications!' Poor, grey, Florence. Since she was unwilling to discuss physical vicissitudes, conversation was restricted at hospital visiting times: but Mel, more fortunate than others in the procession of dutiful sympathisers (whose every grape and flower was recorded in a bedside notebook), could invariably discuss either the last or the next function at 'Bishop's Palace'. She was plied with copious instructions for the cleaning, cooking and laundry arrangements and was a vital liaison. As months passed it became progressively easier to make decisions in advance of Florence's directives and thus cut the corners. Alastair, observing this, was happy to join Mel in a certain duplicity with Florence which allowed them to discuss plans and details with her which were already well in hand. Generally this worked. Alastair was meticulous about everything and his precise, detailed, requests totally reliable. Mel knew that 'lunch for ten on the fourteenth, with sherry at twelve thirty' meant just that – and lunch in those days was usually more substantial than the quiches and terrines of the 'eighties'.

It was an odd feeling to be acting as hostess for Alastair, particularly when, as frequently happened, Adam was not included. There were others in the city who could have deputised for Florence and derived much status and satisfaction in the process. However, Alastair himself found the arrangement uncomplicated and entirely satisfactory. Mel presented no threat to his bachelor life-style and the two of them developed a rapport which confirmed their mutual confidence, while Adam appreciated the fact that the arrangement could well be furthering his career. 'Ten more points towards a see, Mel darling' he would say, flippantly, after one of the social days. Little did he realise how near he was to the truth! There were moments when Mel had naughty thoughts and the uncanny sensation of playing more than a part and actually being translated into the role of the bishop's wife. Not visualising what might be (Adam, not Alastair, at the head of the table), but seeing herself as *Alastair's* wife. Foolish thoughts really: he was already sixty, but celibacy had kept him young. Had there been a woman in his life, she pondered? What would it be like to seduce him – this tall, formidable, priest whose only other female company was that of his ailing sister? He appeared to be as clinically detached from the corporate interest of aspiring widows and spinsters as is a surgeon from the anaesthetised bodies beneath his scalpel. Adam and Mel watched some of them try so hard, and what fools they made of themselves; indeed on a couple of occasions, and very confidentially, Adam found himself explaining as tactfully and as gently as he could, that Alastair neither sought nor needed a wife.

Mel was on very good terms with Mrs Garside (who dealt with the cooking at the Palace) and with Sally, the cleaner, who occasionally turned her hand to childcare and 'children sitting.' It was noticeable that they both performed better when Florence was out of action. Mrs Garside, especially, found Mel easier to deal with and would say:-

'You don't make me nervous like Miss Florence do, dearie: be a love and fill up the salts and peppers...' And she would giggle, self-consciously, before adding, 'I couldn't 'ave asked 'er 'to do that now could I?' She vouchsafed other comments, too, saying one day 'Bishop's never been so 'appy as 'e is with you and Reverend Ellis, dearie – such a relief it is to 'im to 'ave 'er job done proper. She's nothing but a millstone round 'is neck, and 'e knows about them don't 'e. It's in the Bible ain't it!'

With a smile, Mel replied, 'Well, not quite in that context, Mrs G!'

'No, but anyway dearie' (she was pummelling pastry, deftly, slapping it into a swirl of flour) 'she's more of an 'indrance than an 'elp, and she takes up too much of 'is time with 'er aches an' pains. I know they be bad and incurable, but she don't manage to interest 'erself in anything an' she stops 'im too.' Then she glowered and added darkly, 'An' 'e is only 'uman, even though 'e's who 'e is!'

Mel murmured something noncommittal. She could not abuse the trust which had been placed in her and was careful to avoid leading Mrs G on or encouraging her to be indiscreet, but she enjoyed these confidences hugely as they showered in her direction together with hot fat spitting from a sizzling pan. Her escape lines were something like 'Mrs G., I'll just check the flowers,' or, 'have we remembered the napkins?' This would be the cue for Mrs Garside to return to her humming as she manipulated cutlets with one hand and stirred sauce with the other. A marvellous woman!

To many people Alastair appeared distant and impersonal but it was an unfair impression. Whereas he was adequate socially he never overspent in that direction; but in the cathedral he invoked, properly, a certain awe and respect and wherever he went it was his academic gifts which impressed.

'He should have been a don' was Adam's favourite cry, for he and Alastair liked nothing better than an intellectual tussle, and Adam, whose opinions and faith had been nurtured at university during the war years (where, as a scholar, he had qualified for a 'Class B' release) considered himself something of a modern theologian pitted against the establishment. He would return home after a late night of whisky and words with Alastair in a fizzing frame of mind and jump into bed full of nervous energy while Mel, half asleep, was in no mood for anything!

Some of the happiest and most relaxed times with Alastair were when he joined Adam and Mel at Number 12 for an informal family supper. Arriving with slippers in one hand and a bottle of wine in the other he always applied himself first to a good ten minutes chat with Ruth and Sebastian. This was his 'Childrens' Hour'. He genuinely enjoyed hearing about their lives and friends and what was happening at school; so much so that, 'We must remember to tell Uncle Alastair' became a frequent cry between his visits. What had started, initially, as an embarrassing ritual for Ruth and Sebastian soon became a very lively, uninhibited one. Ruth delighted in playing him her latest piano piece and evenings were never complete without an up to date report on the number of scales and arpeggios she had mastered. The assistant organist at the cathedral had taught her to practise properly and when she wanted to learn another instrument, it was Alastair who presented her with a three quarter size cello which he had unearthed from the clutter in his attic. He brought it in to her jauntily one evening with the promise, 'There you are, Ruth! Learn to play it better than I did when I was your age and you may keep it.'

Her eyes shone as she inspected it, pulling gently at the strings and marvelling at their sunken, toneless, sounds.

'I hope I can remember how to tune it,' said Alastair. 'Play me an 'A' Ruth.'

She had not been so excited since the pantomime.

Reverently she sat down and Alastair showed her how to hug it between her knees, at which point she tugged off her school tie, because it might get in the way, before gingerly dragging the bow across the resuscitated gut. As her arm felt the pressure correctly so the amusing assortment of squeaks lengthened into trembling wails of sounds which vibrated throughout the house.

Sebastian appeared – diverted from one of his first real 'preps' by the unusual noises!

'What is that howling?' he asked.

'My cello' replied Ruth, proudly, 'look!' Sebastian eyed it solemnly. 'It looks like a fat 'varlin' and it sounds like a sick fat cat,' he pronounced with all the wisdom of 'nearly seven'.

Alastair smiled with his eyes – a rare, endearing smile, which revealed the man beneath the mask.

'Sebastian,' he said, 'you and I will strike a bargain. You must tell me when the cat sounds no longer sick, and then Ruth may keep him.'

From that day Seb (as he became known around this time) was to call Ruth's cello, 'Your cat!'

This anecdote illustrated keenly Alastair's growing affection for them as a family. In their home he was able to shed his covering shell of extreme propriety for a few hours and to stop being 'The Bishop', and this was something which he was incapable of doing in either the diocese or The Palace. Certainly he would not have played Monopoly anywhere else, or even admitted to doing so. However, it was not all frivolous, this 'humanising of Alastair'. More often than not, as the evening stretched into night Adam and Alastair would again be gripped by some quirk of theology or doctrine which mutually impelled them to sharpen their wits upon each other. It was all beyond Mel; two too brilliant minds. In any debate they were more than equal. She was pleased that they could be so mentally stimulated and exhausted by each other and usually made her excuses, dealt with the clearing up, and went to bed.

As she took the children to swim in the glossy new pools of the higher rate taxpayers for whom an alliance with the cathedral, however tenuous, was as beneficial as their Freemasonry or the Rotary Club, so she longed more and more for those heady days of early married life in Amsworth. Of course she was pleased for Adam that everything was going so well yet she felt a chasm widening between them. As Adam grew in stature, would he grow away from her? Were the signs already there? He was now hospital chaplain, too, and had little time left either for her or the children. He rarely took a day off and she could not recall when he had last said, 'Let's get a baby sitter and go out for the evening.'

She reasoned, simply, to herself that she was far more fortunate than the wives of the Rotarians and Freemasons for she was actually sharing in her husband's career and helping him to shape it. Petulance was unproductive, she told herself, so she channelled excess time and energy into the founding and running of a nursery in the grimy area behind the cathedral. Road schemes and re-housing were still dreams on a drawing board, then. There was plenty to do. The 'chaplain's wife' was enthusiastic and efficient and moreover (which cannot have passed unnoticed), she seemed to prefer the squalor of the back to the splendour of the front, of the cathedral.

In the spring of their fifth year with Alastair, Adam was appointed a suffragan bishop in the same diocese. For the preceding six months he had been edgy and restless, driving himself relentlessly through the appointments in his diary with the discipline of an athlete preparing for a marathon race. His hair was now greying appreciably and his face growing longer and leaner. There were lines there, too, which tensed and wearied those sensitive features into a sharper relief and made him look more like his father.

Paradoxically, on the day that the news broke, he was transformed. It was as though he had won his race... Suddenly the engagement diary was empty of commitments and present cares evaporated into the fragrance of the morning. At forty-five he was one of the youngest bishops ever to be appointed. He was a golden boy of the Church and he revelled in the intoxication that comes with arriving. Certainly he had been travelling hopefully and conjecturing with hope, too, as Alastair let drop the occasional hint, but he had not dared to believe that this coveted prize could really be his. He had arrived! They had arrived!

This time there would be few regrets about leaving, particularly as the abbey town where they were soon to live was much more to their taste. Adam was familiar with it and Mel had liked what she had seen on a couple of visits. The compact, narrow, High Street, with its bustling shops and shabby shoppers, had something akin to the atmosphere of Amsworth, and the abbey, built into precious, historic acres, of lush tree-lined green, was a breath-taking sight especially when the pink tones in the masonry blushed in a clear bright light.

'What is the house like?' Mel queried, as she acclimatised to the news.

'Old and large. It used to be the vicarage until it was needed for the bishop. It's built in the same stone as the abbey and has some interesting characteristics. It last had a face-lift in the 1920s but I understand from Alastair that they are going to do it up for us. You will like it.'

'What about the vicar. Where does he fit in?'

'Oh, he lives across the green in a Victorian monstrosity which was, I believe, inherited by the Church Commissioners from a parishioner who died very conveniently at the time the first suffragen was appointed.'

'When was that?'

'1926, I think, when five new dioceses were created.'

There was a pause. Tongue-tied and floundering in the wake of the news, Mel grappled with her reactions and searched in vain for something more profound with which to end the silence than a prosaic, 'Adam I'm frightened at the prospect of it all,' which eventually came.

'Darling.' reassured Adam, 'enjoy the challenge! Here we are about to start on our most exciting years and you talk of fear. You, who have never faltered – afraid of what? After the slog of the past fourteen years, your role will be easy and, what's more, a lot of it will be agreeable. There are rewards for you, too, with a mitre, cope and crozier... which reminds me that I will need to do something about those items...' The sentence petered out as he appeared to slither away from the conversation.

'You don't understand,' she said forcefully. 'In spite of your confidence, even vanity, I simply can't see myself as one of the 'holy angels bright'.' She laboured the pomposity of the opening line of the first hymn which had sprung to mind but Adam, quick to reply, put an arm round her shoulder and, bursting with happiness, replied, 'Then be one of the saints who toil below and take what He gives...'

Annoyed at his alacrity in gaining the advantage so adroitly, she turned on him angrily, now overpowered by a rising tide of emotion and frustration and shrieked 'So! – I take what He gives, do I and 'praise Him still through good and ill – through good and ill'...' and with a flurry of tears she collapsed into the nearest armchair.

Adam, conciliatory, comforting, caring, was immediately beside her, coaxing her unyielding face towards his, endeavouring to stem the tears and even to kiss her (which he had neglected to do lately) as he murmured sweet-nothings to the accompaniment of her sobbing. Now her tears were as much for her own meanness at spoiling Adam's moment of supreme happiness as for her supposed apprehension. Why was she so wretched! Perhaps he was too puffed up with pride and she was right to deflate him. What had she meant by talk of 'good or ill?' The hymn was a random sample – half-known, sung and endured maybe a hundred times in countless services. Did she have a sense of foreboding, and if so, for what possible reason? Adam was now saying that everyone's life is a series of adaptations to circumstances, and of course he was right. Why on earth should she foresee any problem in adapting hers now? Within a few minutes she had pulled herself together: there was no point in making a meal out of the fact that for some inexplicable reason she was incapable of sharing Adam's joy.

Sniffing, sore-eyed, she offered:-

'I guess I shall make a go of it.'

'Of course you will, darling. Don't worry about it. Just stop fussing!'

'May we discuss it properly when you have time?' she said, archly, the undertone undisguised.

'Whenever you wish.'

He smiled and looked young again, his expression as refreshing as his next sentence:-

'Let's go to Venice!'

'Venice...!' she spluttered.

'Yes, why not? Leave Ruth and Seb and take a holiday. Now, quickly, before things happen.'

'Is there time?'

'The house is likely to take several months and we shall need to be available to show interest. There is paint, and all that sort of thing... Old gas fires to rip out and heating to install. I anticipate that the consecration service may well be before we actually move, so we must act quickly, within the next week, and get things organised.'

Exhilarated, he held out his arms and pulled her to her feet, laughing, carefree, radiating promise...'Venice, my love, in the Spring!'

13

Chapter II

VENICE

And so they went to Venice and as the four night package tour offered the combination they saw Rome, too. It was all very easy, really, particularly as it was schools' half term. The children went to the Bishop's Palace to be spoiled by Mrs Garside and Florence (in one of her 'not too bad' spells) and protected by Alastair, who relished the idea of acting as guardian, and they flew to Rome from Heathrow on a sunny morning in mid-May on flight one hundred and thirty-six. Mel noted the number because it reminded her that she was thirty-six.'

In Rome they revelled in the Coliseum and the catacombs, marvelled at the Piazza San Pietro and the Cappella Sistina, played silly games and did foolish things, holding hands and looking into each others' eyes and saying:-

'Who would guess that you are a bishop?' or, 'You really don't look like a bishop's wife!'

They made love, marvellously, and said, 'Mmmm, not bad for a bishop and mate...'

Mel sat and appraised herself in the fake gilt mirror in their Rome hotel room while Adam, desperate to know the names of the cricketers selected for the first Test Match, was out searching for a Continental Times. She was a reasonably attractive looking woman she decided: no longer a girl – that was sad – but still a 'young' woman! Her face was free of lines; her hair, deep chestnut and naturally crisp and curved, was a little dull in colour but not yet invaded by any white strands; not even an occasional one she noted with satisfaction as she combed it attentively. Her eyes were clear and a pleasant grey blue – a mixture of Windsor and Newton's Paynes Grey and White someone had remarked once. Her nose was a shade too narrow to be beautiful but good in profile. She stretched her wide mouth and bared her teeth ferociously at the mirror image. They were white and even. Her figure, too, was reasonable, though tending to be skinny. She had never had to diet. All things considered, she was very presentable. Was it then so astonishing that she was now the wife of a bishop...? Was it not what she had always wanted, and now been granted, and was not Adam the happiest he had been since the early days of their marriage when they had lived in basic curate's accommodation in Chrysanthemum Terrace - which had boasted neither chrysanthemums nor terraces!

To set foot in Venice for the first time in one's life is to know that it cannot be the last and for two of their four precious days this miraculous grey green, terracotta, pink, and antique white, water-bound city held them under a spell. It proceeded to seduce them with voluptuous facades, cupolas and colonnades, moulded chimneys and minarets, four hundred bridges, one hundred and seventy-seven canals, paddling pigeons, skimming gondolas and crystalline marble.

On their first morning, they were content to wander around St Mark's Square and to acquaint themselves with the vaporetti routes, while, like two mesmerised morons, they surveyed the live Caneletto canvases flanking the Grand Canal. Later they left the throngs of sightseers and began to explore in earnest, dawdling hand in hand from calle to calle to discover secret dark canals and silent bridges of their own, where only lapping water or the rattle of a shutter disturbed the slumbering geriatric buildings. Here were crusty barnacles, dank drainage, and boarded up windows, testifying to another Venetion scenario as moving as its rare monuments.

Insatiable now, and into their guide books, Adam and Mel found fragments of their cultural and historical awareness starting to meet and to make sense spontaneously in this proud city whose very existence made artists and poets inspired parasites, and Mel began to regret that she had not fully appreciated her school's History of Art lessons. After a visit to the Academia on the second day they bought a comprehensive illustrated history of Venice as interpreted by great artists. Adam made some sense of the Italian text, but the glorious reproductions spoke for themselves and led them through the centuries from Bellini and

Carpuccio masterpieces, which they had just appreciated, to those of the twentieth century Dufy, Kokoshka and Masson.

Here was a persuasive new dimension. To be able to see the Piazzo San Marco, Santa Maria Della Salute, and San Giorgio Maggiore through their own eyes and at the same time to share the vision of so many others. It was addictive this place and took possession of them, insignificant though they were, as it had done for countless generations. For two precious days they experienced a transformed perception and joy; a dreaming world too real to lose, too tenuous to grasp. It was more than a mere holiday. It was a revelation. Adam felt it as keenly as Mel did. They had never been happier.

It was early evening on their final day. Relaxed and warm they prepared for a drink on the patio of their small hotel, their minds a constantly moving kaleidoscope of the Tintoretto, Tiepolo and Veronese masterpieces which they had sought out and savoured during the afternoon.

Sipping a 'spremuta' as she waited for Adam (who was trying to wash both his hair and himself in the inadequate wash basin of their 'camera matrimoniale') Mel closed her eyes, wondered momentarily how the children were, and attempted to shut out the trio of north-country accents at an adjacent table. Somewhere she had read that Venice should be savoured like a rare cognac, not gulped, and she was attempting to do just that when she was roused by:-

'Had a good day, then?' The voice belonged to an over-permed fellow guest whose tight white cardigan barely contained her ballooning bosoms and who was now swaying threateningly towards her.

'Yes, yes thank you,' replied Mel, politely. 'Very good. Have you?'

'Aye, we have that,' answered her husband (whom Mel dubbed 'Portly Percy'). 'The wife and her friend here like a boat ride between churches, so we've done a bit of both today. It's a capital place, 'ain't it?'

'Yes, yes it is.'

The wife again (Merry Mabel!) 'Excuse me, it's very cheeky, I know, but are you on your honeymoon?'

Mel laughed. 'No - just our first trip abroad since our honeymoon!'

'There now, Ethel, didn't I say just that' crowed Merry Mabel triumphantly. 'Didn't I say they were too old to be on their honeymoon!'

Ethel, the friend, twiddled her wedding ring (was she a widow?) and simpered nervously, 'Aye, happen you did, but they looked so happy.'

'Likely you've a family then?' queried Portly Percy.

'Yes, two.'

Mel, deciding to be monosyllabic in order to discourage them, did not elaborate. Perhaps they would take the hint if she rummaged in her handbag and started to write a belated postcard to her mother. She bent down to retrieve the bag from the dusty pavement, but Merry Mabel persisted with the conversation, curiosity gleaming through her bright, ornate, non-NHS spectacles.

'When we saw you yesterday, we thought your hubby might be an actor!?'

'No, no he is not an actor!'

Portly Percy slapped his bulging beige thigh and offered:-

'Middle management?'

'Something like that,' parried Mel, before adding, 'actually he's between jobs at present.'

She addressed the postcard. They were game, harmless, insatiable tourists, proving to themselves, more expensively each year, that there is no place on earth to equal Yorkshire. Agreeable and chatty, they would be counting the days until the return to their landscaped luxury bungalows, while discussing last year's runner bean crop, or how long their apples had kept. Sweating, breathy, they reclaimed Mel's reluctant attention as they pronounced on the state of Venice:-

'It stands to reason it'll be sinking with rivers instead o'streets. It's the soggy bottom that does it,' said Merry Mabel.

''Aye, but the water acts like a cushion, you know luv, and there's talk of them replacing the wells with aqueducts to keep it floating,' explained Percy.

'Is that so,' offered Ethel. 'Is that really so?'

Merry Mabel, preferring to address Mel, asked, 'Have you bought any glass, dearie?'

'No, I haven't. I don't think I could afford any.'

'Try the stalls on the Rialto,' advised Percy. 'If there's any bargains in Venice I reckon they've got 'em.'

17

'Some of it's plastic glass, Fred,' (Oh, his name was Fred, not Percy!) 'and I wouldn't give it houseroom, would you Ethel?'

'I don't know, luv. I'd like a small ornament or some such to take back. Tom would have liked me to take something…' and Ethel's eyes clouded (so she was a widow!)

Mabel squeezed her hand as a sop to Tom. The ghost of Tom filled the silence until Mel enquired 'Have you been to the glass museum at Murano?'

'We had to leave out t' museums' confided Fred. 'The ladies find them tiring.'

Mabel had a glazed look behind her lenses – plastic like the 'Venetian glass' she might ultimately take home with her.

'Ah, here's your hubby,' announced Fred, addressing Adam before he had a chance to finish his 'Hello darling, sorry I've been so long' or to sit down. Thank God he was here at last, thought Mel, looking, come to think of it, very like an actor, in the red Marks and Spencer jersey which she had bought for him in a frenzy of last minute shopping.

'The wife's been telling us you're between jobs then!'

Adam, bemused, blinked as Mel's sandal caught his shin under the table, 'Yes, I suppose I am,' he answered, his eyes signalling 'what have you told them?'

'Enjoying the break then?'

'Indeed,' replied Adam.

'Cheerio then and here's to your new responsibilities,' saluted Fred, tossing down the last of his Italian beer and wiping a hand across the dribbles on his chin.

'Come on ladies; time for a little walk before your 'bizzy rizzy!' and he heaved himself out of his seat and gallantly proffered an arm each to Mabel and Ethel.

'It's been nice talking to you,' said Mabel, leaning confidentially towards Mel before adding, 'Your hubby doesn't make glass, does he – in t'factory where he's going to be manager?'

Adam, bewildered, muttered 'glass' as Mel winked in his direction and answered quickly,

'No… he deals with… conversions!'

'Oh!' said Mabel.

As they ambled off good naturedly Percy could be heard explaining, 'that'll be for converting to central heating, or oil or gas, that's what it'll be.'

Mel buried her face in her hands shaking with uncontrollable laughter.

'Kindly explain, Mel.'

'I couldn't tell then, could I! First they thought you were an actor and then they decided you worked in a factory. How could I tell them?'

'I would have told them.' He was not amused, that was obvious.

'Oh Adam, be realistic. Can't you see how acutely embarrassed they would have felt. They thought we were on our honeymoon!'

The final comment went unheard. She knew that she had overstepped the mark, albeit inadvertently. She might as well learn the lesson now since it would be with her for the rest of her life. The incident would prey on her mind. The tautness of Adam's face as he listened to the details of her encounter with Fred and the ladies was ominous and filled her with a pervading melancholy from which there was no immediate escape. She was like someone who has lived with the threat of bad news which, when finally confirmed, brings in its wake a tidal wave of dreadful implications. These flooded over her and through her. She did not drown since she needed to survive, but the damage to her mental landscape was as real as the prose of simile and metaphor as she clawed her way out of the foaming rock-spiked whirlpool into which she had been sucked.

There beside her during those last few precious hours in Venice, Adam failed to see that she was submerged. She was her own whipping boy, lacerating lacerations, festering beneath an enormous resentment which did not strike her as in any way perverse or unusual although it would bear no reasonable or reasoned analysis. Whenever she recalled this episode the intense feelings it had aroused would surge over her afresh and nurture a kind of anger with Adam which knew no bounds.

It was ridiculous of course. Adam had not changed. There was no genuine aggravation: he was boyishly happy; neither absorbed with his 'office' nor suddenly overtly pious. If he was guilty at all, it was in not comprehending the depth of Mel's anguish. It was against her nature to be churlish or spiteful so there was good reason for him to probe more than he did.

As her mood darkened, Mel foresaw an end to all their fun and lightheartedness. Clearly the future was to be an unending routine of the helping hand and kindly word as they utilised their one-way tickets towards the tedious land of the elderly, glowing with piety and goodness, labelled, available, uncomplaining, smiling serenely at arthritic pain or failing eyesight and continuing steadfastly to be seen for what they now were. Senior citizens they would become and Adam, shining spiritual comforter, would doubtless yearn to be one of them long before his wife was prepared to stop wearing trousers or reverted to wearing vests again!

Should she have found the courage to spell it out? To cry, 'Stop, retreat, consider me. I don't seek this gilded future – eschew it for my sake – teach, write, anything but this. People told me when I married you that you would one day be a bishop, but I married you for yourself and not for this. See the threat to the ties that bind us. To you they are of a tough indestructible weave, but to me they are fragmenting, fraying, no longer holding us secure.' It was impossible for her to speak with such fluency and clarity, and pointless, too. This she realised as she wrapped her anxiety in inarticulate stupidities and half-truths that can imitate communication.

She was moody and sharp-tongued as they strolled towards the Riva Degli Schiavoni later that evening. The sun was low in the sky, the light a golden grey, and the air as still as a Renaissance painting.

'You must be getting the curse, Mel,' teased Adam, his arm curving lovingly around her shoulders. 'Indeed, I hope you are after our licentious libido!'

'It isn't due,' she said coldly.

'So what's the problem?'

'This evening is the problem.'

'I'm sorry, I don't understand.'

Impatient and angry, she broke away from him. Since he did not understand she would spell it out. Voice raised, defiant, protesting, she flung at him:-

'It is meet, right, and our bounden duty is it, that we should at all times and in all places be seen to be what we now are.' There, she had said it, and with a certain triumph!

People ambled past as they stood apart, rooted into the panorama like two tawdry statues.

Adam bowed his head. 'Please don't parody those sacred words, Mel.'

'Why not? Why shouldn't I? I'm not the priest called by God to be holier than all his fellow men, preaching goodness and love. OK – I've been reasonably happy to go along with you so far and I suppose it has been interesting and worthwhile, but now we are to be so exposed that normality will vanish forever, and we shall exist in a state of ghastly hypocritical artificiality. Look at Alastair, look what it has done to him!'

Gagged by her own words, she choked to a halt. There were bystanders now, a group of children gazing curiously through vivid black Italian eyes, their immaculate clothes as fresh as the evening sky.

She gesticulated, wildly, towards them. 'Look, they can't understand but they can see that it's serious.'

Seeing a movement towards them they chased off down the street, leggy as young colts fleeing from a sudden threat.

'Yes, I can see that it's serious, but we're not going to discuss it here, nor harangue each other in the street,' and taking Mel firmly by the elbow he tried to propel her towards the hotel.

'Don't,' she exploded. 'Don't treat me like a naughty child or one of your precious sinners. I'm going to the Riva,' and, for the second time, she broke from him and ran in the opposite direction. He was beside her within seconds but neither of them spoke. She was calmer by the time they reached the Piazzo San Marco, even a little sorry for him, but she was dammed if she was going to be mealy-mouthed or beg forgiveness.

They made for a café where the price of a drink would be four times as much as anywhere else in Venice. Extracting a crumpled rubber-banded package of multi-lire notes from his trouser pocket Adam peeled off some likely ones with more care than usual and signalled to a waiter.

'Due brandy per piacere,' he said as he gently took Mel's nearest hand, laid it in on the laundered tablecloth and covered it with his. They sat in silence, avoiding eye-contact until the drinks arrived. If he was praying, then she certainly was not! Indeed she was now nearer to tears than she cared to admit, even though they were tears of frustration.

Finally Adam spoke. 'I accept that I was upset earlier. For me, you see, a bishop's role is merely the culmination of the life of service which I chose, freely, when I was ordained a priest. I don't seek anonymity

21

and if you feel that my being a bishop is a social handicap then I welcome the challenge of proving you wrong, and I believe that I shall quickly do so.'

He was speaking thoughtfully and deliberately. It was easy to interrupt.

'You didn't mind joking about it in Rome – why is it different here?'

''Because other people were involved and a principle at stake. Surely it's as easy to admit to being a bishop as to say that one is a doctor or a lawyer.'

'Don't be ridiculous, of course it isn't,' she snapped. 'A bishop is a very rare bird compared with other professions, and anyway a doctor might well hide the truth if only to save himself from facing a catalogue of ailments.'

'I disagree. One can involve oneself as much or as little as one chooses. That particular episode is now over, but it has served to highlight that you, Mel darling, have a different view of me in this job from the one that I have of myself. I don't see myself as in any way altered from the man I was three months ago – or indeed from the man that you married. I am the same person!'

'Oh God, Adam, don't get so pompous. I wish you were a doctor or a lawyer. You would then be a fairly common phenomenon! The fact remains that Portly Percy and co. would have been frightened off by the truth.'

Adam countered her impatience with a forbearing, 'Portly Percy eh …that, my love, we shall never know shall we.'

She was stubbornly tight-lipped.

'Come on darling, smile! I'm only trying to tell you that I reject both now and for the future any suggestion of shrinking from my responsibilities. To put it bluntly I have to affirm my personal witness even more vigorously. Can you not see this?'

Concerned eyes were willing her to answer that she could, and his hand was pressurising hers. She moved it away with a sigh before finally replying:-

'This is part of the problem. I have the awful feeling that we must be seen to be perfect all the time. How will we cope if there is some dreadful tragedy?'

'Mel you're becoming morbid, and hideously mixed-up in your arguments. To answer your first point, we do not have to be seen to be perfect, but we do have to be seen to be trying our best to live the Christian life.'

'It's our livelihood,' she whispered bitterly.

'Yes – it is, and as such we shall gain any satisfaction in relation to effort, but not always,' and he smiled wryly 'the satisfaction of a large bank balance.'

'You know perfectly well that we shall never want for money since you will have 'the undertaker's' fortune and I shall inherit enough from my mother when she dies.' She was now being bitchy and Adam ignored the comments.

'To return to the points at issue,' he continued. 'How would we cope with tragedy? The answer is that we would face it like anyone else since we cannot be superhuman. We would be devastated by it, endure the pain, and, with God's help, come to terms with it.'

'But everyone does not have God's help,' she said coldly in an attempt to dent his clinical argument.

He leant back in the chair, fingers ploughing through his hair and his eyelids closing for a moment. He looked weary as though troubled by unwelcome shadows.

'It is freely available, my love,' he said. 'That is what my life is about and if you do not like it, you will have to lump it.'

His last sentence was so uncharacteristically prosaic that she had no answer.

'We would seem to have come full circle,' she said.

'Yes, I believe we have.'

Much later, before they fell asleep he whispered, 'I cannot do it without you Mel, you do know that don't you.'

'I suppose so,' she replied, 'but I can't be carried along by your Christianity quite as easily as you imagine. I told you when it happened that I was not so ready to be a Holy Angel...'

'Do you have any particularly crime in mind?' he murmured as he drew her towards him...

Despite the upset they returned from the holiday refreshed and invigorated. It was wonderful to see Ruth and Sebastian again, in high spirits and brimful of chatter. The children were far more anxious to furnish Adam and Mel with the details of their week than to hear about Rome and Venice, informing Mummy and Daddy that they had scarcely missed them! Mel fancied that they had both put on weight – doubtless due to Mrs Garside's 'treats' every evening and Alastair's unending supply of Mars bars. Their appearance seemed slightly altered from her familiar visual image of them: this impression of change was only fleeting, two moments of surprise outside two schools as she scooped them up after nearly a week away, yet it was still two moments of seeing them, briefly, as a stranger would. She was to experience this with them on many succeeding occasions and it never ceased to fascinate her. It was not something which happened when renewing acquaintanceships with adult friends or relatives: it was only with children.

The immediate concern was to get back into the busy routine. Adam and Mel now found themselves in great demand socially; everyone, it appeared, was desperate to entertain them before they moved. Their status had become markedly different. Hitherto disinterested and casual cathedral-goers considered themselves their instant 'great friends' as they competed unashamedly for their company. Mel was astonished to discover how much people to whom she had rarely spoken knew about them and their affairs. Many were folk she had met at the Palace and in these instances their memories, far more accurate than hers, could recall the flowers in the centre of the table, or some minute detail of the food served, or even Mel's apparel! Such observations only served to increase her apprehension about the future.

When she reflected on the holiday, she found herself genuinely saddened. She wished, with a continuing obduracy, that Adam could have laughed in Venice as he had laughed in Rome. Surely then she might have escaped the agony of her own watershed so that the memories of that vain, illustrious, exotic city would have remained as precious as its treasures.

Adam did not refer to the upset, and Mel refrained from alluding to it, yet inside her head there was the primitive instinct of a hunter which would not allow him to extricate himself so silently. She would choose her moment to pounce.

Late in July they were invited to a celebration dinner with Alastair and Florence, the latter fit enough to swallow a thimbleful of sherry and a taste of consommé before retiring upstairs. She had dressed for the evening with care and Mel noticed touches of eye shadow and rouge tinting the pallor of her skin. 'Long' dresses were in vogue again and Florence admitted that she had last worn her floral voile hostess gown fifteen years previously. It all but fell from her. Mel realised how frail she had become and it dawned on her that Florence must have cancer. How unintelligent of her not to have understood before!

'I am going to miss you so much, Mel,' she was saying, in her quiet, affected voice. 'In fact I really don't know how I shall manage after being so spoilt.'

'Mrs G is a tower of strength' reassured Mel.

'Yes, my dear, but being young, and dare I say, uninhibited, you have a way of getting her to cooperate so much better than I do. I find her so extraordinarily difficult sometimes, and I really dread being without you.'

'Come now, Flo', don't make the poor girl feel guilty about leaving,' interrupted Alastair, refilling Mel's glass as he spoke. 'She has enough on her plate without that – which reminds me, have you the er - 'bric-a-brac?'

'Yes I do, of course. Give me a hand dear.'

Alastair bent to help her out of her chair and Mel's heart bled for him in his continuing predicament. He was having to care for a sister as he might have cared for a sick wife, had the cards fallen differently for him. His suit cuffs were frayed and his purple vest stained with greyish blotches. She was reminded that Adam would soon be wearing this conspicuous colour. How did one clean it?

Mel glanced in Adam's direction. He was half out of his chair, offering to help.

'It's alright Adam, thank you,' said Florence. 'I just want to fetch something. I'll only be a moment.' And she moved towards the door slowly, but unaided.

'She is no better Alastair,' observed Adam when she had shuffled out of the room.

'No, I'm afraid not. But she's not in pain and for that we must give thanks. She has a surprise for you!'

His face creased into its cryptic half-smile. The mask half off, the real man half visible.

'I must not spoil her fun,' he said. 'Here, more wine Adam; help yourself. By the way, remind me to let you see those papers later on...'

Mel switched off from a boring conversation concerned with diocesan quotas and looked discreetly around this genteel room with which she was so familiar. It was generously proportioned and sedately furnished with what she had always presumed to have been Alastair's and Florence's parents' furniture. A portrait of their father hung over the fireplace, austere and dark, in a heavy gilt frame, the scrubby beard and moustache slotting it into its Victorian period. Mel recalled hearing that he was 'in tea'. Obviously the many rugs were a part of the heritage. She straightened some erring fringe with the toe of her shoe as she pretended to listen to the men, and wondered idly whether Florence resembled her mother. Certainly the face in the frame, what could be seen of it, suggested no kinship with her although there was a vague likeness to Alastair.

Florence was struggling into the room again, carrying a large square parcel, gift-wrapped, and tied with silver ribbon.

'Ah, here she comes,' said Alastair as he relieved her of the package and placed it, ceremoniously, on a coffee table near to Mel.

'You may undo it,' encouraged Florence, as she eased herself back into her chair, her dull eyes bright with excitement.

Adam crossed the room to join Mel and together they made appropriate noises of protest and appreciation as they undid the wrapping. The faded decorative box inside contained a rare crown Derby tea service. A riot of gold, Prussian blue and patchy rust, it lay in its original presentation velvet, carefully embalmed in order to survive well beyond the generation of craftsmen who had created it. Tenderly Mel lifted a saucer from its moulded crease and reversed it to examine the identifying marks, overwhelmed by its possible value.

Alastair explained, 'It belonged to our grandmother,' adding, with a smile, 'and it will bring you in a pound or two if times get hard.'

Florence commented, 'I think it would look nice in a corner cupboard Mel. It really ought to be displayed and enjoyed. Unfortunately one of the saucers has been riveted. I would like to have had it invisibly repaired for you. These things can be so much better disguised nowadays. Perhaps you can get it done, dear – it is just a question of finding the right expert.'

Mel went over to kiss Florence gently on the cheek and said with real emotion:-

'We shall treasure this all our lives. And it will be a constant reminder of the happy years here with you and Alastair. Thank you for a lovely, lovely, present.'

Adam made a short speech and then, after another extended period of touching and admiring, and inspecting the rivets, they carried the box into the front hall where they gingerly deposited it under a table to be collected at the end of the evening.

Later on, at dinner, after Florence had withdrawn, there was a lull and Mel launched her attack.

'There were these people in Venice, Alastair,' she said, 'who thought Adam was an actor.'

'Not far off the mark eh, Adam,' said Alastair. 'There's a lot of acting in our profession. Dressing up too!'

'I wouldn't tell them what he really did,' she persisted. 'I thought it would frighten them off. Was I right?'

Alastair looked from one of them to the other, sensing the need for tact. Slightly uncomfortable, Adam toyed with his napkin, while Mel gazed brazenly at Alastair, her eyebrows raised in questioning arcs.

Alastair, paused, thoughtful. 'That is a difficult one, Mel.'

'We had a terrible argument about it and Adam ended up buying astronomically expensive brandies in 'Harry's'.'

'It was not 'Harry's' actually,' corrected Adam, 'but nearby.'

'Well, who won the debate?'

'No one,' Mel said, bravely.

'Mel,' said Adam dishonestly.

'I see that I must first preach reconciliation here,' said Alastair with evasive charm. 'You do not seriously ask me to adjudicate, do you Mel, for that will force me between husband and wife, and, moreover, two of the people dearest to me in this world? Forgive me if I am pompous, but let me make some observations, in the role of impartial onlooker, as I perceive that this matter is important to both of you. Whether your acquaintances in Venice would indeed have been deterred, we cannot know, since the hypothesis was untested. There might be a case for arguing so, but you must then work on the premise that you can predict a man's response to a given set of stimuli and that, in our profession, is a little dangerous. As I grow older I am becoming more, not less surprised, at the quirks of human nature and there are moments of sheer joy when the most unlikely response emanates from a truly improbable source. Perhaps your friends in Venice would have been overjoyed to meet a bishop – or who knows, one of their relatives could be a cardinal...'

He was losing himself in his own metaphysics, sitting back now, finger tips touching in a symbolic row of gothic arches which obscured the heavy cross hanging on his breast. He was looking upwards, too, in his characteristic 'I am pronouncing' pose. Mel knew already that she was not going to gain any satisfaction from his words. He continued:-

'There is a broader issue here, Mel, is there not? When is self-advertisement vanity and when is it viable? Is it fair even to ask this question of people in our vicarious position? Certainly Adam and I must accept self-advertising as a part of our trade, from the very clothes that we are required to wear...' (Adam was nodding, so presumably felt the 'cross' swinging his way). You may correctly assume that advertisement is a hindrance in some situations, but I think, and I repeat myself, that you may be at fault in prejudging the ultimate outcome.' He paused for a moment before adding, 'how infinitely more fortunate you are than I have been in having each others' support,' and he looked directly at Adam, a caring expression on his face. 'Cherish her, Adam, she is your greatest asset.'

Mel sensed, rather than saw, Adam's slight annoyance at this paternalistic command.

'Mel reigns supreme, Alastair – on the temporal plain!'

Alastair turned to her again and was about to open his mouth when Mrs G came into the room.

'The coffee is in the drawing room, sir.'

'Thank you, Mrs Garside, and for this magnificent feast our heart-felt gratitude,' and he spread his hands over the debris (which Mrs G would be anxious to get into the dishwasher before her husband arrived to collect her) in a gesture of benediction.

'All my favourites, Mrs Garside,' Mel said, 'bless you!' smiling at her with genuine affection, but inwardly recoiling from her unexpected use of those two unctuous words.

Adam offered, 'Mrs Garside, can we help?'

Hypocrite! He knew full well that if anyone gave her a hand, it would be me, thought Mel, but Mrs G refused.

'Oh no, Reverend Ellis sir, this is your celebratory evening, and I'm only too 'appy to do it for you and Mrs Ellis.' She swept some of the clutter on to a tray, looked at Alastair and queried 'Shall I take the brandy up sir?' Her trained eye had noticed the undisturbed decanter and dry glasses and she wanted the diners out of her way.

'Thank you, Mrs Garside, if you would.'

They retired to the upstairs drawing room where Mel half expected the previous conversation to be picked up like a dropped handkerchief, but it was abandoned, as if forgotten, and it would have been discourteous to Alastair to try to retrieve it. Even so, she wondered what else he had been about to say. He was now talking about Ruth and Sebastian. They had been amusing as house guests and he had stored up several anecdotes.

'Ruth's cello playing is promising, isn't it?' he said. 'I'm amazed at the organised way in which she goes about her practising. She must be the exception rather than the rule, never needing any coaxing or reminding.'

'It's all thanks to you,' commented Adam.

'Nonsense. The talent would have found its way out into the open without my assistance. By the way, Sebastian and I are agreed that she may keep 'the cat' as it no longer sounds sick!'

They chuckled at the recollection of that evening, now more than four years ago, and then transferred to other topics, gossiping as friends, who are also colleagues, do, - of mutual acquaintances, and, inevitably, the affairs of the Church, together with Adam's new role in those affairs.

As they were in the front hall, preparing to leave, Alastair helped Mel into her new Jaeger jacket (good for her image, but it would have to last a long time) with a surfeit of solicitude. Adam, ill at ease, fumbled with the presentation box. It was a poignant moment, mainly because all three of them felt that it should be.

'Well, my children. Out into the world with you. It's a cool night,' said Alastair. He slipped the chain free of its track on the door and raised the antique iron latch. A bulky envelope, addressed to 'Mrs Amelia Ellis' lay on the small oak table by the door. Normally this table was cluttered with incoming or outgoing mail or both, but it was empty today, apart from Mel's flower arrangement of the previous week which wilted apologetically. Several petals scattered as Alastair's hand reached for the envelope. He held it out...

'For you, Mel, with my sincere and deep gratitude for all that you have done for me.'

'But Alastair, you have already given us a truly wonderful present.'

'That is from Flo. This is from me.'

'Come on, Mel, open it,' instructed Adam, but Alastair intervened:-

'No, wait until you are home. Your baby sitter will be concerned for you.'

'But what is it Alastair. What are you giving me now?'

'Nothing that you have not deserved, I assure you,' and his eyes twinkled as he added, 'I do not see why Adam should be the only recipient of new adornments. Come! Away! God be with you both!'

He rested a hand on each of their heads in a 'confirmation' gesture which came naturally to him and did not embarrass them. Then he grasped the backs of Mel's shoulders in his hands, looked into her eyes, and bent to kiss her, holding her firmly and closely. He smelt of dust: the dust from his furniture, or the dust on his clothes – she could not tell. For a timeless instant, he breathed with lust.

Adam and Alastair shook hands. Although the family were not to move for another few weeks, there was a finality about the ritual.

'Come and eat with us again at number twelve before we go, Alastair,' said Adam.

'That I will do, indeed, brother bishop,' he replied, as he closed the door.

They hurried along The Close, their footsteps agitating the silence of the shadows which the vintage street lights cast across the street. Behind them, on the right, towered the brooding mass of the cathedral, animated by its own vastness. It would be better when the new floodlights were working, less oppressive and menacing. Mel would have clung to Adam but on this occasion his protection was centred entirely upon the tea service.

Once home, she went upstairs and undressed quickly, a certain excitement, quickened by the evening's wines, accelerating her movements. She wanted to open the envelope while she was alone. Adam would be more than seven or eight minutes ferrying home the schoolgirl baby sitter and she was in her dressing gown by the time she heard the car leave The Close and turn into The Approach.

She sat on the bed and opened the envelope. It contained a folded note and a small blue velvet box, the latter dulled and smoky with age. She read the note first, not daring to open the box. Alastair's fine, sharp, handwriting stood out on the paper, the vertical strokes neatly angled at forty-five degrees, fixed bayonets in an army of symbols which reflected the precise personality and mental order of their creator. The

30

stilted formality revealed more of his feelings than a chatty note and the careful phrases were charged with emotion. They ran thus:-

'My dear Mel,
Please accept this ring as a token of my regard for you. It has been mine to give for many years now since the original recipient returned it to me. Enough said! I hope that you will wear it and that it may give you pleasure. For your immeasurable contribution to God's work in this place, my affectionate thanks and admiration.
Yours aye, Alastair

Mel opened the box slowly, the small clasp hurting her thumb before yielding to the pressure. It contained a ring at which she gazed in shocked astonishment. A single glowing ruby, smouldering within a circlet of pinhead diamonds which shimmered in a setting of Victorian gold. She was choked by its beauty – and shivered as the breeze from the open window behind her lifted the curtains. Somewhere an owl hooted.

Like circlets from a juggler, the implications of both letter and gift whirled in her mind as she eased the ring on to her left little finger, where it dwarfed the modest, treasured, engagement solitaire which was a little tight on the adjacent finger. She eased it off and slipped it on to her right hand. For how many years had it lain in its dark prison? What a jewel! Reprieved at last and flooded with light. Gift of a husband 'manqué' to a woman young enough to be his daughter and wife of another? Emotively donated, and consummated with a fusty kiss!

She was still staring at it when Adam came up to the bedroom. Silently, she handed him the note and held out her hand which he peered at with interest before reading the explanation.

'Amazing!' was his reaction.

'What do you mean, 'amazing'?'

'Amazing that funny old Alastair should do something like this.'

'Why has he given it to me?'

'He likes you, he owes it to you, and you are female – let's face it, it would look a little strange on me – and possibly, too, he wants to get rid of it. It actually makes more sense to do this than to give you a cheque for a few hundred pounds for your five years' work.'

'He could give it to Florence.'

31

'No! Not Flo' as he calls her. She's a broken reed and may well be ignorant of its existence. She could have purloined it long ago!'

Adam was pulling on his pyjama trousers as he spoke, the sentences arriving spasmodically like those of a sports commentator.

'He didn't tell you he was going to give it to me?' asked Mel as they got into bed.

'No, why should he?'

'You don't mind, then?'

'Mind. Why should I?'

'Well, a ring always has sentimental significance.'

'Savour, the sentiment then!'

'I want to know about … her.'

'Who?'

'The 'original recipient.' Here in the letter.' Still clutching it she pointed to the sentence.

'You will never know,' said Adam, pulling at the bedclothes. 'And you can't ask, can you!'

She was lying on her back now, holding up her hand, the ring on fire with stunning sparks as it reflected the glare of the bedside lamp. Adam raised his head to look again.

'It's very splendid, darling.'

'She was a fool,' said Mel

'A fool?'

'Not to want Alastair! I'm embarrassed by it. Can I give it back to him?'

Aghast, Adam jumped up from his pillow 'Good God, no! Do as he says, my love. Wear it and enjoy it.'

'It will remind me of his misery,' Mel persisted.

'What misery?'

'When she gave it back to him.'

'Maybe she died under a bus,' yawned Adam.

'He'd still be miserable.'

Adam shrugged the sheet tighter around his body and yawned loudly.

'I could sell it!'

'No!'

'Why?'

'Your conscience wouldn't allow it!'

32

'It might.'

'Then I wouldn't allow it!'

'Are you my conscience then?'

'If needs be,' Adam mumbled, sleepily but added, mischievously, 'Perhaps he fancies you.'

'He couldn't could he?'

'Why not? As Mrs. G often says (mimicking her accent) "'e is only 'uman even though 'e's who 'e is,' and he sank back into the pillow.

'His conscience wouldn't let him,' she said, pointedly.

'Touche! Good night my unique Mel – bishop's lady par excellence!' He stroked her hair and fell asleep.

Mel lay awake for a long time, wondering how to thank Alastair and what to do with the ring. She decided that she must behave as he and Adam had instructed. She would wear it. Perhaps it would bring her luck. Yes, she conjectured, it had a deep significance. It was a talisman, to encircle her finger forever, and to protect her from herself.

****

Two days later Mel's Aunt Hester telephoned the news that her mother had been taken into hospital after a heart attack. A period of total rest was indicated, to be followed, inevitably, by a re-programming of her lifestyle.

With the Consecration scheduled for the first Sunday in September, Mel had arranged for Ruth and Seb to spend the preceding week with 'Granny Grant' in her Sussex cottage, thus leaving her free to concentrate on other things, particularly preparations for the move. Now through the long summer holiday there would be no respite from the children who, apprehensive of the impending changes in their small world, were becoming more argumentative and tiresome with each new day.

These weeks were a nightmare.

Mel drove the two-hundred-mile round trip to see her mother four times, twice taking Ruth and Seb with her and spending nights at the cottage. On the other occasions, friends came to the rescue, but she suffered the full fury of the children's annoyance and aggression on her travel-jaded return. Although she could understand their reactions and indeed sympathise for they were now twelve and nine and their roots had gone deep enough during five years to resent disturbance, these were days when everyone's irritability nearly drove her to drink or worse.

Ruth expressed all their feelings when she said, 'Moving's like going to the dentist. You don't know whether it will be nice or nasty so you cross your fingers and hope, but it's always beastly just the same!'

Alastair was on holiday for most of August and Adam too busy to be much support. He was tetchy. They had a couple of rancid verbal exchanges about Mel's need for the car on days when it was simpler for him to use British Railways for short journeys than for her to struggle to Sussex by train. They were not yet a two-car family! Tempers frayed. Thank goodness she and Adam had managed to have the Venice trip, she brooded bitterly, unable to foresee when there would be another.

Mel's mother was not placid in her predicament. Mel's father's death had happened without warning (a massive coronary) during Adam's and Mel's years at Amsworth and had shattered them in different ways - Mel because her father was her hero and Mrs Grant because her husband was her slave. Adam, Amsworth, and babies, sheltered Mel from protracted grief at the time and it was not until now that she fully realised how few demands her mother had made upon her only daughter as she rebuilt her life with surprising vigour and initiative for one who had hitherto seemed so bereft. She had learnt to drive at fifty-five, passing her test the first time, become a competent gardener, studied Italian (though heaven knows why!) and been a pillar of the local W. I. Mel half expected her mother to re-marry and this would have spared her only child the difficult task which now confronted her. Mrs Grant was incensed at the blow to her physical fortune and furious at being in hospital. Unyielding, stone faced, and inert under the disciplined sheets, she wallowed in self-pity. It was impossible to make her smile or to take any interest in anything outside herself. Guilty because of her perceived years of neglect Mel found each visit more formidable than the last. Her mother showed no interest in the family, or their plans, and all she seemed able to say was a bleak 'You have come then.' Mel disguised her irritation, but the fact that she could not shift her mother's indifference was probably an indication of her own depression at this time. Whilst acting the loving daughter she offered new nightdresses, appealing books, grapes, even orchids – tokens of her love! But the grey

34

swathes around her mother's eyes echoed Mel's own mood like a fog in December.

Aunt Hester, her father's sister, came to the rescue. She was practical and uncompromising. To Mrs Grant she said, 'Helen, you are coming to me when you leave here and staying until you're fit to be on your own again. Don't argue because there's no alternative!'

To her niece, she dictated:-

'Mel, your place is with Adam right now. Mine, for a while at least, can be with your mother ... God help me!'

How good it was to be able to share the burden, indeed to shed it, and as they sat talking outside the hospital Mel wept with relief.

'You don't look yourself, Mel,' Hester said, kindly. 'This has been the last straw, hasn't it?'

'It couldn't have come at a worse time,' Mel gulped.

'My dear child, when is there a right time for anything, except a clock! The whole thing is on top of you – I'd no idea you were so low. Have you seen a doctor?'

'No! I'm sure there's no need. I never see a doctor, you know that.'

'Well my girl, you could certainly use a good tonic. Put yourself on Sanatogen and bring the colour back into those cheeks. We can't have you starting your new life looking like a wraith! Promise me you'll do something. You are no good to Adam in this exhausted state.'

Dear Hester. It seemed so little time since Mel's first awareness of her. Bouncy, jolly, bringer of presents and initiator of adventures more wicked and exciting than ever her parents offered, like walking in the moonlight with torches on Christmas Eve to eat doughnuts under the stars and staying up later than ever before. In those days everyone except Hester talked of war, and Hitler, and Mel had a thing called a gas mask and only went to school in the mornings or the afternoons. Hester was something called a landgirl and came to visit looking like a cowboy, still smiling when everyone else was glum. Until one day, jumbled in Mel's memory with ration books, sweet coupons, and starting algebra, something terrible happened and Hester did not come any more. They told her that the man Hester had hoped to marry had been killed by Germans and she was ill because he was dead. Mel wanted so desperately to see her, but she did not come for years, and when she did it was different. She squabbled with Mel's parents and was bossy with her niece. She became more and more the schoolmistress and she constantly introduced Mel to her friends, as 'My niece, Amelia Gaye,' and they all said, 'Ah, Miss Gaye, how cheerful,' and Mel would reply 'I'm Miss Grant, like my Aunt,' which did not seem to please anyone!

Finally, Hester married a retired headmaster and dreamt of a child before it was too late for both of them, but none appeared. They lived amicably until he did not wake up one morning when they were on holiday in Scotland. Now, in her fifties, she was an expert at teaching remedial English and bustled about her county from session to session. Mel did not feel unlike one of her pupils at this moment...!

'Are you sure you can really cope with mama?' She asked.

'Yes, quite sure. It will be good for her, too, that I'm out on certain days. It will encourage her to feel useful. There's no reason for her to become an invalid.'

'Well, I guess you are the best person to prevent that,' Mel murmured.

'I shall be sad not to be at the service – but then, you know me, Mel. It isn't quite my scene.'

Mel shrugged, 'Is it mine?' she ventured, but the question went unheard. Hester was delving into her giant handbag intent upon finding something.

'Ah, here we are! For the children, with Great Aunt H's love,' and she handed Mel two chunky mouth organs. 'Tell them to blow them in the cathedral,' she said.

'Hester, you're wicked – and I love you!'

Mel hugged her and then watched as she got out of the car to return to her own vehicle, straightening assorted garments as she did so and pausing to tie on a tattered headscarf.

'Always drive with the window open – very invigorating!'

Mel smiled and said, 'I'll be in touch. Drive carefully!'

'See the doctor now!'

'Maybe. But seeing you has been a tonic. I feel a new person.' Mel waved, turned the key and started the engine and as she drove home, she began to believe in her 'new person.' She even sang some hymns along the way!

****

Mel bared her soul to the doctor in the privacy of his 'confessional' which was lined with prints by D'Oyly John. He prescribed a combination of tranquillising pills – dolly-mixtures to soothe away her fretfulness. She slept better than she had done for three months.

However, it was a mistake to double the dose on the day of the consecration service albeit she argued that this would stop her feeling sick. For much of the service she was disorientated as she sat in the nominated pew with her two, for once, perfect children. She hoped she was controlled enough to appear normal but there was a moment when Ruth nudged her and whispered,

'Mummy, wake up!' at which point Mel made haste to collapse her knees on to the hassock just in time for the next prayer.

The ritual of the perpetuation of episcopacy wafted its way in and out of her consciousness. Mellow and dreamy she was not part of it except at the moments when her mind caught up in a vivid burst of clarity. It was remote and she was a long way off, like a lonely spectator high on a hillside that sees yet does not identify with, the crowds gathered in the valley below for some spectacular event.

Far away, somewhere in the cathedral, the questions echoed and Adam's voice answered them, confident and clear, as unwelcome rain outside dribbled sorrowfully and laboriously down the stained-glass windows. 'I am so persuaded,' he said - and again, 'I am ready.' And again, later, 'I will be faithful.'

Suddenly, there he was, resplendent in his bishop's apparel and magnificent in the stunning cope embroidered in an orgy of surrealist scrolls and foliage, all white, and gold, and red. Ruby-red, like Alastair's ring. Mel touched it for reassurance. Where was dear Alastair at this moment she wondered, craning her neck in an effort to find him.

She remembered to look at the children as Adam had requested. Seb grinning, his face proud and loving as he clutched her glove which was beside him on the pew; perhaps he would be a bishop too! Ruth, in her excitement, dragging new socks up and down. Mel moved a restraining hand towards her before drifting back into her dream world. In the distance, the choir sang, 'Come, Holy Ghost our souls inspire' the sounds mingling and melting into a restful density. She could find no words to pray for Adam. She lost them in the mists. Not until the end of the Service could she pray and then the words came towards her, ringing their way down the length of the building, 'Prevent us, O Lord in all our doings with thy most gracious favour...'

'Please God,' She cried inside, her forehead pressed into the ridged top of the pew, 'Please God, prevent me! Not just guide me, which is what I know it to mean in the prayer, but prevent me! Dear God, if I need to be prevented then please, I beg of you, please prevent me...'

It was over. Here was the procession and there the mitre perched strangely and precariously on Adam's head, and Adam trying to keep in step with his crozier. She smiled him her love. It was over. There was no going back.

Afterwards, calm and collected, she was charming to the Archbishop and kissed Alastair. There were crowds of people and many old friends including a lovely coach load from Amsworth. The children shone and she was justly proud of them. Members of congregations, past, present and to come, queued up to shake hands and to wish them well. Faces for the future introduced themselves and although none impressed more than another on that day, nor spoke anything more original than, 'What a lovely service,' or 'Such a pity about the weather,' or 'We look forward to seeing more of you,' yet she felt just a tremor of excitement at the prospect of a fresh beginning and new people.

Chapter III

ARRIVAL

A fortnight later the sight of a capacious brown removals pantechnicon parked outside the Tower House, (an imposing building standing next to the abbey in their new home town), announced the arrival of the Ellis family and throughout the day a steady procession of welcoming townsfolk nosed its way into the chaos of the front hall. By the evening they had acquired twelve potted plants, four bunches of flowers, six assorted pies (some more appetising than others) and a fly spray! The last gift came from an elderly lady called Ethel Speight whose current preoccupation was the protection of the new Bishop and family from attack by insects. 'It was.' she declared, her 'Christian duty to ensure a good night's rest for all.' The weather was sultry for early September and the mosquitoes were frightful this year!' She twittered inanely about her allergies and gnat bites while her beady eyes, zippy as one of her mosquitoes, assimilated as much as possible about Adam and Mel, their children, and their chattels. They thanked her for her precautionary kindness and she waddled away on uncomfortable feet preening herself like a bailiff who has just scooped a jackpot. Now she would be itching to share her findings with the parish gossips.

As Mel struggled up the main stairs with pillows and bed linen she could see through a landing window that Miss or Mrs Speight was already chattering excitedly to a man and a few moments later, as she glanced out of a higher window in the imposing master bedroom, she was surprised to see the acquaintance raise her hand to his lips as they parted. Having found this small charade somewhat extraordinary Mel was then a little dismayed to see the hand-kissing man walking purposefully toward the archway into the Tower House drive.

'Adam,' she yelled, her voice echoing through the unfamiliar building, 'There's someone else coming! Can you cope?'

A reply rose from somewhere below, 'OK darling' followed by, 'the men are bringing in the last of the chairs so we are almost through' and even as he finished shouting the frayed canvas bottom of their treasured antique chaise longue came slowly up the stairs supported by what appeared to be two headless bodies. Mel cleared a pathway for this whimsical creature. It spoke!

'In the bedroom, missus?'

'Please. Over by the alcove'

As the couch was being placed unceremoniously on a half unrolled rug, Ruth interrupted;-

'Mummy, shall I unpack my clothes? I've done the books into my bookshelves and helped Seb with his.'

'Put, not done' Mel corrected automatically as the men retreated past her. Mishearing, one of them countered, 'Nearly bloody done, missus!'

Mel grimaced at Ruth, thanked the removals men, and then asked her daughter,

'Is all your furniture there now, love?'

'I think so' replied Ruth. 'It's really super and there's lots more space but I want to put things in the cupboard. Where are my clothes?'

'Well, I didn't empty your chest of drawers but I put things to hang up in the old blue trunk which they've dumped in the smallest bedroom. Please don't scatter everyone else's clothes around while you're finding yours'.

'I won't... Promise!' and she rushed off excitedly, calling to Seb as she went.

They were being really helpful thought Mel. It was a lot easier than the last time and she smiled to herself as her memory flashed back to the nosebleed. This house was in a different league to their previous 'tied cottages' and its solid squareness reminded her of Amsworth; surely that must be a good omen! She trod the new bedroom carpet with tender respect enjoying the silence under her feet after the rattle of floorboards and cold stone flags in Number 12. This was luxury and there would soon be new carpet in the dining room, too, and tight, bright, hair-cord stretched up the wide, imposing staircase.

Humming to herself Mel unpacked the sheets and blankets and made up the beds while Ruth and Seb rushed hither and thither with armfuls of dressing gowns, overcoats and blazers. Seb halted to announce solemnly,

'I've grown out of a lot of these, you know.'

'Yes darling, I shall give them to the first jumble sale.'

'They're not really jumbly.'

'No, but I am sure they will be appreciated.'

Comprehending, he nodded wisely, his shaggy hair tumbling over his eyes. It must be cut before he went to school next week. Where was the barber, she wondered? There was so much to learn in a new town!

'Daddy wants you,' Seb said solemnly a few moments later.

Mel clattered down the stairs to find Adam in the front hall.

'The men are bringing in the last of the stuff,' he said. 'Come and meet the Abbey layreader.'

Mel mouthed, 'Must I?' but Adam was already propelling her into the spacious study.

The lay reader rose to greet Mel from his packing case perch.

'Welcome', he said, 'I don't believe I've had the pleasure of meeting you though I have had the privilege of meeting your husband before. Piers Tarrant-Jones.

They shook hands.

'How do you do. You've been talking to Adam, have you?'

'Indeed! Putting him in the picture, one might say, and also incidentally, bearing abject apologies from Felix and Ellen Hughes.

'Ah, the vicar!'

'They deeply regret their absence, but they are on holiday in Wales. However, fear not, for I am here to minister to you instead. Indeed, I have with me some very necessary refreshment.'

As he spoke he extracted a bag of rice from one pocket of his leather-patched tweed jacket, and a bundle of courgettes from the other.

'You will need to find a casserole, ma'am. And a pan.'

'A casserole?' Mel queried.

'For the steak', he announced as he triumphantly produced yet another package 'Bourgignon!'

Mel was mesmerised.

'Last, but by no means least, a bottle of wine, Nuit St Georges. Naughtily uncorked in case your corkscrew is not to hand!'

He smiled jubilantly. Mel was disconcerted, partly by his unusual approach but more by the black shade which covered one eye. The intensity of his gaze, concentrated into one gravy brown iris and ink-blot pupil, unnerved her as she was conscious of every detail of her lank, tired, hair, grubby shirt and tatty trousers being scrutinised.

'You're too kind', she stammered. 'A casserole, you said?'

'A pair of casseroles. The beef and rice are cooked and merely require re-heating, and you may do you own thing with the courgettes.'

She regained her composure.

'You're a modern Aladdin's genie!'

'Without a lamp, dear lady!'

'Please thank your wife.'

'No wife ma'am' he twinkled. 'I am the cook. Bon appetit!'

He moved to go.

'I must leave you holy folk in peace.'

'Certainly not,' stated Adam, producing a bottle of sherry. 'Celebrate with us Colonel. We shall drink a toast to a long and happy life here. Can you lay your hands on something to drink out of, Mel.'

Colonel Tarrant-Jones was delighted to join in the inaugural toast and as Mel went to find glasses (and casseroles) she heard Adam explaining that his 'wine–cellar' had been first into the van and last out in order to spare everyone temptation!

Mel found three cups.

'I've a nasty feeling that one of you is sitting on the glasses,' she said on her return. It was not strictly true but struck the right note.

'To drink sherry from a cup is an entirely new experience,' mused their guest. 'I shall savour it.'

'Well, here's to you, sir,' said Adam raising his cup.

'And to you and your enchanting lady' came the reply.

Ruth and Seb sidled in, uncertain.

'Can we ride our bikes?'

'Yes', answered Adam. 'Go out on to the grass.'

'Is that alright Colonel Tarrant-Jones?' Mel queried, 'is cycling allowed?'

'Now that you mention it, dear lady, I believe there's an unfriendly and forbidding notice tucked away in a corner, but I should not let that worry the two of you'. He winked towards them with his one eye.

As is the way of children with strangers, they studied him suspiciously for a moment before running out to act on his advice.

'A bright pair!' commented their visitor.

He did not stay long but the three of them consumed two thirds of a bottle of Amontillado. It was useful to talk to someone who obviously knew everybody and everything and Mel sensed that he and Adam had established a quick rapport. Her intuition was confirmed immediately.

'I will return in the morning to help you with all this,' he said, waving an arm over the colony of packing cases. 'I'm especially good with books and pictures. We will arrange a date, too, for you to dine with me. I'll gather in some of the flock to take sherry-wine beforehand.'

'How very kind,' Mel murmured politely.

'A splendid idea,' said Adam. 'We shall look forward to it.'

'And so shall I. Until tomorrow then. Au revoir!'

He lumbered off, a big, ungainly man, somewhat flat-footed, and with an apologetic stoop. He looked like an unemployed Army Officer if that, indeed, was what he was. He raised his hand in a friendly salute before disappearing.

'Slaughter the insects,' he shouted from in front of the high stone wall flanking the entrance.

'Good heavens, how does he know about the fly spray?' asked Adam.

'Miss 'what's her name' must have told him. I saw them talking.'

'He's bit odd,' Mel ventured, 'but good for a free dinner.'

Adam put a hand on her shoulder. 'Everything under control, darling? The day has gone well, hasn't it?'

'As well as it could have done I think. I shall like living here. The house feels solid and dependable and it's wonderful to have so much space again.'

She leant against the door lintel and surveyed the spillage of possessions which resembled an orderly rubbish dump.

'When everything is in place,' she said slowly, 'it will make a good set.'

Adam looked up from his unpacking. 'Set?' he puzzled.

'Stage set, for our continuous performance. Venice...Remember! My feelings haven't changed.'

He opened his mouth as if to speak, but closed it again, teeth banging together, cheek muscles tightening. She heard him sigh, however, the sharp retort that her comment deserved did not materialise. For the character that he was playing, the stage directions did not include exasperation.

****

Untroubled by mosquitoes, they all slept well. Mel awoke early.

The temporary curtains, hastily fixed the previous evening, were like mini-skirts over the deep windows and cheeky September sunlight danced through the naked lower panes. This room, on the front of the house, and facing east, was going to be sunny. She eased herself out of bed and on to the precious new carpet. Oh dear, was it too blue? She recalled her mother's telephoned advice before her heart attack:-

'Choose mid-tones, Mel. Better safe than sorry and a mid-tone is always good tempered'.

Mel doubted whether this would be 'mid' enough for her mother but she liked it. It was hyacinth blue. It would fade in the sun to match the rolls of heavenly chintz she had bought for the curtains. Once the children were settled into school she would concentrate on the house. Its wide, lofty rooms asked for elegance. What a lot there was to do. She must find a 'cleaner' too. Later on today she might call on the woman who had cleared up after the painters. She had been recommended by their predecessor, seemed a bouncy soul, and knew the form. Mel would probably engage her. How many hours could they afford and what would the rate be down here? It would be a pleasant change to be relieved of housework, providing the woman was easy to have around.

She crept over to the windows and bent to look through the seductive gap. She guessed it must be nearly seven o'clock and as if in telepathic communication with her, the abbey clock chimed its acquiescence. Marvellous! They had slept through all its nocturnal counting. She liked the timbre of these chimes. They did not boom and reverberate in one's head like those of the cathedral; gentler on the ear they were a pleasant, tactful, reminder that one was a quarter of an hour older and

44

the day that much shorter. The cathedral clock had laboured its message with unremitting clangour.

A secretive mist veiled the view of the distant hills, a view which would so soon become commonplace but which affected an early autumn modesty at this hour of the day.

It was a scene of peaceful serenity, not so much dominated by the abbey as enhanced by it. There was so much green around the building that it did not need to assert itself; it almost apologised for its own beauty. She decided to study books and pamphlets about it so that she could answer any questions which might come her way in the future. No doubt Adam had already done his homework. One must be au-fait with the history of such a monument when living with it cheek by jowl and perpetuating its message.

Adam stirred.

'Are you up?' he asked in a still-asleep voice.

'No! I'm looking out of the window.'

'Nice view?'

'Very.'

'Anyone about?'

'A man with a dog and a boy on a bicycle. Ah – it's the newspaper boy and he's riding straight across The Green.'

'I don't think he should. Nor should they.'

'Who?'

'Ruth and Seb, even though our new friend gave them permission.'

She turned to look at Adam who was now scratching his head, yawning, and pulling early morning faces.

'What is his name?'

'Piers Tarrant-Jones.'

'I do hope he doesn't go on calling me ma'am and dear lady', said Mel pulling on her pants. 'Did he say he's coming this morning?'

'Yes. He'll be useful. Let's employ him!'

'He's a good cook, I'll grant him that. His stew was super'.

Adam was sitting on the edge of the bed, still scratching. 'Did you hear what Seb said about it?' he asked.

'No, what?'

'He said it tasted like beer smells.'

Mel laughed.

'Poor Seb. It was too advanced for him. He had set his heart on sausages.'

She gave her hair a perfunctory comb and swilled her hands under the new taps in the re-furbished bathroom.

'Come on love, rise and shine,' she said as she opened the door.

'Yes – time I was up,' he said, obviously savouring the unfamiliar ambience. 'Nice to have the luxury of a dressing room,' he added, as he shuffled his feet into his slippers. Then, retrieving his bible and prayer book from the floor where he had left them the previous evening, he ambled into the adjoining room to do whatever it was that came first in his day.

'Make me a cup of tea, ma'am,' he teased.

'Certainly, your grace,' she mocked, before going to see whether the children were awake.

Colonel Tarrant-Jones arrived soon after ten and the two men settled into the business of marshalling the study while Mel tackled the mountainous agglomeration of assorted crockery, ironmongery and stores which rose from the kitchen floor.

Ruth and Seb had quickly decided, during tentative exploration of the town, that it was going to be a great place for cycling and although she was not happy about their wild circuits of The Green perimeter path or the diagonals carving into the grass from corner to corner, Mel left them to their sport. The bicycle bells, squeaking brakes and excited squeals would soon set tongues wagging. 'Those children of the new bishop ought to know better – little urchins!' But it suited her to have them out of the way for a couple of hours. A gang of camera-festooned tourists gazing at the Abbey gargoyles would not identify them. If Ruth was acting young for her age, her mother sympathised: she could hardly be expected to settle to cello practice today. They tired, predictably, and came to find squash and biscuits.

'Why is that man who came yesterday here again?' asked Ruth, her mouth full of shortbread. 'Is he a clergyman?'

'No darling, he's what's called a lay reader. Someone who helps in the Abbey. He's being useful with Daddy in the study and it's good that they're getting down to it. '

'What does lay mean?' pondered Seb.

'Just an ordinary person, not a vicar,' replied Mel before diverting the chatter with maternal ease and instructing 'there's a dairy at the bottom of the High Street. Go and buy half a dozen eggs and some milk.'

Ruth pouted. 'Must I? If *he's* so helpful,' - she pointed aggressively towards the front of the house – 'Why can't *he* go?'

'Ruth and me want to go on exploring,' supported Seb.

'Ruth and I,' intoned Mel, 'you can go exploring after you've shopped otherwise there won't be any lunch!'

She chased them out, armed with purse and shopping basket. How many more years, she wondered, of this interminable debate with Ruth. Every decision warranted discussion, half the discussions ended in indecision, and the indecisions frequently triggered trauma. She was tense, Meg knew that, and facing up to a new school as well as the unfamiliar environment, and she was desperately anxious, too, to know her latest music exam result which her teacher had so far neglected to communicate.

'If I haven't got distinction,' she brooded, with all the agony of some athlete fearing defeat, 'it will break my record.'

When Mel had a moment she would telephone someone, somewhere, and put her out of her misery. Hopefully the phone was connected! Seb was so calm and straightforward compared to Ruth. Two factors made all the difference. First, he was male, and second he had, as yet, no particular talent.

The larder shelves looked filthy and Mel decided to scrub them before unpacking the provisions. Dust had collected since the coats of white paint and the floor was revolting. She was on her knees, scouring, and trying not to look too closely at tangled spiders and flies or strewn mouse turds when Adam and Colonel Tarrant-Jones interrupted.

'Piers is just going, Mel. He has very kindly invited us to dinner on Monday.'

Embarrassed at being caught scrubbing, she straightened up and peeled off her rubber gloves.

'That will be lovely,' she said, 'especially if it means more of your delicious cooking.'

'Ma'am it will be my pleasure.'

Another 'ma'am'!

'I'm Mel,' she said awkwardly. 'At least, that is what everyone calls me. It's Amelia really.'

How lame it sounded. Why was she behaving like a schoolgirl?

47

'A beautiful name! Too beautiful to shorten, and more beautiful in the French tongue. I shall call you Amelie, if I may. I am Piers as you know.'

'An elegant gesture, Piers,' said Adam sensing Mel's discomfort, 'but she will probably answer to 'Mel' more quickly. How about lunch, darling?'

'Yes, of course. Do join us ... Piers?'

She spoke the name with difficulty and almost made it 'Pierre', but did not wish to humiliate him. 'It's scrambled eggs.'

As she was speaking, the front door slammed, voices muttered, and energetic feet scuffed along the passage.

'Here are the children, I hope they've brought the eggs.'

'Yes,' said Ruth, entering on cue, 'ages ago. They're in the fridge.'

'Good morning, young lady,' said Piers.

'Hello,' said Ruth, somewhat sullen.

'Do you have a name as enchanting as your mothers?'

'We think so,' rescued Adam. 'She is Ruth, and this horror here,' (Seb had followed Ruth into the kitchen and Adam's shadow boxed him playfully as he spoke), 'is Sebastian.'

'No one calls me that, only masters at school,' said Seb. 'Most of my friends just call me ...' and he paused briefly to spit out the consonants with some force, 'Seb!'

'Well,' said Piers, smiling. 'Ruth is a very special name, and it cannot be shortened, can it! I am sure that you are every bit as pure and graceful as your Old Testament namesake and may nightingales sing arias for you!'

He turned to look at Sebastian, who was not really listening.

'And you, Sebastian, majestic martyr, transfixed by arrows, you are equally distinguished ... I shall call you Sebastian, like your masters, but I shall be a friend as well! Let's shake on it, shall we?' and he and a stiff, poker-faced, Seb, shook on it!

'Yes,' enthused Seb 'and I've got an engine that puffs real smoke.'

'As for lunch, Amelie, sadly I must decline. I'm disappearing for a couple of days this afternoon and meanwhile my faithful Miss Biddle expects me.'

'Miss Biddle?' Mel echoed, questioning.

'I call her my batwoman,' he explained. 'I inherited her from my mother. Incidentally, she will be happy to sit in with the family here

48

while you are honouring me with your company on Monday. Her bark is worse than her bite, and she knows her way around here because she used to help out on occasions.'

'How very thoughtful,' Mel said. 'I'd forgotten about the babysitting problem.'

'I go to school the next day,' protested Ruth, resenting the fact that her parents were going out.

'Then we must be sure that you have everything ready by Monday afternoon,' Mel snapped briskly, ignoring the innuendo.

'And when does your term start, Sebastian?' asked Piers.

'Wednesday. I'm going to be a weekly border at my old school.'

'Ah - the Cathedral school?'

'Yes.'

'Are you looking forward to boarding?'

'Only a little bit,' he admitted.

'The little bit will get longer,' comforted Piers. 'One weekend when you are home you must come and visit me. Do you know that from the top floor of my house I can almost talk to the men in the signal box by the level-crossing. I have a feeling you might like trains. Is that so?'

'Yes,' enthused Seb, 'and I've got an engine that puffs real smoke.'

'Now that is really something. Will you show it to me one day?'

Seb's eyes sparkled. 'Yes I will certainly!' he said.

Mel suspected that Piers had spotted the pile of cartons and OO/HO railway boxes amongst the chaos. Seb's allegiance would be won speedily this way.

Piers turned to Adam. 'Well, sir, I must be on my way.'

'I'll see you out,' said Adam. 'Sorry we can't persuade you to share the eggs! I am most grateful for your help this morning.'

'My pleasure. Until Monday then, Amelie. I have explained to Adam where I live and I will despatch Miss B to you for six thirty. A bientot ...' With a gallant flourish he raised her hand to his lips, and although caught off guard, she now understood that this particular gesture was a characteristic of the man. He was probably the darling of every woman in the parish!

'Goodbye,' she said.

Adam and Piers were barely out of earshot before Seb asked, 'Mummy, why did that man kiss your hand?'

49

'Because he is unusually polite,' she answered, 'I expect he does it to everyone. I saw him do it on his way here yesterday.'

'He didn't do it to me,' observed Ruth. 'I thought it was silly, and why on earth does he call you a 'May leaf', Mummy?'

She laughed. 'Oh Ruth, you fool! He is saying Amelia the French way. A may lee ... try it.'

'A-may-lee, a-may-lee,' she chanted. 'And it does sound just like a 'May leaf', doesn't it, Daddy?' she appealed, as Adam rejoined them.

'A May leaf!! That is what you are exactly my love, isn't it,' replied Adam, lightly kissing her hair. 'Come on, who's for lunch? Wash your hands, troops, and get moving!'

'Can I break the eggs?' asked Ruth.

'Yes. Carry on. Here's a bowl.'

'Does that man play cricket, Daddy?' asked Seb, thoughtful as water spilled over his hands into the sink.

'Why Seb?'

'Well, he said he had a batwoman and I thought p'r'aps it was something to do with that bad eye.'

Adam roared with laughter.

'Well bowled, son, but not quite on the wicket! A batman is an Army officer's servant really, so I presume this Miss Biddle to be a kind of housekeeper. Understand?'

'Sort of.'

'What did he mean about nightingales singing for me?' asked Ruth.

'That,' replied Adam, 'is a reference to a famous poem by Keats called, 'Ode to a Nightingale'. The poet suggests that the beautiful song of this bird might have cheered up Ruth when she was pining for her homeland. You remember the story of Ruth – we've told it to you often enough?'

Ruth nodded. 'Can you remember the poem?'

Adam thought hard.

'I can't,' Mel said defeated. 'I can't get beyond, 'Thou wast not born for death, immortal bird'...

'Wait, I've got it,' said Adam, jubilant, and now able to recite:-

'Perhaps the self-same song that found a path
Through the sad heart of Ruth, when sick for home,
She stood in tears amid the alien corn.'

50

Ruth was listening intently. 'I see,' she said. 'It's clever.'

'When the books are all unpacked I'll find it for you,' offered Adam.

'Mmm,' she murmured, nodding slowly.

The chatter continued as eggs were scrambled and the table laid in a haphazard kind of way and when Adam eventually located an opener, a cool lager had never before tasted so good.

Suddenly Ruth said, 'I wonder what's wrong with his eye?'

I expect it's a sty,' Seb answered wisely. 'There was a boy at school who had a great big sty …'

'Seb,' interrupted Adam between protracted sips of lager, 'describe the sty more carefully. To use 'great' and 'big' is to abuse the English language! Think of a second adjective or, better still, use only one!'

Adam could be pedantic about mental sloppiness!

'Well, huge,' Seb continued, 'an absolute whopper.' Adam flinched.

'Cupfuls of poison came out of it. I'll bet he's got a sty under that cover. What do you think, Mummy?'

'Probably,' Mel said, buttering toast.

'Well, I have no idea,' said Adam. 'But one thing I do know is that I am starving.'

Ruth was pensive.

'It will not be as simple as that with him,' she said slowly. 'He is kind of filmy and different. With him it will be something much much rarer.'

'Why should it?' argued Seb.

'Why indeed?' thought Mel.

****

By Monday, the house was more or less straight and the pieces of the new life shaking into a clearer pattern after the kaleidoscopic upheavals of the past few months. Mel had engaged Maidie Sloggett to help in the house – with such a name she would surely prove to be 'a treasure' - and Adam had found a part-time secretary who would start at the beginning of October. They had also alerted local garages to be on the lookout for a reliable small car, realising that they could no longer escape the fact that the moment had arrived when a second vehicle was a necessity.

Uncertain as to what to wear to the party, Mel found the Tarrant-Jones number and telephoned to enquire. She found herself speaking to a deep, but female, voice which she assumed to belong to Miss Biddle. The dialogue was stilted.

'The Colonel is out madam. He will not be dressing for dinner. He expects you for sherry at six thirty and I shall arrive to sit in for you at six twenty-five. Is there anything special about the children, madam?'

'No, nothing special at all. I'm very grateful to you for volunteering to come. It's extremely kind.'

'I do not volunteer, madam. Anything which the Colonel asks of me I am ready to do for him.'

It was a formidable introduction. Mel sensed an undercurrent of hostility but dismissed it as nothing more on her part than a reluctance to come to terms with a new situation. It would take time for the Miss Biddles of the town to accept that the new bishop and his family were human. Adam's face was already known around the Abbey, but hers was not. She was determined to make as good an impression as possible and to avoid any gesture which could be interrupted, albeit incorrectly, as a desire on her part to usurp the position of the vicar's wife. She judged that she would be neither fish, fowl, nor good red herring! Instinct must help her to discover the right habitat. She had already been both vicar's wife, and 'substitute first lady'; now as the actual 'first lady', she might find herself not figuring in the parish popularity charts! Ellen Hughes, whom she would meet that evening, was firmly entrenched in the vicarage. She need fear no salvos from across the abbey green.

'The Colonel is not dressing for dinner!'' Mel giggled at the idea of turning up undressed but Adam was in no mood to be flippant as he rumpled through his clothes piles.

'Darling, don't get so frantic, your suit is in the cupboard and your beautiful new mauve 'vest' on the chair in the dressing room.' Adam grunted!

'What do bishops wear when one does dress for dinner?'

'G.O.K.' he said.

'What is that?'

'God only knows! Probably gaiters!'

'Don't forget the cross.'

'Do I wear it?'

'Alastair wore his the whole time.'

'Yes, I suppose I do then.'

The cross was the gift of the Cathedral clergy. Adam had asked particularly that it should be simple and the local silversmith had complied with his wishes though not without protest. 'Only the plainest of representational symbols,' Adam insisted. 'Not a pretty piece of jewellery.' Deprived though he was of the excitement of creating an ornate and original masterpiece, the long-suffering craftsman admitted, in the end, to being pleased with the result. Presumably, it should be dunked in 'silver dip' from time to time! Where his other vestments were concerned Adam was almost casual – happy to leave the colours and design of his cope to the whims of others and to those of the Jewish seamstress who worked it with such meticulous care.

'What are you wearing, darling?' Adam called from next door.

'My favourite skirt?'

'Which one? You have so many!'

'The green one.'

It was still warm enough to look summery and Mel felt good in the fine swiss cotton which fell in soft, generous, folds from a neatly belted waist. The rich jade and blue floral motifs were broken by tapering spirals of russet tendrils which complemented her newly washed auburn hair. She had shampooed the latter, but it was not looking its liveliest. She would search out the best-groomed head at the party and discuss the merits of the local hairdressers. Her pale jade silk shirt was elegant, and the pearls which her parents had given her for her twenty-first birthday just cleared the scalloped collar. She remembered to wear Alastair's ring.

Together they stood in front of the long, lacquered, 'sale-bargain' mirror and admired themselves and each other.

'Will I do?' asked Adam, stroking his violet chest, a little coyly. He looked distinguished in his charcoal grey bishop's suit, like a scrubbed, rather old, school prefect. Mel kissed him lightly on the cheek. It was so incongruous, but, perhaps, after all, they did look the part. Yes, they would do!

Their preening was interrupted by a ring on the front door bell.

Mel vaulted down the stairs in stockinged feet. 'You must be Miss Biddle,' she welcomed. 'Do come in.'

She was a plain, but powerful, middle aged spinster and exuded competence. She could have played Mrs Fairfax in a dramatised Jane Eyre.

Ruth and Seb were watching television.

'We are perfectly well able to look after ourselves,' growled Ruth, after the introduction.

'Hush Ruth, dear, you know Daddy and I never leave you alone. Be sure to look after Miss Biddle, and be in bed, and I mean 'in' by nine. Seb, you go up half an hour earlier, OK?'

'Yes alright. Don't talk, this is the best part!' His face was cupped in his hands and his attention riveted on the shoot-out between 'goodies' and 'baddies' in some mediocre cowboy film.

'Are the telephones in the same places, madam?' enquired Miss Biddle. 'In case there are any messages.'

'Yes, they are. Ruth will show you the new layout of the kitchen. Do please help yourself to coffee and sandwiches.'

'Thank you. I expect there are some changes in the house. It certainly needed painting, madam,' and she wrinkled her nose as though testing for pollution!

'I don't expect we will be too late', said Mel. 'Good night Ruth, good night Seb. God bless. Goodbye Miss Biddle.'

She escaped to collect smart shoes, coat and handbag while Adam made his number with Miss Biddle and kissed the children. He banged the front door. Mel smoothed his hair into place as she might have done Seb's. She was proud of him. She wanted to hold his hand, but he kept it tidily in his trouser pocket as they walked briskly to the first social engagement of the new life. On the way they talked eagerly about the folk they might meet at St Mark's Lodge.

****

'Lovely to see you both,' Piers greeted on their arrival before showing them into a reception room. It was oppressively sombre and full of people all focusing in their direction and suddenly silent. As Mel hesitated she felt touch on her arm.

'Courage, Amelie, they do not bite!'

Energy returned. Conversations resumed, picked up like dropped stitches, patterns continuing. She was thrust into a trio of females.

'Mrs Amelia Ellis,' introduced Piers, 'Hannah Weston, Elizabeth Hughes, Prudence Ogilvie.'

They acknowledged each other with stilted middle class formality.

'My god, the new bishop's wife. Why didn't I wear my hat or my veil!' wailed the jolliest looking specimen.

'Not for me please,' Mel laughed. 'I never wear hats.'

'What a consolation!'

Piers edged in with a glass. 'My own classic brew, or would you prefer sherry, ma'am?'

'Thank you,' she smiled, 'I'll sample the brew.'

'Bloody potent, Piers, what's in it?' demanded the chatterbox.

'My blend of magic,' he replied. 'Guaranteed to keep you on the straight and narrow path Hannah.'

'Well, I shall be off course any moment now, you bastard,' she chaffed. ' He needs watching, Mrs Ellis. These girls will vouch for that, won't you?'

'I stick to sherry, anyway,' said Elizabeth Hughes, ignoring the invitation to join in the banter. 'I'm delighted to meet you Mrs Ellis. My father is the vicar here. We have all been looking forward to your arrival.'

'Oh yes, it's lovely for us to have a family in the Tower House,' simpered Prudence Ogilvie, nervously sipping a tomato juice. No brew for her! They conversed awkwardly for a few moments and then Hannah, who was obviously popular and snatched the conversation at every opportunity, declared that 'Mrs Ellis must be shunted on to meet more of the town riff-raff.' Here was a character, Mel realised. She was to become her greatest friend.

'Old Piers asked me to make sure you meet everyone,' Hannah explained. 'Mustn't miss a body, must we. Look! He's dragging your old man all round to say hello, too!'

Mel was deftly manoeuvred from group to group until finally, with the tour complete, she rejoined Adam and the few selected guests who were obviously staying on to have dinner.

'At last,' said Piers. 'A party of more manageable proportions. Adam and Amelie, are you clear as to who pairs with whom in this conclave? Let me recap,' and he swiftly presented their fellow diners, most of whose hands they had already shaken, so that they were assured of their identities. He then left 'to attend to the feast' as he phrased it, and during this interlude Mel found herself sitting next to Hannah, which pleased her.

'Tell me about yourself, dearie,' she said. 'How old are your brats?'

'Ruth is twelve and Sebastian nine.'

'Kittens! God, you're young. My two are nineteen and sixteen. I'm an old hag, a nervous wreck, too, after running a sodding school boarding house for ten years.'

'Ah! You must be at the Queen's School.'

'For my sins – and Giles over there is the HM. We're Direct Grant, you know, in or out depending on the bloody government and right now, almost out! I can't say I care much what happens so long as Giles gets his pension. His successor will have to go completely independent.'

'When does your husband retire?'

'Eleven more bloody years! He's older than he looks. Eight years older than me, too, poor bugger!'

'Take heart. Adam is nine years older than me.'

'You're a mere chicken', she pronounced. 'By the way, I'm Hannah in case you've forgotten after so many new names!'

'And I'm Mel.'

'Now that's what I call sensible. Amelia is a bit of a mouthful, at the best of times, duckie, so I thoroughly approve. Parents ought to consider their children's feelings before saddling them with outlandish names.'

Mel smiled and changed the subject. 'How long have you lived here?'

'Over twenty years now. It's a good place to live. The quality of life thing is quite special.'

'You must know everybody. Like Piers.'

'I suppose we do. Old Piers is a bit of a mystery really, you know. As a matter of fact,' and she lowered her voice, 'we all expect him to shack up with Elizabeth over there one of these days. She's eating her heart out for him, poor lass.'

'He strikes me as a confirmed bachelor.'

'Very likely. I tease him. It's good for him to imagine he's a womaniser, but he isn't really. He has this kind of old world charm... But you never quite know what is going on behind that 'Dead-Eye-Dick' stare!'

A trifle shocked by this blatant reference to his disability, Mel decided to wait until she knew Hannah better before pursuing this particular conversation, although her curiosity was already aroused.

Over dinner, she studied the others. The vicar, Felix Hughes, on her right, talked fervently about the history and present state of the abbey as they sipped ice-cold vichyssoise from heavy Victorian spoons. The launching of an appeal for repairs to the roof and fabric featured prominently.

'I hope I live to see the work completed and the debts paid,' he said. 'It is going to take years.' He looked exhausted already.

His refined, aesthetic, countenance was echoed in the face of his daughter, Elizabeth, who sat opposite, but fuller, softer, lines gave her more than a hint of a hidden sensuality which, if satisfied, could unmask real beauty. The dependability of her expression appealed to Mel. From that first evening, she liked her. She guessed that they were about the same age. Every now and then Elizabeth looked towards Piers as though she expected something. Time would not be her ally for much longer.

Ellen Hughes, her mother, a dumpy soul, solid as a Henry Moore sculpture, exchanged a few sentences between courses across Piers' temporarily vacated chair. She struck Mel as a shy woman, still very much on her best behaviour. Made anxious, maybe, by this meeting with strangers who must of necessity become intimates. She found reassurance in appraising and talking about her daughter.

'Elizabeth is probably discussing medical things with Ian Davidson next to her,' she surmised. 'He is one of our doctors and she is a theatre sister. She so loves her job!'

'Does she work locally?'

'No, in London. At present she is on night duty so it is worth her while to come home for her four days off.'

There was a silence, embarrassed by a mutual focusing on Elizabeth.

'Did you have a nice holiday in Wales?' Mel asked politely.

'Very restful, thank you. Do you know Wales?'

A reply was unnecessary because Piers squeezed back into his chair at this moment and castrated the conversation.

'Salade, Amelie – verte!'

He held the bowl and she helped herself. She was aware suddenly of an unnatural absorption with lettuce as the bowl tilted towards her. Tough, sand coloured, skin stretched over the tracery of veins and bones on the backs of the hands which held the bowl. The fingers were wide, rounded and strong. The nails squared by scissors. What was it her mother had said long ago? 'A man's hands, eyes and teeth, in that order, will always reveal all that you need to know.' There seemed to be an earthy power in these hands. Somewhere, inside her, something tightened. She needed reassurance. Glancing up, she found it in Adam's agile, tapered fingers as he gesticulated, characteristically while making some point to Mrs Davidson, who was listening intently. Yes! These hands, cradling the bowl, were undoubtedly larger than life. They were giant-sized. They frightened her.

'Enough Amelie?'

'Sorry, I was dreaming! Yes – lovely, thank you.'

Sleek, glazed, coq au vin lay steaming on the plate in front of her. A culinary masterpiece!

'God, Piers, this is bloody delicious,' called Hannah, across the table, relishing the first mouthful. 'Fanny Craddock and her old man are still in cookery kindergarten compared with you!'

Everyone laughed.

'Do you grow your own chickens, Piers?' teased Felix.

'Of course, and ring their scrawny necks!'

More laughter. Yet suddenly, for no reason at all, Mel felt a strangling sensation.

Her own first morsel of chicken churned in her mouth and she could not swallow it. In the end she flooded it down her throat with a large gulp of wine. She felt an overwhelming, blind, fear. She wanted to leap from the table and flee, she knew not where, from this slow suspended moment of strangulation. Whether it was the effect of 'the brew' or the sight of the rich food, she could not tell, but somehow it was also to do with large hands and necks and death.

All around voices chattered, knives and forks clattered.

A shiver, in the nape of Mel's neck, crept upwards to inch round the back of her head like a furtive, sinister, caress. My God! she thought, surely I'm not going to pass out! She concentrated on breathing deeply, her eyes fixed on her plate, her hands automatically breaking a chunky crust of bread into silly small pieces. She held on to her consciousness and willed her vision to stabilise. Her head felt as though it was spinning on some terrifying fairground machine. She seemed to rise above the table and to see the chewing, jeering, dinner party faces beneath as they jerked up and down and from side to side like mechanical leering puppets, until the seconds of weird panic passed and she was secure and nearly normal on her chair again.

She reached for her handbag which was on the floor.

'Can I help?' asked Piers.

'Just my bag – for a handkerchief,' she said as casually as she could.

'A little more wine, Amelie?'

'Thank you', she said. She was in control. The crisis was over.

'Tell me about those two special children,' he said.

So she did.

****

On the way back to Tower House, Adam said, 'You looked rather pale during dinner. Were you alright?'

'I felt peculiar for a moment. It was probably the cocktail.'

'Are you still taking tranquillisers?'

'No. Perhaps I should be.'

She clung to Adam as they ambled back to the Tower House. A mature cheesy moon presided over the deep blue-black velvet of a gentle September night. They had been the last to leave, but not by long. Away across the Green, upstairs lights glowed in the vicarage. Felix, Ellen, and Elizabeth Hughes were going to bed. Hannah and Giles and the Davidsons all lived at the northern end of the town and had travelled by car. 'You must come and see us', they shouted as they left and Mel confidently anticipated that they would call or phone quite soon. The Davidsons had a son, Tim, who was the same age as Seb and might be a good contact. It was always a business finding the right slots for one's children.

'I enjoyed the evening. Did you?' said Adam.

'It was interesting. I like Hannah Weston.'

'A character! I wonder why she is so loud mouthed?'

'Just an act. Harmless enough.'

'What did you make of the Hughes trio?'

'He's nice. And Elizabeth. But I can't see myself having much in common with Ellen!'

'Piers' house is a bit grim, isn't it?' Adam continued, 'all that heavy Victoriana.'

'It goes quite well with him,' she commented.

She had not studied it all that carefully. She would have a better look next time. Certainly the navy blue velvet curtains and dark chair covers had been depressing but she had been unusually unobservant of the rest.

Mel scribbled in her diary at midnight while Adam retraced his steps round three sides of a square to escort Miss Biddle back to St Marks.

The entry reads thus:-

Monday, 15 September 1962
'Good evening at St Marks, Piers' house in Saints Avenue. Dozens drinking before – dinner afterwards for us plus Hughes, Davidsons and Westons. Fantastic food, all cooked by P. Felt strange during dinner – seemed to float above the table – most odd! Not much in common with E Hughes – seems dull. Like Elizabeth. She likes P. Is he attracted to her? Think Hannah W will have the answers. She is a good sort. When we need a doctor will sign on with Ian D. He and wife Mary have son, Tim, who could be friend for Z. Feel we are launched!'

Early the next morning as Adam slept peacefully beside her she added the following paragraph.

'I seemed to dream all night. We were dancing around a huge beast, roasting on a spit. It was the size of an elephant but had the limbs of a turkey. It lay, sizzling; flames scorching its flesh, the searing skin erupting into glistening glycerine, globules of phosphorescence which burst, then glowed, like blind albescent eyes. With long leaden weapons, we stretched out to pierce the pulsating incandescent bubbles, but a heavy chain held us back. We were secured both in front and behind. I dragged at it. It was icy. Vivid sheets of red and orange splashed the grey shadows and brilliant coruscations blazed into the circle of silhouettes. We were all there. Adam, me, Felix, Ellen, Piers, Elizabeth, Hannah, Giles, Ian and Mary, gyrating, struggling straining to be free of the fetters and to puncture those oozing orbs. Piers had a huge oxidised key which he threw and I caught. The others signalled with their iron staves that a padlock hung down from the chain and was swinging behind me. But although I picked up the key, I could not twist to reach to padlock and the more I tried the more the chain tightened

60

as the others heaved and pulled. Frantically I tried again and this time the key rammed home, but even as I gasped with relief it fractured and fell in pieces on to the lava tinted ground. It was made of clinker...'

She put down the pencil, lay back on the pillow, and closed her eyes again until a long unending scream bored its way into the pervading horror of this grotesque dream and its macabre cremation rite. It was the alarm clock, ringing into the silver tapers of light strung across the bedroom. It reminded her that she had to get up and take Ruth to her new school this morning.

Chapter IV

DISCOVERIES

For several months the new life felt temporary. An impression, not unlike that of being on holiday, bred a sense of limitation, and a niggling urgency that there was another place, cosy and familiar, to which Mel and the family must soon return. But gradually she acclimatised, and the cognisance that this home was likely to prove more permanent than any of its predecessors steadily grafted into her awareness until, like a strong new shoot, it became a part of her. They embarked on a series of satisfying years, often overfull of weeks so committed that they bulged and expanded like elasticated parcels. Adam worked long hours and hard, capitalising on the opportunities brought by his enhancement, while Mel learnt that many of her fears and much of her 'future shock' syndrome had been ridiculous.

To some extent the community protected them. It was not vanity to admit that they were popular but their prestige was not won without tact. Mel reminded Adam, occasionally, of his good fortune in having her for a wife. She felt, too, that she controlled the balance between approachability and over-familiarity. This was not something at which she worked consciously, yet she knew it to be so, and it helped to make their position in the community secure and comfortable.

A strange glow pervaded the recurring recollections of the bizarre experience over dinner and the ensuing surrealist dream which had been features of that first visit to St Mark's Lodge. The choice of dinner guests was not accidental, that was certain, and through the early years the support and friendship of this chosen group brought, like an unexpected gift, a happy bonus into their lives. Individually, or in pairs, they all became real friends, although, as Mel quickly realised they were far from being in each other's pockets.

Hannah, for example, was very absorbed in her life as a headmaster's wife and tended to embrace the folk connected with the school. A great 'do gooder' she was everyone's ally, yet admitted, when she and Mel came to know each other well, that Mel was her first real confidant since school days. Mel believed her. Tough and extroverted she could ride any crisis. Her refreshing outspokenness, colourfully interpolated with epithets, made her an amusing companion for an away day to the theatre or the coast. Even shopping became stimulating in her company. Giles, her husband, had seemed remote at that first meeting, but Adam and Mel soon understood that his detachment, twin-born of dedication to his job and Hannah's domination of any conversation, did not imply disinterest. Some found Hannah irritating, even overbearing. Others rated her a gossip: probably they were right!

Adam enjoyed being with Ian Davidson and if they went anywhere as a foursome, it tended to be with him and Mary. They would drive out to a country pub and tuck into late night steaks or scampi, their professional identities temporarily discarded and discretion diluted by alcohol. Ian called them our 'bugger all nights.' 'Bugger the souls and bugger the bodies,' he declared scurrilously, one evening when both he and Adam were delayed and they all reached the Rose and Crown too late for his favourite whitebait.

He was healthy for Adam.

'Do you know, you are the only one of my patients with piles to match his vest,' he would joke, and Adam, brought down to earth, was easily encouraged to mimic some of the more obsequious of the diocesan clergy, with side-splitting realism. He claimed that he and Ian had a special dispensation to say outrageous things to each other and to behave with a measure of abandon which would have been unpardonable elsewhere. This promoted a confidence and freedom which enabled them to divulge the sacred secrets of their own confessionals if such betrayal could be of positive benefit to some 'stricken soul'.

Bereft of their husbands, Mary and Mel had little to discuss apart from their sons who did, in fact, become good friends, using and abusing each other as their moods dictated. Temperamentally they were opposites. Tim Davidson was short, rugged and surprisingly brusque, his banalities bordering on insolence. Seb, lean and rangy, became, during his adolescent years, brooding, melancholy, and pale-faced, like some frustrated poet. They went to different boarding schools and when holiday weeks found them in need of company, a game of tennis, or visit to the cinema, sufficed to sustain the liaison.

'Elizabeth and Piers' provided another talking point but so far as one could ascertain their relationship remained static, at the point of take-off, prevented, for some reason, from ever leaving the runway.

Hannah expounded her theory. 'Damn shame! It's ma Biddle and those moth-eaten Hughes parents that are the problems. Ma B makes Piers too cosy and, ultimately, if you bed Elizabeth you are saddled with old Felix and Ellen, too!'

'Perhaps,' Mel said flippantly, 'when Elizabeth is an orphan, and Piers an old man without a batwoman, it will all come right.'

'You are a romantic, duckie! I've been saying now or never for the past five years. Now I'm finally plumping for never!'

'Do they go out together?'

'Lord, yes! Platonic platters in the pub – or perhaps the theatre. Piers is dotty about plays! She is there if he wants her and he if she wants him. It's beautiful, bloody, and wasteful, but she is too good to complain... or do the other thing!'

'She is good, I agree' mused Mel, 'In a noble kind of way.'

'That makes two of 'em, Mel.'

'Oh, I'm not so sure about Piers!' Mel quibbled.

'Pure as lilies, love! Virgins both!' She pronounced.

Hannah's dogmatic conclusion lodged in Mel's mind and her phrase, 'virgins both' prompted caution when she was tempted to pry or pressurise her friendships with Elizabeth and Piers which developed side by side, yet individually. True she was a romantic, but no useful purpose would be served by aligning with a cajoling crowd too anxious to tidy two nomadic lives into a neat married whole. Better surely, to stand aside, and let things take their course. If, along the way, some startling event powered the relationship into the air, so much the better.

When, rarely, Mel dared to tease Elizabeth about Piers she just smiled, somewhat wistfully. If there was a secret between them she intended to keep it. One certainly gained the impression that she considered Piers to be her property; there was never a hint of any other man in her life.

Mel encouraged Elizabeth to come across for a chat and a cup of coffee whenever she was home. She enjoyed talking about the famous London hospital and Mel was a ready listener, easily projected into a life with which she could relate. Elizabeth tried, unsuccessfully, to persuade Mel to practice as a physiotherapist again but Mel believed everything to be changing too rapidly and did not relish the idea of refresher courses or managing new techniques. For Elizabeth, the tenets of her job extended beyond a mere day's work. There were times when one could detect that she was suffering and worrying over a patient and willing her days off to be over so that she could get back to the hospital. She admitted that she carried her brief too far but she was unable to accept a body which left the operating table as just one more butchered hunk of diseased or damaged flesh. She felt compelled to visit it, afterwards, still semi-anaesthetised, in its ward, and to identify with it. She must have been held in some esteem by other staff to be allowed on to their territories. Possibly she confided to them, as she did to Mel that she might have found more fulfilment as a social worker.

'Their bodies are not enough for me, Mel,' she explained, 'I need to become involved in their lives. The irony is that while their bodies often recover, their lives can remain rotten – and others, whose lives are good, lose out when their bodies let them down. My job in the theatre can be done by a mechanic. That's why I try to do more.' Mel was impressed, although uncertain where such sentiments might lead.

At first Elizabeth seemed genuinely interested in Ruth and Seb and Mel would chatter happily about their exploits, believing that these would also be fed back to Ellen in the vicarage. However, when confronted by the children face to face, Elizabeth was peculiarly awkward and ill at ease and this niggled. It strengthened a growing feeling that Elizabeth forged relationships on her terms and her behaviour at the hospital seemed to support these findings. Because she was attracted to her she assumed a need in Mel's role, as a mother, to discuss family matters and went along with it until it had served its purpose.

Mel was quite objective. It did not worry her if her friends did not care for her children! Even so, Elizabeth's paradoxical behaviour was interesting and, in the context of her alliance with Piers, it posed some conundrums.

It became rare for more than two or three days to pass without Hannah and Mel communicating, either by telephone or by calling in on each other. The friendship was precious to both of them, the more so perhaps because the nature of Giles's and Adam's vocations deprived their wives of their undivided attention for so much of the time. Mel was fascinated by Hannah's life. Being married to a headmaster, who was also housemaster of the school's large boarding house, was more than a full-time job. Hannah's routine was like a circus act. She was forever juggling. One moment she would be rushing an injured boy to the hospital to be stitched, and, the next helping to cook for her sixty lodgers because one of the kitchen assistants had 'had a turn.' Twice a week one found her playing snap with hundreds of clean tumbled socks, the intertwined fuzzy grey navy mass gradually shrinking as she matched colour to colour, nametape to nametape, with jubilant shouts. A sudden free hour would find her chasing to the Cash and Carry to fill the old Morris Oxford estate car (already crammed with broken Hoovers and polishers) with huge giant's breakfast tins of fruit, or baked beans, known in the catering business, so she enlightened Mel, as 'A 10's'. A spare few minutes before lunch just allowed her time to compose a reassuring note to a worried mother with the news that 'Jeremy's diarrhoea is better and his verruca being treated by Dr Davidson.'

'How do you cope with it all, Hannah?' Mel marvelled.

'Easy when you know how! Like a game of chess! Make the right moves and you win. Wrong moves, check mate! Start again! It's a piece of cake now the kids are off my hands, bless 'em.'

Her easy dismissal of 'the kids' which referred to Susie and Guy, belied her maternal pride in two of the happiest and most relaxed young people Mel would ever know.

Felix sometimes called at the Tower House but found it more satisfactory to catch Adam out on the Green, or as he drove off in his car. The windows of the living room at the front of the vicarage afforded Felix a clear view of the archway and a quick sprint through his own back gate to the corner by the bus stop meant that he could waylay Adam, providing the car turned left into East Avenue. If it turned right then Felix either pushed a note through the letter box or telephoned later in the day.

Ellen, unlike her daughter, never visited unless invited. As Mel had foreseen, her timidity made it difficult to get on terms. Her alliance with Felix was a strange one. There can have been little mental affinity in it, but she was busy, kindly and dutiful and made hundred-weights of marmalade, tomato pickle and crab apple jelly! She had a compatibility with the country folk from the villages, perhaps because she was more akin to them. Mel never managed to persuade her to call her by her Christian name. It was always 'Mrs Ellis'. Maidie, Mel's precious cleaner worked out her own compromise and always addressed Mel as 'Mrs Bishop', which was quite endearing. She was a tough little Liberal, and Welsh, like Piers' mother.

Not that Piers talked much of his mother. Hannah and Maidie did so instead. Maidie's revelations were interesting for her aunt had worked for 'the General's wife' and Maidie gleefully recounted many an anecdote form those days. Like most of her sex in the town, she had a soft spot for 'Captain Pears' as she called him and as he frequently visited the house when she was there, she had plenty of excuse to feed me background. It was not only 'Captain Pears' about whom she gossiped, it was every other local caller, too. 'Maidie', Mel would remonstrate, 'don't tell me all these naughty things…!' Fortunately for Mel she enjoyed the telling too much and any protests went unheeded.

Mel learnt that St Marks had been home for Piers for the whole of his life. His father had purchased the angular gothic Victorian house for his bride and himself during the euphoric period which followed the armistice in 1918. A professional soldier, he had survived some of the worst horrors of the trenches to return, victorious, to claim his fiancée. They were of mature age, and no time was lost. Two sons were born in rapid succession and duly christened Andre (a tribute to the French which Maidie pronounced 'Handray') and Piers.

When Adam and Mel arrived on the scene, the General had been dead for fifteen years, but he was still affectionately remembered and many of the older generation could reminisce about him. He had been a real character. Incensed that retirement from the army overtook him before the outbreak of war in 1939 he threw himself into Civil Defence and Home Guard activities with all the enthusiasm of a young subaltern and martialled the defences of the community to withstand every form of attack. It must have been frustrating for him that the only threat to the nestling town, tucked so snugly into untroubled Wessex Downs, came from a couple of stray bombs which a lost, lonely, Messerschmitt evacuated before crash landing further west.

Piers once said that his parents were more like grandparents. For most of his childhood, his father had overseas postings. Mrs Tarrant-Jones chose not to accompany her husband, occupying herself instead with a formidable array of causes. In the town she *was* the Red Cross, the Mother's Union, and the Girl Guides, becoming, eventually, a tyrannical local Commissioner. Her sons were first nannied and then boarded, into a school system which in 'the thirties', implied that home was a place for holidays only. Piers always expected to follow his father into the army and his own baptism of fire, straight from school, took him through the North African and Italian campaigns. By the end of the war in Europe he had a row of medals and the rank of acting major.

Andre became a lawyer and ultimately settled in Chiswick with his wife and three daughters. Piers liked his brother, loathed June, his sister-in-law, and laughed at his nieces. Mel and her family met them all when they visited Piers for weekends; he would invite them in after Matins – so that his sister-in-law could 'name-drop' at her next Thames-side cocktail party. Viola, Serena and Lydia (who was Ruth's age) were all as whimsical as their names, Andre pompous and overbearing, and June only interested in her new 'William Morris' chair covers or the next fashion show at Peter Jones.

Piers, a generous uncle, always sought Ruth's advice on Christmas and birthday presents for the girls, until one day, caught at one of her most fractious moments, she snapped, 'Oh, for heaven's sake Uncle Piers, give them frilly undies! It's all girls like them understand, and all they are fit for!' He never asked again. 'Mr Handray was not the old lady's favourite son, Mrs Bishop,' volunteered Maidie, 'Captain Pears was always her boy, mind. Oh, but she was a tiger, and when Mrs Handray had a third girl she would not even send the babby a present.'

Hannah, who had known Mrs Tarrant-Jones quite well, revealed:-

'The old bag ruled Piers with a rod of iron. She was a real martinet. Never wanted him to grow up, poor sod. Tried to make him into a Wodehouse 'poof'. He pandered to her – had to, I suppose, as she was pushing it a little. She was a fierce old bitch. Either you were accepted or you weren't, and the test, as likely as not, was whether you were wearing gloves on your first introduction to her. Bloody funny really! Poor old Piers was devoured by her – hardly had time to go to the loo, let alone get to the altar like Brother Andre.'

Maidie offered another titbit:-

'When Captain Pears lost his eye, that nearly killed her, Mrs Bishop. She was in a terrible state and went very funny in her ways. Indeed to goodness, you would have thought it was *her* eye the good Lord had taken, the fuss she made. There was the lovely Captain, his face all spoilt, and she could not bear to look at him. Terrible it was.'

Hannah chuckled over her demise:-

'Thank God the old cow choked over her grapefruit one morning. I'll bet she was shocked to discover she hadn't finished it and absolutely livid that old Piers was still on terra firma. She would have preferred him to kick the bucket with her!'

It did not dawn on Mel for some time that Mrs Tarrant-Jones had actually died only a few months prior to the first meeting with Piers or that the years preceding her death had created such a revolution in her son's life. The accident to his eye (which, according to Maidie had been caused by 'a foreign explosion' but 'not a war one') brought premature retirement from the army, and the return to St Marks, during this unkind period of adaptation to his changed fortunes, meant that he had to cope also with the athero-whims of a distraught elderly parent. It cannot have been easy and accounts for the exuberance of his welcome to the Ellis family, she thought. It was not that he sought sympathy, far from it, it was more a question of his need for new faces and new causes. For Piers, the family materialised at the right psychological moment.

Mel decided that her family must have a fatal fascination for eccentric bachelors, although any similarity between their friendships with Piers and Alastair ended with that statement. Alastair was guide and guardian, Piers more of a follower – an amusing companion, a sagacious advisor, but, when the occasion demanded, always deferential to Adam. Piers made no secret of his faith. Indeed, one of his first positive actions on returning to live at St Marks permanently was to take the steps to become a lay reader, a move which apparently received every encouragement and support from Felix. Piers himself argued that the obligatory study would build up confidence in his 'one cylinder sight' as he termed it and also help the right eye to compensate quickly. He made light of problems and rejected restriction of any kind.

It was clear that Piers, both able and available, was the best person to administrate the Abbey Restoration Appeal so dear to the heart of Felix. His mission brought frequent contact and made him an integral part of diocesan debate. He was almost one of the Clergy. Certainly his perception and acumen (though military at times) was vastly superior to that of many of the rural incumbents who barely rose from their rectory beds in time to administer the chalice.

A few months after the family moved into the Tower House, Piers and Mel were standing in the front hall and Mel asked Piers whether he had any regrets about his lost army career. His answer was definitive.

'At the time, Amelie, yes! I was offered an office job in the Ministry of Defence, but, on balance, decided that it would be wiser to quit. I believed there to be a reason for this graze' (he indicated his patched eye) 'but I would be unlikely to discover it playing out time behind a desk. I needed to be free of the army... only now am I beginning to understand just how and where I was being directed.'

Astonished, Mel queried:-

'You believe that this is how God operates?'

He smiled.

'I never said anything about God, Amelie, now did I? But, frankly, yes – I suppose I do believe just that.'

'So, if one has an accident, as you did, He has a reason for it? It's all there, in the master plan for your life, and why not a blueprint for the response, too? Surely this is fatalism, not faith?'

Piers, sensing her aggression, replied swiftly,

'You miss the point. I don't see God as actually introducing misfortune into a life – ie 'My servant Piers will be sent various vicissitudes on the first of March and these are the details.' It's entirely a question of utilising what happens to one in a positive way and making it available to Him, for His glory.'

Mel turned away, cringing, a Ruth-like expression on her face probably betraying the stubbornness which rose inside her at this righteous twist in the argument. She was surrounded by pietists; he, and Adam, as pragmatic as each other, equally adept at causing allergic blisters of guilt and inadequacy to swell up inside her. It was not fair.

She looked up and saw the bafflement on his face. He spoke again, more gently, almost in an undertone.

'Also, my Amelie, it is only in Christ that we know God.'

70

The air between them was charged with a mixture of emotions and Maidie, hovering on the staircase behind with Hoover and dusters, seemed poised to spring. They might have been two surreptitious children engaged in some unacceptable intimacy!

What Piers was feeling, she could not know, yet she sensed his embarrassment and surprise at being drawn into such a confrontation. It was an affront to Adam. Surely, she, Amelia, Adam's wife, should of all people, be 'au-fait' with such basic truths!

The cynic in her asserted itself as she saw Piers out and nodded her 'Good bye for now.'

'Many are called, but few are chosen,' sang the refrain in her head. It would seem that of the 'few' here were two, her husband and a friend, from whose superiority she would be wise to barricade herself in future. Was it just possible that she might need a little help with her own salvation one day? To whom, if so, would she turn? Another phrase echoed, quieter, but insistent. 'My Amelie' he had said. It was an improvement on 'dear lady' but it smacked of patronage and a possessiveness which irritated, especially in view of the context in which it had been uttered. However, when 'My Amelie' became commonplace, she warmed to it. As she did to Piers, as the years went by.

Amongst their many revelations, neither Hannah nor Maidie ever mentioned the grave. Mel found it purely by chance. It happened during October at the start of their fourth year. Late one afternoon she drove her small car to the nearest garage ready for a service the following morning. Normally she would have enjoyed the brisk return walk to the town down the mile-long curve of the main road, but the wind was biting and a deluge threatened at any moment as staccato raindrops struck the tarmac and a low-slung slate- coloured canopy unrolled across the sky. A small unlatched gate banged apprehensively in the breeze as she hurried by. Flush with the rusting borough railings, she had not noticed it before but perhaps it offered an irreverent short cut through the cemetery and the chance to escape a soaking. She slipped through, closed it solicitously, and negotiated a dark narrow track pressed between ungainly leaning gravestones and unkempt mounds. Scraggy grass grew spitefully around capsized urns and decayed vases and she was thankful to reach an asphalt footpath which led across to the main drive. When she had nearly reached the main gates the name

'Tarrant-Jones', high on a large, yet discreet, slab of stone, caught her eye. Deep carved, it stood out clearly, distinctive on its placard amongst undistinguished modern marble and granite memorials. The inscription was long, and she stopped, curious.

It read:-

Gerald Anthony Tarrant-Jones, MC TD died 1st August 1951, aged 76 years

Euphemia Tarrant-Jones MBE died 5th February 1961, aged 80 years.

No loving or treasured remembrance supported the names, but some way below them, in smaller script, were chiselled these lines:-

'Remember friend who now pass by,
As you are now, so once was I.
As I am now so you shall be,
Prepare for death and follow me.'

Their effect was immediate. They transmitted, as was doubtless the intention, unwelcome disturbance into the detached complacency with which a living human being dares to wander amongst so many dead. Mel was not accustomed to studying tombstones but now glanced furtively around to see whether any adjacent ones bore similar cautionary verses. They did not. A second and a third time, and repeatedly until it was memorised, she read and re-read the coercive rhyme. Then, suddenly languid, like someone listlessly transfused with a strange narcotic, she turned from the place and sauntered uneasily on her way, oblivious now of her earlier desire to hurry.

It was raining hard. Although she could feel wind on her face and water trickling down her neck from saturated hair, she now sensed a strong reluctance to reach the shelter of home. Discomfort served to highlight the impact of each cryptic line as she mouthed it again and again into the murky grey wetness, as the sky sealed its horizons with premature night. *'Remember friend...* that's me' she whispered, *'Who now pass by...* that's me too! *As you are now, so once was I.* That's true, indisputable. Moreover I, Mel Ellis know a good deal more of what you were than you could conceivably know about me! *'As I am now, so you shall be'...* this is nasty, she thought, it reminds me that in *x* years (hopefully at least as many again as I've already enjoyed) I'll be a box of bones or a puff of ashes, or indeed whatever she is now, and that is impossible to ascertain! *'Prepare for death and follow me.'* This was the nastiest line of all. It suggested a kind of power. Inescapable: and the *'follow me'* was too personal. The lines whirled around Mel's brain and she perceived a haunting presence -an eminence grise - beckoning with insidious persuasion and challenge in that final six-word ultimatum. Mel did not like it, not any part of it. If she wasn't careful it would prey on her mind... as though, craftily, this grave had adopted some kind of a hold over her.

She crossed the road outside the main gates of the cemetery and a pile of pallid crumpets in the window of the Cottage Bakery caught her eye. It was out of character for her to stuff herself with starch, but she dripped into the shop, nevertheless, to buy a couple, hoping (with optimism, but no realism) that Adam would be at home to share them. Business was scant, closing time near, and Mrs Tidd, the baker's wife, erect as one of her eclairs, already bearing away ransacked trays of buns and cakes to some unidentified region at the back.

She recognised Mel instantly, twittering as she dealt with the small purchase:-

'Oh dear, you got caught in the shower, madam. Let me lend you an umbrella.'

'It's very sweet of you Mrs Tidd, but don't worry. I can't really get any wetter if you see what I mean!'

'Dear, oh dear! Don't catch cold now. See you have those crumpets piping hot, mind, with lots of butter to warm you up.'

'Thanks for the advice, I will,' Mel replied cheerfully as she closed the door, its bell tinkling pertly over a large Hovis advertisement which had seen fresher days. Adam's car was not in the courtyard she noted on reaching the Tower house. Damn! She set about changing out of the wet clothes and as she sat down to peel off her tights she wondered whether the experience in the cemetery had jolted her so much because of the wild weather, but then realised that she was shivering violently. The whole episode had unnerved her and she needed Adam's reassuring presence to help a return to normality. It was nearly six when she eventually checked the engagement diary, only to discover, as she might have guessed, that a diocesan committee and school governors' meeting would keep Adam busy until much later. It was the normal pattern and she was accustomed to it. Frustration was futile, but she sighed none the less.

Under the grill, the crumpets slowly heat-dried and darkened, the undersides to a cardboard evenness, the upper ones to mottled brown honeycomb. She basted them with butter, added a sprinkle of salt, poured a solitary cup of tea, and wandered through to the room known as Backs View where she felt most at home and where it was easiest to be alone. She sank into a comfortable faded chintz armchair, lodged her feet on a stool, and made a pig of herself. When had she last consumed two crumpets, she wondered? Had '*she*' ever indulged as Mel was doing…Now?

Backs View, at the rear of the house, had proved its value by its versatility. For the first couple of years it made a marvellous rumpus room for Ruth and Seb. Currently it was full of potted plants, leaked from the adjoining conservatory, and it was Mel's expressed intention to change it yet again into a music room. It housed a strange cosmopolitan mix of furniture, mostly inherited, respectable enough to keep, but not up to the standard of the more public rooms. An ugly, squat-faced television stood in one corner, cheek by jowl with a bronchitic vintage record player sitting precariously, on a pile of long-playing records. These were fast becoming redundant as Ruth and Seb constantly reminded her. Orphaned chests and tables, battered books, magazines, games, mounds of mending, empty Spanish flower pots and even gardening implements found a haven in such a place. In her mind's eye, Mel saw the room transformed by Habitat basket chairs, bright blotchy cushions, modern prints, hanging plants, and Ruth in a dress of Suggia red playing the cello in one corner, but she held back from actually realising her dream for fear of destroying shabby comforting warmth with superficial packaged décor.

They had called it Backs View because the vista through its wide windows and adjoining conservatory glass, which led to a backcloth of patterned rear facades of tall 'Saints' Avenue' houses, was exactly that! Some of their acquaintances in these houses cursed their three floors and upstairs drawing rooms, yet cherished unpainted elegance, managed without the servant-cushioned comfort of days long past, and maintained a discreet external silence on lowered status when circumstances forced them to convert into flats. As a family they loved this room. It meant privacy, access to the garden, and a panoramic view of the architectural phenomena behind them. It breathed normality. It never reminded them of their obligations.

Still shivering slightly, despite the crumpets, Mel turned on one bar of the electric fire and huddled into Adam's gardening jersey which had been carelessly hung on the conservatory door. She needed to relax. Resisting a temptation to phone Hannah and ask whether she knew about the grave, she flopped into the chair again and, alone with her thoughts, coaxed them to wander away from the dictates of a deceased geriatric and into the happier company of her family and friends.

Ruth occupied her mind for a while. Soon, now, they must make a decision. Those who knew about these things told them that she should move to a specialist music school for the sixth form years. There was talk, too, of scholarships and bursaries. Currently, she went daily, with a posse of other local day girls, to a quite smart independent school twelve miles away. Each day they stayed until the end of evening 'prep'. Mel looked forward to her duty weeks of driving them all to and fro and enjoyed having Ruth's company during the late evenings. Recently Ruth had insisted that she must borrow a second cello so that she could practise at home as well as at school though she moaned continually about its inadequacies compared with her own instrument, which it was obviously impractical to transport daily. She practised in her bedroom and as Adam and Mel ate their evening meal in the kitchen below, they became used to an accompaniment of scampering phrases or stately soliloquies. To be honest, they could hear no difference between her own cello and the one loaned from Giles's music department and when they dined in state in the dining room the sounds were out of earshot anyway. Dear Alastair would be retiring in a couple of months but they had not caught up with his future plans. Florence, of course, had died. On this particular evening, Mel did not wish to think about the dead!

Seb was blissfully happy with his lot as only a young boy can be. He was not really small anymore and would move to public school in another year. When the time came how Mel would miss his weekend visits home, and regret, too, the passing of balsa wood models, mustard and cress farms, scalectrix, railways and conkers! The recollection of a recent escapade evoked a smile. Mel had kissed him a ritual goodbye outside the Cathedral School after his first weekend of the term. A bell was already tolling for evening chapel and an anxious friend was scooping up gumboots and anoraks from the back of the car.

Suddenly Seb gabbled, 'Mummy, will you feed the animals?'

'What animals?' Mel asked, aghast.

'Just some baby mice. A boy gave them to me. They are quite alright. In a box. I brought them home yesterday. I forgot to show you.'

He was appropriately crestfallen and apologetic!

'Where on earth are they?'

'In my bedroom', he called as he backed up the steps towards the bedlam of boy noise and banging doors that was his preparatory school on a Sunday evening. 'Bye, mummy, they're quite friendly!'

Mel had remembered at midnight.

'What's happening, darling?' grunted Adam as she switched on the light.

'I have to feed Seb's pets!'

Unmoved, he grunted again.

She crept past Ruth's room and along the dark passage, fearful of putting on more lights until she was safely into Seb's territory. Gingerly she opened the door. There was squeaking and scuffling and something scratched across her bare foot. She shrieked and found the light switch. Adam rushed from the master bedroom wielding an antique shepherd's crook which he sometimes used instead of his crosier!

'Quick, it's got away', she shouted.

'What has? What in God's name is the matter?'

Dumbly she pointed in the direction of the tiny creatures streaking down the stairs.

'There's one,' she whispered hoarsely, 'and another!'

Ruth appeared, wide-eyed, dragging at her crumpled shortie nightdress to be decent.

'Daddy, you look ridiculous,' she said.

Suddenly it had all been ridiculous, as anyone who has searched for a troupe of mice in a rambling house, at dead of night, will appreciate. Ultimately, the only solution was to give up the chase and to return to bed, in the fervent hope that no fretful intruder had found its way into your bedroom. The following morning the game of 'hunt the mouse,' which they now felt bound to play, proved infinitely more demanding and demoralising than 'hunt the thimble.' Two they eventually caught (and without the aid of a mousetrap!), one leapt between the bannister supports, plunged to the hall below, scurried round in a last frenzied circle and collapsed, and one was never found. For a couple of weeks afterwards there was a strong, suggestive, odour in Backs View.

Mel opened her eyes, smiled to herself and sniffed analytically. Yes, the smell had vanished long ago together with the mice! However, as she now recalled, Adam had been irritated rather than amused by the incident, adopting the line that Seb's behaviour in depositing mice in his bedroom in the first place was extremely stupid. Nevertheless, he had since dined out on the story many times and once it found its way into a sermon!

Both Adam and Mel were apprehensive about Seb's school work at this time; especially in Maths where he was regularly at the bottom of the form. He would need extra coaching for the Common Entrance examination. English, on the other hand, was going well and he admitted to a liking for poetry – possibly, Mel suspected, because he found it less of a chore to read than prescribed prep-school prose.

As a five year old he had preferred 'Cruel Frederic,' 'Harriet and the Matches' and 'Johnny Head in Air' to the less poetic dramas associated with 'James the Red,' 'Thomas the Tank,' and others from the notable collection of animated engine stories. He could probably have recited Struwelpeter's 'Merry Stories' from cover to cover! Now in the most recent school magazine they could read his own first published work. Entitled 'A Poem by Sebastian Ellis' its sixteen lines ran thus:-

Two feet walking
See the grass talking
Insects stalking
Careful! Feet walking.

Two wheels spinning,
Past hedges grinning
At birds winning.
Careful! Wheels spinning.

An engine spluttering,
A driver muttering,
At butterflies fluttering.
Careful! Engine spluttering.

No foot churning,
Wheel or engine turning.
Just a sunset burning,
And nature yearning.

Like her son, the composition was sensitive and adorable!

'It's super darling,' she had said. 'You are very clever.'

Adam had insisted that the last verse was nonsense which upset Seb. The English master praised its lilt and thought it showed 'a maturity beyond Sebastian's years.'

Piers had considered it remarkable, though more for its philosophy than its rhymes. The next time he came round he brought a pile of poetry books with him and he and Seb spent an absorbing afternoon studying them. This was the first of several sessions which made Seb feel very scholarly and important. As a gesture of thanks, Seb wrote out the poem in a laboriously neat hand and presented it to Piers with appropriate solemnity.

'My poem', he said. 'For you.'

Piers was very touched and this particular exchange marked the beginning of the special relationship which developed between them. It had his parents blessing and seemed wholly desirable although Mel did have some misgivings initially.

'It's alright, is it?' she asked Adam.

'How do you mean – alright?'

'This claustrophobic closeting to read poetry!'

'Darling Mel, Piers is virtually one of the family. Surely you don't think...'

'No of course not', she had said quickly. It's just that they do seem to be getting awfully...' she hesitated, stuck for a word, 'well, wrapped up in it together.'

Adam's reply was fluent.

'Look! Seb is experiencing a little healthy hero worship and if, while he is this young, he can acquire a measure of appreciation and judgement for a great art form then surely it can only be to his advantage... Since Piers would seem to have the knowledge and patience to capture his imagination in this way, then so be it.'

She nodded agreement.

'I'm quite glad for him really,' she said. 'But Piers ought to get married and have his own son.'

'His and Elizabeth's! Some lad that would be,' said Adam enigmatically.

Hannah said much the same, plus a little more.

'Don't fret yourself Mel. Is it the choirboy thing you are fussed about?'

'What choirboy thing?' Mel asked, dismayed.

Hannah was brisk.

'Long before you came. Never a word of truth in it. Busybodies making mischief!'

'What happened?'

'Nothing love, nothing happened! Old Piers just put an arm round Darren Smith – long ago, when the beastly child was a round faced cherub. It was Christmas. Piers was on leave. He just put his arm round him and said 'Happy Christmas, you sang like an angel' or some such thing. The youth's a bloody 'Hell's Angel' now – all leather fringes and studs!'

She fumed, silently, remembering,

'And people stirred it up?'

'You know what those people get like when they want to be nasty. The other choirboys teased him, he told his mum, she suddenly got all uppity and vile and the fact that she cleaned for old Millicent Green, who hated Mrs T-J's guts, meant that her filthy insinuations went all round the town.

Seeing the concern on Mel's face, she spoke still more forcefully.

'Forget it Mel. You know as well as I do that you could entrust Piers with the key of your daughter's chastity belt and he'd hide it somewhere so safe that she'd be locked into it for evermore.'

Mel had half smiled, not entirely reassured.

'It's not my daughter I'm talking about, Hannah.'

'No, I know. It's that precious son of yours. He's clean, good living, and dashed handsome – and if he wants to spend his time reading treasuries of verse with uncle P, good luck to him. The poems won't turn blue, I promise you!'

Mel's becalmed face twitched with amusement at the recollection of Hannah's wit. There was a consolation dividend, too. Hannah was nearly always right!

By now Mel was very tired, wearied by her non-transcendental meditation. Somewhere between thought and no thought, wakefulness and sleep, the landscape of her mind yielded its vigilance and lost itself. Just as the persuasive charm of waning golden sunset light will soften layers of jagged mountain edges into blotting paper reliefs and finally suffuse them with a grey brown softness, so her consciousness dimmed into blank bronze pink oblivion, and warm, stretched out and comfortable, she slept soundly.

Two hours later she was rudely awakened by Ruth who came blustering into the room.

'Help! What time is it?' she asked, needing a moment to adjust to the situation.

Glancing at her watch Ruth answered tritely, 'Huit heures et demi', flung her music case into a chair, wrestled with the toggles of her duffel coat and finally showed some concern.

'What's wrong? You were fast asleep!'

'Yes,' Mel yawned, 'I realise that. Is Daddy home?

'No! How long have you been asleep?'

'Too long. I must go and cook,' and Mel struggled out of the chair feeling nearer to eighty years old than forty.

'It isn't like you, is it?' persisted Ruth.

'Not really. It's been a funny sort of day.'

'How?'

'Oh, I got wet after taking the car to the garage… and maybe I was a little lonely, too!'

'Don't be silly, Mummy. And you look a fright in that jersey. It's filthy!'

Mel looked down at herself. True it was grubby and torn. But it was all of Adam that had been available at the time when she needed him.

'I was cold,' she explained, 'after getting wet.'

Ruth lost interest.

'J'ai grand faim,' she said (her usual cry). 'Is there something to eat? Supper was vile. Macaroni cheese without cheese or sauce – just thick drainpipes of sticky stodge. How I hate school food!'

'There's some apple pie,' Meg called on her way through to the kitchen.

'Yummy,' said Ruth.

Mel was all behind with their meal and it would be convenient if Adam stayed away for another three quarters of an hour. By then she should be ready and free to recount the events of the afternoon. She pondered its unusual happenings (the cemetery discovery, the crumpets, and her uncharacteristic nap) as she shoved chops and tomatoes into the oven and sliced carrots into a pan. That wretched rhyme! How had it begun? *'Remember, friend…'* she halted at the word 'friend.' It must have escaped her attention previously. It had not registered at all. 'Friend' was a precious, companionable, term, evoking a feeling of affection, and a sense of caring. How could she be filled with such foreboding and suspect that Mrs T-J was threatening when she addressed one so amicably? How foolish to read the opening line and neglect to stress the cordiality of that all-important second word. She had got it all wrong. She was her *friend*. She, Mel, had totally missed the point: the rest did not matter. She threw salt on to the carrots and watched the scalding water bring them dancing up the pan. She turned down the heat and clamped on the lid. There was no need to tell Adam about her day. It was already irrelevant.

Chapter V

PASSING LANDSCAPE

Mel came to terms with her existence. Much of the social side was palatable because she liked entertaining and was good at it. Nor did she mind being at the centre of attention. The years with Alastair had prepared her well. She preferred summers to winters. In the middle months of the year there was a lull in certain services and Adam's load was marginally less - once the annual spate of spring Confirmations had swelled the numbers of communicants for a few brief weeks. Occasionally they got away together. Nevertheless, as Adam, Ruth and Seb all reached towards new horizons there were many moments when she felt herself to be the only member of the family without a destination, seemingly stranded on a plateau in a wasteland of endless space.

From time to time, Mel opened Fetes or presented prizes on Sports' Days and she was regularly a guest of honour at Garden Parties. If the occasion warranted a short speech she heeded the advice given to her once by a senior bishop's wife.

'My dear,' she had said, 'adopt the Queen's ship-launching tactics! Bless them and all who sail with them and if that is not quite appropriate, make up something just as short and equally sweet. Look cheerful. Only stay as long as *you* want to. Once you have done your stuff, you're a bit of a drag to them, and they'll be relieved if you have to rush away.' It was good advice, though not always easy to follow. It would have been obscene, for example, to rush away from a 'Hunger

Lunch' in order to fry bacon and eggs! So, when it was necessary Mel not only chatted brightly and bravely, but also fasted!

She steadfastly refused to discuss church politics and never became involved in debates about women priests or the three prayer book series though, over the years, the latter, rites one, two and three, drifted like phantoms into assorted conversations. As a bishop's wife, it was much easier to say 'No' than it had been during the probationary years and for many functions attended by Adam, Mel was an 'optional extra,' invited, but not necessarily expected. She was now less of an extension of Adam and had all the ingredients to be her own person. She admired the courage and authority of another 'wife' who had entitled her autobiography, 'A bishop's wife and still myself.' Yet for Mel, in spite of some emancipation, it was still difficult to find self-recognition in the efficient, plastic, semi-public figure which she had become. There were times, deserts of frustration and futility, when repetition, ritual and rubric almost drove her to climb on to her pew and to scream abuse at the neat, self-satisfied, Christians, who sat so piously in their seats. Their hypocrisy, and her own, overwhelmed her. How many of them would have taken Jesus seriously had he wandered, a hairy hippy, into their midst? What did they know of suffering or sacrifice? How much did they care? Doubtless a pleasant mask covered her real face as she considered the possibility of such an outburst and conjured up the crude headlines in the newspapers which would inevitably follow such an event. In one squealing desecration she could destroy both Adam and herself. For what? To become a candidate for the baying passion of a crowd hungry for scandal. 'We always thought there was something funny about her,' they would hiss – 'Poor man, what cross he has to bear.' No, no. She held her tongue and fashioned herself, instead, into a model parochial matriarch.

Deserts there may have been on Mel's plateau, but there were oases, too; times of family happiness when all seemed right with the world and it their oyster. In Mel's imagery some of the family holidays ranked as oases. Two, especially, in successive years, when they camped first in France, and then in Spain. Piers went with them on the second trip. He and Adam lay inert for hours beneath a garish giant umbrella, remarkably content for two men who had claimed aversion to any form of beach life: picking themselves lazily from the sand with just enough energy to reach the sea and muster a middle-aged crawl apiece. Seb, weaving and flailing, like a playful dolphin, harassed them with his underwater antics, while Ruth and Mel, passive on gentle lilos, drifted lazily out to sea. It was always Seb who stormed through the water to pull them back into their depth, never the men!

There were beacons, too, on the plateau, lighting the way as Ruth and Seb strode through their teenage years. Ruth passed all her 'O' levels, won a valuable scholarship to a specialist music school, and from there graduated to London. As Adam and Mel listened to her performances at more and more events they agreed that she was outstanding and accepted, with some measure of pride, that she had a future as a cellist.

Although Seb had a habit of scraping through examinations his beacons burned none the less. He wrote more poetry, much more, and acted in plays, content to be some stammering soldier or simpleton servant in order to be part of a drama. But his greatest triumph, when he was just sixteen, was as Horatio. Wracked with nervous tension at playing, for him, so large a part, he made a noble sensitive friend for the school's best actor who was too bumptious and overbearing to be a memorable Hamlet.

And there were cacti on the plateau, prickly and uncomfortable, yet not too damaging. George Ellis died after several months of debilitating senile confusion. He failed to recognise Adam and Mel when they visited him yet he was not, they decided, unhappy. He would tell them that he 'entirely understood their requirements and shared their grief. Real brass handles on the coffin would cost more as they might appreciate, but he could recommend them...' Sometimes he presumed Mel to be 'the lady from the florist's' and gave her complex orders for wreaths and sprays. It was easiest to go along with him, trapped as he was in muddled mortality. On their last visit (with Ruth and Seb who were anxious to pay homage to their forbidding and largely absent grandfather) a cheerful little probationer nurse, giggling and over confident, tittered brashly, 'Poor old man, he's a scream, isn't he. Do you know, he thinks his son is a bishop!' Adam, casually dressed, bit silently into his lip, his eyes glazed. Could he be angry at last wondered Mel as she commented 'Really,' with frigid politeness while somewhere deep within her an unwelcome memory of an evening in Venice vibrated like a viper.

The nurse's unwitting lack of tact served to highlight the duplicity of George Ellis's attitude to Adam. The disdain with which he had viewed his son's committal to a career in the church had never left him and yet, with strangers, he would boast of Adam's success with a father's pride. It was a consolation, but small compensation for the breakdown in communication which his pettiness had destroyed over the years. Now, at his death, Adam was troubled. He borrowed a sober striped shirt and black tie from Piers and wore a traditional dark suit to the funeral service where for all the world he might have been just one more fellow undertaker, apart from the fact that he read the lesson with a certain flair. Mel was staggered; but she understood. Adam was both humiliated and humbled and on this final occasion in his childhood home town, he opted for a profile which his father might have found tolerably acceptable and allowed the local vicar and his father's old firm to manage this last farewell.

Afterwards, for a time, tension and guilt irritated Adam's few, normally unobtrusive, mannerisms. His foot tapped with added impatience, his lips pursed more tightly, and his brow, scrambling into fresh furrows, brought a sculptured anxiety to his characteristically alert expression. Mel wanted him to talk about his father – to help him through this patch. But they found so little opportunity to be alone, or to converse, and her attempts at sympathy were not very convincing for, as Adam well knew, his father had not been one of Mel's favourite people.

In another prickly area, Mel's mother died. Hester was convinced that she worried herself into the second fatal heart attack which came just six years after the first. Certainly her impatient nature and total self-absorption had done nothing to delay the inevitable. She left Mel her cottage and the bulk of her estate, thus providing a welcome hedge against inflation and a source of income for which Mel was grateful, especially as Adam's inheritance from his father was significant. Their joint financial future was assured.

A letter which her mother wrote during her time with Hester after the first heart attack, demonstrated that she had cared more about her daughter than Mel imagined. It had been a revelation when it arrived. Prophetic in its way, it told Mel nothing that she did not already know, but she felt a good deal closer to her mother after receiving it. Previously she had not appreciated that in many ways they were very alike, nor had she credited her mother with much vision beyond the vista of her village. Mel kept the letter in a small drawer and re-read it occasionally. It provided a kind of solace in a funny sort of way.

'When the children are older,' it read, 'you will need other interests. It will be lonely being a bishop's wife. People will be on their best behaviour with you. Real friends will be few. Adam will be away a great deal and life will not be easy. Now is the time to find something that will occupy and interest you. I am not suggesting that you go back to your physio, but you might think of studying a language, or even doing a degree through the Open University! Give it some thought. I know I am right and I want you to be happy. Think about it in time...'

Mel did think about it and she and Adam talked about it. 'People' were her forte, they decided. When the children were older, and 'the time came,' she graciously rejected an invitation to become a magistrate and chose instead to devote more time to her Marriage Guidance Counselling. It was interesting and time consuming and at the various courses she learnt unbelievable and extraordinary things. Even so, she still wondered whether she would remain on her own particular plateau for ever. At heart she was still as disenchanted as the beleaguered curate's wife, who, with her blotchy children, had a pained 'It's alright for you' look on her face whenever they met.

Chapter VI

REQUESTS

It was the middle of May. Weather pundits predicted a long, hot, dry, summer and already in the press and on television, farmers and water board officials were manifesting early symptoms of drought neurosis. There had been little rain for a month but in the garden elegant lupins crowded the borders, peonies and rhododendrons were in flower and the air was fragrant with a pot pourri of roses and warm baked grass. Backs View and the conservatory looked more attractive than they had done for years. Maidie and Mel had spring cleaned early and slopped a coat of paint over the peeling conservatory timbers. Adam was growing fuchsias and geraniums in there now and the mauves and vermilions, singing against the new brilliant white, lent the place an exotic continental ambience. On this particular evening Mel was busy watering plants and trimming shrivelled geranium heads. Curious bees flew in and out through the open doors; somewhere a hedge-cutter whined, and local bird and insect populations chirped and chirruped companionably. It was nearly half past six, and Thursday. The weekly ringing practice would start at any moment. The Abbey bells were company. Mel enjoyed hearing them peal out their 'grandsire doubles' or whatever they were. Maidie's husband, Alf, (who did the heavy work in the garden) was one of the most experienced of the campanologists and Mel believed him to be the source of at least half of the gossip which Maidie vouchsafed...acquired, Mel deduced, during those ominous silences from the belfry!

Footsteps sounded in the front hall. Adam was in London. Only certain people would walk straight in so they must belong either to one of the curates, or to Hannah, or Elizabeth, or Piers! Too slow and heavy for Hannah or Elizabeth, and no polite clerical tap on the door, so it must be Piers - as indeed it was!

'Greetings, Amelie. Blessings upon you!'

'Hello Piers. How nice to see you.'

'I've brought you a brace of stickers for the cars,' he explained. 'As you see, 'County Orchestra' writ large, and 'Soloist Ruth Ellis' writ nearly as large!'

'How embarrassing!' laughed Mel 'But of course we must display them.'

Ruth was to play the Saint-Saens cello Concerto at the end of June – her debut in the Abbey. It promised to be a memorable evening for everyone.

'Have a drink?' Mel suggested. 'I could do with one.'

'Delighted to join you on such an idyllic evening. Adam not in yet?'

'No, he's up at Church House. An important committee. Felix went with him. Be an angel and fetch the decanters from the drawing room. I'll get us some ice.'

He bowed, teasing. 'Your servant, ma'am.'

On his way he called out:- 'I should have remembered. It's the synod planning committee. But I don't understand why Felix has gone.'

'For the ride,' Mel shouted, her head in the 'fridge. 'He had some business in town.'

Piers poured himself a whisky and provided Mel with a gin and tonic, plus lemon, which he insisted on locating and slicing. Used by now to his eccentricities, she was happy to let him wait on her.

'And how is my good friend Sebastian, does he flourish?' he asked, as he spread himself over the narrow old sofa.

'He's fine. He phoned us at the weekend.'

'When is the dreaded, yet honourable, Ancient History examination?'

'In three weeks' time.'

'Then I must not omit to pen him a felicitous note.' He took out a diary from the pocket of his light linen jacket, and wrote himself a reminder ending with a flourish of his silver pencil.

'In Greek?' Mel enquired, mocking him.

'Naturally,' he retorted, smiling.

'Poor Seb,' she said. 'He's not the world's best examinee and I tremble to think about the other 'A' levels next year.'

'Sufficient unto the day is the evil thereof, Amelie. Leave next year to look after itself. Our noble Sebastian may yet surprise us all.'

'I'll concentrate on this year, then,' she said obediently, 'there's plenty happening... especially with the Abbey Music Festival!'

Piers nodded, sipping his whisky appreciatively before remarking;-

'Rather too much for Felix, I fancy. Have you observed how ill he looks?'

His comment surprised Mel. Men did not usually notice such things. 'Pale and a little drawn, perhaps,' she acknowledged. 'But it hasn't struck me that he may be unwell. When is his holiday?'

Piers leant forward to consult the diary again.

'Not yet awhile. September if I remember correctly. Yes, here it is.' He indicated the entry. 'The first half.'

'August should be quiet for him, when the Festival is over... it usually is.'

Deformed, descending, scales from the abbey tower were more interesting than this banal exchange thought Mel as she sipped her drink, a trifle restless.

'No holiday for you in Spain this year, Amelie?'

She brightened.

'Sadly no, Piers. That was fun that time when you came with us. We ought to repeat it.'

'It could never be the same again. Ruth and Sebastian would be too old now for those frolics we had together...'

'They've finished with family holidays,' she interrupted.

'Quite so – and to phrase it a little clumsily, I hardly think you and Adam would welcome me as 'Piers the gooseberry'!

Mel felt her cheeks flush. He was looking at her, a shade wistful perhaps. She knew him too well to answer with some trite cliché. His comment harboured something deeper. They were very close as friends and he must know perfectly well that their relationship could survive a holiday 'a-trois' if the occasion arose. So why the remark? However, any reply which she might have made was forestalled when he added:-

'You must promise to tell me, my Amelie, if I should become a burden.'

'Don't be ridiculous, Piers. Whatever do you mean, a burden?'

'An intruder then. Yes... an intruder into this, my most precious family... For that is what you have become, all four of you. My family.'

He stressed the 'my' his gaze focussed on the glass in his hand, and then spoke again, this time more quietly and deliberately:-

'My love and admiration for each of you,' he said, emphasising every word and separating it from the next, 'is so total that I fear for it sometimes. Indeed I fear for its very survival if it is indulged.' He looked up at her. He was attempting to say something (just what she was not certain) which did not fit easily into a procession of words. His eye searched for some sign of help from her.

'You might, with every right, weary of me,' he said quietly.

She rounded on him.

'Piers, don't be so morbid! We are as fond of you as you are of us. Each of us needs you, too, in our different ways. To Adam you are clerk of the works and confidant. To Seb literary inspiration and tutor. To me,' she shrugged, 'light relief.' She hesitated before adding 'and to Ruth...' but the sentences no longer tumbled out. She was unsure of his role with Ruth.

'Well, what to Ruth?' he pressed.

'An enigma, I guess. I don't think she has ever known whether to regard you as a wicked uncle, or a potential lover!

He laughed and leant back. The tension eased. They both relaxed.

'Time will tell,' he pronounced. 'But meanwhile I greatly look forward to her virtuoso performance in June.'

There was always plenty to recount about Ruth and they chatted amiably about her life at Music College. She was now into her second year. Piers wanted to mull over Felix, too, genuinely convinced that there was some problem. He had noted a 'transparence' about him which surely had not always been there.

'What does Elizabeth say?' Mel asked.

'She's worried', he replied. 'That I do know, but nothing more.'

For a few seconds there was silence between them; no thread of conversation waiting to be tidied away. Mel studied Piers as he toyed with his glass on the old ebony table. He was essentially a brown person whereas Adam was grey and white. His hands, now spread eagled over the frayed flowers of the sofa cover were tanned, like his face and neck, by the May sun. He had been gardening hard. Those hands were still larger than life and as different from Adam's as amber to alabaster. His whole person was a contrast. She had never forgotten the strange feeling of levitation at that first dinner party (so long ago now) nor the weird dream which had followed. In some uncanny way, she held Piers responsible for those events over which, in all innocence, he could have had no control. Now he was rubbing his right eye, smoothing the lid sideways with the fingers of his right hand. Momentarily he brushed the dark patch on the left as if to check that it still securely covered whatever lay beneath. It was a familiar gesture. Years ago he had recounted the stark but horrendous details of the accident. It was not, as Maidie had said, an explosion, but a collision between a staff car and a jeep during NATO exercises in Belgium. The corporal who was driving Piers along an unmade track, at night, tried desperately to take avoiding action when lights careered towards him through a field. He miscalculated, not realising that the driver of the jeep was slumped over the wheel, blind drunk, with his foot on the accelerator. Piers' side of the car took the full force of the impact and the left hand side of his face was impaled on a tangle of glass and metal. He, himself, remembered nothing of the crash, only learning afterwards exactly what had happened. 'I was lucky' he had said simply, when he narrated these details, 'the other chaps were killed.'

'You are pensive, my Amelie,' he said recapturing her attention.

'Your eye,' she said, 'I was thinking about it.'

'Aaah, the one that sees you so beautiful and bewitching before me, I trust!'

'Don't be a fool. The other one!'

He drained his glass, and looked at his watch.

'I should go,' he said. 'Adam will be back.'

'Not before nine,' she said. She did not actually want him to go just yet. They seemed to have been on the brink of something important a few minutes earlier. She did not know what it was, but wished to pursue it.

'Is it painful?' she asked.

'My eye that sees you not?'

'Yes.'

He hesitated. Fidgeted. 'May I have another whisky?'

Of course. Help yourself.'

'And for you?'

'A little,' she replied. 'Mostly tonic.'

He stood up and poured them a second drink each, methodically placing the decanters on the lower platform of the funny old table. It was an odd piece of furniture with its marquetry top and lower deck. No doubt someone's art nouveau treasure once. Mel could not recall how they had acquired it but she had an idea that they had found it in the Tower House attic when they first arrived. It was usefully round, and typical Back's View furniture. Piers sat down again without speaking. He raised his glass to her and drank half the contents before replacing it on the table. For some reason her heart was pounding. It must be the gin. She rarely had more than one. Suddenly she knew what she was going to do. She repeated her question.

'Well, is it painful?'

He remained silent, his passivity unnerving, but she was not to be deterred. For years now, in idle moments, she had wondered what lay beneath that concave triangular seal. Was it a neat scar, a pair of eyelids machined together, an unsightly distended wall eye, or, more grisly, a gaping cavity? Her curiosity at this particular moment was so intense, that, come what may, it must be satisfied.

'Please Piers,' she insisted, 'answer me. I want to know. And tell me what it looks like, too.' Her speech sounded normal and calm. Yet within her there was a growing quivering, excitement. She had become a preying beast. A cat playing with a mouse; a spider trapping a fly. He was cornered. She felt no pity. She would not be denied.

'Let me see, Piers,' she persisted. 'You have never let any of us see, not even in Spain. Please show me. I would like to see...

He was quite still, his head bowed, as though he was concentrating on some silent entreaty. When he raised it to look at her she met his gaze. Unflinching, her two-eyed challenge held steady. It was impossible to interpret the look on his face. She hoped that it indicated trust and acquiescence, but, in its inscrutability, it could just as easily have signified reticence, or even refusal. Silent seconds stole by. The bells had stopped.

At last, Piers spoke:-

'You have asked me questions, Amelie. I will give you answers. To your first question, the answer is that it only hurts on those more rare occasions when something moves me so much that I feel disposed to weep. There is a terrifying upsurge of pressure. It is indescribable.

Something akin to suffocation – a blind, arid, suffocation, a welling up of psychological tears which cannot overflow, a dam which cannot burst: a ghastly impotence. The whole agony of the aftermath of the accident returns... There is no escape.'

It was difficult for him to talk about it. His voice betrayed the emotion that he was experiencing.

Gently, she asked, 'how long does the feeling last?'

'Until I can bear it no longer,' he replied, tightly, his glance straying upwards as though relating somewhere else.

'It subsides,' he added, simply, 'through supplication!'

'How dreadful,' she said. 'I'm sorry!'

She waited. They were not finished.

Piers swallowed hard and breathed deeply before he spoke again.

'As to your other concern, Amelie – the answer to that is that it is not pretty.'

'Go on,' she murmured.

He looked perplexed 'On?'

She indicated the shield.

'Take it off. For me!'

He shook his head, and, in an attempt to curb her insistence gestured with the palms of his

hands, like some frantic policeman.

'I am your family. Remember!' she said.

His shoulders slumped. He knew that he was beaten.

Now Mel was silly with exhilaration and sick with apprehension. Immobile, she sat watching his every move. His hand shook as he picked up his glass again, drank from it slowly, and then, almost absent-mindedly, replaced it on the edge of the table, pushing it to and fro until the base found itself in the centre of a convolution of crazy marquetry cones. He stood up slowly and looked down at her, his face frozen with tension.

'Are you sure, dear friend, that this is what you want?' he asked.

'Quite sure,' she answered.

He bent down to move a couple of floor standing Spanish flower pots, heavy with geraniums, and then edged awkwardly round the table until he was beside her, and now in front, facing her. He leant over her, his hands gripping the arms of her chair. He was very close, his mouth half-open, his breathing laboured. Sweat ran down his forehead and trickled over the eye shade. His speech was thick as he surrendered.

'If you are so sure, my Amelie,' he said, 'then you must move the patch.'

'Kneel down,' she whispered...

Until then as she eased the shield away she had not fully appreciated just how much of Piers' face the patch covered. Once it was replaced, the sutured seams, weathered into the repaired lower part of his face, would have a new meaning for her. Pale, and hardly noticeable now, they were the tidy perimeter ends of a knotted, tangled, skein of cobbled flesh which sank, deep and hideous into his skull. No cosmetic embroidery this eyelessness! No cosy, furry, teddy bear emptiness, one bright shiny eye unfixed, nor clean   doll's socket, vandalised by tiny fingers into a china emptiness! Face to face with the sickening revulsion of this livid bilious devitrification, Mel felt her stomach heave as she absorbed the full horror of it and at the same time tried to imagine his face as it once must have been. Confronted with so ravaged and vile a disfigurement, such visualisation was impossible. For a few moments she held his head between her hands. He was trembling, blind to her scrutiny, his right eye closed. Silently she repositioned and adjusted the eye shade. Freed from her touch, his head sagged on to his chest.

'Piers,' she whispered. 'It is over. I have seen.'

She heard him sigh, gasp almost. Suddenly he fell forwards on to her, his arms, brutish and awkward, trying to prise a space between her body and the back of the chair.

As he struggled, he was muttering;-

'No one, no one outside a hospital, no one but you has ever seen... no one but you!'

The arms became very powerful. He was a strong man.

'Now,' he said, his voice rising in a crescendo, 'now, my beloved, my most cherished Amelie, - now it is your turn to show me!'

One arm tore from the gap it had made and a hand curved over her breast, tight, strong, firm, kneading... needing, tamed into the lightest of caresses as his fingers fumbled with the buttons of her cotton blouse.

'Show me', he pleaded, his mouth close to hers, his tongue licking his lips, his weight heavy upon her.

'Show me,' he begged.

She struggled to push him away.

'No, Piers, no,' she protested, 'please, no!' She could feel his ribs as her hand pushed hard into his flesh – 'Please!' she screamed.

Rebuffed, he broke from her and crumpled to the floor, a heap of dejection. Neither of them spoke. There were flies on the wall. Had they been able to interpret the scene they would have marvelled at the sight of these two wilted humans who had so recently generated such a plethora of emotion; but they merely buzzed from one surface to the next in mindless unconcern.

Eventually Piers picked himself up, his frame heavy with humiliation, like a schoolboy who has been belittled by a prefect. There was nothing she could do. Yet at this moment she yearned to comfort him. As he straightened up, his elbow caught the edge of the table and his glass flew through the air, shattering as it hit a bare patch of flooring, unprotected by any of the rugs.

Mel jumped up, practical as always, feigning composure.

'I am so sorry,' Piers mumbled as she brushed against him and opened the door on her way to collect dustpan and brush.

Embarrassed and uncertain, he watched as she swept up the fragments. There were slivers of glass everywhere.

'Don't move,' she said. 'There is some on your shoes.' The splinters glinted on the buffed dark suede like diamonds in a dusty jewel case. He was stammering and uncertain.

'Was it a good glass, Amelie?'

'No, Piers, of no value. Think no more about it.'

But he was too observant not to realise that it was of the finest crystal. Now, like the evening, it lay in fragmented pieces.

Mel was quick to take control of the situation. Something must be salvaged. The blood had drained from Piers' face. He was the colour of clay. Somehow she must take his mind off what had happened and restore the status quo. Later she would try to conjecture what it was all about.

'I'll telephone Ma B and tell her you are staying for a bite of supper,' she stated. 'There are eggs on the kitchen table. You can make us one of your omelettes. Go on. Get cracking!'

She gave him an unceremonious push, and he revived a little.

'Cheer up,' she said. 'You like making omelettes, and I'm hungry!' She had never felt less like eating.

By the time Adam arrived home they had regained some semblance of normality. Piers, who had in fact partaken heartily of his Spanish omelette (chopping the onion, tomato and pepper was therapeutic for him, while Mel laid the table and coped with a couple of phone calls), appeared to be recovering his equilibrium. Afterwards, swapping trivialities, they discussed the idiosyncrasies of certain townsfolk, never for one moment conceding that they might have a few themselves. To make him chuckle again she recounted Hannah's latest disaster at a recent dinner party when her new puppy had piddled all over a pair of patent leather sandals belonging to an elderly female, and a cockroach had crept out from the fruit bowl! Only once did he refer to what had happened. 'Amelie,' he said, 'I beg your forgiveness, most humbly. I cannot think what came over me.'

She brushed his words aside. 'Forget it Piers. The whisky went to your head. Forget it. It was my fault.' He was still a little distracted but she sensed that no irreparable harm had been done, though she was loath to let him go home until she was certain.

Adam arrived home soon after ten to find them lingering over coffee in the garden and snapping at midges in the grey pink light of a setting sun. Tomorrow promised to be another good day. He deposited a ritual kiss on Mel's brow and acknowledged Piers with a cheerful, 'Good to see you Piers. Keeping Mel happy, I hope,' as he flopped into a creaky garden chair.

I'm weary,' he added. It's a tedious drive on that everlasting motorway.'

'Darling, would you like an omelette?' Mel asked.

'Bless you, but I've had the usual round of dreary sausage rolls and sandwiches. I'm really beyond eating.'

He turned to Piers. 'Have a brandy with me?' he suggested.

'Thank you Adam, but no. I must be on my way. Amelie has been most generous and kind.'

He stood up and looked across at her, fondly, half-expectant, uncertain in the fading light. Surely he did not want her to recount the events of the evening to Adam at this moment when it was time for him to leave? Without moving from her deckchair Mel dangled a hand upwards and, as was his custom, he raised it to his lips in the familiar farewell. Did he hold it fractionally longer than usual? The salute was so well established that she had long since ceased to notice details, yet on this occasion it felt different. Was there a slight pressure? Did his thumb normally close warm over the backs of my fingers? If he was trying again, in this way, to express his regret, then she understood.

'Bye Piers,' she said, feigning nonchalance. 'See you soon and thanks for keeping me company.' After such an evening, how trite, over-casual and pedestrian she sounded.

Adam got up.

'Mind your head,' he said, as Piers forgot to stoop to avoid the clematis trailing carelessly over the conservatory door. It was almost dark now and suddenly chilly.

'There's just one thing, Piers,' said Adam, following him into Backs View. 'Felix! He saw a consultant in town today, and there is some question of him going into hospital...' The words drifted out of earshot as they reached the further door, but for several moments there was a murmur of conversation from the passage beyond.

So there *was* something wrong with Felix. Mel shivered and got up to fetch the gardening jersey from its usual perch. It was holier that ever but reasonably clean. She washed it occasionally. She sat down again. Adam's brandy would bring him back to tell her about Felix. No doubt he was already making contingency plans with Piers. Both curates were due to take their holidays shortly. The Summer Festival would fall squarely on Piers' shoulders if Felix was laid up for long.

Adam was soon back with his nightcap (Napolean style). He was obviously concerned.

'It looks bad for Felix,' he said.

'How bad?'

'Trouble in his lungs. He's had various tests and X-rays today. There is nothing definite yet. He didn't make a lot of it on the drive back, but enough to prepare us for the fact that he may be out of action.'

'Ian sent him to London, did he?'

'Yes. He and Elizabeth homed on a consultant together. Sounds a good man.'

'Poor old Felix!'

'Piers has just offered to do all he can to help. He's away for the weekend but back on Monday and more or less free to take over the admin. What would we do without him!'

'Another of Piers' mystery trips,' Mel commented, ignoring the rest of the sentence.

'Mmm. I suppose so,' agreed Adam, savouring his brandy.

For as long as they had known him Piers had melted away for a couple of days at regular intervals, without giving any indication as to his whereabouts. The Ellis family had long ago eliminated assignations with Elizabeth or polite calls on brother Andre in Chiswick and could only presume that he had a regular commitment which was both personal and private. There were few clues. The favourite supposition was that he retired to some 'Retreat' of which he knew Adam would disapprove: a freak fringe religious community housed in a bleak forgotten Priory – with Piers, in all probability responsible for the upkeep!

'Did you have a good day?' asked Mel, displaying interest.

'Not bad. Ecumenically encouraging but still exhausting. We are living with a church which has to rethink its structures. I must scribble some notes before I come to bed.' He paused. It appeared that there was nothing else to say about his day and he switched to Mel's with the question.

'Did Piers bring any news?'

'No, not really. Just Festival stickers for the cars.'

'Nothing else of interest?'

'No!' she lied. 'Nothing.'

Adam was too tired to listen and Mel needed time to martial her thoughts before she could narrate the events of the evening. She would have to tell him soon and explain, too, why she had postponed her confession. Tomorrow would be the time to tell him. They would both be fresher tomorrow.

She collected the cups and Adam's glass.

'It's cold and dark out here,' she said. 'Are you coming in?... I'm going to bed.'

'Mmm,' he said. 'I shan't be long. You go on. I'll lock up.'

Normally she slept well, but this Thursday night was an exception. While Adam breathed metronomically beside her, the events of the evening hijacked her mind and held her whole body to ransom. She was unwilling to accept that what had happened had been entirely her fault and yet, as she could clearly see, her persistence may have been the trigger which released the spring within Piers which, in its turn, because of their very proximity, and the nature of the extraordinary intimacy which had occurred, caused the finely tuned mechanism of his person to run amok.

Yet what construction should she put on his talk of being a burden? Is it possible that this was a primary ploy in a carefully laid plot to discover where he stood. Impossible! It was unthinkable that he had been waiting, patient but prurient, for an opportunity to seduce her. Unlikely, too, that the chivalrous, upright, Piers, whom they all knew so well should suddenly turn philanderer. Did not the Ellis family hold the title deeds of his loyalty and devotion? If he were a seducer at heart then he had made poor use of the past eight years! Personally, she did not feel that she had been unduly obsessed by him. He had interested her, yes, but only as a 'character' who had become a friend and for whom, as such, one felt a certain fondness and affection. She had not woven fantasies around him, like an adolescent schoolgirl, nor spared him an excessive amount of thought when he was not actually in her company. So what did it all mean?

It was a night of mental turmoil. Images which she had not invited came writhing into view and the long hours were punctuated by a series of aberrant visions in which her normal sane and ordered self seemed to be witness to another self, cavorting and contorting with a dream figure Piers, sometimes grotesque, sometimes brutal, but bound with her in a terrifying, glorious, emotion. 'Show me,' he breathed, as this wanton self trembled again for his touch. Revelling in the liberation of this fantasy world and its erotic rituals she half-woke, half-slept, begging for more in her anguish to preserve the delirium for longer. She was uncertain of anything until the supposedly honest and normal self became more and more aware as darkness paled to dawn and dawn to day that, for all its inward protestations to the contrary, she may have both wished for, and precipitated, a climax in the relationship. She had used his eye as a means to this end. In itself this zenith was all she had sought. Now she had to determine whether it had already led anywhere else, or whether it would have led anywhere else had she 'shown' him whatever it was that he craved, or whether, indeed, it would yet lead anywhere else. The whole episode had been, quite literally, a duel of personalities, she reasoned painfully. The honours were even. A permanent truce, hopefully already achieved, was desirable... Presumably no hand, either large or small, would move towards a trigger again... The alarm went at a quarter past seven. Mel struggled listlessly into a dressing gown and sat on the edge of the bed, throbs of pain measuring the distance from a point somewhere inside her skull to the right temple.

Adam noticed her sighs.

'Are you alright?' he asked,'

'I've a wretched head. I'll take something in a moment.

'Stay in bed for a while, darling. I'll go and make a cup of tea.'

'No. It's OK. I'm up now,' she said resignedly before adding, 'by the way, Ruth phoned last evening. She's coming home for the night tomorrow.'

'Good,' he yawned, 'I can give her all the up to date news on the Festival concert. Felix was saying that the ends are more or less tied up.'

Mel was preoccupied and miserable. She would need to clear this head before talking to Adam. It shouldn't be too difficult. Adam would be able to rationalise the whole wretched business. Quietly, over a drink this evening, this good man, who was her husband, would ease away her guilt and tease away the tension. Our love, he would say, could encompass Piers still. It was big enough, and strong enough... It could survive. We could all survive this one insignificant emotional upset. Yes! This is what he must say. She would seek his absolution this evening.

After a breakfast of a cup of coffee and a couple of aspirins, the head eased. Adam was at his desk by eight-thirty (his secretary came on Fridays) and Maidie breezed in at nine-thirty full of some chatter, (fresh from the belfry!), about another pregnant schoolgirl. Mel made suitably shocked noises and then strolled up to the High Street to collect a few necessary provisions. She felt disorientated. The sandals clattering on the pavement seemed to belong to someone else and her response to half a dozen morning greetings was in an unfamiliar voice. On the spur of the moment, she called in on Hannah who was busy counting out wages for her domestic staff.

'I saw Piers' eye,' she said. 'He showed it to me.'

'Really, duckie. Has he got it pickled in a preserving jar then?'

'No, you fool. I mean I saw underneath the eye shade.'

'Good lord, how did you manage that? I always thought it was cemented in. No-one has ever heard of it being removed. What happened. Did the elastic break?' Hannah was being flippant. Mel wanted her to listen. She spoke seriously:-

'I asked him, and he showed me. It's a frightful sight. I'm a bit worried now though, because he was rather upset.'

'How, upset?' Hannah gave Mel a searching look, her eyes echoing the question.

'Well, he seemed to need comfort, or reassurance, or something, afterwards.'

'Poor old boy,' she said sympathetically, 'it probably embarrassed him as much as showing you his privates.'

'I hadn't thought of it quite like that,' Mel remarked slowly.

No one but Hannah would have done so and there seemed little point in pursuing this particular conversation.

Back at the Tower House, it was mid-morning before Mel remembered that this Friday evening was a counselling night. Her regular sessions, on Tuesdays and Fridays sometimes lasted a full four hours which, with the fifteen-mile drive to the Centre across the diocesan boundary, where she could be one more anonymous do-gooder, meant a maximum of five hours away. Damn! There would be little opportunity for a comforting hour with Adam today. Not for the first time, she cursed the Marriage Guidance Council, wreaking vengeance on the shell of an innocent egg and causing the saffron yolk to flood into the white, making separation impossible. She was making slow progress with Ruth's favourite pudding, lemon soufflé, she reflected, as she tipped the streaky slipperiness into the sink, turned on the tap, and collected three more eggs. How wasteful not to scramble those others – or make crème caramel… her thoughts were not on the job in hand!

Maidie interrupted the soufflé struggle.

'Is it a glass that was broken in Back's View then, Mrs Bishop?' she asked, her Welsh lilt fluctuating with her tenses.

'Yes Maidie. Didn't I clear it all up?'

'There's a jagged piece under the table, mind. I might have cut myself real bad.' Her voice reflected her lucky escape and Mel's carelessness. 'I'm down on my knees on the floor,' she continued, 'when I see it. Indeed to goodness I hope it was not a best glass.'

Mel shook her head and made some dismissive comment. 'Knees… floor… glass' – Maidie's words stung like sparks from a furnace and she burned under their heat. She was in no mood for further conversation and addressed her in her most authoritative voice.

'Maidie, when you've finished in Back's View would you check Ruth's room, please. And lay lunch for three in the dining room.'

'Ah,' she twigged, 'himself and Miss Fellowes is in today, is it!'

'It is,' Mel replied mechanically.

No sooner had she successfully folded in the whites of the second trio of eggs than she heard a ring from the front door bell. She took off her apron and finger-tidied her hair. It was probably another tramp wanting bread and cheese and a glass of milk. One of these days such regular customers would leave a legacy of nits or lice!

Maidie put her head round the door.

'Miss Biddle it is, to see you,' she informed. 'It's in the hallway I'm putting her.'

'Coming,' Mel said. (What could Ma B want?)

Miss Biddle was standing just inside the door, her usual stiff, unsmiling self. She carried a large cone-shaped package, pinned into floral wrapping, which was obviously a bunch of flowers. She spoke archly, implying disapproval.

'The Colonel asked me to drop these by, madam. He went away early this morning but left me his instructions. He said I was to give you this letter, too.' She separated the two items and held them out awkwardly, one in each hand.

'How very kind, Miss Biddle,' exclaimed Mel feeling somewhat foolish as she received the items. 'What a lovely surprise and how good of you to call.'

'Not at all madam. I understand the Colonel enjoyed his evening.'

'I'm sorry if you were inconvenienced over his dinner.'

'It is not my place to be inconvenienced, madam,' she smirked as she moved to pass Mel considering the interview to be at an end. But Mel sensing a need for some further conversational gambit, queried, 'when do you expect the Colonel back?'

'Monday evening, madam. In time for dinner.' She sniffed, scornfully, as though something displeased her. Perhaps it was the flowers.

Mel opened the front door clumsily. Her hands were full.

'Goodbye, Miss Biddle. Goodbye... thank you again.'

'Good morning, madam.'

Mel watched her retreat across the courtyard and through the archway. She did not look back. The belt of her scrawny rayon dress was twisted and her grey stockings laddered. How did Piers stand her Mel wondered as she closed the door.

While she was standing in the front hall removing the wrapping paper Adam came out of the study.

'Did I catch a glimpse of Ma B through the window?' he asked.

'Yes,' Mel answered, 'she brought these from Piers,' and she removed a bunch of splendid roses from the inner cellophane wrapping. Adam looked at them approvingly.

'Those are superb, Mel, 'Josephine Bruce' if I'm not mistaken. Does Piers think it's your birthday? It isn't is it? I haven't forgotten something vital, have I?' For a moment he looked genuinely worried, and Mel was quick to reassure him with a smile.

'No darling, another three months to my birthday!'

Lowering her voice, so as not to attract the interest of either Maidie or Miss Fellows she added, 'Piers is getting romantic in his old age!' The remark was tossed off lightly and Adam, with an amused raise of his eyebrows, returned to his ministrations with Miss Fellowes.

She took the roses through to Backs View and laid them on the old round table. A classic offering. Red roses. White 'Iceberg' might have been more appropriate! She gazed at them, uncertain, and then at the envelope. It was formally addressed in neat blue-black ink to 'Mrs Amelia Ellis' with 'By courtesy of Miss Biddle' in the top left-hand corner.

She undid it slowly and extracted a plain white correspondence card on which was written the following message:-

My Amelie
I cannot bear to have shattered something so precious.
Please forgive me
Yours ever
Piers

From the sofa where he had sat the previous evening she surveyed the bouquet, conscious that her normally quiescent heart had altered its pace and was again asserting itself. To what could she contribute this

103

quickening? He had sent an apology and a bunch of roses. Nothing further was implied. Or was it?

She inspected the roses. There had to be a dozen. She counted them. There were. They had to be perfect specimens, long stemmed, lush with dark glazed leaves. They were. The diameter of each bud was no larger than a liquor glass, yet in a day or two, the uncurling surrender of every layered petal would yield up the secrets of each stamen studded centre and bring a chalice's circumference to every bloom. In less than a week each petal would fall, a tissue of humus, to decay in solitude, still fragrant in demise. There had to be thorns, too. There were - below the sepals, embryonic, apologetic, scarcely more than thick hairs, but lower, on each stem's spine, strong, vindictive, and sharp. Above all, the buds had to be red. They were indeed. A deep velvet crimson.

Two alternative explanations presented themselves. Either she could accept the roses for what they were, reparation for a glass worth no more than a few pounds; or she could read into this dual offering an invitation not only to restore the status quo about which she had been so anxious, but also to progress. She was not naive enough to interpret his 'something so precious' as a reference to a mere glass. He had apologised for that at the time... and later for the other thing too. Here, in these blood red roses, lay visible evidence of his devotion, offered on unconditional terms. For this sign, she was unutterably thankful. She realised that his friendship meant more to her than she had dared to acknowledge and that the past eighteen hours had shown her a spectrum of emotion of which, until now, she had been unaware. The intensity of the situation excited her: she felt all powerful.

She found a slim, elegant glass vase (a rarely used wedding gift from some wealthy undertaker), filled it with water, arranged the roses, and stood them in the centre of the ornamental table, with the card propped up for all the world to see. Then she set about preparing a lunch of pate, fruit and cheese for Adam, Miss Fellows and herself.

Pert, pretty little Mrs Prosser did not have Mel's full attention that evening. She was concerned for her that her husband's urges never coincided with her own and more so that he could only perform effectively, sexually, on the rare occasions when they were in an alien bedroom, and never within the confines of their own four and a half feet of bed...! She listened, consoled and encouraged but was thankful to be behind the wheel of the Mini again speeding for home. She had problems enough of her own which made her less enthusiastic to listen to those of other people. She looked at her watch and accelerated hard. With luck she would be home by seven. She hoped Adam would be ready to listen.

As she drove in through the archway he emerged from the front porch with Elizabeth. They were deep in conversation. Mel stopped and got out of the car, leaving it at the front of the house instead of driving on round to the garage. She sensed that they were discussing Felix. To save a repetition of all that he had just been told, Adam gave a quick summary.

'Elizabeth came home this evening,' he explained. 'She is to take Felix back to London on Sunday. They want to operate as soon as possible.

'My dear,' Mel commiserated. 'I am so sorry.'

'It couldn't be worse Mel. Primaries in one or both lungs, almost certainly. They will know when they get to them but I've seen the X-rays and I'm not optimistic.' She was telling her friend that, irrevocably, since yesterday, her father was under a sentence of death.

'Does he know?'

'Not yet. I needed advice. I wasn't too sure what to tell him. With your own flesh and blood it isn't all that easy! When I arrived home this evening he and mother were watching a TV soap, so I made an excuse to pop out and came straight over here to discuss it.'

Mel nodded, understanding.

'You would like Adam to talk to your parents.'

'Not to break the news exactly. But to prepare the ground.'

'And I'm just on my way,' said Adam. 'Give me half an hour or so. I'll prise your father's

engagement diary out of him if I do nothing else!'

He strode off purposefully. He coped admirably with this kind of situation.

'Come inside again, Elizabeth,' Mel invited, 'I'll pour us a drink.'

'Adam said you were over at the M G Centre.'

'Yes, rather a long afternoon!'

They wandered through to the kitchen, collected a chilled bottle of wine and a couple of glasses and took them through to Backs View.

'This is desperate, Elizabeth', said Mel as they sat down. The words sounded hollow and inadequate and added to Elizabeth's anxiety as she controlled herself, defied an urge to weep, and valiantly sipped her wine.

'The moment of reckoning has come,' she choked. 'I have known in my heart that it was coming and been powerless to stop it.'

Mel moved across to the sofa and put an arm gently around her shoulders in what was, she hoped, a comforting gesture.

'Your father is not a man to give in without a fight.'

Elizabeth shrugged. The platitude belonged nowhere and altered nothing.

'This will mean giving up my nursing for the time being,' she said, voicing her thoughts aloud. 'I must be with him if he comes out of hospital.'

The 'if' was significant. Mel latched on to it, but spoke too brightly, with false confidence.

'Of course he will come out of hospital. We must believe that.'

She shook her head, slowly, emphatically, miserably certain that he would not.

'We are all around you,' Mel continued giving her a gentle hug. 'We'll help you – and pray for you.' How limp she sounded!

Aggravated, Elizabeth broke free, flouncing away from the despair and breathing deeply as if to gain strength. The professional nurse was in command again.

'You are very kind, Mel,' she said automatically.

'How will your mother take it?' Mel asked.

'She won't realise it is happening.'

The words sounded harsh but Mel could appreciate their meaning. Long long ago she had outgrown Ellen's pedestrian absorption with the next jumble sale and whilst Felix and Elizabeth meant a great deal to her Ellen had remained a hindrance. Dull, insecure, and obsessive about petty unimportance, Mel had never been able to achieve a relationship with her. She reminded her too much of her grandmother's housemaid. Now that Elizabeth had taken a grip her face was composed again, the features as tidy as her neat tailored shirt and linen skirt. Her gaze was steady, her eyes dry and she could speak with near clinical detachment.

'Papa has been spitting blood for the past three months,' she said. 'I have known since then.'

'I had no idea,' Mel said quietly. 'I'm so sorry.'

Elizabeth sighed, resigned. Looking straight at the roses she suddenly appeared to see them for the first time. She smiled appreciatively, her expression brightening.

'What beautiful roses, Mel. Is it an anniversary?'

'Just what Adam said,' Mel tittered rather stupidly, as she reached out to recover the card, which had tipped on to its face, and carefully propped it up again. 'No! It isn't actually!'

Imperceptibly Elizabeth raised her eyebrows and seemed to look away. She had recognised the writing on the card!

'Piers sent them', Mel gabbled, embarrassed. 'He was here last evening while Adam and your father were in London. They are his peace offering. He broke a glass.'

Mel felt Elizabeth's scrutiny. Disconcerted she studied her finger nails and ran a hand nervously around her collar. Elizabeth was too silent for comfort. Did she have to say more? Must she endure this torture?

'He brought some Festival notices and we had a drink and a chat.'

'Quite a long drink,' Elizabeth said flatly. 'I tried to phone him several times. I knew he would be away today and I wanted to talk to him. I would have gone to see *him* this evening, instead of coming here, if he'd been at home!' She stressed the him.

There was no accusation in her voice but the implication was quite clear. In catching Mel out she had deemed it necessary to state her claim to Piers and, in the process, to remind her that she and Adam were only second best at a time of crisis.

'He'll be sorry to have missed you,' Mel said as they stood up.

Elizabeth inclined her head but did not comment.

'Let me know if there is anything I can do,' Mel said. 'Anything at all.'

'Yes. Thank you.' The voice was cold.

They walked through the house in silence and said their goodbyes quickly.

The interlude had not ended quite as Mel would have wished and she realised acutely as she returned to collect the wine and glasses that Elizabeth had every reason to feel hurt. She had not been very clever. She, Mel Ellis, who had everything – husband, status, success, children - had betrayed her. That Elizabeth still hoped that Piers would settle for her ministrations one day, in preference to those of Miss Biddle, was obvious. What comfort could Elizabeth draw from the knowledge that he had spent the evening with me, thought Mel, when everyone else was safely out of the way, and showered me with roses to boot! She had been tactless in the extreme. It would have been so simple to spare her the pain and to toss off the flowers as the gift of some visiting cleric or a distant relative. In the circumstances a white lie would have been a small price to pay for a wretchedly shabby moment of vanity. By bungling the whole incident she had bred suspicion where there need have been none. Indeed, why had she not told her the whole truth...

Mel vented her anger on the cheese grater as she prepared lasagne for supper. She was guilty. More guilty than she dared to admit. She had flaunted her roses in front of Elizabeth. Steeped now, in such guilt, it was unlikely that she would find the courage to unburden her soul to Adam even though she could hear his returning footsteps; anyway, there was Felix to discuss!

The following day the weather broke. Relentless rain spilled into the day, changing the Abbey Green into a landscape of lilliputian lakes as the downpour accumulated on a hard heat crusted surface. Umbrellas bobbed to and fro and folk splashed about disguised in plastic macs and gumboots: refugees from the sun, preoccupied and anonymous. For the time being the continental heatwave was over.

Mel made three fruitless trips to the station before finally scooping Ruth off a late afternoon train. Vague as always about times of arrival she was hardly apologetic that her mother had spent the afternoon playing taxi driver.

'You shouldn't have bothered, Mum, I could have walked.'

'In this weather! Suppose you had brought the cello.'

'Ah! You have a point there.'

Half an hour later Ruth and her parents stood in the kitchen drinking mugs of tea. It was almost 'drinks' time!

How is the concerto, Rufus?' asked Adam, using his favourite nickname for his daughter.

'OK,' she replied, with youthful economy, 'Viv says it will sound groovy in the Abbey.'

'She will not have used that particular adjective,' said Adam, a schoolmaster's look on his face. Viv was her professor.

'Sorry, Dad! But it will be good I promise you.'

'I have every confidence in you Rufus,' he smiled.

Later, sipping cider in Backs View, Ruth, who fidgeted with everything in sight, saw the roses and picked up the card.

'My God,' she said, 'what has got into Piers? What precious thing has he broken?'

'A glass,' Mel stated.

Ruth stared at her mother in disbelief.

'Just a glass. Why the fuss?'

'It was Waterford crystal.'

Ruth's brow contracted, scoring the smooth elastic skin with lines which would vanish as quickly as they had come. By middle age this tracery would have weathered. Nothing could erase it then. Protective of her beautiful daughter's fleeting precious youth Mel smiled at her lovingly and said,

'Don't frown. It doesn't suit you.'

Ruth handled one of the roses, sniffing it perfunctorily like a shop girl testing cheap perfume.

'Well, it is overdoing it a bit isn't it. I mean he's always been keen on you. Everyone knows that. But surely this is a bit much... Aren't you embarrassed?'

Mel laughed.

'Good heavens, no! It's his way of doing things isn't it.'

Adam had just come into the room to join them and Ruth appealed to him as he poured himself a gin and tonic.

'What do you think, Dad?'

'About what, Rufus?'

'This rose thing!' She gestured towards the vase, dramatically, teasing him with a theatrical pose which demanded response.

'I don't have any profound thoughts on the subject', he said, retaliating with amused mockery as he settled into a chair. 'Why? Should I?'

'Well, if you don't mind about Mum's roses, you ought to care about Piers and Seb. It's unhealthy the way he takes such an interest in him and something ought to be done about it!'

Ruth spoke aggressively and the moments of what could safely be interpreted as light-hearted banter were past. She was serious now and the twist in the conversation startled Mel. Never before had Ruth expressed such sentiments though she had often been cool and even insolent to Piers. If these were her true feelings then Adam's answer was important.

He did not hesitate. Ruth's comment was diminished with a swift rebuke and his impatience with her for voicing such an opinion brought irritation into his voice as he replied:-

'If Piers and I, or Piers and Seb, played golf together you would not query our motives. It's intolerable to read sedition into an acceptable and normal relationship. Piers and Seb happen to enjoy walking and literature. In these shared pursuits they find stimulation and friendship. It's as simple as that.'

Ruth looked ready to interrupt and protest but Adam, with the repressive salute of a Victorian autocrat, commanded silence, and continued his pronouncement.

'One thing is absolutely certain, too. We and this whole town would be the poorer without Piers. And particularly just now. He'll be taking on a lot of parish responsibility while Felix is indisposed, and may I remind you, my girl, that this includes the Festival arrangements.' He emphasised the paternal endearment with admonitory jabs of his forefinger.

'You're not up to date, darling,' intervened Mel, noting that a puzzled look had replaced the stubbornness on Ruth's face. She was a little old to be peremptorily chastised and maybe she had a valid point. Perhaps they should be more concerned about Seb and Piers. But Adam had been categoric and in a way this was a relief. There was no point in questioning. One did not, after all, tear up a healthy plant to look at its roots. Since two days ago an up- to-date analysis of Mel's own relationship with Piers might be a wholly different matter! A fleeting vision of his grisly defacement came into focus and she nudged it forcefully to one side.

'Daddy will put you in the picture about Felix', she said as she emptied her glass and stood up. 'I'll go and cook the peas and whip the cream for the soufflé.' She rumpled Ruth's hair as she passed; it was good to have her with them for the weekend. What a pity Seb could not be here, too, instead of sweating over Ancient History.

The rest of the weekend passed without further allusion to the roses. They were now fully unfurled and a splendid sight. Half of Mel would be thankful to see them withered and tossed on to the compost heap, but the other half longed to preserve them – to embalm their exquisite

110

elegance and to wax it into an everlasting reminder of an evening of earth shattering significance in her own existence. She did not question Ruth again about her comments. She had seemed subdued after Adam's straight talking and Mel retreated from upsetting her further. In her present delicate state she shrank from hearing anything either controversial or unpalatable and she could not seriously believe that Ruth had any evidence to substantiate her remark about Seb and Piers. Surely it was no more than feminine pique! Piers had always identified more easily with Seb. Perhaps her pride was hurt. Ruth could not accept that she might come to regret the fact that she had never captured Piers' attention and confidence like the rest of them. There was still a formality about their relationship. She had responded to his gentle teasing with haughty indifference and given an impression of wishing to keep him a proverbial arm's length away.

With Alastair, Ruth was quite different. He had won her heart on the day that he gave her the cello. She had kept faith with him as she might have done with a grandfather, had a suitable one been provided. She still wrote him long chatty letters and whenever she saw him she was loving and communicative, and Alastair was becoming an old man now. Mel realised that she ought to be interested as to why Ruth's response to Piers was so angular but now that she gave it some thought she was unable to reach any conclusions. However, she was left with the sensation that Ruth's unease was born of a feeling of danger and that in some indefinable way she saw Piers as a threat. Mel did not wish to pursue it...

Ruth and Mel went to Choral Eucharist together the next morning, leaving Adam to apologise for his wife's absence from a big ecumenical gathering forty miles away in the cathedral. Few would miss her amongst that eager hand-shaking throng and it felt poignantly appropriate to support Felix at this time. He had obstinately refused to relinquish his responsibilities one hour earlier than necessary. The news of his impending hospitalisation had travelled fast and one sensed, in the larger than normal congregation, a keen awareness of his presence. Undoubtedly some had come to form their own opinions as to the seriousness of his illness; others to wish him good luck as they filed past him at the end of the service; a few to thank the Almighty that they were not in his shoes; and the rest because they always came.

Mel knelt at the altar rail. The wafer stuck to the roof of her mouth until its rice paper texture melted away in a ladylike swallow. The shoes peeping from beneath the cassock and surplice in front of her now belonged to Felix. His hands offered the chalice. She breathed an 'Amen' and drank from it as he urged her to 'preserve her body and soul unto everlasting life.' Then she dared to look up at him, wanting him to notice her and to recognise the concern which was, she hoped, visible in her expression. But he was already administering to Ruth and gave no flicker of recognition. His eyes could have been two grey pebbles. If they were seeing anything at all, it was a long way distant, beyond the great west door. Did this deeply religious man sense that he might be performing this sacred ritual for the last time? Was he already elsewhere? A feeling of despair caught Mel as she gripped the brass rail and stood up slowly. He was her pastor and she needed him. For a moment she was tempted to throw herself at his feet and to confess before it was too late for both of them, but the idea for such a dramatic exhibition drained away as she returned to the pew, her heels echoing on the chancel steps.

She knelt again, as people do, but she was neither renewed nor refreshed, as people are. She tried to pray, as people pray. Words crept into her head and spoke noiselessly in the silence. But sentiments tangled with sentences and she could make no sense out of it all. There was a gripping ache in her body. Was it because she had wronged Elizabeth? Or concealed things from Adam? Or persuaded Piers? Or was it to do with dreams? Surely they did not count in quite the same way as ordinary sins...! Or was it because of Felix. In her supplicatory position her hands covered her face. But she spied on Felix through the chinks between her fingers and watched him drain the last of the consecrated wine. 'Dear God, here is a precious friend,' she prayed. 'Please, if there is any way in which medical science can save him, then please, bring him back to us for a while': and she prayed more simply for Seb and Ruth, and for Adam, too, but in the end, because she was weary of searching for phrases, she wandered away from trying to pray for herself and allowed her mind to dwell on other things.

Beside her, Ruth stirred. The last pairs of feet tapped along the nave. It was a relief to be standing up and singing the last hymn. Mel was pleased that it was rousing and powerful. In the final verse, the organ and the congregation swelled into a great duet – of praise.

'Angels help us to adore Him,' they sang, and as Felix passed by on his way to the abbey's great west door she and Ruth could observe that, although his mouth was almost closed and his face drawn with fatigue, he seemed to understand that they were singing their hearts out for him and he smiled a strange, tired, mystic smile.

Chapter VII

PIERS

'My dears, I have things to tell you,' he said.

Adam and Mel were sitting over coffee after a Monday evening supper of macaroni cheese and apples when he appeared at the kitchen door. He had phoned earlier. Would they be in, he had asked, and could he call round later?

He leant rather than stood, apologetic, anxious to account for his presence. More formally dressed than usual – he wore a navy blue blazer and light trousers which were ringed round the thighs with car seat creases. A gaudy regimental scarf was tucked into the neck of his shirt and a cheerful green silk handkerchief sat tidily in his breast pocket. They had not heard his footsteps. He had crept through the house like a cat burglar, as though unwilling to disturb them and although he had returned from wherever he had been, and Mel was secretly overjoyed to see him again, she sensed in his bearing the reluctance of a man who finds at the end of a long journey that his day's work is only just beginning.

'I am back. I came straight here,' he stated - the clipped phrases displaying a tired urgency.

Mel jumped up.

'You must be starving, Piers. Let me get you something to eat.'

'Thank you, but no, Amelie. A 'Services' near Tewkesbury fulfilled my needs. It was from there that I telephoned.'

'A cup of coffee then, old chap,' suggested Adam, pulling out a chair from under the table and patting the seat invitingly.

'That sounds very agreeable. Thank you.'

He sat down awkwardly on the pine kitchen chair. It seemed too small for him this evening and he did not know where to park his legs. Noisily Mel brewed more coffee, clattering crockery as an antidote to her nervous tension, while Adam, who had obviously realised that Piers was not his normal self, made various attempts to put him at his ease. But the small talk drew little response. Piers toyed with his coffee and Adam embarked on the protracted ritual of emptying, cleaning, and refilling his pipe. Abstractedly, Mel stacked plates, shuffled knives and forks, put away glasses which normally stayed out, emptied the rubbish bin, and wiped over the work top. Sick with apprehension, she could not look at him. Why had he come? What did it mean? What 'things' must he tell? Why, oh why, had she not confessed...?

Now Adam was looking for a match and she handed him the box from the cooker. The flame burned with a hypnotic intensity as he held it against the tiny pyre of tobacco in the cedar barrel of his best Dunhill (the one Mel had given him for his birthday). New smoke puffed upwards. It had a calming effect. Through the haze Mel scrutinised Piers and suddenly, again, she remembered her long-ago dream and the dream aroma of that sizzling creature; it had not been unlike the smell of burning tobacco. Piers seemed to emerge from a trance as the smoke wafted across his line of vision. Waving it away he looked from one of them to the other and repeated what he had said already.

'I have things to tell you.'

Adam stood up. 'Then we'll find some more comfortable chairs,' he announced, and, like three middle aged committee members engaged on some official business, they adjourned to Backs View.

It was a balmy evening. The doors through the conservatory and into the garden were open. The heatwave had returned – the bonanza of good weather an unexpected bonus. The air in Backs View was stifling and the precious roses looked sick, their outer petals shrivelled into a tatty blackness and their stems sagging like old necks.

'Let's sit outside,' Mel said. 'There's some of the weekend Sangria left in the fridge. I'll get it.'

'I'll go darling,' called Adam, still puffing his pipe and bringing up the rear.

Piers and Mel carried out chairs and a table and put them on a patch of old paving stones which merged into the lawn. He was very quiet, his nervousness communicating itself like the early symptoms of some illness.

'It's a lovely evening,' Mel offered, as cheerfully as she could, but he only nodded as he adjusted the metal ratchets on the arms of a garden chair.

They sat down and she willed him to look at her. She could hear Adam coming back, the jug and glasses knocking against each other as he balanced them on a tray.

She leant across to Piers and momentarily her hand brushed against his wrist.

'Are you alright?' she whispered.

Startled, he straightened his legs, and flicked at his arm as though her touch had left dust on his sleeve. His eye met hers at last.

'There are things that you should know,' he said. 'So that you may understand.'

Unasked and unanswered questions clamped into circuits in Mel's mind as Adam poured the sangria. The glasses glowed like giant rubies and she thought nostalgically of their last Spanish holiday. Piers picked out a slice of orange and nibbled it, his hand trembling slightly as it had done at their last meeting. Mel caught Adam's eye. He, too, had noticed the tremor.

Piers cleared his throat:-

'I should have told you these things many years ago,' he began. 'You, my adopted kin, should not have been left in ignorance for so long.'

He stopped. The pause, after his stilted opening, was prolonged and, now under some stress, he was unable to continue.

Adam, used to confidences, spoke to him gently:-

'Piers, whatever it is that you wish to tell us will in no way separate you from us. Nor shall we question the wisdom of your decision to refrain from speaking about it until now. If it will help to unburden yourself then share the load, but if you prefer, even now, to remain silent then be assured that both Mel and I will understand.'

Mel cringed. He, too, spoke unnaturally and with a sickly professionalism. But Adam had realised, as she had, that some purging of the soul was to follow in which, almost certainly, Piers was going to expose something of a very personal nature. In a flash of intuition she realised that they were about to be let into the secret of the mystery trips. What Adam did not possess as she did, was the uncomfortable knowledge that it was almost certainly the events of the previous Thursday evening which had prompted this desire in Piers to communicate the 'things' to them. She shuddered inwardly. There was still the forlorn hope that something had happened on this recent trip to make the revelations imperative: that his intention was in no way connected with what had happened between them. She hoped against hope that this might be so for she did not want her world to fall apart.

The spluttering of a Saints Avenue lawn mower which choked repeatedly as it buffered their boundary wall, distracted attention from the absence of any immediate response to Adam's sympathetic, albeit pompous, comments, but after two or three minutes, Piers braced himself for a second attempt. In view of the length and content of the narrative his initial hesitation was understandable. This time he did not waver.

'It started in 1952,' he began, 'I was over thirty at the time and housed at battalion headquarters in North London. Existence was drab between postings. I considered that the time had come for me to search for a wise and eligible virgin, and, as luck would have it, fortune smiled upon me and I fell in love.'

He continued. 'She was the daughter of friends of friends whom I had met through a brother officer. She was a student at Westfield College. We were introduced and I took her out on several occasions. The more I escorted her the more certain I became that this for me was 'it'. I had found my 'Juliet'.'

Warming to his story, Piers was able to smile at Adam and Mel a little sheepishly at this point before continuing:-

'Alas! There were problems. As a potential lover I was inhibited and untutored. I was not unacquainted with the bawdiness of the Mess and had overheard my share of barrack room smut, but I was green... victim of my God-fearing Victorian upbringing and my own puritanism.

The object of my affection was of impeccable background and a retiring disposition. So although I held her hand, put my arm around her and confessed, as we walked, that she was the temptations of Eve, she made no initiating moves towards me to facilitate my advances. A seductress would have spared me what followed. To put it simply, I needed to prove myself... (here he was momentarily lost for words) as a male animal, before I could escape the physical impasse in which I found myself. It may sound absurd to you but I had to know how to make love. I was factually and anatomically ignorant. For me there had been no sordid encounters with little girls, no sisters, no female cousins, no forays with ladies of the night or pornography. I was unprepared to offer such gross naiveté, to so perfect a partner. In cold blood, I decided to quest for an opportunity to acquire the necessary knowledge. Please understand, I had no lust. It was a 'melange' of curiosity, innocence and idealism that led me into such a torrid adventure. In a risky attempt to resolve my problems without resorting to Soho, I began to visit seedy pubs in less salubrious suburbs. Would I had shopped in the normal market!

However, one fateful evening, somewhere near the Oval, my search appeared to be over. I chatted up a pert faced little number. She was nineteen, she told me. Her name was Teresa and she worked as a machinist. She lived 'just down the road' with her mother and sister. I bought her a few drinks. It became encouragingly obvious that she was not unfamiliar with the manoeuvres which were taking place, and after a final gin and lime, I was invited back to her place for a cup of coffee! 'She was able to entertain' she explained. Her mother worked at night! I warmed to my intentions and went home with her.

An hour or two later I took a taxi back to HQ a wiser and happier man, initiated by a little cockney girl, well-skilled in the art of fornication. My baptism was complete, the libido released. I was ready to advance. I experienced feelings of great relief and intense happiness.'

Here Piers paused for a long drink of his sangria. He was sweating, and so was Mel. Neither she nor Adam spoke. They were listening to a painstaking account which did not need any comment. The silence was bustling with images – of postures and of people. And of Piers long before they knew him, unscarred and unscathed, encumbered only by his own innocence and seeking to dispose of it in as seemly a way as his upbringing would permit. The story continued:-

'The following month, I learned to my chagrin that I was posted to Korea. It was very vexing. The enforced absence of two or three years meant inevitably, that my matrimonial plans must be deferred. However, it was imperative to ensure that my intentions were understood. This sortie did not go at all as planned. My beloved divulged what I believed to be the details of another suitor and I had to content myself with chaffing her not to marry before I returned from the East to claim her. In retrospect I believe that she may have been trying to help me to be more decisive, but the inescapable fact of my imminent eleven-thousand-mile exile cast a shadow over us at those last trysts and ends which should have been tied up were left fluttering. Ashamedly I was still emotionally inept and unable to press my suit effectively. But in my heart I was convinced that she would wait for me and her letters during those first few months away supported my hopes. I was mastering the courage to atone for my cowardice and cable her a proposal of marriage when the romantic idyll exploded around me.'

Piers paused again. The effort of remembering and recounting was taking its toll, but he was now, also, removing a tattered envelope from his pocket and extracting a letter. A soft, ragged letter. Discoloured and age-crumpled. It had been read many times!

He held it out to them and Adam leant across to take it.

'It speaks for itself,' he said bleakly.

Adam smoothed out the cheap notepaper and together he and Mel struggled their way through the round childish script smudged on to Woolworth's lines. The spelling was atrocious.

'Deer Left tenant,' they read. *'I am going to have a baby. It is yaws becouse you are the last one I was with befor I new. If you like I will kepe it and you must send munny. My mum blams me and says you must pay. What will you do abowt me and the baby? Plese rite soon. From Miss Teresa Travers.'*

Unable to restrain herself, Mel cried out.

'Oh Piers, how absolutely terrible!' But Adam laid a restraining hand over hers, handed back the letter, and quietly encouraged Piers to continue, which he did after he had meticulously replaced the letter in its envelope and returned it to his pocket. He was like a performer. It was impossible not to watch him.

'I was utterly dismayed by this turn of events,' he continued, 'the possibility of such a biological accident had simply not occurred to me and I was profoundly shocked. Unnerved, too, that the redoubtable Miss Travers had been canny enough to remember my name and to write to me via the War Office with a 'plese forward' on the envelope. Security considered it expedient that such a letter should reach me safely in

Korea. I passed through various stages of decision and indecision. Ultimately I made a clean breast of my folly in a letter to my mother although I could not bear to imagine the anguish it would bring her.'

He paused again before continuing:-

'It was some weeks before I heard from her. Her reply was a concise record of her actions on my behalf. She was a remarkable woman. The fact that she did not censure me made me feel the more culpable. Mummy had gone to Kennington to locate Miss Travers and had negotiated the ransom that my indiscretion demanded. The baby, when born, would be supported until it was of age and would then receive an amount of not less than a thousand pounds. To Miss Travers and her mother such offers smacked of fortune and they were apparently satisfied. My regular contribution, credited to them at the beginning of each month, would be more than enough to assure security for the family. They would not attempt to contact me again. The necessary arrangements were concluded and Mummy produced a document for them to sign, agreeing the terms and accepting that there would be no further demands made upon us. She thus 'nipped in the bud' any likelihood of blackmail by the Travers ladies. Personally I doubt whether this would have entered their calculations. But she left nothing to chance. The terms were generous. A hefty slice of my subaltern's salary was mortgaged for my misdeeds. The price was high, but the torment much worse. I was tormented by my mortal sin. I badly needed forgiveness and felt that it would never be mine. I was haunted by the enormity of my action in creating, so carelessly, a human being – and besieged by indistinct images of babies and small children, neither of which species was at all familiar to me. Dimly I saw a child growing up with the now hazy Miss Travers – my child! I had been interested only in her body and what it could teach me. I knew nothing of her personality or the life she would create for our child. In the Korean heat, I steamed in agony. In my effort to come to terms with my guilt, it dawned upon me, one day, with excruciating clarity that this calamity demanded the sacrifice of my plans to marry.

For a few weeks, I carried on the precious correspondence. The letters from my dear one had become love letters in the fullest sense – I could not bear to lose her, but knew that it must be so. For me, in this pit, there was but one road to salvation. I allowed some time to elapse and then wrote, harshly. It was the coward's way, but there was no alternative.'

Mel interrupted him a second time at this point. 'Piers – what kind of letter did you write? Did you explain?' But Adam restrained her again, shaking his head to silence her questions. All the answers were on their way. Now Piers was fidgeting, disturbed by the intervention, and, for a moment, engulfed. Temporarily he had lost the next piece of the jigsaw to fit into the picture of his ruined life. Adam was right. They could help only by listening.

Piers found the 'jigsaw piece' and continued:-

'It was a difficult letter and took many drafts. In the end I wrote in general terms, preparing the way for a retreat. I conveyed an impression that my own feelings had changed. It was unthinkable to tell the truth, yet I have asked myself countless times since whether I would have behaved differently had we actually been betrothed. She replied intelligently, as I would have expected. She was shocked – and unconvinced by what I had written. I wrote a second time. How I betrayed her. Yet it had to be. Now the only way was for her to think me the biggest blackguard that ever lived. This time I convinced her. There were no more of her dear letters. She deserved great happiness. I hope she found it.'

At this point, Piers stood up, removed his jacket, finger-combed his hair, fiddled with his eye shade and stretched his limbs. It was as though he needed to check that his body was intact

'Excuse me', he said. 'I am discovering that I am not yet heat-resistant to these reminiscences. Also, I think I must have a pee!'

He lumbered off to the lavatory, leaving Adam and Mel in a limpid vacuum, their faces taut with concentration.

'It's beyond belief,' Adam remarked quietly.

'The child!' Mel stated.

'What do you mean, the child?'

'That is where he goes. It must be.'

'Yes. You could be right.'

Mel's mind was busy with calculations. 'My God, Adam. Do you realise. Don't you see?'

'See what, darling?' He was a calculation behind her.

'The child', Mel repeated. 'It must be almost the same age as Ruth.'

Adam caught up, and nodded slowly.

'Born in 1952 or three. Nearly the same age.'

In the distance, a cistern flushed.

'Make some more coffee,' suggested Adam, 'There's the rest of the confession to come and this is a good moment for a break. I won't let him start again until you are back with us.'

Mel retired to the kitchen. Foremost in her thoughts was the child. Piers's child. Where was it? What was it? A boy or a girl? What was his contact with it now, and the obliging Miss Travers? The other woman did not concern her. She had been dismissed from his life, sacrificed as a part of his penance. She was a nebulous figure, anyway. Too good to be true. She merited no more concern. But Teresa Travers – and her child! They were another matter.

The coffee was welcome. While they drank it they remembered Felix in hospital in London. Soon there would be news. His illness was a sombre topic but a chat about the Music Festival, now only a month away, afforded a measure of relief. Piers was confident that he would have all the arrangements under control within a few days.

After about a quarter of an hour he seemed ready to continue. Well into his stride, now, he did not falter again. Shadows crept into the garden as he spoke. The sky, diffused with rose water pink, melted into an oyster candescence. By the time he had finished it stretched over them and all around them, a thick padded midnight blue, injected with a million floating stars.

'The baby,' he said, 'a boy, was born on the last day of 1952. Mummy wrote to tell me that the Travers had informed her of the birth. Providing the money supply was regularly maintained, we could rest assured that they would make no further demands and that the boy would have a stable home. Mummy did not visit the child. Full provision had been made and honour satisfied. After her death I learnt that she had consulted a lawyer on the matter to verify that we were legally protected. She was not a woman to do things by halves. I was, I confess, uneasy that she had not visited Kennington again, but was in no position to call the tune. My problem had been alleviated. It was now my patent duty to make a success of my career.'

While Piers was speaking a clearer picture formed of this efficient parent whose acquaintance Mel had made through hearsay and a tombstone. She dominated the scene like some powerful figure from a primitive painting: flicking up into one's imagination a static, cardboard presence; uncompromising in a dress of sable and inky grey ruler stripes relieved only by stiff neat cuffs as white as her anaemic cheeks. Mel imagined the features on her pallid face, drawn dark and sparse, making the expression unyielding and austere with hair that fell from the centre of her forehead in bare ebony curves. Here was a formidable figure indeed. Not grandmotherly in any way... But the story continued:-

'It was another two years before I returned home after what proved to be an extended tour in the Far East. When the war in Korea ended, I moved to Japan, and was content to stay there for as long as the Army decreed. I enjoyed myself. I was grateful for the opportunity to learn something of the country's culture and heritage. It was adapting quickly to westernisation and I was fascinated to see something of this metamorphosis at first hand. I made many friends, found peace of mind again, and, incidentally, Adam, (he addressed him directly at this point and received a reciprocal nod of appreciation), it was at this time in my life that a saintly padre helped me to rediscover my faith.

It was good to be in England again and home with the family in time for Christmas. Andre had married while I was abroad and he and June stayed with us for the festival. Mummy was in especially good spirits, I remember' (so she could be convivial, thought Mel) 'and I was glad to meet June after relying for so long on news bulletins in letters. It was strange to have a sister-in-law and to view my young sibling as a staid married man. I became acutely aware of what I had squandered. Moreover, as an obvious 'catch,' I was now pursued without mercy. Everyone gave parties that year. I was inundated with invitations which it would have been churlish to refuse. Suddenly there was a fleet of potential brides in this, my home town, displayed before me like racing yachts under full fail, any one of them mine for the asking. Somehow I steered a steady course through them all but some of the turmoil and anguish returned engendering with it a great desire to see my son. Since I was obliged to stifle my natural urges because of him it seemed to make good sense to utilise the fountain of unused love within me for his benefit. The compulsion grew. At a propitious moment I communicated my inclination to Mummy but she would have no truck with it. 'Let it rest,' she said. 'The financial responsibilities are settled. I do not recommend you to try to see it. It is now over two years old and has an established pattern of life. There is nothing that you can add. Stop being sentimental.' She spoke firmly but I was politely irritated! It was unchivalrous of me but she talked of my son as 'it' and I found this uncharitable of her. He was male, and one half of him was me! I yearned to see him. Remember, beloved friends – I did not even know his Christian name.

It was in late February, finally, that I retraced those fateful steps from the Victorian pub. I had the address of course and the house took little finding. In daylight it revealed itself as a smaller and meaner dwelling than I remembered. Distance had lent it a cosy enchantment which it did not possess. I hesitated before ringing the bell. I could still retreat. But somewhere inside the house a pseudo chime tinkled its major third and seconds later a rather tawdry young woman opened the door wearing, I recall, some sort of eastern dressing gown. I was quite clear in my mind that this was *not* Teresa and she turned out to be the sister. Teresa was away, she volunteered. She didn't know when she would be back. She often went away. 'Is the boy with her?' I asked. 'The boy?' She repeated, and then replied quickly. 'Oh, yes, the boy is with her!' adding, as she realised who I was, 'You must be *him*!' 'Correct,' I acknowledged. 'I wanted to be sure that everything is alright and that she is managing.' 'Managing?' She queried. 'Oh yes, it's all OK. She's managing.'

'When will they be back?' I asked. 'Back?' She said. 'Maybe next week. Maybe next month. She works away.' 'With the boy?' I persisted. 'Yes, she takes him', she said. 'Do you have an address?' I asked. 'An address? No! She wouldn't want to hear from you.' 'Will you be so kind as to tell her that I called and that I am pleased to know that all is well with her and the boy.' 'Sometime,' she said, 'when I see her.' As I turned to go, I remembered what I had forgotten to ask. 'There is just one more thing,' I said. 'About the boy. What is his name?' 'His name?' She said, repeating my words yet again and I recall the impatience that these uncommunicative echoes aroused in me – 'His name is Monty. Montgomery that is. She thought she should give him a soldier's name!' 'Monty,' I said, catching her disease. 'Monty,' I repeated again. 'Thank you, Miss Travers. It's an heroic name.' A blank stare indicated that the adjective was beyond her comprehension. She shrugged her shoulders and slammed the door. For the rest of the afternoon I tramped the streets of the area reflecting on my findings. Any disappointment which I may have felt in not actually seeing my son was tempered by the triumph of discovering his name. He was, so far as I could ascertain alive and well. But why had I not pressed for more details from the other Miss Travers? How could Teresa work away from home? What sort of a post could she have with a two-year-old that did not have the permanence of an address? Had she married? If so, surely she would have an address? I began to realise that the sister had been cagey with me. Maybe she was hiding something – indeed perhaps there was no little boy called Monty and never had been – was it possible that we had been duped? I became quite frantic with worry but I knew there was nothing to be gained, at least for the moment, by returning to the house, but I was more than ever determined to get to the heart of the matter. A little boy called Monty could be quite a chap and, when I found him, he was going to have all the support that I could give him.

Patience is my non-favourite virtue, but I had to cultivate it. Mummy refused to help, apart from substantiating that at her sole interview with the Travers family one of the young women had the normal swollen belly associated with procreation.' (Dear Piers, thought Mel, how comically he puts it!) 'The payments through the bank account were also being collected regularly. Nothing seemed to be amiss. I had to bide my time. I lived with the hope that when the day came for me to implement my resolve to visit Kennington again it would be the right Miss Travers who would open the door to me. Meanwhile, in my heart, I formed a bond with Monty which nothing could destroy.

Army circumstances intervened, as was likely, and I was unable to pursue the enquiries again until after my return from the debacle of Suez. Then, on an impulse, I called at the house one evening, only to find that it was inhabited by new tenants who had no idea of the whereabouts of the Travers family. However they were kindly folk and directed me to a neighbour's home a few doors away. It was here, at last, that I learnt the truth. Monty, my son, was born grossly disabled and was totally rejected by his mother after a few months when she realised the full significance of his crippling disabilities. One can argue that he should never have been allowed to breathe but I have been told that the extent of impairment would not necessarily have been all that obvious at birth. I do not wish to bore you, dear friends, with the details. They are harrowing. His life is not a life as we know it. He has to be supervised twenty-four hours a day and is, as people so cruelly describe such unfortunates, a human cabbage. Even so, for now, and for all eternity, he is my son.'

He paused, briefly. He was picking at his fingernails in the darkness, lost for a time in his own life history. He had not quite finished. He seemed to be seeking some conclusion or postscript. When it came, his voice was tranquil, almost humble, and the phrases fragmented as though they were drifting from him and he could scarcely catch them.

'If I have ever done anything,' he breathed, 'which has hurt either of you... in any way... then I ask that this explanation... may conjure up some expiation on my behalf... I beg most penitently for your mercy... and the continuing gift of your most precious friendship.'

No-one spoke but Mel wondered whether Adam was frowning, uncomprehending, as dusk sheltered her own blushes and warm night air evaporated her tears.

Suddenly, in an exuberant gesture, Piers slapped the arms of his chair, the frail metal joints protesting noisily and stinging the twilight out of its silence. He spoke again, his voice jovial and normal. He did not wait for assurances. For now he was totally confident of his friends' sympathy and understanding.

'And that, my dears, is that,' he stated. The things are told...'

Adam was the first to speak.

'This has been your burden for far too long, Piers. Is there anything more that you would like us to know? Tell us everything about Monty. Perhaps we can help.'

Mel murmured agreement.

'No, Adam. No one can help. The people who care for him are dedicated and efficient. No one can add to the dimension of his existence.'

'Do you mind us asking questions?' Mel enquired gently.

'Of course not, Amelie. Now that I have told you, at last, ask anything you wish.'

'Is he – Monty – in some sort of mental hospital?'

'No, he's in a residential home near Shrewsbury – one of the best of its kind. It's a long way from here, but as he does respond to his surroundings and his keepers, I have no plan to change the arrangements.'

'So that is where you go, when you vanish so mysteriously,' she commented.

126

'Yes, it is, and I apologise for the subterfuge.'

'These neighbours of the Travers,' queried Adam, 'did they tell you where to find Monty?'

'They knew that he had gone into a home, as they put it, and they thought it was in Eltham. It did not prove too difficult to find him, although he was actually in Brixton at that time.'

'And did you take over?' Mel asked.

'Well, to all intents and purposes he had been consigned to the institution and abandoned. His mother had visited on a couple of occasions, so I was told, but contact was quickly lost and I cannot say that I blame her.'

'Did you ever see her again?'

'Never. I stopped the money immediately of course. There was no comeback. How could there be? She enjoyed a nice little source of income for those years and would still have it today, but for my cussed curiosity. In a strange, and even wonderful way, it has been a worthwhile endeavour. Through Monty I have experience of an area of life about which I would have remained totally ignorant. He has taught me, paradoxically, something of the true meaning of what it is to love… it is difficult to explain… perhaps you can understand…' He signalled his impatience with himself for a temporary lack of eloquence.

'Does he know you, Piers?'

'Yes, I think it would be true to say that he does know me although he is virtually blind and does not really speak. But he recognises my voice and when this happened (presumably he was touching his eye patch but darkness hid the movement) 'I tried to explain it to him by putting his fingers against his own eyes and then against mine. Since then, he has never failed, when I visit him, to reach out to try to touch my face, and then to feel his own, and it is almost as though he laughs: as though we share a joke together.'

Now it was Adam's turn again.

'Does anyone else know about Monty, old boy?'

'Ma B, Adam. She has always known, but, as you know, she is the soul of discretion. I have been reluctant to share the secret. The only other person au fait with it is Elizabeth.'

'She will have helped you, I'm sure,' said Mel.

'Yes, she has. There have been medical problems from time to time and I have been grateful for her counsel. That is why I told her in the first place. I fear though that I have not admitted to her the fact of Monty's illegitimacy... I saw no reason to sadden her and sheltered behind some white lie about an early and catastrophic marriage. I have lacked the courage to tell anyone else the full facts. Possibly this is why I have not married Elizabeth!'

'You never doubted?' asked Mel.

'Doubted what, dearest Amelie?'

'That Monty is your son, and not someone else's!'

'No. I have never allowed myself to doubt. I believe him to be mine. And for the little that I am able to do for him I have come to comprehend that he was always meant to be mine, uncertainty has no meaning for us.'

By this time Mel was very moved by the things that Piers was saying, but it would not have been fair, after his epic soliloquy, to collapse in a sentimental heap.

'What about your Mother?' she asked, suddenly, not wishing to end the questions, which were helping to fill in the gaps, and complete the story. 'How did she react?'

'She was dreadfully upset. She would have preferred the anonymous existence of a perfectly healthy grandson whom she would never know or see, to the hard facts of reality. She was also, I believe, very angry with me for adding to the burdens of those who care for the disabled. She instructed me to subscribe handsomely to relevant charities particularly as I was no longer required to support Monty. She did not need to regulate my behaviour over this.'

She certainly did not, Mel thought to herself! Piers, the most generous of men will have emptied his pockets for them, especially the home in Shrewsbury.

'So did your Mother ever see Monty?' enquired Adam.

'No. She showed no further interest.'

Mel fumed at her again, inwardly. The cruel old bitch! The lines from the tombstone came back into her mind. When she last considered them she had convinced herself that the woman was friendly, but now the tables had turned again. What was it she was saying to them all – '*Prepare for death and follow me*'. She was vile, vile, vile... And Piers, gentle, marvellous Piers... through all the years of friendship he had carried this silent cross day and night, while he loved them and laughed with them. No wonder he had felt so drawn to Seb. No wonder, too, that he had held back from Ruth, a girl the same age as his stricken son. In a terrible revelation Mel knew that she must redeem him from his deprivations, his disappointments and his distress. She alone could atone for them. She alone would show him...While her thoughts ran amok Adam and Piers continued to debate various details and implications of the astonishing story. Piers seemed relaxed now, ready and happy to talk, and the discussion lasted well into the night. They stayed outside. It was warm. It was easy to talk in the dark and there were not too many mosquitos. Piers was reluctant to leave. He was now in a near celebratory mood and Adam and Mel had to draw on their last reserves of energy in order to complement his new-found happiness.

After he had gone they were drained of all emotion. They locked the front door behind him and clung to each other. There were no words left. The shocks of the evening were still being digested.

'Poor brave, ingenuous, Piers,' murmured Adam as Mel leant against him, her damp cheeks pressed into his shoulder and her arms around his neck.

'Dear, dear Piers', she sobbed. 'What a waste, what a terrible waste!'

She felt the rigidity and excitement in Adam's body. She knew that he was going to make love to her. He could pretend that she was Teresa, and Mel would dream that he was Piers...

Chapter VIII

FELIX

During the following week Piers called several times. It was not necessary for him to frequent the Tower House so much but he deemed it courteous to keep Adam informed about parish affairs and Adam himself wanted to assist wherever he could. When he appeared on the Wednesday morning Mel was up to her elbows in flour preparing for a large ecclesiastic dinner party that evening. She never made pastry in small amounts, always in large ones, so that she could stack it away in the freezer and be spared the chore for another couple of months.

'It is Colonel Pears who is coming this way Mrs Bishop,' announced Maidie (who must have seen his approach from the window in the dining room where she was supposedly laying the table) 'and himself has just gone out!'

'Tell the Colonel I'm in the kitchen Maidie.'

'Very well, madam.'

Mel continued to rub fat into the shapeless flour mountain, concentrating on the movement of her hands as adrenalin buzzed her fingertips.

'Greetings Amelie!'

'Hello Piers.'

It was their first meeting since Monday evening. He came and stood next to her and peered interestedly into the huge mixing bowl:-

'My busy little Amelie,' he chaffed, 'so industriously preparing pastry for an entire congregation!'

'Busy is right!' she said, concentrating even harder and postponing the pleasure of looking at him.

'I wanted to catch Adam. I hope he may have the time to call at the Alms Houses later in the week. Felix never misses this engagement and in the circumstances the veterans might appreciate a visitation. I have the impression that they do not consider John (the younger of the two curates, the other was on holiday) to be of any significance!'

'I'm certain Adam will be happy to do that, Piers. Friday morning might suit. He is usually here with Anne Fellows then.'

'Good. Tell him to liaise directly with Matron. There's no need to contact me unless he can't do it.'

'Anything else?' she asked, half looking at him as she pulverised more greasy lumps of margarine between her fingers. She liked hearing him talk. The rather high-pitched military voice had become ridiculously important to her.

'Just a reminder from James Adler about the timing of the rehearsal with Ruth. He suggested two thirty in a note to Felix. How does that sound?' James was the founder and conductor of the County Orchestra.

'That sounds fine,' replied Mel. 'Ruth will come down the day before, anyway, and I know she's hoping to practice on her own in the abbey, too.'

'Ah! We shall have to slot that in around the flower ladies.'

'Help!' Mel exclaimed. 'I'd forgotten that we are to be festooned with flowers. They are a fearsome breed those floral females.'

'And you, the fairest flower of them all, are you not one of them?' he mocked.

'Shut up,' she snapped good humouredly. 'You know I'm not.'

He was back to his usual form, missing no opportunity to tease affectionately. But this was his way with everyone and revealed nothing of his real feelings. Only when he dropped this pose, as he had done twice within the past few days, was the real Piers exposed. She wanted him to drop it now for surely they had moved beyond such flippancy.

The pastry was a pile of pale powdered yellow.

'Come on Amelie,' he encouraged, 'time for the water!'

'I'm not adding that while you are leaning over me,' she said. 'You make me nervous.'

Little did he know just how nervous as he stood there too close for comfort. She moved away from him, scrubbed her hands under a running tap and dried them on the kitchen towel.

'Would you like some coffee?' she asked, hoping to persuade him to sit down and relax. But she was disappointed.

'Bless you, but no. I must go back to the vicarage and take the dog for a walk.'

'Oh goodness, Tertia,' she said, comprehending. 'Felix always takes her.'

'Either Felix, or Elizabeth when she is here. The hound is a handful for Ellen.'

'There's no news?'

'Of Felix? No. Not yet. Elizabeth will phone as soon as there is anything to report.'

They were by the kitchen door. As they reached to open it simultaneously their hands met on the old brass knob. Mel's was underneath. His lay on top, quiescent, covering hers completely. His face was close, his eye scrutinising her.

'Thank you for Monday evening,' he said. 'Thank you for listening.'

She felt transfixed. His powerful hand was warm and strong. She wanted it to stay where it was for a precious moment longer so that she could decide whether it was his pulse or hers which was thumping so persuasively, or whether it was just one huge magnetic beat throbbing between them, like an unseen, silent, pneumatic drill. He seemed to tower over her. Was she shrinking? People said that the cartilages in the spine compressed in middle age. Hers must have started quite recently. Their hands separated, peeling away from each other, reunited with their respective arms. She opened the door just as Maidie appeared from the dining room carrying a tray.

'Is it white wine you will be drinking then?' she asked, 'so as I can lay the proper glasses?'

'The hock glasses, Maidie,' Mel said sternly.

'It's careful I must be not to break any,' rambled Maidie, 'after last week!' And she fixed Piers with a wily, knowing stare!

'Ah, Maidie, you winsome Welsh witch,' he wailed, 'what punishment shall the penitent culprit perform for you? Shall I lie on a bed of glass and swallow nails...?'

'Go on with you, Colonel Pears,' she said, titillated by the attention. She was ready to flirt with him, as anyone could see. Mel's proximity was a hindrance.

'It's lucky I was not to cut myself, mind,' she added pertly, waddling on her way past them, and adding as an afterthought, when she was well into the haven of the kitchen, 'but the flowers was nice. Just what I would expect from a real English gentleman like you, mind. What a pity they've died.'

Oh dear, thought Mel, as she and Piers ambled towards the front door, here was Maidie advertising her awareness of the roses donor. Mel knew that she had not told her. Presumably she had read the card: her inquisitive eyes missed nothing.

'I should have thanked you earlier, Piers,' Mel said gently and quietly. 'They were beautiful. I was very touched. But you shouldn't have sent them.'

'My pleasure, Amelie,' he said. 'I hope you understood.

'I like to think that I did,' she replied, looking him straight in the eye. 'Everything!'

As she unlatched the front door he turned and looked hard at her a searching, questioning,

expression on his face. He scratched his head, thoughtful, and sighed as he met her direct gaze.

'It's a mess, Amelie,' he said.

She nodded, but she had no idea whether he was referring to the eye, or to Monty, or to his relationship with her.

'May I come with you sometime,' she asked, 'when you go to see Monty?'

He did not respond immediately. He was collecting together various papers which he had scattered over a chest in the front hall a quarter of an hour earlier.

'I'll give it some thought,' he said slowly. 'It's an attractive suggestion.'

'When will you go again?'

'Probably in August.'

'Oh dear,' she frowned, 'that will be difficult.'

'How – difficult?'

'Explaining it away to Ruth and Seb. They'll be home then.'

'Ah yes,' he said. 'Understood! I would prefer them not to know.'

'There's always another time,' she said, as she unlatched the front door.

He acquiesced with a quick nod, murmured something, kissed her hand perfunctorily, and left swiftly. His departure was abrupt, as though someone had called to him. When she looked through the window he was striding across The Green towards the vicarage, but his head was bent and his arms wrapped around the papers held against his chest. There was no breeze. Surely he could not be cold on such a beautiful morning.

Mel returned to the pastry. There was no way of discerning whether or not his mind was finely enough tuned to hers to foresee the opportunities which a trip to Shropshire together would offer. What was the word he had used? 'Attractive'. It was reasonable to assume then that he could appreciate the possibilities…Her body tensed with excitement. She would become a scheming woman. Somehow, somewhere, she must be isolated, insulated and alone with him…

On Thursday, Ian's and Elizabeth's brilliant man in London finished diagnostic tests and made a decision to operate the following day, and Ellen, anxious to be near Felix, went to stay with her sister in Wimbledon after deciding against lodging with Elizabeth in her tiny maisonette. Piers, in touch by phone, relayed the news on Friday evening that Felix was round from the anaesthetic. Elizabeth had given no other details. It was some relief to Adam and Mel to know that he was as well as could be expected but the flat hospital jargon, functionally manufactured to display hope, was as efficacious as a dry biscuit and merely teased a nagging ache.

On Saturday Piers learnt that the whole of one lung had been removed, that the other one was already diseased, that the prognosis was bad, and that there was scant room for optimism. As Elizabeth had feared, it was as bad as it could be.

On Sunday, at all the Services, special prayers were said for Felix. Piers led the congregation at Matins, his strong clear voice echoing its way into each forgotten corner of the Abbey, to the certain embarrassment of the antique dust which had lain there throughout Felix's ministry. Was it really only a week since Mel had knelt in front of him, she mused, choked by her own impotence to confess? Surely she had not sinned much more during the interim – just a little in thought! She buried her face piously in her hands in order to peep irreverently again through the cracks between her fingers. Piers, standing on the chancel steps, intoned the proscribed rubric. The lay reader's medallion hung down over his surplice which glowed bright white from Ma B's laundering.

'Oh God', he chanted, 'whose nature and property is ever to have mercy and forgive, receive our humble petitions; and though we be tied and bound with the chain of our sins, yet let the pitifulness of Thy great mercy loose us...'

'The chain of our sins.' Another chain jangled somewhere. The one from that haunting, nightmarish, dream that had lodged so obstinately in Mel's mind. It was advisable not to listen too carefully to the words. Better to let them float over her! She hoped Piers was going to preach but was disappointed. John Elliot delivered one of his light weight chats which would have been flattered to be called a sermon. He would never be a bishop!

'Come and have a sherry,' she said casually to Piers after the Service. 'I'm all alone. Adam is over at the Royal School Commemoration and lunching with the headmistress and governors.'

'Sadly I must decline, Amelie,' he said. 'I've promised my girlfriend that I will take her for a walk.'

Mel's face must have registered bewilderment for he burst out laughing and patted her on the shoulder.

'Tertia, my Amelie,' he explained. 'She is a house guest while Ellen is away.'

'I see,' she said, feeling rather foolish. This was not a moment to offer to accompany him.

Groups of people chatted together outside the Abbey in the way that congregations do after services. It was good to be alive on a warm summer Sunday morning, especially after attending church. Smart summer cottons were sprinkled amongst the drip dry shirts and striped ties. Children tugged at each other and jumped on and off low walls. Men, who had just collected their papers from the newsagent cast sly glances at the sports pages while their womenfolk gossiped together. From time to time someone glanced at the vicarage. It had an abandoned look. There was no tail-wagging Tertia by the gate, no Ellen to usher a parishioner into the house for a jar of her crab apple jelly, no kindly pastor, with a good-weather word for everyone, and no week-end visiting Elizabeth.

'Is it true the vicar's got cancer?' they asked. 'Has he had a stroke?' 'We hear he's had a big operation!' 'Will he be paralysed?' Any ploy was fair in order to be able to return to the High Street, or the pub, or the front garden to recount to the next person you met that you had the prized details from the bishop's wife herself, and she *must* know the facts.

'Yes, it was true he had had an operation,' she said. 'No, she didn't know exactly what the trouble was, but it was in his lungs.' 'No! He certainly wasn't paralysed and we must all hope and pray that he would soon be restored to health.' She wanted to shield him from their excited speculation. They savoured his misfortune with such hideous relish: they would know soon enough that he was dying.

That evening the loyal adult congregation returned to the Abbey for a special Compline Service which Piers had announced earlier along with the Banns and other notices. Many of the parishioners were unfamiliar with the short service and mumbled self-consciously into their leaflets. But Adam's mastery was supreme, his lines rehearsed, his memory sure. So sure, indeed, that he was able to convey, with consummate skill the timeless power of faith put into words and uttered at a specific moment of need. It was a staggering performance. But something within Mel rebelled as the words were spoken and the prayers said for it seemed to her that here in the Abbey, in the midst of this meditation, that they were despatching Felix, and sending him too quickly, without demur, upon his one-way journey to eternal changelessness. Perhaps she was interpreting it incorrectly but she was disturbed. She wanted Adam to talk to her about the implications of this particular service. She wanted to be tutored in depth. To understand as he understood and to see as he could see. Doctors were renowned for ignoring symptoms in those closest to them and bishops no less careless for she could recall little in the way of family religious debate. It had always been taken for granted that they were all healthily Christian and required no treatment!

Her desire to talk with Adam was real and urgent and she hurried home ahead of him, barely acknowledging Piers as he wished her goodnight.

It was half past nine, a sulky time of day. The brightness had dimmed and the Sunday evening people, trailing shadows on The Green, were loth to linger for long. Even so, it was a full forty minutes before the front door banged its warning that Adam was back.

'Sorry, darling,' he said as he came into Backs View. 'I was chatting with Piers and the churchwardens.'

She shrugged her shoulders, petulant.

He showed concern.

'Is there something wrong?'

'No! Well, yes! I have been waiting for nearly an hour to talk to you.'

He sat down, feeling in his pocket for a pipe as he did so.

'Talk away, Mel. I'm listening.'

'It isn't that easy to explain really. I'm in a muddle!'

'A muddle? ... With your tapestry?'

'Oh Adam, be serious. How can I talk to you if you are so frivolous?'

Drawing on his pipe, he answered her in short, puff-punctuated phrases:-

'I assure you, darling...I am not being frivolous...Come on...Fire away...What is the problem?'

She took a deep breath and began to explain.

'It's about Felix,' she said, 'and death, and life after death, and Christian belief, and why we have to pray so hard for him now. Surely if anyone has the necessary credentials for eternal life, he does, so why must we keep reminding the Almighty about him – speeding him on his way like a registered parcel?'

The simile did not amuse Adam.

'I don't agree with you that this is quite what we have been doing,' he said quietly.

'Well, what have we been doing then?'

The pace was more measured now, the structure of his reply supported by patter that was familiar. She found it tedious and let her eyes rove around the room as he spoke.

'In the Service we have just completed, we have been commending Felix to God and asking Him to support and sustain him in his present suffering. We have also. as at all times of prayer and communion with God, through Christ, been commending ourselves and asking for continuing help and strength. We have been drawing closer to each other and to God at this time.

137

'I still don't understand,' she said perversely. 'Why do we have to remind God. Surely He knows. And death has no sting for such as Felix, does it. Why must we fuss so?'

It pleased her to see that Adam was perplexed by this sudden bout of questioning. Now there would be more clever words for her doubting soul!

'You have lost sight of one basic Christian truth, my love. The power that comes from God comes only when we ask, through prayer, and through the sacraments. It does not come automatically, clocking in when needed, like a thermostat. Surely you can recall the sermon in which I use the analogy of a pipeline?'

'I have ceased to listen that closely to your sermons,' she snapped, 'and I don't want one now.'

He frowned and looked a little hurt. There was a moment or two of uncomfortable silence.

'Your aggression troubles me,' he commented. 'What have I done to deserve it?'

Mel groaned.

'Oh, nothing! I didn't mean to be personal. I'm sure it's a marvellous sermon, like all the others.'

He tried again.

'I can understand your sense of wretchedness over Felix. It's natural. We are all concerned for him and the service has brought him clearly into focus.'

'It was the service itself that upset me,' she said in a low flat voice.

'How can the sacred office of Compline distress when it is so gloriously filled with hope and trust?'

'It may be for you. I have no doubt that it is so for you. But can you not see how difficult it is for me to comprehend why we must all pray so much for a good man who has led a blameless life? If we have to labour like this for someone so saintly, what chance does a guilty person have in such circumstances...Would you, for example, say Compline for a convicted criminal at such a time, and is the end result the same?'

'I must repeat,' Adam said seriously, 'that the saying of Compline is a corporate act. Try to grasp this, Mel, and what do you mean by 'the end result'?'

'The quality of the everlasting life, I suppose,' she mumbled, now somewhat embarrassed by her own handling of the conversation.

'You must turn to another basic Christian truth for your answer. Namely that forgiveness and reward for a sinner depend on his own repentance. Such repentance may be initiated by the prayers and actions of others but the motivation must come from within. St Luke, fifteen, verse seven, says the rest, 'joy shall be in heaven over one sinner that repenteth more than over ninety and nine just persons which need no repentance.'

The text, tossed off so glibly, incensed Mel and prompted the kind of swift retort that Adam did not expect.

'So that cuts Felix down to size,' she said sharply.

He was startled.

'Whatever do you mean?'

'He is one of these so-called, just men,' she enlarged bitterly. 'But there will be no surfeit of joy in heaven for him when he arrives...'

'Dearest Mel, you are twisting the truth. One of the great truths. Misinterpreting it and manipulating it.' He puffed on his pipe, maybe playing for time, and then asked, 'for what reason... To prove something?'

'I don't know. In order to sort out my thoughts I suppose.' She shrugged, pouted, like a cornered teenager, and drummed her fingers on the coffee table.

Adam stood up and smiled benevolently. 'You are right my love. You are a trifle confused. And why this sudden obsession with sin? Could it be that approaching middle age is making you melancholic?'

Half serious, half playful, he bent towards her and tilted her chin upwards, coaxing her to meet his gaze. But she resisted and stared sullenly at the cross which hung level with her eyes, suspended against its purple backcloth. She drew away from him, closed her eyes and lay back in the chair, cocooned in red blackness.

His voice sounded distant. 'I am concerned about you. You look tired and miserable.'

Her reply, too, came from far away. 'Maybe I am tempted.' she heard myself say in a small, weak, voice.

'Tempted by what?' he asked. 'Explain. What do you mean by 'tempted?' His sharpened voice stung the grey silence.

She opened her eyes and looked at him as she gripped the arms of the chair, brazen with challenge.

'Tempted to sin,' she blazed at him. 'It could be worth it if I repented afterwards!'

He hesitated, uncertain of his next move, his face betraying the dilemma in which he found himself. He did not chastise her or fall on his knees in front of his wife to comfort her.

Either course of action could have been preferable to the one he chose for by one of them he might have salvaged her. No! He opted for the easy way. He chose to paper over the cracks and effect a quick return to surface smoothness. She was a perverse, emotional little wife to be teased out of her premature menopausal melancholy. He was gentle with her and proferred a hand to help her out of the chair.

'Now it is you who are being frivolous,' he said. 'Come, my Jezebel!'

She sighed and let him pull her up. How small his hands were, almost apologetic in their contact. They were hands made for blessing...

When her tears came, as inevitably they did, he was tender and loving and held her close. But she wept the more for she now suspected that these hands no longer had the power to persuade her...

Chapter IX

DAYS IN A WEEK

Monday

As Mel walked home from the hairdresser's the following morning, she was astonished to see Ellen with Tertia. She looked harassed and Mel could see that it was Tertia who had her on a lead! She called out to her, 'Ellen! How are things? I'd no idea you were back.'

'Hello Mrs Ellis,' she panted, 'oh this dog is hard work; she'll never hold still for me. Tertia, sit a moment there's a good girl. I really don't know how Felix and Elizabeth manage her, she's such a fidgety one. Sit, I say! Oh, I'm so sorry, Mrs Ellis.'

'Let me hold her for a moment, Ellen. Come on, Tertia! Good dog!'

Panting much less than her mistress, Tertia allowed Mel to take the lead and then stood quietly by her side, licking and sniffing around her ankles. Mel patted her and she sat down meekly, her tail flailing the pavement like a huge fin.

'You have a way with her like all the others,' commented Ellen, 'she's as much as I can manage. Dear, oh dear!'

'Poor Ellen,' sympathised Mel. 'I expect she's over excited. Have you just collected her from Piers?'

'That's right. I came back on the late train last night. There didn't seem a lot to stay for now that the operation is over. Felix wanted me to come home. There's Tertia, and the garden, and I've loads of plums to bottle, and the phone keeps ringing... people are so kind. You've had your hair done, haven't you - how nice it looks, and mine is such a mess! This last perm I had was a waste of money... half my head is frizzy and the rest as straight as it ever was. What a sight I must look!' The disordered phrases tumbled out as she self-consciously mangled her hair into a worse state with a series of frantic gestures.

'Don't worry about your hair,' said Mel, 'it's fine. Come on, I'll walk back to the vicarage with you. Here, you take my bag and I'll hang on to Tertia.'

'Oh that is kind of you,' she said gratefully as Mel took her arm with her free hand. How podgy she was. One could feel the dimpled flesh through her pimply yellow cardigan!

'It's lovely weather isn't it,' said Ellen tritely. 'Almost too hot.'

'Very hot to be in hospital,' replied Mel bringing the conversation round to Felix. She hoped to hear some first-hand news.

'It's very nice where he is. There's air conditioning. Very modern. It's the new part of the hospital. No expense spared.'

Mel cared about Felix, not the air conditioning.

''Good,' she said briefly, but not unkindly, 'how was he when you left him yesterday?'

Now, almost at the vicarage, Tertia was starting to tense and jerk towards her familiar territory.

'Stop that pulling, Tertia!' fussed Ellen. 'I'll open the gate Mrs Ellis and then we can let her go. She'll be happy to be back in her own garden, won't you doggie.' She seemed to be addressing them both at once and Mel smiled to herself as she unclipped the lead and released the Labrador who bounded off across the flower beds, sending up a shower of dusty soil.

Ellen apologised. 'There now, she never does that if Felix is with her. She stays on the paths when she's with him. How she does let me down!'

Mel tried to make light of the embarrassment as she leant casually against the garden gate to keep it shut. 'She'll settle down. She's as worried as you are, I expect. She wonders where Felix is. She can't make it out.'

'Well she did see him go off in the car with his case,' Ellen declared.

'And then you went. She went to St Marks. You came back. She came home – and Felix is nowhere to be seen,' Mel offered, smiling.

'Yes,' she conceded. 'I can see that it's a bit puzzling for her. Poor doggie!'

'Anyway,' (this was a last attempt and Mel injected some urgency into her voice) 'how is dear Felix?' The endearment obviously registered and for the first time in the encounter that morning Ellen's conversation was properly controlled.

'He's not very well, Mrs Ellis. Not very well at all. But he had a little nourishment yesterday and managed to keep it down. His breathing's bad. It will be, won't it, working twice as hard with only one lung. You don't realise what it means until you see it. But folk pull through don't they, and he'll do his best. He's all tubes and can't talk very easily. It may be better at the end of the week, they said. I'm going back to him on Thursday.'

Her simple statement of the facts, as she saw them, brought a lump into Mel's throat. She squeezed Ellen's arm gently.

'Promise me you will let me know if there is anything I can do.'

'Yes, I will, I promise.'

Mel retrieved her bag, and turned to go. 'How about Tertia?' she asked.

'I'll manage now she's home,' Ellen said valiantly, 'and Piers, bless him, will take her walkies in the evenings.'

'I'll look in and see you in a day or two. Don't hesitate to phone if you need me.'

'Thank you,' she said warmly. 'You really are one of the best, Mrs Ellis. One of the best. I'll look forward to seeing you again soon. Very likely there'll be a pot of plums for you by then, too.'

On her way back across the Green Mel half turned, in anticipation that Ellen might be watching and hoping for a wave. Amazingly there was already a cluster of people around the gate talking to her. Word that she was back had spread quickly, doubtless activated by early morning sleuths. Today it was unlikely that she would be left alone for long enough to set about the business of preserving her plums.

Tuesday

The air was appetising with a hybrid fragrance of toast, coffee, and breakfast eggs just on the boil when the phone rang. Mel glanced at the kitchen clock. Five to eight. It was early for a call, unless it was to cancel one of Adam's appointments for this warm June Tuesday. She clicked the extension button and picked up the receiver.

'It's me, Piers,' said a familiar voice before she had a chance to identify herself.

'You're an early bird this morning,' she trifled.

'Amelie! Grevious news I'm afraid.' Mel felt her heart lurch and stomach tighten:-

' Felix!'

'He died suddenly at six o'clock this morning.'

'Oh no!'

'Elizabeth phoned me five minutes ago.'

'What happened?'

'Heart failure, almost certainly. There'll have to be a post mortem.'

'Poor Elizabeth,' she said. 'How was she?'

'In control of herself. She's going to phone Ellen at eight thirty and asked that one or other of us might be there, or, better still, prepare the ground before she telephones.'

'I see,' said Mel, suddenly apprehensive. (Was this woman's work?) 'Which one of us?'

'I had the impression that she would like it to be Adam. Is he there?'

'Just coming, Piers. Hold on for a moment.'

Mel laid the receiver on its side. Adam was on his way down the stairs and she met him in the passage. Her voice, sensitive to its message, had become a whisper. 'It's Piers on the phone. Felix is dead. Can you go to Ellen?'

His reaction was immediate and he sprinted to the telephone where short staccato replies indicated that he would go at once to the vicarage. Mel laced a cup of coffee with a generous splash of cold milk and buttered a piece of toast.

'There isn't time for an egg,' she said practically. Adam was bending down to lace up his shoes and already perspiring a little. He was obviously going out later as he was wearing his bishop's suit. He helped himself to a spoonful of marmalade and perched on a chair.

'The Lord gave and the Lord hath taken away; blessed be the name of the Lord,' he said.

Egg pan in hand (they were now hard boiled but could go on a salad) Mel stood looking at him as he gobbled his toast and gulped his coffee. She felt sick and could not have swallowed anything. Death was all a part of a day's work to him.

'Shall I come with you?' she asked.

He crunched noisily and thought for a moment.

'I'll do my best with the help of the Holy Spirit now my love, and you can pour out some human comfort later on.'

'It will have to be this morning because it's my big marriage guidance week. The others are on holiday.'

He nodded briefly before conjecturing:-

'Piers thinks Elizabeth will be home by lunchtime, so she and Ellen will be together then which should help.'

Mel sat down while he finished his emergency breakfast, and until he pushed back his chair, and looked ready to leave.

'It's a bit sudden, isn't it?' she remarked.

'Yes,' he agreed. 'How prepared is Ellen do you think?'

'Not unprepared. But she may want to weep on your shoulder.'

Adam nodded again, grunted, glanced at the clock, and checked his watch.

'She will need all the solace we can give her. I must go. Can you phone around and tell the obvious people. That way the whole town will know by mid-morning.'

'Yes,' she replied, before asking, 'shall I draw the curtains at the front of the house?'

'Definitely not,' he said shortly.

She saw him out of the front door and watched him as he walked briskly towards the vicarage, looking around as he went, savouring the warm air and his own vitality. He had shown no emotion! He strode across the Green to the far gate, ignoring the path to trample on the daisies. Now he was opening the gate. Bleak emissary, armed with a message of emptiness on such a morning which still held a few last precious seconds of hope for Ellen! How would he tell her, and what other words would he use as they waited together for Elizabeth's phone-call? How absurd it was that in this grim terrain, in these dark valleys of death, he could find his path so easily. He hated to be reminded and disliked a parallel to be drawn, and yet, true professional that he was, he was also, in his own way, very much the undertaker's son!

Mel sat over a mug of black coffee and reflected. An experience of death was not unlike a bout of 'flu! - When it came close to you, you thought about it and worried about it, but in between whiles, you put it out of your mind. During the periods free from contamination there was no point in fretting oneself since one was still a survivor, and after one ceased to exist the cause of concern would be eliminated! The human psyche was well adapted to being able to forget the inevitable during the long healthy periods because close friends and relatives did not die all that often! But when an attack came, it was not just the bereavement, the separation, the loss... it was also this renewal of the knowledge that one day it would be one's own turn; an uncomfortable reminder, niggling for a while, making one less certain, more careful.

Even so, the realisation that Felix was dying seemed to have affected her disproportionately. Was it because of her morbid preoccupation with sin? Somehow the two had become knotted together in her mind and at this moment it appeared difficult to disentangle them. How complicated life could be! Now that events had reached a climax and Felix was actually dead, maybe she would be capable of drawing some conclusions if there were any to be drawn. But she would not seek Adam's help again. She would unravel it for herself. She was sad that she would never see Felix again unless she was bidden to see his corpse when it arrived from London. She did not relish the sight of another waxen inanimate face – she had seen several. The last had belonged to her mother. For Ellen and Elizabeth she felt genuine concern. Especially for Elizabeth. The bond with her father had been strong, and nurtured, for the whole of the time that she and Adam had known them, on their mutual and equal regard for each other. Piers could very easily become all important to her now. But wait! She and Ellen would only be able to stay on at the vicarage for a limited time and, if they uprooted and moved from the town, maybe to their cottage, then 'out of sight' might come to mean 'out of mind'. She could not seriously believe that Elizabeth presented a threat (dear God, why did she use such a word), but she knew about Monty...and it was just conceivable that Piers, in a surge of protective chivalry, might suddenly opt to marry her! Maybe Felix would use his influence from beyond the grave! She wondered where his soul was now – that faithful, upright, Christian soul! Were the angels ready for him, or would he just drift in, unannounced, while some miserable sinner's soul (absolved in time, of course) wafted in to steal all the heavenly limelight, chat up the saints, and receive a hero's welcome.

Mel drank the last half inch of her coffee. It tasted cold and bitter. Maidie would arrive presently and there were phone-calls to make. She would start with Hannah. She picked up the receiver to dial the number, but momentarily her hand faltered. The numbers were clear and neat in their holes on the dial, yet a form was flickering in front of her eyes, on and off, like something out of a disco. It came and went, speedily, many times until she could discern that its shape was not some kind of emblem dragged from her subconscious, but a bright white tombstone – and splashed upon its garish, staring, surface there were six dark crimson words, '*Prepare for death, and follow me*'. She blinked, and blinked, and shut her eyes until the movement stopped. This was not a day to have a migraine.

After a couple of minutes, she was able to call Hannah...

After telephoning Hannah, Mel broke the news to Maidie who was genuinely distressed and had to sit down and have a little weep.

'It's a good man, he was, the vicar,' she sniffed. 'Always teasing me for being brought up chapel and telling about the valleys and the cottage in Wales he loved so. What a dreadful shock it is to be taken so suddenly... such a terrible shock to everyone...' and she helped herself to another wad of tissues and blew her nose loudly. Rapid footsteps signalled Adam's return and the sight of him prompted fresh floods of grief. Unless Mel was firm she would spend the morning consoling Maidie.

Adam spoke quickly, barely acknowledging Maidie's prostration.

'Darling, I must rush. I'm late already.'

Mel followed him to the study. 'How did it go?' she asked.

'All right,' he replied automatically, as he stuffed files and papers into a briefcase and rammed a pipe and some tobacco into his pocket.

'Yes, all right,' he repeated, 'but there are two points. First, Ellen hopes to have Elizabeth home within a few hours and feels they will be better left alone today. She herself wants privacy, so anything you can do to suppress callers will be appreciated.'

Mel nodded.

'Secondly,' he continued, 'can you contact Piers – I said I would but I haven't got the time – and ask him to alert Reg Stanton (the undertaker) and John E. They would like to see all three of them later in the day to discuss the funeral arrangements. They hope for next week – depending on the post mortem, delivery of corpse, etc – but it appears unlikely that there will be hitches.'

'I am worried about Ellen,' said Mel, 'being on her own this morning.'

'Better to keep away, even so,' he dictated curtly. 'But you might phone Ian at the surgery. Don't be put off by that officious receptionist. Insist on speaking to him. Alert him and ask him to look in at the vicarage.'

'I'll do that. Anything else?'

'Not immediately. I shall see various fellow clergy today, so the news will travel.' Agitated, he frowned at his watch. 'Where are my car keys?'

'Here on the hall table,' she said, handing them to him, together with the morning post which he crammed into the bulging case. As likely as not it would return unopened at the end of the day. He kissed her perfunctorily and she ran with him to the garage to heave open the heavy wooden doors and watch him throw himself and his case into the car. The engine spluttered, then roared, and the car swung into the courtyard. He poked his head out of the window.

'Back around six,' he shouted, 'another engagement at seven! May I have an early bite of supper?'

Mel nodded again, on the point of asking him when he would tell her more about Ellen; but the car was already turning right through the archway and accelerating towards East Avenue. She wandered slowly across the courtyard, mentally listing the various calls she must make. She felt cheated! Adam had virtually ordered her to keep away from Ellen today, yet he, and Ian, and Piers, and John and Reg, were all acceptable as callers. He had given her no details of his encounter and she was more than a little curious to know how Ellen had reacted and what they had said to each other during that grim breakfast hour. She toyed with the idea of going across to the vicarage to assert her own claim to first-class citizenship: to position herself at the door as a kind of deterrent sentry and thus protect Ellen physically from those who sought to intrude on her raw isolation. Yet Adam had made it plain enough. She had no right to override Ellen's specific wishes. What would one do oneself in a similar position? How would it feel to find oneself suddenly a widow on a sun-drenched morning such as this? For how long would tears flow, and upon whose shoulder would one shed them...? Such a question was impossible to answer. It stirred up images too dangerous to heed, possibilities too compromising to risk. Impatient with herself she endeavoured to push such thoughts aside. There was no reason to suppose that Adam would die! He had no symptoms! But accidents could happen. Without doubt he frequently drove too fast and could even be considered fortunate to have steered clear of the law for so long. As Seb had drily remarked recently, 'It won't look so good in the papers, dad... Bishop caught speeding to sacrament.' She smiled to herself. Dear Seb... He and Ruth would be sad to hear about Felix. She would write them a couple of postcards when she had finished telephoning. As for Ellen, she must contain her impatience. She would see her tomorrow.

Evidently Mel made a good job of her sentry duties albeit they were carried out vicariously. When she relayed Ellen's message to Piers, he suggested that a discreet notice might be a good idea and sanctioned her to creep across to the vicarage and fix something to the front gate. She found a piece of card and a thick felt pen and wrote in clear, square, capitals;-

MRS HUGHES IS NOT AT HOME TO CALLERS TODAY
PLEASE RESPECT HER PRIVACY

The vicarage was silent. Expressionless. The curtains almost drawn and the front door tightly shut. One rarely saw the door closed – normally it was open, friendly and welcoming, and windows, too, even in winter. Today, despite the June sunlight the house had taken on a brumal aspect. It was cold with grief.

The verger, Eddie Black, spotted Mel as he parked his vintage bicycle in its diagonal slot by the abbey notice board and hurried across the Green for a chat.

'Mornin' Mrs Ellis, ma'am,' he greeted cheerfully, 'what news of the vicar?'

'The vicar died during the night, Eddie' said Mel quietly. Eddie's expression changed to one of solemn concern and he bowed his head...

'Oh no, oh dear! That is very heavy news. Very heavy indeed,' adding in a shocked voice, 'I am very sorry to hear that. Very sorry indeed.'

'It's a sad day for us all, Eddie,' said Mel, affected by his banality.

He was still busy absorbing the news and lost for words until he reverently offered, 'The Lord has taken him then...' and Mel continued with 'and spared him further suffering.'

Eddie scratched his ear, anxious to say something more but not sure what! Finally, and doubtless remembering to whom he was speaking, he offered:-

'They say God grants an easy death only to the just.'

'Do they Eddie? I've never heard that before.'

'Well, ma'am, in his case it is true, I reckon. Here last week and taken so quickly and quietly this week... Yes,' and he scratched his head again more fiercely until dandruff showered his shoulders, 'yes I reckon it has proved true for him.'

For a moment he was silent, then he signalled towards the vicarage and asked:-

'Is there anything I can do?'

'Tell everyone you see Eddie, and also tell them not to disturb Mrs Hughes today.'

'Don't you worry. I'll keep them at bay,' he said. 'I'll make sure she's not troubled.'

'You can start over there,' indicated Mel as she spotted Prudence Ogilivy advancing across The Green, pulling her tartan shopper drunkenly behind her. She bid Eddie a swift farewell and hurried back to the Tower House fully aware that some of the diverted callers would be unable to resist ringing her own front door bell. Sure enough, the first one arrived within a quarter of an hour. By then the flag on the abbey tower, hoisted to half-mast, was fluttering its woeful tidings across the roof tops. Eddie had lost no time. With a morning of callers and phone calls, Mel had none to lose either, especially as she was due at the Marriage Guidance centre at half past one.

Wednesday

Mel's own close encounters with the chief mourners began the following morning and lasted until the funeral. The dragging routine of the aftermath of death seemed interminable. The whole town was affected and the Abbey Green respectfully subdued, as folk suppressed their voices and children were made to walk tidily and to wait, until they were past the vicarage, to suck their ice lollies. The body was to be brought back at the weekend in time for it to lie in state in both the house and the abbey. This was a macabre business. Mel had no previous experience of a home inhabited by a corpse; a corpse powerless to communicate yet all-powerful in its dominance of every decision and awesome by its very presence. Her own death experiences had lacked this patrician approach. They had been neat affairs, the cadavers unobtrusively stowed away by undertakers in vague chapels of rest, to be produced, clinically neat, along with the hearse and wreaths! Ellen, the new widow, showed a toughness and certainty which was unfamiliar. Indeed, she and Elizabeth became duplicates of each other, for Elizabeth was so swamped by grief that her nurse's fortitude deserted her and she became pathetically irresolute for a few days. She spent hours alone in her room, leaving Ellen to handle the torrent of condolence with good sense and dignity and, for the most part, dry-eyed.

'Ellen you are being truly marvellous,' Mel said on the first of several visits, aware that Ellen was making it easy for her to appear helpful as she arranged a huge display of peonies, which had been picked early that morning by the chemist's wife, and just delivered by Eddie.

'You and the bishop have always been so considerate, Mrs Ellis, and when you first came,' she closed her eyes, bit her lower lip and paused before continuing, 'Felix... was worried. But many were the times that he thanked God for the way you treated him and respected his position; this was his life... nearly thirty-five years... he was set in his ways and knew it, but he never ceased to be thankful that your husband understood him and took him as he was.'

Without doubt this was the longest sentence that she had ever delivered to Mel. Now she was ready to overflow - and did so on to her well-scrubbed wooden draining board. Another reminder of those thirty-five years! Mel held her close. 'Cry, Ellen, my dear. Let it come.'

When it was over she apologised. 'Yesterday, your husband was so comforting and wise,' she gulped, 'that I hoped to be able to control myself today. Just by remembering his kind words and by knowing that Felix is happy. I am sorry.'

She did not lose her composure again and for Mel there was a certain satisfaction in knowing that Ellen had wept in her arms. Her innate simplicity made it easy to give comfort. It had probably been relatively straightforward for Adam, too!

Later Ellen begged her to go upstairs to Elizabeth. 'You are so sympathetic,' she said, 'and she is so fond of you. I don't have the words to help her. She is like Felix - deep thinking. When you are just ordinary and dull like me, it's difficult to get through.'

She gestured helplessness and motioned Mel towards the stairs as the doorbell heralded the arrival of another mourner. Mel climbed up to Elizabeth's room and knocked politely.

There was no response. Eventually she found her in her father's dressing room - a small room in which Mel suspected he had normally slept although the larger adjoining room, with its sagging double bed, presented a marital image. The tired blue candlewick bedspread matched the sad drabness of the whole house. Elizabeth did not hear her enter the room. She was sitting in a faded armchair gazing at the carved crucifix set above the narrow single bed. Tertia who lay beside her in silent communion, barely twitched her ears, and only showed interest when Mel put a hand on Elizabeth's hunched shoulder.

'My dear, is there anything I can do?'

There was no reaction. Elizabeth appeared to be in a trance. Mel pulled across a painted wooden chair which, like most of the contents of the house, had seen better days and sat down. Tertia padded over and nuzzled her head in Mel's lap.

'Good girl. Lie down again,' she whispered. Tertia responded immediately and Mel sank fingers into the warm fleshy folds of her neck before trying again.

'How long have you been here, Elizabeth? Would you like to talk? How about a cup of coffee?'

She shook her head. Her face, ravaged by grief and fatigue, was a barometer of despair. The silence was total, measured solely by the tick of a small carriage clock on the bedside cabinet: it was a poignant reminder that time, for its owner, had ended. Eventually, Elizabeth lowered her gaze and looked at Mel. There was misery in her voice when she spoke.

'He is still here, Mel. Everywhere!'

'I know Elizabeth. A part of him always will be.'

'Is that what we believe, we who call ourselves Christians?' she asked with resigned weariness.

'Well,' Mel answered, 'We believe that he is now at peace with God - a step ahead of the rest of us, but merely a step and only separated by the confines of this world...' (Oh, Adam, she groaned inwardly. You should be here to answer her. The daughter's need is far greater than the mother's. You have the appointed words for this situation... They are all a part of your routine...)

'And love?' she whispered.

'God's love, you mean?' Mel queried gently.

'No!' her voice was sharp with anguish. 'No! Papa's love for me and mine for him. What of our love?'

Mel was in deep trouble now but must reply somehow.

'That lives on,' she said, lamely, 'sustained by memories and faith.'

'Fed on dreams. Like all one-sided love,' Elizabeth said bitterly. 'All I have now is dreams.'

Mel became aware of an extraordinarily passionate and intense grief which was raging inside Elizabeth and was fearful of it. Her own gut, too, was being invaded with unsettling nervous turbulence.

'You were not unprepared for this,' she said quietly, leaning towards her friend with a gesture of sympathy. But the comment was ignored. Elizabeth's train of thought would not be side-tracked so easily.

'Why has God let him die,' she moaned. "Why? I needed him. Who is there now to show me love...?' Gradually her voice faded and she mouthed the last words in a despairing cadence – 'Who is there no... no-one... I have no-one...'

'Dearest Elizabeth,' Mel encouraged, 'you have us, your friends, your mother and...'

'My mother,' she spat out, interrupting with the force of a fire cracker. 'My mother! What communication do I have with her? Papa and I could talk - about anything - everything. Mother, model of propriety and mediocrity that she is has nothing to say, unless it is to comment on the rise of fall of her next Victoria sponge...'

'Hush Elizabeth. Don't say such things.'

'You know I'm right! What contact do you have with her? Any minute now she will be baking cakes for the funeral feast... What has that to do with communication - or love?'

'Everything,' Mel said with conviction, although she would have been pressed to explain exactly why! 'I have nothing but admiration for the way in which she is coping today.'

'Which infers, I presume, that you despise my reaction.' She took a deep breath and Mel shook her head in protest as Elizabeth continued;-

'God knows, Mel, I have seen death hundreds of times at the hospital. I know the marks which it leaves. No-one is ever the same again. The dead steal from the living. They take something with them which is never returned. Death initiates the erosion of happiness. It ends relationships.'

'That can't be true, Elizabeth. There must be a revival of happiness after the grief. Time heals. No-one escapes experiences of death, though some, I am sure, can accept them more comfortably than others. Adam has often said that one can feel great joy and wonder in the presence of death, and surely our faith can help us through the agony of parting... can you not reconcile the agony with the ecstasy of knowing that your father is at peace and in a state of everlasting joy...?' Mel petered out. Her armpits were soaked and her heart racing with the effort of trying to project something of value to Elizabeth. It was all too much like an unexpected examination for which one has done no preparation. She was intelligent enough to ridicule Mel's efforts if they sounded pious or banal, and Mel knew that she had almost certainly failed her with a string of pathetic clichés. There was no reaction from the huddled figure, apart from a weary reach towards Tertia who thumped her tail in a sympathy more articulate than Mel's attempts. She sighed again.

'Someone will have to befriend the dog,' she said in a dull monotone. 'She loved papa, too. She is as bereft as me.'

'Shall I take her?' Mel offered gamely.

'I don't think she would go with you,' she said. 'It is either me now, or... (there was a long pause as she raised her eye-lids and looked straight at Mel, her blood-shot, violet grey, eyes not registering any reaction) a man! Tertia enjoys a little male company too!' There was no escaping the implication. The death of her father had added insult to the injury Mel had inflicted less than a fortnight ago. It was as though Elizabeth held Mel responsible for her total bereavement. She stared at her, almost brazenly, and now, between them, Mel felt the presence of an invisible bunch of red roses. Back at the Tower House they, too, were dead. Mel stood up, avoided the scrutiny and spoke as naturally as possible.

'I'm sure Piers will take Tertia for you. Shall I ask him?'

She sighed once more; an embarrassingly long exhalation which lengthened the silence between them.

'No thank you. I suppose I should have mentioned it when he called, but there were other things on my mind.'

'He'll do anything he can to help you,' Mel said.

'It's magnanimous of you to say so,' she snapped.

With what appeared to be a studied lethargy she moved from her chair and over to the bed where she sat down reverently. For a second time she challenged Mel with her searching gaze. But her mood was less aggressive when she spoke again.

'Do you believe, Mel, that along with the everlasting joy, papa might be aware of all that is happening here? Or are the ties that bound us, as I so fear, now totally severed...? When we spoke earlier of love which only flows one way, I wanted to hear you say that you believe it possible for communication to be maintained both ways. I need to believe that his love and care and understanding are still there, still available... It is so difficult to put it into words, but tell me, please, that there is hope.'

The profound and searching questions were more specific than the earlier one had been and now, more than ever, Mel needed Adam's intervention. What would he make of this vision of Felix - as fully aware as he was insensible. A species of ethereal, eternal, eavesdropper?

'I guess that anything is possible, Elizabeth,' Mel said slowly. 'There is still so much to be discovered about the relationships between the living and the dead. Maybe there are new senses which spring into being when one dies... It cannot but help to believe in whatever gives you the greatest comfort.'

This was no answer to Elizabeth's questions. Scorn and disdain were apparent in her expression. She stood up and looked as though she was about to make a pronouncement. For some reason, Mel began to tremble slightly; she steadied herself against the lintel.

Elizabeth spoke. Her voice was like white acid.

'As I am now, so you shall be, Prepare for death and follow me.'

Mel's blood ran cold. 'The tombstone,' she whispered. 'Mrs Tarrant-Jones.'

'Exactly,' Elizabeth confirmed. 'Precisely! And she, too, may be waiting and watching in the heavenly wings. Good sport don't you think!'

Somehow Mel extricated herself, clumsily tripping over one of Felix's shoes as she did so: it had a large hole in the sole and would not have lasted much longer without repair.

'I'm so sorry,' she stammered, replacing it under the chair.

155

The tear-reddened eyes never wavered, boring through Mel as she opened the door and staggered from the main bedroom out on to the landing. Somewhere, beyond, she was conscious of too many animated forces arming against her. She clutched the banister. On the staircase, shrouded from the sun by dark curtains, the air was cool, yet she felt stifled. She was overcome by a need to escape into fresh untainted outside air.

Feigning a pseudo normality Mel called through to Ellen from the front hall and said that she would be in again soon and that Elizabeth was going to contact Piers about Tertia's walks. Out on the Green she gulped warm air and blinked at the prismatic brightness of a coachload of tourists surveying the abbey. Between the vicarage and the Tower House she must have encountered half a dozen acquaintances and enacted as many duologues on the theme of Felix's demise. When she opened her own front door she sighed with relief, kicked off her sandals and sank into the nearest comfortable chair. She was not displeased with her handling of Elizabeth but was very disturbed by her behaviour and the curious episode of the sudden recitation. It was all becoming too uncanny for comfort. Possibly she could rationalise that Elizabeth, sick with grief, hardly knew what she was saying and might not even recall saying it in a few hours time. Mel hovered between apprehension and scepticism as she sat and meditated, trying hard to convince herself that she had exaggerated the importance of Elizabeth's words, or misunderstood their relevance. She all but convinced herself that she was being foolish and reading far too much into a few casual comments... But a haunting unease had crept into her body...She was being warned, that was certain, and if she did not heed the warnings then she must suffer the consequences. Certainly she must compensate for anything that she had done to hurt. She must continue to be a good friend to Elizabeth - and, yes, to Ellen, too. She would play her role undefeated! Her resolve heightened, and her confidence returned. Slipping on her sandals again, briefly, she wept for Felix.

Thursday

One way to forget one's own problems is to concentrate on those of others and this first week in June, when Mel had undertaken to stand in for two other counsellors with long standing family and holiday engagements, was a strong dose of analgesic in itself. One by one the wretched clients came in - to perch on their seats like dry loofahs until afternoon armchair probing penetrated their porous fibres and prepared them, now soft and pliable, for the damp process of squeezing out emotions. By this time Mel was fully experienced. Even so protracted sessions on consecutive days proved something of a marathon and after hours of listening to the victims of unstable, unsavoury and unsatisfying alliances, she had little energy left for nagging personal worries and certainly none with which to confront herself with the dichotomy of her own position.

It was still incredibly warm. In the squat box-like room the air was satiated with stale sweat. Between interviews Mel made neat notes for colleagues, studied the Citizens' Advice and other bureaucratic posters which papered the walls with a bizarre offering of services, and refreshed herself with iced coffee. The extraordinarily elegant flavour reminded her of long forgotten visits to Wimbledon and tennis heart-throbs of bygone days, like Frank Sedgeman and Jaroslov Drobny...

There was a great sense of relief on this Thursday when the final session ended. The normal Tuesday afternoon and alternate Friday evening routine could now be resumed and Mel drove home with a sense of jubilation. She felt like a school girl at the start of half-term: a long weekend lay between her and her next counselling appointment at the Centre. Tuesday was a full five days away. She had done her stuff nobly this week, though it was hard to know whether one achieved much success in this business - for at the heart of most of the difficulties, as Mel secretly perceived them, was a suffocating boredom. In the symphony of her own life at this time the tedium of the long slow movement was past and now the scherzo had taken over, teasing, mocking, daring her to succumb to its charms. The excitement of the finale was still to come. There was considerable counterpoint in her life! She must remain strong enough to direct her own score for there were still themes to be played.

Soon after seven Mel arrived home to find a scribbled note on the hall table. '*Late pm meeting with ordinands at St A. Had beer and sandwich. Back late. Love A*'. ' St A' stood for Saint Anselms, the theological college fifty miles away. Mel would be in bed and asleep when Adam returned!

She sighed, removed the litter from the kitchen table, swept up the crumbs, poured herself a glass of wine and wandered through to the garden where marshmallow tinted peonies in full flower, exotic as a troupe of geisha girls, shuddered and swayed imperceptibly as rapacious ants invaded their secret places. Down by the lavender hedge a squadron of bees hummed happily and above the pond, shivering in solitary ecstasy, an exquisite dragonfly hung suspended in space. Mel squatted down to search for any pond life - a legacy of the various shoals of goldfish and shubunkins which Ruth and Seb had imported from time to time. Some, hideously swollen, died fishy deaths: others were devoured by a scavenging heron: still others disappeared without trace. Surely there were survivors? She dumped her glass and knelt down to poke about with a twig to disturb the stagnant undergrowth. The dragonfly took flight.

Inevitably the phone rang to divert her. It was Piers who launched straight into conversation with 'Amelie, I know you too well to dissemble!'

'Indeed, I hope so,' she replied, balancing on the edge of the telephone stool in the kitchen and wondering what was to follow. 'Come on. Out with it. What's the problem?'

'The funeral,' he answered. 'I have spent the post prandial hours with Elizabeth both yesterday and today...'

Mel interrupted, saying, 'I was there yesterday morning!'

'Yes, I know. You were of immeasurable comfort and brought real consolation. Bravo my Amelie.'

Did that brittle, plastic, telephone voice convey mockery, a touch of sarcasm or genuine congratulation? Surely only the last for it was unlikely that Elizabeth would have divulged all that had passed between them and thus risk compromising Piers. He must be smiling at her along the wires from St Marks. It was fortunate that he could not see her fluster. Apologising for the intervention, she urged him to continue.

'The funeral lunch is the rub,' he explained. 'The service is timed for two thirty and normal practice would be for those nearest and dearest to the departed to foregather beforehand and possibly take a bite of lunch together. Elizabeth states categorically that she wishes to confine this to the immediate family, id est herself, Ellen, Ellen's sister, a brace of cousins, a godson and'...there was a pause and whisper of embarrassment rustled the line... 'me.'

'That's fine Piers,' said Mel brightly. 'There's no problem! Can I help with the lunch?'

'That's generous of you but it won't be necessary. They have accepted the offer of Ma B's assistance with the vittels. What concerns me is the absence of you and Adam, and, indeed either of the curates, from this ritual feast. It would be right for you to be there, but I fear that Elizabeth is adamant.'

'Don't fuss, Piers. We shan't take offence.'

'Dearest Amelie, I know you will not,' he persisted, 'but I want you to know that I consider Elizabeth to be at fault and that nothing I can say or do will make her change her mind.'

'We'll go to the abbey incognito from here,' Mel joked, 'it isn't far! No doubt Elizabeth has her own good reasons for excluding us and we must respect her wishes.'

'She is singularly obstinate in her grief,' he mused.

'What happens afterwards?' Mel asked, cheerfully. 'If I am let off lunch do I provide tea?'

He was still apologetic. 'It's the same story, Amelie. I'm very sorry. However she and Ellen would like Adam to talk about Felix and to do the committal at the cemetery.'

'I see. So I scoop up any spare arthritic mourners who are in need and bring them back here for tea and a pee while you all bury Felix!'

The slight irritation which Mel now affected did not pass unnoticed.

'Obviously that would be greatly appreciated,' he said, 'but, believe me, I would prefer it otherwise.'

'Don't worry about it, Piers,' she said, and then, choosing her words carefully, and speaking more quietly and seriously, she added, 'Elizabeth needs you more than anyone else just now. This is her way of showing it. I fully understand. Honestly!'

The phone crackled derisorily. He did not speak. Mel addressed the silence. 'Piers, are you still there?'

'Still here, Amelie.'

'She needs *you*,' Mel reiterated, emphasising the final pronoun.

He hesitated before commenting and then said, 'I know, but this campaign is not without its territorial complications.'

'What campaign? What complications?'

'I have to assess where and why I am most needed,' he said slowly. 'My strategy needs care.'

159

The enigmatic innuendos were music to Mel's ears, but she did not stop to revel in them, nor did she consider that there could be any alternative interpretation of his remarks to the one which she was so ready to accept. His next enquiry only served to strengthen her conviction.

'And you, Amelie. You will be content?'

'Of course, quite content.'

'Then so be it,' he said.

This was amazing! There he was at the other end of that ridiculous length of communication wire, submissively awaiting her instruction. What did it mean? How dare she react? She must preserve this magic.

'Piers,' she said, 'I implore you to stop being frivolous! Go and be a nice boy to Elizabeth. You must support her. Fate will reward you. Have faith!'

'Amen to that, my Amelie,' he murmured. And again, in a whisper, 'Amen to that!'

A metallic double click from his receiver signalled the end of the conversation. Gently, almost reverently, Mel replaced her own receiver. She felt a renewed sense of triumph. If she was reading his dithering mood aright it marked the end of Elizabeth's hopes. What words had he used? 'Campaign,' 'Strategy'. Elizabeth was the enemy! (It did not cross Mel's mind that she, too, might be an enemy!) Piers was not concerned with the scope of his own support nor if he were honest, did he mind that much whether she and Adam were among the chief mourners. No! His solicitude transcended etiquette! It was to do with her and her feelings. She clung to his words. They sustained her. They had filled her with glorious hope.

Later in the evening, after she had nibbled a solitary salad, watered the roses, tied back the lupins, and finally counted three frail fish in the pond, Hannah phoned. It was good to hear her voice.

'Been trying to get you all day, ducky, where the blazes have you been? Are you free on Saturday? Let's go down to the coast and get a whiff of the old briny. I need a breather before the end of term jollies!'

Mel checked the diary. The following day was cluttered but her only Saturday engagement was a courtesy visit to Prudence Ogilvie's coffee morning and 'Bring and Buy for the Blind'. She could be free by midday.

160

'Bring for yourself and buy for me first then,' quipped Hannah, 'and I'll pick you up when you've done your good works. The old Ogilvie bag could use a couple of cataracts... eyes like telly cameras... don't miss a wriggle! Come to think of it our buggy's a bit bronchial just now. Can you be taxi?'

'Yes, I'll drive and we'll keep off the main roads. They'll be busy at a weekend.'

'OK luv! I'll bring grub - and you have the gossip ready. I want to hear all about Felix, poor bastard. One way to cool down in this heat isn't it!! Haven't had the guts to pay my respects to the girls yet - only popped a note through the door. Is it all Greek tragedy in there? Widows weeds and wailing? Not quite my scene! Tell me all on Saturday then - bye for now.'

Dear incorrigible Hannah. A few refreshing hours of her company would blow away the cobwebs. Yes, a day away could be therapeutic.

Friday

At breakfast the following morning, when Adam drew Mel's attention to the death announcement in The Times, she realised, as he indicated the position of the Hughes entry on the relevant page, that this was their first communication since the previous morning. Sometime he might like to know something of her visit to the vicarage and there were the funeral instructions from Piers to pass on, too. They would be able to talk in the car today, on their way to a big lunch at County Hall - the opening function of a weekend of celebration and thanksgiving to mark the six hundredth anniversary of the diocese. The smart embossed invitation pronounced Mel an official guest, and she also intended to claim her status seat for the great service in the cathedral on Sunday morning. Indeed this particular weekend had warranted the purchase of a stunning dress in garlanded Liberty cotton - a rare extravagance.

Mel glanced at the notice. 'Beloved of Ellen and Elizabeth,' she read out, 'what odd wording!'

'Is it?' said Adam, barely listening.

'Surely it would be more normal to put husband of Ellen and father of Elizabeth,' she persisted.

'Why?'

'Well, this way it could mean that Felix had two sisters, or two daughters, or even two wives, couldn't it?'

'Really,' said Adam, mildly, as he scraped back his chair, 'the eccentricities of the female mind never cease to amaze me!'

'Mine or theirs?' she asked, irritated by his lack of interest.

'All and every one,' he retaliated good humouredly as he left the kitchen.

Mel kicked the table. Adam's remarks appeared to disparage her own harmless observations. It would be senseless to argue about such a petty thing, but more and more these days, she had the feeling that her opinions were of little interest and her function comparable to that of a reliable domestic appliance: like the refrigerator or cooker, she rarely gave trouble.

A couple of minutes later, Adam reappeared. 'Can we leave promptly at eleven, Mel?'

She nodded, robot-style!

'By the way, we're giving Edmund (the rural dean) and Sybil (his wife) a lift. They'll be here at five to.'

Mel hunched into a protracted shrug. Adam frowned.

'Something wrong, darling?'

'Oh nothing,' she groaned, 'except that I was banking on being able to talk to you in the car. I hardly see you these days.'

'It's a busy time for both of us. Things will calm down in a few weeks.'

'Roll on August,' she said in a bored voice.

'Cheer up,' he called, on his way back to the study, 'and be ready on time!'

The leg of the table suffered its second assault and Mel bent down quickly to make sure that it was unharmed. Like a faithful dog it was an old friend and deserved better treatment. At this moment she understood the breed of despair which can drive a wife to hurl her crockery across a room. However, she was attached to her Denby coffee pot and when Maidie walked in shortly afterwards, she found Mel humming 'All things bright and beautiful' as she rinsed it out tenderly. Her irritation had evaporated quickly. After all, the sun was shining; she was looking forward to wearing her dress; the banquet might be appetising; and it would be fun to be able to chat to Alastair and other old friends and acquaintances. But there was another reason for the lightning change of mood. It was the simmering warmth of the secret incubating within like a fast-maturing embryo. In its fever to exist it

162

radiated incandescent ripples of excitement through her body and demanded to be noticed. It could not be ignored. It was sensational!

Maidie had started to sweep the floor and was blethering about her overweight neighbour who was weaning her first-born on fish and chips and Guinness. She had only half Mel's attention. The other half was planning a quick courtesy visit to the vicarage before the rural dean and his wife arrived. She glanced at the clock. She would change first. It was a bit mean to call on Ellen and Elizabeth in all her finery but it would make it obvious that she could not spare them much time today. Honour would be satisfied this way and she would also be protected from any further skirmish with Elizabeth. As it happened, when Mel arrived Elizabeth had gone out to buy dog food, so she was able to pass the time of day peaceably with Ellen, comment appropriately on her 'lovely letters of sympathy' and escape gracefully at a quarter to eleven.

The day away was unexpectedly tiring and being on one's best behaviour for so many hours an uphill task, particularly on the return journey when Sybil, who was sharing the back seat with Mel and who, like so many clergy wives, had developed an ability to jabber incessantly, obviously deemed it necessary to divert Mel with an unbroken barrage of words. Her diatribe banged on like a pop record and ranged from what antiperspirant to use in a heat wave to the state of the Archdeacon's prostate. Her rhythmic refrain was, 'But of course you are so young my dear,' and compared with her Mel certainly was for there was a good twenty years between them. She could have been Mel's mother - in a hot climate! Hopefully extreme youth excused the dryness of Mel's responses. They were like the grey dust which puffs out of old nuts two months after Christmas. Sybil did not seem to mind. She was the sort of woman who filled all her empty vases with dried and artificial flowers in the autumn, in order to make them feel loved in winter. As Mel murmured, nodded, and said 'Really!' she realised that she had long ago rejected the trap into which Sybil had fallen. Mel did not believe that one established any kind of relationship by talking at people and if she gave an impression of diffidence it was because Mel liked to talk if there was something to say and not just for the sake of it. Sybil's pastoral patter was a self-perpetuating addiction.

They flashed past the signpost three miles from home. Adam and Edmund, oblivious of their wives' presence, discussed various diocesan problems, including the gap created by Felix's death. Mel agreed with whatever Sybil was saying and smiled politely. People like Sybil were a part of her life as Adam's wife. But now there were other parts, stimulating, dramatic and capriciously exciting, which more than compensated for the tedium of this particular drive.

Back at Tower House, they fortified Edmund and Sybil with a late cup of tea before waving them on their way. As their elderly Morris spluttered through the archway, Mel sighed with relief and turned to go inside.

'Several people commented on your appearance,' said Adam. 'That dress suits you.'

'It ought to. It cost enough,' Mel retorted.

Habit, born of good manners, halted his steps in the porch to allow her to precede him through the doorway. He was watching, appraising.

'What a fortunate man I am to have such a wife,' he said fondly.

She moved towards the stairs. 'It's nice to be appreciated,' she said ungraciously.

'Where are you going?'

'To have a cool bath. I'm hot and my feet hurt.' She kicked off her shoes.

'Wouldn't you like to talk about the day?' he asked, trying to restrain her with one hand while hanging up his jacket with the other.

'Come and sit in the garden. I'll make us a Pimms.'

'I might have done, if you hadn't saddled me with that bloody woman,' Mel replied as she swept past him and went slowly up the stairs. She was aware of a mixture of frustration and anger fermenting inside her. Half way up, where the banister curved to the left, she turned to look down at him, and waited. He had loosened his collar and was fumbling with his cuffs. Lately he had admitted to needing his spectacles more often: he could do with them now. His leaden grey hair, spiky and thin over the crown, had lost its lustre and his face, when he looked up at her while repeating 'Come to the garden, darling,' was strained, drained of its morning vitality. In his sagging stance there was the weariness that shows at seven in the evening. He could use a stiff drink, this upright husband who now, through a pang of conscience, regret, or remembered neglect, was inviting her to sit and talk to him. Suddenly he looked much older than his fifty-four years. Older and more vulnerable. Fatigued by his own industry. Here was an opportunity for Mel to dismount from her high horse and go down to him. He beckoned her to the safety of all that was familiar. Momentarily she let her head fall forward and tightened her closed eyelids in a grimace of indecision.

'Come on darling. Come downstairs. Have the bath later.'

Wretchedness spilt into her. A dreadful wretchedness that manufactured its own fetid cheap nastiness. She had to hurt him: he warranted it. He challenged the power of her glorious secret. She had too much to lose...

'So,' she spat at him, 'you have time for me now, have you! Bribing me with Pimms to be cosy in the garden! Another half hour of your precious time to add to the measly quarter I begged from you on Sunday. Well! It's bloody well Friday now. After waiting around for a whole week, I'm damned if I'll come running now at your bidding. Holy Rural Sybil has exhausted all my conversation! Even your almighty God must know what a fucking bore she is. Christ! a fucking prostitute would get more change from you than I do. You can bloody well find out for yourself what has been happening to me while you've been buggering around for the blasted church!'

The sentences spilt out of her mouth and parachuted down to attack him. One by one he caught them, blanching visibly, wounded and outraged. She stamped exaggeratedly on her way: she did not recognise herself. Never before had she used such language.

Angry and indignant, he shouted up at her:-

'You had better make peace with yourself and your maker before you say anything else. Such profanity ill becomes you and has no place in our home.'

'Shit!' she screamed back, and, for the first time during their life in the Tower House she heard him slam the study door in fury.

She locked herself in the bathroom, ran the water, poured in bubble bath, and dragged off the expensive dress and flimsy underwear, chucking them on the floor in a heap, together with her handbag and tights. Trembling from a mixture of triumph and terror she submerged in the luxuriant warm foam and tried to empty her mind as thousands of tiny bubbles, each one existing for a puny burst, fizzed around her body.

Mel was reluctant to analyse the full meaning of what had occurred for it had happened on the spur of the moment and there had been no premeditation. Yet she knew that she must face herself. She refused to feel ashamed. The whole thing could be rationalised perfectly easily as something snapping at the end of a long day. But that was too simple. From the private and solitary look-out post deep within herself, she could see several Mels, each one offering a different explanation. There was the one ruthlessly ready to deceive and even destroy in order to sustain the hope which was growing with her secret; another sought to expiate her guilt by making Adam's shortcomings the scapegoat for her own. A third, balanced and sensible, should heed warning voices, no matter whence they came, and the fourth, loving and unselfish would have gone gladly to the garden and welcomed a tumbler of Pimms!

Languidly she exercised her toes and played water games with the sponge, squeezing it out repeatedly so that spray splashed on to her bosom and tummy. Then, impulsively, she decided to wash her hair, dripping across the bathroom to collect the shampoo and shower attachment and fixing the latter on to the taps.

As the hidden quadrangular conflict persisted, reason, the arbiter, decreed that she must make peace with Adam. To allow such anger to erupt was foolhardy: it demonstrated the danger of losing control. Clearly, if there was to be progress, there must be reconciliation. It would be expedient to apologise, and fair to Adam. Amazed and troubled by his wife's behaviour he was doubtless busy considering at this moment how best to placate her. He wouldn't sulk, nor be angry again; nor ask questions; nor make any demands. Instead of Pimms he would offer a measure of his compassion. Damn his compassion...! But he had looked so old standing there in his shirt sleeves. Old, and worn, and starved. Starved not of calories, but of time. Time for himself and time for her. It was ironic that 'time' should be one of his favourite themes, manipulated so adroitly into many a talk and sermon. Indeed he had written a book of short essays entitled 'Time and Time Again' which was published as a paperback in the early nineteen sixties and bore a garish cover depicting what appeared to be, but obviously wasn't, a simple child's drawing of a church and clock tower.

Precious time! Haemorrhaging away, unimpeded, towards eternity!

She stood on the bath mat and let lazy runnels of water trickle over her skin while savouring the warmth of a thwarted silver white early evening sun which mocked her through the myopic frosted glass of the sash window. She pushed the lower frame upwards. If she leant out a little way it would be possible to see the ornamental gabled roof of St

Mark's Lodge. She felt ridiculously naughty and as free as a bird. She sat on the windowsill and invited the sun and warm air to caress her body. If this were a scene in a French film, she smiled dreamily, her lover would now be seen wrestling his way over the high stone wall at the far end of the garden. Or, alternatively, he would tip toe into the bathroom (unlocked!) and plant exquisite kisses on her esurient nakedness. Sadly, her lover, if he existed, was out of sight, beneath those stiff gaunt chimneys. It would be her husband who would come to the bathroom. A surge of emotion poured through Mel as desire for Piers engulfed her. The memory of that wild sensual evening encounter in Backs View flooded back. The weight of his body. The power in his hands. The sound of his importunate voice as it begged her to show him. She stayed on the sill until the glow went from her and she began to shiver, and she asked herself over and over again, 'When will I be able to show him?'... because she knew that her body was becoming impatient, and for all that there were several Mels, they all shared this one body.

When Adam tried the door, as she had anticipated he would, she was sitting on the bathroom stool wrapped in a towel.

'Mel,' he called. 'Mel are you in there? Unlock the door!'

Of course she was 'in there', but normally the door would be open. She made no sound. Perhaps she had slashed her wrists and was lying in a pool of blood!

'Mel, darling,' he coaxed, urgency tightening his voice, 'do you hear me?'

This was becoming more and more like Eli and Samuel!

Eventually she said, 'Yes, I do hear you.'

He rattled the door knob. "Let me in. We must talk - I know I am largely to blame.'

'I'm in the bath,' she lied.

'How long will you be?'

'I don't know.'

'May we talk later?'

'No,' she said. 'I'm tired. Not today.'

'Tomorrow then?'

'Hannah and I are going to the sea tomorrow.'

He was silent. What a curious experience it was to converse through a locked door. Adam's distant, disembodied voice appeared to have left his person to come on a solo expedition of its own like a lone pilgrim.

It spoke again.

'What about eating?' he asked, adding, 'Would you like to go out somewhere?'

A rare invitation. He must be desperate.

'No,' she said. 'There's some cold chicken.'

The phone rang. She turned on all the taps because she did not want to hear him talking, even if it was Piers at the other end. When she turned them off he was waiting by the door again.

'That was Ruth,' the voice said formally. 'She wants a chat. She'll phone back in a quarter of an hour. It's about Monday.'

'Alright,' Mel said, resigned.

'Mel,' it called, with more emotion. 'Forgive me for making you so unhappy.'

Later on, after supper, she would tender some sort of apology. It would be about as drab as the cold chicken. The hitch in communications had delayed transmission of the message about the funeral arrangements, so she resolved to wait until their next drive to the cathedral, for the anniversary service on Sunday, to relay that information. It would make a suitable topic of conversation, prepacked, like a frozen dinner for two, and if, meanwhile, Adam saw Ellen and Elizabeth, his current ignorance of the plans would be his own misfortune.

Time might drag its feet for Mel over the weekend. She would chase it along in a frenzy of activity. Garden. Write letters. Turn out drawers. Sew new cushion covers. The last thing she intended was to make herself available for a heart-searching interview with Adam. Monday was the day. She would goad it here. She wanted it to come quickly. Because on Monday, at the funeral, she was certain of seeing Piers again, if only at a distance. For the moment, that would suffice. After Monday acres of days, like the Yorkshire Moors, would stretch away to the far horizon. Time enough then, after the funeral, to sort it all out.

'I got your postcard,' gabbled Ruth on the phone ten minutes later. 'Isn't it frightful! How are Mrs Hughes and Elizabeth? I'm coming to the funeral. Is Seb? How's daddy? What about the festival? It won't be cancelled will it?'

168

The questions sped on, as though clinging to a bobsleigh, until the one which demanded an answer.

'By the way, some friend of Viv's is coming on Monday. I told Viv about Felix 'cos I've had to change my lesson because of the funeral, and she sent me a note about this friend who phoned her because she had seen the death in the paper, and she, this friend, knew about Viv teaching me, and us living in the same town as the Hughes family, and Dad being the bishop and so on. And her father, Viv's friend that is, is ill, and he knew Felix, and he wants his daughter to represent him at the funeral and if she comes she'll give me a lift!'

'Steady on, Ruth. I can't keep up,' Mel protested. 'Let me recap. This is a friend of Viv's whose father knew Felix. Right?'

'Yes. She'll bring me down on Monday morning and I thought we'd give her lunch. I mean, I will. Because you'll be all involved, won't you?'

'Oh Ruth, what a moment to have a visitor!'

'I'll boil her an egg,' she offered. 'It'll be worth it to save the train fare!'

'Actually, we'll be having lunch here. The Hughes are playing it very quietly.'

'But dad's doing his stuff?'

'Some of it.'

'And Piers is comforting Elizabeth?'

'Well, yes. I expect so.' Mel bit into her lower lip. It was an effort to talk.

'Is she very upset?'

'Naturally.'

'You sound a bit low, Mum. Are you OK?'

'We've had a long day, darling. I'm very tired. Big happenings for the six hundredth anniversary of the diocese.'

'Golly. Poor you! Did you see Alastair?'

'Yes, as a matter of fact we did.'

'How is he? I hope you gave him my love.'

'He's very frail. Daddy and I saw a big difference in him.'

'But he isn't ill?'

'I hope not. He loves your letters. Write as often as you can.'

'Mmmm. I do. He's a darling. I hope he'll come to my concert.'

'We'll try to organise it.'

169

'Super! Well, I'll see you on Monday then. With this woman! I suppose the whole parish will be there, plus God knows how many 'dog collars'!'

'I expect so. You won't be staying the night?'

'Heavens no! We'll drive back afterwards. Seb's not coming is he?'

'No! His exam is on Thursday and he's revising furiously. You can represent him.'

'OK, I'd better send him a good luck card! See you on Monday. It'll be fun, even though it's all so gloomy! See you! Bye!'

Hissing noises and the rattle of the receiver supported her farewell and Mel had a fleeting mental picture of her banging the door of the phone box and swinging her way back along Exhibition Road to the flat where she lived with a group of fellow students whom they knew affectionately and collectively as 'the royal mini orchestra'. It would be good to see her and people would be pleased that she had made the effort. Useful, too, to have a lift from this friend of Viv's. Certainly the woman's ingenuity in contacting Ruth as she had done, would warrant more than the basic hospitality of 'a boiled egg'.

Saturday

Adam left the house early the following morning. He and Mel had been politely careful with each other since the contretemps the previous evening. He did not press her to talk, but she knew, from the uncharacteristic way in which he sat around doing nothing after her brief apology, that he was shocked and distressed. The previous evening when they had gone to bed, he had tried to cuddle up to her, but she had eased away to lie inert, uncomfortable and too near the edge, until she knew from his breathing that he was asleep.

Maidie did not come on a Saturday except for 'something special and important' so Mel busied herself with household chores, collected weekend groceries, called at the vicarage, took a garish cake plate, glass candlestick and tin of biscuits to the 'Bring and Buy', purchased a chunky hand knitted dishcloth, packet of outsize envelopes (for Hannah!) and jazzy bracelet (for Ruth!), changed into a trusty denim skirt and striped summer 'top' and drove up to Hannah's gates five minutes before the agreed time.

Hannah greeted her with blustering affection. 'You're bloody early. What's got into you?'

'Desire for your company and a wish to be free,' declared Mel cheerfully.

Hannah threw some wild-looking greasy packages into the back of the car (the picnic?) dumped a bulging beach bag decorated with comic cats and sandcastles onto the floor and squeezed herself and her voluminous skirt into the passenger seat, gasping, 'God it's hot!' as she banged the door. Only Hannah would wear such ghastly clothes!

Mel clicked into gear, drove up the hill and headed west on the top road out of town. A genial breeze stroked them through the open window as heat from the sun scorched the landscape. She moved into top gear.

'Now come on ducky,' said Hannah, finally settled in her seat, 'how about this blow by blow account of the widow and orphan? Then I'll be able to gird up my loins and trot in with my condolences before Monday!'

Mel spoke at some length about the events of the week, but omitted details of Elizabeth's passionate outburst. Such revelations might have led into all sorts of trouble and Hannah, too shrewd to be fobbed off with some slick diagnosis, would not have rested until she had probed deep into the centre of Elizabeth's suffering. Living as dangerously as Mel now believed herself to be, she did not intend to present Hannah with the evidence and invite a prognosis. She valued the friendship too much; this day was special. She concluded the account with a description of the vicarage visit earlier that morning when the mourners had been embarrassed to be caught around the breakfast table. Ellen's sister had arrived the previous evening and the three of them were chatting over coffee. Elizabeth had offered to show Mel Felix, but she declined the invitation, telling Elizabeth that she preferred to remember him as he was the last time she saw him.

'When was that?' asked Hannah, who had listened intently without interrupting.

'Evensong. A week last Sunday.'

'No time at all ducky, is it! Here yesterday. Gone tomorrow. Poor sod! What's going to become of the girls? They'll have to move out of the vicarage, won't they?'

Mel nodded. 'You and I would have the same problem if our husbands died.'

'Too true!' she said - before changing the subject abruptly. 'Where's old Adam today then?'

'With hospital chaplains at a centenary celebration.'

'Bully for him! But it's not much fun for you, Mel, is it! When did he last drag you out to a pub for a noggin and a bite to eat, or ravish you in the orchard?'

The amusing turn of phrase inferred no more than friendly frivolity. However, it was not always easy to interpret the implications behind Hannah's waggish language. Mel braked, and then pulled out to overtake a milk tanker, the moments of silent concentration enabling her to compose an answer which left the options open on both sides.

'It must be six months since we went out,' she said, 'and, as you know, we don't have an orchard.' She refrained from divulging that she knew exactly when Adam had last 'ravished' her. It was after hearing about Monty.

'Well, under the cherry tree, then,' she baited.

The remark warranted no comment. Mel pulled a face in her direction and waited.

'Seriously, ducky,' she began, breaking off to rummage through the beach bag for her sunglasses, and accompanying the search with a string of expletives. 'Seriously, I think that man of yours is neglecting you. Between you and me, I've thought so for a long time but haven't plucked up the old whatsit to say so.'

Sensing danger, Mel answered quickly. 'Oh, I wouldn't say I was neglected, Hannah. My life is exactly what I expected it to be when Adam got this job.'

She spoke convincingly. The second half of the sentence was certainly true. But Hannah was not to be deterred.

'Of course I suppose it's a bit much to expect old God to have a day off now and then to let people like Adam off the hook. I mean, He never shuts up shop, does He! Here, have a bit of Crunchie!' She pushed a large tacky cube into Mel's mouth and then carried on ruminating about God's lack of concern for his 'staff' ending up with, 'I s'pose *He* can't really have hols 'cos there's nowhere much for *Him* to go. And anyway, what would *He* do?'

One had to smile at the comic impiety and her seemingly childish view of the Almighty. But Mel knew Hannah too well. Her friend had a tough respect for 'Old God'. She also had a hunch that things with Mel were not quite as they should be and Mel was obliged to comment somewhat lamely:-

'I think Adam's a bit tired. He's infernally busy and I never seem to get round to telling him the things I should.'

'Pity that' champed Hannah licking the Crunchie paper, 'you might miss something important one of these days. Now old Giles is always bumbling in and out. Pops back between lessons sometimes for a natter. It's easy for him. Living on the job.'

'You're in your job as a partnership, aren't you. Interdependent!'

'Yes, ducky. But I would have thought that you are much the same. Perhaps I'm wrong. But whatever your terms of reference I know it's bloody important to have time together, and total communication, don't think I'm prying, luv, I'm not asking you to tell me secrets. You know Auntie Hannah's here to help if you ever need her!'

Mel turned right to bump down the private track which led to a rocky cove. Each year they feared for its seclusion and they breathed a joint sight of relief when they saw it tucked beneath them, basking innocently in the sun, and still undisturbed by ravaging holiday crowds. Hannah's clumsy attempts to persuade Mel to unburden herself had brought a lump into her throat and she knew that she was being watched as she leant forward to negotiate the difficult terrain. She drove slowly down to park the car, with half a dozen others, where the track narrowed to a footpath and disappeared between boulders. Backing on to a patch of grass, she switched off the engine and said, cheerfully, 'Well, we're here!' She turned towards Hannah and smiled knowing that Hannah was waiting for some acknowledgement of the sentiments which had been expressed. 'Thanks for the concern,' she said, 'there's nothing to worry about. Honestly...!'

As they struggled down the path and across the rocks, carrying all Hannah's supplies between them, Mel congratulated herself on her reactions. She was grateful for Hannah's concern and curious to know what had prompted it. She had rallied to Adam's defence automatically. To admit to the obscene behaviour the previous evening would have brought the sternest condemnation, for despite her own colourful vernacular, Hannah would be shattered by Mel's use of the real thing;

173

and having taken her to task she would have been placed under Hannah's motherly wing until the whole idiotic muddle with Adam was sorted out. To tell the truth about Piers, or the roses, or Elizabeth, or guilt at the feet of Felix, or the tombstone coincidences, or that dream of long ago, would be to introduce her to a stranger. Such an introduction would put at risk Mel's whole secret life in addition to destroying forever the image that Hannah had of her friend. Mel was intent on enjoying the day and she cherished her respectability. There was no way that she could take Hannah into her confidence.

However, Hannah was not quite ready to call a ceasefire. The second salvo landed in the middle of the afternoon after they had washed down scrumptious home-made pasties with Chianti and laid themselves out, warm and relaxed on a couple of plastic lilos which Hannah had produced from the bag with the remark, 'easier on the bums, luvvy, at our age, especially on these blasted stones.' She had puffed them up vigorously before lunch in order to win her pasty. She was constantly trying to slim, but never succeeding. They had caught up on each others' children (Susie was happily married to an architect and pregnant, which was exciting for Hannah, and Guy had just completed his law exams) and exhausted local tittle tattle. Mel was delightfully semi-conscious: lulled, but not disturbed, by the rhythms of the cove - an occasional shout- creak of a boat- gulls overhead - sea dribbling over shingle...

Suddenly, Hannah's voice disturbed the idyll. 'Funny old Piers taking off his Guy Fawkes mask,' she said, 'what happened?'

'What? Oh!'... Mel yawned to conceal her consternation. 'Well!... He just... took it off!'

'Did you ask for a peep?'

'I suppose I did. In a sort of way,' she admitted drowsily, not at all anxious to proceed with the conversation.

'And he was kind of peculiar afterwards?' she persisted, heaving herself around on the lilo and forcing Mel to open her eyes to see what was happening. 'Tell me more,' she ordered, as she finally landed on her front with an outsize gasp. 'God, I ought to have brought my bikini! Come on! Tell me, while I tan the backs of my legs.'

'There isn't any more to tell,' Mel prevaricated.

'But when you saw me afterwards you said he acted funny. Upset you said.'

'Well, yes. He did get a bit emotional, I suppose. Worked up, one might say. It was... well... embarrassing.'

Mel was thrown. Replies to these several questions had not been rehearsed and the memories which they prompted brought a sheet of heat to her already sunburnt face. She had to do better than this. Hannah's curiosity must be eradicated.

'Look Hannah,' she said firmly. 'I'd rather not talk about it. It's all over and forgotten.'

'That's OK old girl. But one of these days, Piers is going to make a fool of himself. Forewarned is forearmed as they say, so don't let him start to get fresh.'

'Oh Hannah! After all this time.' (This sounded better. More convincing!)

Hannah gave Mel what might be described as an old-fashioned look - half amused, half concerned - before struggling to roll over again and to sit up, moaning as she did so, 'God, why did you give me these great boobs. You try heaving 'em around!' Still she had not finished.

'He must be pretty frustrated you know, Mel. I wouldn't want him to go overboard for you. He's damned fond of you, you know.'

'He's fond of all of us,' Mel said, sitting up and bending forwards to touch her toes. 'Anyhow, he has to marry Elizabeth. More than ever now.'

Hannah shook her head.

'That's a lost cause, ducky, and you know it as well as I do. We've been waiting since old ma T-J died! You only need a modicum of the old common sense to see that it's hopeless.'

'Well,' said Mel, standing up, and stretching in what was, she hoped, a nonchalant way, 'well, I shall go on hoping!'

Neither of them referred to Piers again.

Mel hoped that she had muzzled Hannah, not only verbally but mentally, although she felt a certain unease. Somewhere she had picked up the scent. She suspected something. Her friend was sniffing at her secret. She must be wary!

When Hannah got out of the car at the end of the outing, Mel ignored a remark from her that she would 'chivvy old Adam' next time she saw him. She leant across to hand her a stray flip flop and invited her to come for a cup of tea after the funeral. 'I shall be fortifying thirsty lingerers,' she said, 'and you can help to entertain this female who is bringing Ruth.' She had explained Ruth's travelling arrangements earlier.

'Yes, I'll come and give you a hand, duckie. What are you going to wear? It's so bloody hard to look sombre in the summer. All funerals should happen in November! National Funeral Week. You know - like 'Bob-a-job' week. All the bodies despatched together!'

The flippancy went unanswered. She heaved the gear out of the back of the car and banged the doors.

"Bye, duckie,' she said. 'Smashing day! See you on Monday.'

'Charcoal grey,' Mel said.

'Charcoal - who?'

'That's what I shall wear.'

'Happy choice! I'll find some old rag. Trouble is the M.A.S!'

'Maz?' Mel queried.

'The perishing middle age spread. These days, most of my little numbers are two sizes too small. Still, it's not your worry. See you luvvie. Bye!'

'Goodbye, Hannah. And thanks for enticing me out for the day.'

Hannah weaved her way through an informal game of cricket taking place in the school yard, spilt her belongings into a side door and gave a jaunty backwards wave. Mel pulled away from the kerb to drive the short distance home. When she pulled up at the traffic lights at the bottom of the High Street she became acutely conscious that she had been at a symbolic crossroads with Hannah today. A safe well-used road had stretched ahead. Hannah would have trod it lovingly and patiently with her, until all that was concealed had been aborted, expunged, and scattered in the hedgerows. With Adam, too, Mel had considered that road - only last evening. She had wondered about travelling it with Felix. But Felix had died. Even Elizabeth might have assisted her some way along it...The car behind hooted. The lights had turned green and she had not noticed. She jerked into action. At that imaginary crossroads where she had waited, indecisively, with Hannah, with Adam, with Felix, and with Elizabeth, the lights were now stuck at red. Along the unknown track they glowed, invitingly, green and green again, as far as the eye could see. One by one she was spinning past them...

Chapter X

REQUIEM

'Mum, we're here!'

Ruth's shout echoed through the house. It was eleven thirty in the morning. Mel had survived the preceding thirty-six hours with the impatient desperation of a child awaiting a birthday, but Monday was here at last. She hugged and kissed her daughter with 'Hello, darling,- lovely to see you,' and extended a hand to her companion whom Ruth introduced as Mrs Armstrong. Mel was slightly flustered. They had arrived earlier than expected and she had not yet changed into discreet grey.

'We've had a fantastic drive, babbled Ruth, 'a record run! I'm famished. What's for lunch? Oh! Just a minute – I've brought a load of washing with me. It's in the car. I'll put it in the machine now and dry it in the sun while we are burying Felix.'

She vanished.

'Give it to Maidie,' Mel called after her, 'she'll deal with it.'

Doors banged in all directions. Mrs Armstrong smiled with an attractive warmth.

'What a charming daughter you have,' she said, 'and how delightfully practical!'

Mel laughed. 'Actually, that's the last thing she is, and she's certainly the only member of the family who would mix laundry with lamenting.'

She shepherded her guest upstairs to show her the geography of the house.

177

'This is a frightful imposition, Mrs Ellis' she apologised. 'I promise you that I will melt into the background. My father and the Reverend Hughes were friends for many years and I felt I owed it to them both to make the effort to be at the funeral. Knowing about your talented daughter through my friend Vivien Jackson seemed to make it so easy somehow...' She tailed off a little helplessly to be reassured by Mel who said that they were delighted that she had made contact with Ruth and to make herself at home indicating the way down to the garden and intimating that she would join her there as soon as she had changed. Meanwhile Maidie would bring her a cup of coffee.

A few minutes later Ruth bounced into the bedroom to borrow tights and a slip.

'Washing's away! Fabulous! Maidie is quite chirpy isn't she. Looking forward to the funeral, and the tea-party afterwards!'

'She'll revel in it,' said Mel zipping up the charcoal linen dress and inspecting herself, unenthusiastically, in the mirror.

'That's hideous, Mum!' declared Ruth.

'I know. It does nothing for my ego, but it's the only thing in the wardrobe that's both cool and gloomy.' She did up the cuffs and glanced at Ruth. What a scarecrow she looked in her frayed cheesecloth shirt, patched jeans and Scholls clogs!

'Go and change, darling. We can't leave Mrs Armstrong alone for too long.'

'Dad has just come in. He's talking to her.'

'Oh, good! What are you going to wear'

'I haven't got anything either. I've just looked. Except that brown pinafore thing.'

'That'll be fine,' Mel said abstractedly.

'Are we going to have lunch in the garden?' Ruth asked.

Her mother remonstrated 'No! This is hardly the moment for an extended picnic. We're going to a funeral. Remember?'

'Golly, yes. Poor Felix. He died awfully suddenly, didn't he!'

She peered through the window, straining to get a clear view of the vicarage.

'Shouldn't you be there? With them?' she asked.

'They're only having a few people to lunch,' Mel replied briefly.

'I'll bet they've snaffled up Piers.'

'You could put it like that,' Mel replied offhandedly, while searching the jewel box for something to cheer up her appearance, and adding, irritated by the chatter, 'do go and change darling.'

'OK, OK. Pity you and Dad aren't out to lunch though! We could have gone to the The Tavern. That would have given the regulars something to gossip about. 'Fancy t'bishops daughter being in t'pub before t'funeral!' and she went off to change, chortling to herself at the thought of this imaginary scene.

Mel sighed. Ruth had distracted her. If she were honest with herself she would admit that part of the reason why she had delayed her own changing until now was because she wanted to keep an eye on what was happening on the other side of the Green. She glanced at the clock on the abbey tower. Five to twelve. There didn't appear to be much sign of life over there yet. Piers must be with them by now. Probably he had left the car in East Avenue and entered through the side entrance. She was only half concentrating. On appraising herself again, she had to agree with Ruth. The dress really was awful. Too tailored to be currently in fashion; too nipped in at the waist; and too long! She must remember to buy something else before another summer funeral took her by surprise! Hannah was right. Winter requiems were more manageable.

She found Alastair's ring and slipped it on her right hand. Years ago the shank had been enlarged so that she could accommodate it on the fourth finger of either hand where it sat more happily than on either little finger. The presence of this precious ruby never failed to conjure up vivid memories. Indeed the mere tiny private ceremony of removing it from its velvet case, and handling it, aroused the same nostalgic emotion every time. This rare jewel was a testimony to the loyalty and devotion of the recipient, Mel Ellis, from an energetic period of her life when she had not been found wanting! She treasured it almost more than her engagement ring. It told her favourable things about herself which, from time to time she needed to hear... A final check in the mirror confirmed that the glowing adornment had added the touch of colour that was missing. She hurried downstairs to make polite conversation with Mrs Armstrong.

Lunch passed off affably enough, although Adam's brow contracted with annoyance a couple of times when Ruth's behaviour bore more relationship to the showing off of a fourteen-year-old than the

179

'maturity' of twenty. For her the day's ritual was a welcome break from routine and something to be thoroughly enjoyed and she tucked into the paella and pineapple with festive fervour, secure in the knowledge that neither parent would censure her in front of a stranger.

While they were sipping a quick pre-lunch drink in the garden, Mrs Armstrong insisted that they call her Diana. The name suited her. She proved to be a woman of some sophistication with whom it was easy to identify, particularly when she talked about her job with a firm of publishers. As her work frequently involved the editing of religious books Adam was especially interested. Her father had not been ordained as they had presumed; his friendship with Felix dated from childhood and had weathered long ago into a mutual exchange of greetings at Christmas. Mel studied her as an antidote to what might, or might not, be happening in the vicarage. She was probably older than Mel and much better dressed. Her immaculate appearance matched the quietly confident personality and Mel coveted her beautifully styled blouse in a pale grey and pinky beige design. Was it pure Italian silk, she wondered? It was stunning and toned with the deep burnt umber of her matching coat and skirt. The expensive shoes and handbag were in the same burnished price range as was her hair which, although greying, curved down the sides of her face in a becoming youthful style and flicked up level with her neck as if caught by a light breeze. She wore a narrow gold wedding ring but no other jewellery. She seemed a nice woman; had she lived in the area, Mel decided , they might well have been friends.

Adam left promptly after lunch and the others followed shortly afterwards. By the time they took possession of their appointed pew the abbey was filling up fast. Diana, embarrassed by the 'V.I.P.' treatment, offered to sit on her own in the nave but Mel and Ruth insisted that she accompany them. The sidesmen were already directing folk to the side aisles and apart from the churchwardens' pews and those at the front reserved for the chief mourners, the only central spaces were isolated gaps between people reluctant to move along only to find themselves squeezed between thighs and elbows.

The coffin, supported on trestles, commanded a dominant position in the sanctuary pointing towards the altar where Felix had walked and waited so many thousands of times. It was draped with the festal cope, a theatrical touch which brought tears to the eyes, and a single, eloquent wreath of pristine white and cream flowers lay on the floor in front of it. It was not Ellen's or Elizabeth's choice to be lavish and the local florists, acceding to their wishes, had encouraged sympathisers to donate money, which they were prepared to spend on floral tributes, to the Restoration Fund. .

Mel knelt on her hassock. She could not bear to think of the shrouded, chopped about, body that was all that was left of Felix, packed into that claustrophobic box. Where was his immortal soul now? Seeing fresh things with resurrected sight; sensing with surrealist senses; hearing; communicating... To whom? With whom? His deceased relatives? Parishioners at whose funerals he had officiated? Crabby old Mrs Tarrant Jones? Assuredly he had obeyed the summons, and 'followed', to the place where she was now... He knew 'her', too, and would need no introduction when he happened to 'float' into her. But the idea of that good and saintly man in perpetual scheming, heavenly communion with her offended one's sensibility!

The activity in the building stilled into a sacramental silence resting in the grip of the steady, invocatory, tolling, of the great tenor bell. The life of the town had been suspended for an hour while its heart, condensed into a contemplative mass of black ties and dreary dresses, waited to beat out its homage. A rustle shivered the mass as the small group of mourners, which had entered through the side door opposite the vicarage, straggled, almost apologetically, into the front two pews. Mel had eyes only for Piers as he guided them to their places and then crept away, reverently, to the vestry to robe. The sight of him filled her with happiness and as a lingering tintinnabulation lengthened the reverberation of the final chime of the bell, there was no corner left in her thoughts for Felix. The organ sounded the melody of the processional hymn. The service had begun.

People talked about it for months afterwards, even after the departure of Ellen and Elizabeth and the installation of the new vicar. For this was no ordinary service. It could easily have been a routine affair. The words were those which the Prayer Book ordered for the burial of the dead and the hymns were popular Sunday hymns which everyone sang with confidence, and people might have been thankful to get it over in as short a time as possible because their formal clothes were uncomfortable and the heat made one sleepy at siesta time. But tangible and intangible things made its dimensions nobler and more sublime than some run of the mill affair and for the majority of the townsfolk, whose fragmentary and episodic religion was confined to the sensitive moments in their personal lives - weddings and funerals, christenings and carol services - this was something altogether more grand and awesome and transcended normality.

Unlikely people found their way there. Like Ephraim Hobbs, the postman, who had faithfully delivered mail to Felix six days out of seven - and rested on the seventh! And 'Tommo' who trundled the streets with his council barrow, clearing the gutters, and open spaces of the litter left by mankind and nature. In the autumn, when the leaves blew over the Green he heaped them into piles, like huge helpings of cornflakes, before spooning them into the cart and spiriting them away; and Felix had often stopped for a sympathetic chat on those irksome October days, and made another friend who came, uninvited to this funeral. Half way down the nave, at the end of a pew, sat one of the constables who was noted for his brusqueness and intolerance of even the tiniest infringement of the Highway Code: and he clutched his helmet, nervously, throughout the service, and blew his nose loudly when it was over. And at the back, by the historic west door, a group of tramps, looking like the prisoners at the end of the first act of Beethoven's 'Fidelio' stood silently and wearily before shuffling out at the end of the service ahead of the coffin.

Piers always sat by the lectern. From her position in an elevated pew reserved for the bishop's entourage, Mel was able to feast her eyes upon him without arousing any suspicion. It was just as easy as focusing towards the organ console and general, cavernous aspect, of the abbey beyond. When he approached his place during the singing of the first hymn, he acknowledged them with an unhurried devotional nod, and Mel was the only one (with the possible exception of Ruth) who would realise that this particular gesture was not a part of the proscribed ritual. Stealthily, she too, inclined her head, to reciprocate the barely perceptible greeting.

The service was taken by John Elliot, the younger curate, who never failed to look as poor as he actually was; the Lesson was read by Piers, and the Address and special prayers delivered by Adam. When Piers first began to read, Mel did not pay any attention to the content of the Lesson. She only heard the strong, expressive timbre of that slightly arrogant soldier's voice which, after the long days of waiting, brought

182

instant and exquisite pleasure. But soon the sentences began to hammer at her brain, forcing her to interpret their meaning. All through the prayers which followed the Lesson, and the responses that followed the prayers, haunting fragments, morbid little texts, repeated themselves, and her mind throbbed with them as she continued to gaze unashamedly across the chancel. Temporarily she was oblivious of anyone, or anything else; of Ruth and Diana to the left of her, the choir members in front, or even Adam, who was now proceeding from the sanctuary to the pulpit, ritualistically escorted by a subdued Eddie, hidden inside his formal verger's robes like a holy highwayman.

Adam's tribute to Felix was a brilliant eulogy, laced with apposite phrases, personal reminiscences, and humorous anecdotes which Felix himself would have been delighted to hear. Such oratory would send the large congregation away well satisfied with the character and humanity of its bishop, as well as of its lately departed parish priest. Throughout the ten-minute address Mel's own disturbance continued. She should have listened more closely to the whole of the Lesson. Later, she would look it up in Adam's bible in his dressing room. Clearly it was all about the final reckoning! The triple spectres of sin, forgiveness and judgement had been bugging her for long enough. This was the last straw! Piers himself had now delivered some extremely bothersome snippets, with the complements of the apostle Paul, and phrases such as 'lives laid open', 'each must receive what is due', and 'for conduct in the body good or bad', had clattered against her conscience to lie in uncomfortable heaps and crystallise into deposits which were unlikely to evaporate. No longer was she going to be able to rationalise that what she yearned to do with her body could not be wholly bad, because she would be doing it for the good of Piers and from the purest of motives. Love!

She struggled fiercely against this latest threat. Yet she knew that unless she had already divorced herself completely from the sacred abbey and all that it stood for - which was unthinkable - she could not leave it today without confessing, on her knees, that she had understood the ominous words of warning. This much she owed to St Paul – to Felix, to Adam, to Piers and to herself. Each for a different reason. Also, by some strange quirk or coincidence she owed it to that old witch, Mrs Tarrant Jones. By such a gesture she would demonstrate her obedience to that wily command to *'Prepare for death'*...

The choir rose to sing a setting of Felix's favourite hymn, 'Praise to the holiest in the height'. It was a moving performance. Geoffrey Salter, the organist and choirmaster had rehearsed it to perfection and although the fresh faced choristers and boys from the Queen's School were quite matter-of- fact about it, some of the choir men had tears running down their cheeks; and Mel wept, too, but her tears were not for Felix. They were for herself and the desolation of her own dilemma. When it was time to pray again, she crumpled on to her hassock, and, in a miasma of mixed emotions she asked God to quench her desire and to give her the strength to sacrifice the love that had taken possession of her. All things considered this was probably as good an attempt at prayer as she had made for some time...

'For all the Saints, who from their labours rest,' they sang, relaxed and relieved because they had no doubt, at the end of the service, that Felix was now crowded into the hereafter and safely numbered amongst the countless host. One hoped, however, that he would not be tramping the endless planes of eternity, forever, to this energetic, pulsating, tune!

The congregation knelt for the final prayer and blessing. Adam's voice rang out with words which Mel knew by heart after so many years of repetitions. At this moment they affected her as they had never done before.

'O Thou', he intoned, 'from whom to be turned is to fall, to whom to be turned is to rise, and in whom to stand is to abide for ever. Grant us in all our duties Thy help, in all our perplexities Thy guidance, in all our dangers Thy protection, and in all our sorrows Thy peace...' If one was allowed just one prayer on a desert island, to add to the chosen luxury, single book, Bible, and Shakespeare, then this must be it for it said everything for everybody! Mel was proud of Adam and proud of Felix. She rose from her knees and looked down the Abbey past Piers to where Ellen and Elizabeth were sitting, and in her heart she echoed the sentiment that they would find peace in their sorrow.

The bearers moved into position. The choir stood and waited until the coffin had been carried as far as the nave before beginning a gentle last Nunc Dimittis for Felix. As soon as the singing started, Piers and John left their places and went over to the front pew to escort Ellen and Elizabeth and the relatives on their processional walk in the wake of the coffin. Piers bent to murmur something to Elizabeth, took hold of her arm and helped her out of the pew. This steadied her and encouraged her to pull back her shoulders and face the congregation. Mel monitored their backs as they retreated down the aisle and the distance between them lengthened. But she was distracted by Ruth who was fidgeting around behind her in an attempt to rescue her handbag and a stray tissue, and she was puzzled, too, by Diana who was straining forwards, over the pew, almost indecently, as though there was something that she still wanted to see. Not that it seemed important. Probably she was merely compensating for a forgotten pair of glasses.

The funeral was over. They emerged from the Abbey into the pellucid heat of the afternoon sun and walked slowly back to the Tower House to engage with the pre-arranged tedious tea party This comprised less than a dozen clergymen, half as many wives, a gaggle of elderly female parishioners who had hung about expectantly until Mel was obliged to invite them, Mary Davidson (Ian rushed off - he could not stop for anything as frivolous as tea during his medical working day), Hannah, Giles, Ruth and Diana. The crowd outside the Abbey had dispersed quickly. People could not wait to get home to change back into informal clothes and, apart from the embarrassment of not knowing what to say to the vicar's widow, if one bumped into her, the whole business was over and duty done.

In the dining room at the Tower House supporters stood around in small subdued groups sipping tea and nibbling shortbread. Rural rectors steamed inside their shiny dark suits while their handbag dangling wives twittered amongst themselves. Hannah and Mary chatted animatedly and Ruth flirted with John Elliot out of sheer devilment; she preferred Edward May, the other curate but he was still away on an extended holiday visiting a sister in New Zealand. Maidie and Mel congratulated themselves on having estimated the number more or less accurately. Maidie was wearing her best polyester dress and her hair had been newly tinted. The addition of a fine cotton and lace apron, kept for important occasions such as this, made her look like some bossy proprietress of a south coast tea shop. She bobbed in with a fresh pot of tea, surveyed the scene and prattled excitedly:-

'The funeral was lovely, Mrs Bishop, really lovely it was. Everybody says so – lifted us up on high it has!' Her face glowed. Mel had to smile at her enthusiasm as she replied, 'It was a great tribute to the vicar, Maidie, but I hope he is the only one who has been 'lifted up' as you put it.'

Maidie was asserting her right to be a part of the proceedings and one had to remember that Felix had always treated her 'a bit special like' and that Alf, her husband, led the bell ringers. Mel decided that this was not a moment to engage her in further conversation and moved away before Maidie got careless with the tea. She noticed Diana looking a little lost and examining porcelain in a corner cupboard so squeezed her way through to her to be greeted with 'What a moving service that was. The abbey is magnificent and I'm so glad I came.' Mel acquiesced and they swapped generalities for a few minutes (including the history of the porcelain) until people began to drift away and Mel's presence was needed elsewhere. This enabled her to move towards the entrance and to catch a glimpse of the undertaker's Daimler pulling away from the vicarage. They must be back from the cemetery and Adam and Piers, still aiding and abetting, would now be tucking into cucumber sandwiches and Ellen's best chocolate sponge!

Mary Davidson caught her attention to ask about Seb and to report that Tim was doing no work at school and dividing his attention between his girlfriend and his motor bike.

'I'm worried about him, Mel,' she confessed. 'These wretched 'A' levels are so important aren't they. Count yourself lucky that Seb takes his seriously and get him to knock some sense into Tim for me when they meet up in the holidays.'

'I'll try,' Mel promised, although she knew full well that Seb would be fed up to hear about Tim's latest liaison. Any current girlfriend invariably took precedence over any claim which Seb might have to Tim's company.

By the time the rest of the hangers on had left, Hannah, Ruth, and Diana had found their way on to garden chairs. Ruth, back in her student attire, had rolled up her jeans and tucked up her shirt to expose maximum leg and midriff – doubtless encouraged by Hannah. Oddly enough when Mel appeared they were talking about Adam for which Diana apologised by saying, 'Forgive us for discussing your husband. It has been a pleasure to meet him and I am now being initiated into the secrets of a bishop's life.'

'Being a bishop's wife is bloody lonely at times from what I've seen,' interjected Hannah.

'And being a daughter a social handicap,' stated Ruth.

186

'It's a full-time job' Mel said, somewhat pompously as she settled into a deckchair longing to remove her shoes and tights. What a pity Diana was here. Decorum decreed that she maintain her image!

Ruth smiled across at Diana. 'Dad says that one of the prerequisites is a good digestion. He's a connoisseur of sausage rolls!'

'There are days when you face a non-stop round of refreshments,' elaborated Mel. 'Milky coffee and ginger biscuits at a diocesan seminar followed by salmon and strawberries with the Mayor…you can imagine the sort of thing.'

Diana nodded before asking 'Does your husband spend much time away? And what exactly is a suffragen?'

Hannah nodded vigorously in reply to the first question but allowed Mel to reply.'

'He's away a lot during the day but not all that often at night, and a suffragen is the official second or third bishop in a diocese with his own title and a specific function. It varies from one diocese to another. Most people are surprised to learn that there are more suffragens than full bishops. It's something like sixty to forty and of course only twenty-six sit in the House of Lords. Adam has autonomy in certain areas and he's away somewhere or other about once a month I suppose – next week for example he'll be in London for three days attending synod consultations... it's a varied life – for him!'

Hannah, who had been fidgeting with zips and buttons while Mel was speaking and was now loosening her belt, flopped back in her chair, noted the glazed look in Mel's eye, and obligingly changed the subject.

'We made a good job of despatching old Felix, didn't we girls!'

They agreed and she rambled on with, 'Poor old boy! He was a duck! Always had time. Never gave an impression that there was another soul in the world to worry about. Wonder what the poor sod's up to now. She then turned directly to Diana and ventured, 'He was a buddy of your old pa's, was he?'

'Yes. But I don't recall meeting him. He was a name and a signature on a Christmas card.' Diana looked bored and spoke rather primly, as though she did not wish to field any more questions. However, Hannah persisted:-

'Where's your nest then?'

'I've a tiny house in Richmond.'

'Fantastic,' commented Ruth who was at the age at which one believes London to be the only place worth inhabiting.

'Any brats?' flashed Hannah. There was no stopping her when she turned inquisitor.

'Sadly, no! 'I've been a widow for a long time. My husband was killed in a car crash. He was a brilliant architect.'

There was a pause – even a pregnant pause – while each of them considered how best to follow such a conversation stopper. Diana herself broke the silence after a moment's hesitation.

'Tell me,' she said, 'who is the clergyman who read the lesson so beautifully – with something wrong with his eye?'

'Piers!' they chorused.

'Colonel Piers Tarrant-Jones,' informed Ruth with a hint of sarcasm in her voice. 'He's only a reader, not a clergyman, and he's the local playboy.'

'That's a bit rough Ruth,' disagreed Hannah, jumping to his defence. 'He works damned hard for the abbey and his heart's in the right place. He's bloody generous too. He'd never let you down. But as I was saying to your ma the other day, the thing between him and Elizabeth is a squeezed out lemon!'

'Elizabeth?' queried Diana.

'Elizabeth Hughes,' replied Ruth, 'Felix's daughter. She's a nurse. She and Piers have had a vague sort of affair for years but nothing ever happens. I think he's gay. He's always been keen on Seb – my brother that is - and I was told some grisly story some years ago about him and a boy called Darren Smith.'

'Who is Darren Smith?' enquired Diana keeping the topic in play.

'Some town boy,' snapped Mel. 'That story is a load of rubbish, Ruth. I'm surprised you've heard it.'

Ruth shrugged and looked surly. Hannah supported. 'Nothing in it duckie. Old Piers is no homosexual. Problems with his hormones or his hydraulics, maybe, but nothing nasty.' Turning to Mel she added 'You'd agree with me Mel, wouldn't you?'

This was an exposed moment. Mel waited for Ruth to say that there was nothing nasty about being gay but she didn't. Why oh why must they analyse him in public. Why were they even talking about him? She had just made brave new resolutions…what she craved was time to adjust. Not the torture of hearing his character torn to shreds! And why did Ruth continue to be so antagonistic towards him? She gathered her threadbare thoughts together and spoke directly to Diana.

'This small town gossip can't be of any interest to you, Diana. The man in question has a certain (she hesitated, stuck for a word) flamboyance! It makes him a little controversial.

Diana signalled with her hands and also her facial expression that she understood and realised that her innocent questions had caused a minor furore. Mel frowned at Hannah, hoping that her friend realised that her crude remarks had overstretched Mel's patience. Ruth appeared to be dozing! Mel glanced at her watch. Neither Ruth nor Diana gave any sign of movement. She had understood that they would be leaving around half past five. Adam had said 'goodbye' to them at lunch time!

Ruth woke up.

'How's your sex counselling, mum?'

Hannah guffawed and Diana looked taken aback.

'Marriage guidance,' Mel interpreted tersely. She was becoming more and more exasperated by Ruth who was in one of her perverse moods. However, this subject was a more serene choice than the previous one and she could wax eloquent if necessary.

'Ruth!' intervened Hannah, 'did you hear about the cheque for the organ fund? From a grateful client. Damned appropriate don't you think!'

Ruth nodded. She *had* heard about it and appreciated being considered mature enough for the vulgar innuendo, but she now had the grace to curb Hannah with a curt, 'Mum wouldn't want that repeated, Hannah.'

One way and another Mel's daughter and her good friend had put her through it during the past half hour and she regretted that neither of them had shown her proper respect; they would not have behaved so fatuously had Adam been around.

Diana decided that it was time to make a move and stood up. Hannah did up her plackets. Ruth yawned and dragged herself out of the deckchair.

'Don't forget your washing, darling,' said Mel. 'Maidie has left it folded ready for you in the kitchen.'

'Thanks. I'll get it. Can I pinch some food?'

'Help yourself, but not to our supper.'

'They're all the same, Mel, aren't they,' puffed Hannah, as she struggled to tighten the belt around her spare tyre with a characteristic groan about her size, 'Skint! And hungry!'

'But how fortunate they are, Mrs Garside,' said Diana, 'to be so uninhibited. Life was very different for us at their age.'

Hannah was unconvinced. 'Too bloody soft now! I dare say not for Ruth, though. Don't envy her all those hours shut up alone with that cello. Pretty unnerving!'

The three of them walked through the house, Mel, thankful that Ruth and Diana would soon be gone.

'You ought to come to the Festival Concert, Mrs Armstrong,' Hannah was saying, 'to hear Ruth. She's damned good you know.'

Diana looked interested. 'Ruth was telling me about it on the way down. I'll think about it.'

'Well, let me know if you need a bunk. I dare say I'll be putting up the odd bod to help old Mel here.'

Diana unfastened her handbag. 'When is it exactly?' she asked. 'I'll make a note of it in my diary.'

'The last Saturday in June,' said Mel, helpfully, 'Ruth has all the details. Viv will be coming of course and you know her – do try to make it.'

Diana pencilled it in. She might come thought Mel but after the pantomime in the garden she was in no mood to pressurise. After all, they had only just met. It was entirely up to her. Within a short while they had all departed and Mel heaved a huge sigh of relief. Some- where in her mind something was waiting to be processed. It was producing the same intermittent, but persistent, prompting that she recognised from schooldays when she was wont to procrastinate over the writing of a difficult essay! Whatever it was had to be faced. It was no use pretending that she was ignorant of it. It was to do with her experience in the Abbey this afternoon. She had asked for help. Now it was up to her to prove the integrity of her intention by restoring Piers to the tidy slot in her existence that he had occupied before that fateful evening when she had divested him of his chastity.

Like some enfant terrible that one has allowed to escape from restraints and run amok, he must be clamped back into a safety harness; she must suffocate her desire...and douse the molten, nerve searing passion, which was still smouldering inside her, aching, with white heat, for the sight of his face or sound of his voice. In this great purge, she would learn to play truant with herself until all danger was past. She must bury her secret and hide away in the grey isolation of bitter bereavement. The Mel who was Adam's wife, the Mel who was mother to Ruth and Sebastian, and the Mel who busied herself with all manner of things would continue to function in her little world. No-one must suspect as life trudged by, that for her, at this time, it was as though she was alone on some desolate Cornish beach, waiting to be washed sand-clean and pure by the tide, until her mind, scourged of all flotsam, was firm enough to withstand the pressure of treating him forever as a stranger who once came too close…!

She lay on the bed and sobbed. To be alone on such a beach was a mortifying and unendurable prospect.

Chapter XI

MEL

By the time Adam came home on that Monday evening, a reconditioned Mel was waiting to welcome him. She had spent an hour watering the garden while the going was good. The heatwave was causing reservoir panic, and any day now hoses would be banned. Gentle early evening air soothed her eyes and dried out swollen red cheeks. If, by any chance, Adam noticed that she had been crying, she would say it was for Ellen and Elizabeth! She realised that there was no longer any reason to weep for Felix.

She made a supreme effort with Adam. They talked freely over supper, and, afterwards, when they carried coffee out into the garden, a therapeutic twilight, drenched by a sky of amethyst and mother of pearl, closed around them and lulled their conversation into a quiet, curative, harmony. He told her about the interment and the tea at the vicarage. There had been iced coffee sponge, not chocolate, and home-made eclairs, to which, as he reminded Mel, both he and Piers were addicted. It had all been very straightforward. Nothing untoward had occurred. Mel congratulated him on how well he had spoken and on his choice of prayers... and when he tentatively raised the subject of her violent outburst the previous Friday evening, as he remembered to do, because she had said that she would talk after the funeral, they discussed it all objectively and drew up new agreements about communicating more and having time to listen to each others' point of view.

He decreed that they should spend more time together and do things with Ruth and Seb –which was exactly what Mel had been saying for a very long time; but she let him believe that these were his own, original, thoughts. They discussed the possibility of a trip to Scotland in early September. Ruth and Seb might like to come with them. And Adam, in all innocence, suggested that they could take Piers along, too, but Mel pointed out that this was not a very sound idea. For some reason Ruth didn't like Piers much, and, anyway, it would be an impossible crush in the car; and if the young didn't come, surely it would be best just to be on their own. Adam took a lot of convincing! He was anxious to visit Monty, and they certainly couldn't do that unless Piers was with them. She suggested that it was just morbid curiosity which made him want to see Monty and he agreed that this might be true... Finally, after nearly twenty-three years of marriage, he offered to discuss the precepts of Christianity with her but she assured him that, after all, this was not necessary. Was she certain, he asked, that she was no longer in a muddle? 'Pretty certain,' Mel replied; but when, a few moments later, he reached out, sympathetically, for her hand, he could not possibly know that she was surrounded, within and without, by a massive grey emptiness.

For a whole week she lived a blameless life. Every time she was tempted to exhume her secret she drove it from her mind expurgating it with the same force that she had once employed against a swarm of flying ants in the old back kitchen at Amsworth. On that occasion she had waited far into the night to ambush the last stragglers as they crawled furtively into the rotting wood around the window frame.

As well as routine engagements, she found extra things to do - like helping Ellen to go through Felix's belongings and parcel them up for 'Oxfam'. It was a heart-breaking task, but somehow, stoically, they finished it. Elizabeth, who had gone back to London, was coming home again at the weekend to finalise plans for the future. They had three months grace in which to adjust to their changed circumstances and solve the problem of where to live. For Ellen this was essentially a choice between moving to new accommodation in the locality, going to live with her sister ('I'm not really at home there, Mrs Ellis; people don't speak; they draw the curtains at teatime and watch TV all the evening!'), settling permanently into the tiny cottage in Wales, or living temporarily with Elizabeth. Ellen had even begun to consider other alternatives such as the possibility of some sort of residential post.

'I know I'm not qualified,' she said wistfully, 'but I'm sure I could be useful somewhere; in an old peoples' home, or a school, or maybe as a companion. I wouldn't mind what I did!'

Storage of furniture was another worry, and so was Tertia. But Ellen divulged that Piers had offered either to foster, or adopt, the Labrador if the need arose, and meanwhile he was calling every day to take her for a walk.

'He's a dear, kind man, Mrs Ellis. I've often thought there must be something in his life that has stopped him from marrying. He and Elizabeth have seemed close to it at times. Or perhaps it was just that Felix and I wanted it to happen... what do you think?'

Mel, who was pairing off Felix's well darned, matted, socks and rolling them into neat woolly balls (Hannah would be proud of her!) tried to ignore the seething mass of thoughts which buzzed excitedly around the closed area of her brain at the mention of his name. She answered dispationately with, 'I think he's a confirmed bachelor Ellen, some men are you know.'

Even so, she could not stop herself remembering that both she and Elizabeth knew things about him that Ellen would never know. There was even a tiny temptation to unburden everything to this simple, warm-hearted woman. It would have been a form of purification. But Mel had to remain strong. Felix, by his death, had shown her the way... and now, here she was, neatly folding his faded clydella pyjamas ('Those are the winter ones, Mrs Ellis. They'll do someone a good turn, won't they.'), and dingy pullovers, and packing them into cartons as a gesture of her good faith. It was odd the scent of the pullovers. They smelt like Alastair. Perhaps all elderly clergymen developed this same aroma. Was it something to do with spending so much time sealed inside fusty cassocks and dusty churches?

During this week she saw Piers three times, which was about average. On the first occasion he called at the Tower House to discuss an imminent smart county wedding for which the last-minute arrangements had been 'much inconvenienced' by Felix's death. Adam was in, for once, and after Piers had hovered uncertainly in the front hall, held Mel's hand for far too long after the ritual kiss, and presented all the signs of being overjoyed to see her, she ushered him into the study with uncharacteristic speed. It was unbearable. But courageously she fled from him on the pretext of having to take the car to the garage for a tyre check. Their second encounter was at the vicarage. Mel was there when he returned Tertia after her daily exercise, and again she was able to resist the temptation to prolong the confrontation. The third meeting was at Parish Communion on Sunday morning. She knelt at the altar rail, between Seb and Adam (who had no suffragen engagements) and waited for Piers to edge sideways until he was level with her and offering the chalice as Felix had done. On her knees, at his feet, she begged God for more assistance, much more, and the fortitude to survive another week. And the stark realisation of the excessive amount of strength that she would need depressed her...

Seb had come home for the weekend. His exam was over and he was extremely relieved. It had not gone too badly. He was not proposing to do much more work this term. There was barely a month of it left! Yes, he might write a few English essays and read some books; that was enjoyable! Did they mind desperately that he had started to smoke, he asked? They probably did but accepted that this was just one more of the cults pursued by the young and they hoped it would pass. Obviously it would be rash to be caught out by the housemaster...'

'When did you start, dad?' he enquired, puffing away a little self-consciously before lunch and allowing the ashtray to enjoy the larger share.

'At university,' replied Adam tersely. 'A pipe. Not cigarettes. My generation couldn't afford them. A little tobacco went a long way.'

Seb grinned. 'You don't approve Dad, do you!'

'It's not a question of approval or disapproval. I'm sad that you find it necessary while you are still at school. And concerned about your reason for doing it.'

'Same as yours at Cambridge, I suppose! To prove one is grown up! This is the trouble today. Parents don't realise that their kids are adult a good two years earlier than *they* were. At seventeen, I'm like you were at nineteen! More worldly, too, I would guess.' (For Seb, this was an amazingly long speech!)

'You are less protected in this permissive society, Seb,' replied Adam, 'but not more 'worldly'. My generation was being weaned on a diet of armed conflict, and facing up to being prepared to die!'

'Oh God! All that war stuff again,' moaned Seb. 'It gets boring. Except the poetry. Now that really is something. The first war stuff is great and there must be some from your war, too. I'll call in on Piers while I'm home to see whether he's got any books.'

'He'll be a bit shattered to see you smoking,' offered Mel.

'Oh, I dunno,' he said. 'He's probably got the odd vice or two we don't know about. He won't mind. I'll call at tea-time, before I get the train back to school.'

'Yes, do,' said Mel, in a matter-of-fact voice. 'Piers would like that.'

This was the kind of remark that Adam and Seb would find absolutely normal. They could not know what it cost her to make it. To speak his name, or to visualise him, was to exacerbate the insupportable torment of her self-imposed seclusion. To speak was to remember. And to remember was forbidden...!

Chapter XII

AMELIE

Mel had a nasty feeling that her next spell of abstinence was going to drag intolerably and whilst she could not entirely equate her situation with that of a reformed alcoholic left in charge of a crate of whisky, the strain was not lessened by the knowledge that Adam's synod commitments would keep him in London for three days, or, that for the time being, she had done all that she could to assist Ellen. Her reputation with Ellen, at least, was running high. Hannah, immersed in the business of making and fitting costumes for the school production of 'HMS Pinafore' (to which she and Adam were going on Friday night) was in a 'Sorry, can't stop to talk now, duckie,' mood, and Mary, with whom Mel might have spent a little time, was in Devon visiting her elderly parents. She was tempted to go away herself, to stay with Hester for two or three days, or to camp in Ruth's flat in London, but there was no way of shedding her marriage guidance engagements, and she had also promised to say a few words at a Christian Aid lunch in the abbey hall on Thursday.

After a customary bout of dithering, Adam opted to travel to London by rail. He didn't really need the car in town and parking was a terrible problem, even in Dean's Yard. So on the Tuesday morning Mel drove him to the station in time to catch the early train.

'With reasonable luck I'll be back on the seven thirty on Thursday evening,' he said. 'If I'm held up it will be the later train.'

'Don't waste money on filthy British Rail sandwiches,' Mel instructed. I'll have some supper for you.'

The carriage jerked forwards and he raised his hand. 'Look after yourself,' he said through the window, before sitting down to put on his glasses, undo his jacket, smooth the purple vest across his chest, and open The Times.

Mel nodded. He had made no attempt to kiss her. Either he hadn't thought of it, or he was conscious of being rather conspicuous especially as they had both acknowledged various acquaintances who were also travelling on the train or seeing people off. Sometimes he kissed her, and sometimes he didn't: she was used to both. But today she felt a certain disappointment. A tinge of regret. A sense of something missing which it would have been comforting not to have lost. As though echoing her frustration, the Mini took a lot of starting outside the station. On the short drive down, ten minutes earlier, Mel had drawn Adam's attention to the fact that the engine had lost power, spasmodically, several times lately. 'Probably the plugs,' he had said, 'I'll look at them when I get back.'

Three hours later, when she was ready to leave for the Centre, she cursed her stupidity for ignoring the recent symptoms. Surely she had learnt that a sick car never recovers spontaneously! This time, despite repeated twists of the ignition, there was no way of encouraging it to start. Damn! Now she would have to transfer to Adam's car, which handled like a bus after the Mini and which she hated driving. She went in to collect the keys but they were in none of the obvious places and for the next quarter of an hour she and Maidie scoured the house for them. She was forced to the conclusion that they were in London by now, in one of Adam's pockets - and the duplicate hidden in some nook known only to him.

The question was, what to do? Time was still on her side. She had allowed plenty in order to collect a load of groceries from the large Sainsbury's situated conveniently near the Centre. She dismissed the idea of enlisting the help of the professionals; there was no point in inviting garage costs unless it was absolutely necessary and, so far as the Mini was concerned, it would be sensible to allow Adam a first look under the bonnet. In the past he had been known to correct mechanical faults, though more by luck than expertise! Hannah would lend her their car. She had done so before. But Mel was deterred from approaching her because she knew her to be heavily involved at this particular time. For a split second she hesitated. Then she rushed to the phone. Piers! Piers would know what to do! Her hand shook with apprehension as she dialled his number. Perhaps he was out... But no! He answered promptly and Mel explained her predicament.

'It sounds like the regulator or the starter,' he diagnosed. 'But chin up, Amelie. I can drive you wherever you need to go. And while you are dispensing wisdom this afternoon, I'll use the opportunity to distribute some Festival posters around. Good publicity! No problem! Be with you in ten minutes!'

Suddenly the whole day presented a new dimension. Niggling, whispering voices told Mel that she was playing with fire but she did not heed them. Yes, alright! She could have gone by train but it would have meant changing and she couldn't be certain of a connection in the middle of the day to get her to the centre on time. Anyway, the eleven thirty had already left!

She shouted to Maidie who was ransacking the unlocked drawers in Adam's desk. 'It's alright Maidie. Panic over. Colonel Pears can drive me.'

She sounded relieved as she replied, 'There's nice. Goodness knows what has happened to those keys. Only himself knows, very likely.'

'Only himself,' Mel endorsed cheerfully.

Tempted to change out of a sober striped cotton dress into something less formal she raced upstairs to the bedroom. 'No!' forbade a fierce small inner voice. 'No! You will not change. Be dignified! You are Mell Ellis, wife of Adam. Never forget it. Not for an instant. This man is banned. Beyond reach. Your love is buried. Dead! Remember the warnings. Heed the words. Your actions will be exposed. You will be judged... Be strong. Be vigilant.'

The voice, or reason, persuaded her that she could not turn up at the Centre looking as though she was going to a barbecue. After all, Mrs Prosser (Mr Prosser, too, now), and everyone else foundering on the tricky rocks of marriage, must continue to view her as a model of middle class propriety...

She contented herself with undoing the top two buttons and folding back the collar. This gave a more sporty image and allowed air to circulate. She was sweating profusely. She waited by the bedroom window until the navy blue car swung cheekily into the courtyard and announced its arrival with a friendly 'peep, peep'. Piers jumped out to polish the windscreen.

Mel ran downstairs, told Maidie that she was leaving, asked her to lock up at the end of the morning, collected handbag, file of notes, and a light blazer, and, sick with excitement, went out to join him.

His face creased with welcome as he kissed her hand, and, with a flourish, held open the door of the Lancia.

'Greetings, Amelie. I am at your service.'

Momentarily incapable of speech she got into the car. It was hard to believe that this was really happening. She reached across to put her belongings in the back. What a fabulous sports car! She could not recall sitting in it before although recollected Seb's enthusiasm when Piers had first acquired it.

Piers squeezed into the low-slung driving seat, switched on the ignition, bent forwards, and turned his head until he was able to see Mel with his right eye.

'Seat belt, Amelie,' he reminded her.

She fumbled and he leant across to grab hold of it. Her heart thumped uncontrollably. Surely he was so close that he was bound to hear!

He straightened up. "Do we have time for a quick pub lunch ma'am?' he enquired. Mel pretended to consult her watch. 'Yes Piers,' she said. I think we do.'

They drove out of town.

For a short while the busy, officious, voices inside Mel behaved like meddlesome interlopers. However, there was so much to talk about and, moreover, a pub lunch to enjoy, so their jibes were treated with disdain and summarily dismissed from her mind.

That afternoon Mel's counselling went astonishingly well and she derived as much satisfaction from the knowledge that she was being of real help to the Prossers as she had done in former physio days when a patient's pain was substantially reduced, or even cured, by her efforts. Contrary to expectations she was able to concentrate superbly during the three hours away from Piers. Her happiness at having been with him and the pleasurable prospect of the return journey created a unique sense of peace and well-being. But on the drive back the tranquillity was gradually replaced by a certain urgency and feeling of defeat, and, moreover, she began to be haunted, yet again, by misgivings and a sense of 'déjà vu'.

A simple comment from her about the quality of the choir's rendering of 'Praise to the holiest' at the funeral, prompted Piers to ask whether she was familiar with 'The Dream of Gerontius'.

'No,' she admitted. 'All I know is that it was composed by Elgar.' He shook his head in disbelief.

'A masterpiece,' he pronounced. 'We must ensure that this gap in your musical education is filled with all speed, my Amelie.'

'What makes it so special?'

'It is a visionary work. Elgar himself inscribed it with the words, 'This is the best of me; for the rest, I ate, and drank, and slept, loved and hated, like another; my life was as the vapour and is not; but this I saw and knew: this, if anything of mine, is worth your memory'.'

Mel was temporarily silenced.

His hands were firm round the steering wheel, his eye on the road ahead. They were going at a law breaking speed. Because of his limited sight he was unaware of her scrutiny as she studied every detail of the scarred blind side of his face. Obviously he found it difficult to shave this area. Tiny ridges of stubble grew around the edges of the scar tissue like scrub beside a dried-up river bed. His ear was unscathed. So, too, was the side of his nose. The eloquent recital of Elgar's sentiments called for some comment! Who but Piers would have such a ready and accomplished memory? His mind was a storehouse of unusual items.

'It's obvious that Elgar was pleased with it. What is it all about?' she asked eventually.

'It's based on a poem by Cardinal Newman which is concerned with death, judgement, and the passage of the soul into immortality. It embodies the prayers of friends on earth, personal entreaties, demons of hell, angels and archangels and the final moment of facing one's maker. Believe me, Amelie, it *is* inspired.'

Despite his enthusiasm, Mel did not have the stomach for much more of this. She licked her lips. The day, like her mouth, was beginning to turn sour. At any moment the voices would start to harangue her again!

'So who was Gerontius?' she asked politely.

'An unidentified Christian. A worldly man, but a penitent! A likeable character who left it a little late to come to terms with the implications of death...'

'Not a Felix then?' she offered.

'No. Definitely not a Felix, Amelie.'

She sighed before saying, 'I find this sort of thing very depressing.'

Piers made an abortive half turn in an attempt to see her face, but reverted immediately, to watching the road.

'Why 'depressing?, my Amelie?'

'Oh, I seem to go round and round in circles - and quite frankly, I've had a basinful of it all during the past few weeks...' She tailed off, her voice registering genuine misery.

He sensed her frustration but had the tact and sensitivity to keep his own counsel. She sighed again. They were nearly home. Suddenly he reached out, touched, and found, her right hand.

'Help me to change gear,' he ordered. 'Come on - we're going into overdrive!'

The contact sent an electric charge through her body and her mood lightened. No wonder 'shock treatment' worked! Neither of them spoke. His hand blanketed hers on the short gear lever. The pressure altered with each gear change, and several times, as their hands lay sandwiched together, he changed his grip so that his thumb and fingers explored the contours beneath, massaging and caressing. Was there something that he was trying to tell her? She wished that the drive could go on for ever. He pulled into the courtyard and turned sharply to the left. They moved into neutral and he released her hand. She made a trite comment about not realising that he had five gears and he said that it was a feature of the Lancia Fulvia. They undid their seat belts.

'Come and have a bite of supper,' Mel ventured, tentatively.

'I dare not, Amelie. Much as I would like to. Ma B is cooking steak au poivre, and her wrath will know no bounds if I'm not there to appreciate the fare.'

Mel had a quick intuitive image of what her anger must have been on a previous occasion when he played truant:-

'Well, thank you for the life-saving lift. And the lunch.'

The last treasured moments of opportunity were rolling away like a broken string of pearls. Had she missed a cue? Was there some initiative that she should take? She felt a mounting panic at the prospect of leaving him and facing the long lonely evening ahead. He was ominously still, and silent. She opened the door and began to get out.

'Thanks again, Piers,' she said. 'Be seeing you!'

He clambered out of his seat and bounded round the rear of the car to hold the door for her, helping her out, solicitously, and handing her the articles from the back. The car had been parked in the shelter of the wall, and parallel with it, so that when the nearside door was open a kind of semi-enclosure was created. It was a very private place. He looked down at her, his expression inscrutable. Tiny pinpricks of sweat dotted his brow. A bronzed left arm lay casually along the length of the top of the door and his right one hung limply by his side. His feet were firmly planted in a commanding position in front of her. She was imprisoned by his presence. He gave no sign of being ready to allow her to pass. Indeed the angle between the door and the car seemed to be growing smaller. She was weak at the knees. Why was he waiting? Did he want to kiss her? Should she kiss him? There was no-one to see... His breathing was rapid and his lips parted a couple of times as though he was about to speak but thought better of it. Magnetism filled the space between them. Finally he spoke, very quietly.

'Would you care to spend the day with me tomorrow?'

It had happened! She wanted to throw her arms round his neck and crumple against him. Her whole body filled with an erotic tension such as she had not felt for twenty years.

'There is nothing I would like more,' she answered, equally quietly.

'Bravo!' he said affectionately, his eye crinkling into a strange half wink. 'And where will you choose for us to go? To the sea? Or the hills?'

Mel had a quick vision of the advantages and drawbacks of either landscape. The countryside held more appeal than the coast. She could not imagine them lying on a beach, or swimming. Yes! They would choose the peace of a rural setting. He had ordnance survey maps imprinted on his mind - he would know where to go!

'The hills, I think,' she said. 'Take me to one of your favourite places.'

'My little Amelie,' he said, 'I shall give it my earnest consideration. It will not be one of my favourite places until I have visited it with you. After that,' - he moved his left arm towards her as he was speaking and laid it gently on her shoulder, smoothing his thumb up and down her neck while he delayed the rest of the sentence – 'after that, it will be my most favourite place.'

He moved aside to let her pass, bowing with mock gallantry. 'Until tomorrow, then, my Amelie. Shall we say ten o'clock. I'll call round after I've taken my girlfriend for a walk!'

Mel had been doing some quick thinking. Although she had the car as an excuse, she was concerned about Maidie's reaction if Piers collected her for a second time during Adam's absence, particularly after her remarks about the roses.

'Ten o'clock will be fine,' she said. "But I'll walk round to St Marks. I don't want Maidie getting ideas.'

'Ah Amelie. You think of everything,' he said. 'How wise you are.'

'Whether I'm wise or foolish remains to be seen,' she said provocatively.

'It does indeed, and either version will enchant me.'

'And how long will the enchantment last?'

'So long as men can breathe, or eyes can see', he quoted.

There was no need to prolong these teasing exchanges. They reflected the relief of a decision made; a relief coupled with a reckless headiness. Nothing, now, could stand in their way, decided Mel; tomorrow, tomorrow at last, she would show him.

The following morning she awoke in time to hear the abbey clock strike seven. She had slept soundly. On the few occasions during the night when she was semi-conscious, an undercurrent of excitement lulled her back to sleep with the gentle persuasion of a moonlit summer sea splashing softly over luminous shingle. Such a night enhanced the pleasure of opening one's eyes to the glare of the new day.

She had a leisurely bath and removed excess hair from various stretches of her body. The results of the sunbathing on the expedition with Hannah were still visible. Would they lie in the sun today, she wondered? Perhaps she should have offered to provide a picnic lunch. No, she reassured herself! Piers had issued the invitation and it was up to him to make the decisions. A second pub lunch would be very acceptable. She opened the bathroom window. Another azure sky. How long could it last? She leant out, searching for the chimneys of St Marks: this morning they were hugged by a flattering silver haze. 'Wake up, my beloved,' she breathed. 'Wake up. Today is ours. Every minute is as precious as a diamond.' She tried to visualise his bedroom. She had seen it once, years ago, when Piers had some virus and she and Adam went along to cheer him up. It was in keeping with the rest of the house, she recalled, sombre and oppressive; cluttered with military objects, like regimental swords, old pistols, and prints of famous battles, and crowded with books bound in drab dark colours. Did he remove his eye shade in bed? Would she ever know? She made the bed quickly. It was so easy when only half of it had been used. There were stray hairs on Adam's pillow. She smoothed them away and allowed him a brief thought before putting on fresh clean underwear and selecting a soft grey shirt and comfortable emerald green skirt to wear, after she had breakfasted in her dressing gown. Later, well pleased with her finished appearance, she rubbed oil on to her bare legs because they looked horribly dry. An occasional spot on the carpet no longer worried her. Long years had passed since the concern about the tone of the hyacinth blue; it had faded a little, but not as much as one might have expected and, to be honest, she was tired of it.

She opened drawers and found a narrow leather belt, maroon like her sandals, and an emerald spotted square which she knotted round her neck. She could not quite decide whether this particular accessory made her look any younger than her forty-four years and ended up creasing it back into the drawer! Today inside, she felt the same age as her daughter. Intrinsically, one's psyche altered very little Mel conjectured. Additional years and responsibilities produced congestion in the brain and memory, making it more difficult to single out a particular feeling, but it was still possible to do so and, this morning, as she glanced repeatedly at her watch whose tiny gold pointers were creeping steadily round towards ten o'clock, she was the same young woman who, twenty-four years earlier, had counted the minutes to her next rendezvous with Adam.

If any further confirmation was needed that it was already past nine-thirty, assorted sounds from below (footsteps, running water, and various bangs associated with Maidie's daily raid on the cleaning cupboard) were sufficient. Mel inspected her hair and face. Her complexion was in good shape and now that she had a light tan there was no need for make-up. She slipped on her engagement ring which had been lying on the dressing table. The gesture was automatic, but something prompted her to pull it off, quickly, and to substitute Alastair's ring. She had a vague sense of wishing to be fair to Adam... of not wanting to be caught cheating! And the slight unease prompted a faint, aphasic, scared voice to begin its halting chant of familiar words:- '*So... you... shall... be: Prepare for... death!*' Ignoring the interruption, she located a handkerchief and polished the iridescent gem on her finger until it glinted in the light, a splintered spectrum of rubescence. 'I hope that you will wear it, and that it may give you pleasure,' Alastair had written. 'I do. And it does, dearest Alastair,' she whispered. The inner voice grew more distinct. '*Remember, friend... Each must receive what is due...*' 'Shut up!' she said sharply in a cross voice. 'Just leave me alone and let me enjoy today in peace!'

When one thinks about it, it is not always easy to differentiate between the many voices, or thoughts crystallised into words, that invade the absolute privacy of the inner self. They are legion! Controlling, advising, forbidding, encouraging, reasoning, doubting, remembering... There is the well-mannered one for praying, and another, more holy than the rest, there by special invitation and never far away... But since they all come from the same untraceable place, and speak in a conflicting way, it can be extremely confusing! On this momentous day in her life, Mel did not intend to concern herself with any one of them more than another

After tidying the contents of her handbag, and choosing a cardigan, Mel went downstairs. Ephraim had just delivered the post which included a 'bread and butter' letter from Diana Armstrong, thanking them for looking after her on the day of the funeral, and intimating that she hoped to come to the Festival. 'If it will help,' she had written, 'I could drive Ruth, Vivien, and the cello, down to you on the Friday evening. Mrs Garside kindly offered me hospitality but I have no wish to impose upon anyone and will happily stay at a hotel. Please fit me in wherever is most convenient. Meanwhile I shall look forward to meeting you again, to hearing Ruth play, and to seeing the display of flowers in your lovely abbey. My best wishes to you. Yours, Diana'.

It was a pleasant letter. She might as well stay at the Tower House. They were expecting a crowd, and even if Hester and Alastair both came, there were still enough beds. Ruth's surplus friends and supporters could unroll sleeping bags in Backs View and Seb would not be coming, so his bed was also available. He was in the school squash team and probably glad of the excuse of an away match which would prevent him from getting home in time for the concert. 'Wish Ruth luck for me, Mum,' he had said, sheepishly. 'I'll send her a card with a black cello on it!'

The phone rang. Mel picked up the receiver in the study. It was Piers.

'Good morning, Amelie. I trust this sublime forenoon finds you well.'

'I'm fine, Piers. How are you?'

It was ten to ten. She was fearful that his courage had failed him and that he was about to cancel their plans.

'Fighting fit, Amelie, but there is something I must attend to before we leave. In the cemetery.'

'The cemetery!' Mel blurted out.

'Yes. A regrettable business.' He sounded indignant. 'Some joker has been in there with a tin of paint and defaced several graves.'

'How vile! Is there much damage?'

'Enough to warrant concern. My parents' grave has borne the brunt of this scandalous attack.'

'Oh dear! What are you going to do?'

'Clean up. Before we go out. We must postpone our departure for an hour or so. My apologies, Amelie!'

An hour lost! The day's capital depreciating. Mel was experiencing the chagrin of an investor powerless to stop a slide on the stock market.

'I'll come up and help you,' she said quickly. Needless to say, she was curious to know exactly what had happened. Especially to the Tarrant Jones's grave. 'I'll walk up,' she continued, 'in a few minutes.'

'Bless you! Are you acquainted with the grave?'

'Not really,' she lied. ' Where is it?'

Piers gave explicit directions, to which Mel pretended to listen, and asked her to bring some steel wool if she had any. He wasn't quite sure what would be needed but had assembled a cleaning kit.

'I'll see you soon,' he said, in a business-like voice, and rang off.

Mel searched for steel wool. Her thoughts fluttering like a venetian blind in the wind. She tried to quell the disturbance while foraging in the cupboard under the kitchen sink. Eventually she located some Brillo pads.

'It's out you are, Mrs Bishop, is it?' enquired Maidie who had followed her into the kitchen.

'I'm just going, Maidie,' Mel answered as she stood up and shut the cupboard doors.

'There's nice,' said Maidie in a mystified voice as she caught sight of the Brillo pads.

'Partly business and partly pleasure,' said Mel by way of explanation. 'I shall be out for lunch, so will you lock up as usual and note any telephone messages on the pad?'

'Very good. Have a nice time mind. Take care now.'

Mel made her escape. Poor Maidie! She would spend the rest of the morning wondering why on earth her employer was going out to lunch accompanied by a packet of Brillo pads. Mel hoped she had not looked too guilty. She had been made to feel like a shoplifter!

On this Wednesday, the weather had a markedly different aspect from the thick damp greyness of that day years earlier when Mrs T J had first wheedled her way into Mel's life. She did not hurry. Her longing to have Piers to herself had suffered a setback and she was intensely aggravated with the old woman for interfering yet again. She fervently hoped that on this day, of all days, she and Piers would not be required to spend too much of their time pacifying her. It must be a coincidence, this paint on the grave, but by now Mel was so sensitive to the oblique connotations of that beastly poem that this latest threat could not be minimised. Shivering slightly, she quickened her pace up the hill. To allow the old girl to spoil the day would be to concede victory. There was still some fight left in Mel... indeed, if it became necessary, she was prepared to challenge her for her son!

Piers's car was parked outside the main gates. The nearside door was unlocked and Mel deposited her cardigan in the back where she was pleased to see a picnic basket, cushions, and a rug. This looked promising. Slowly she retraced her steps along the path to the grave, an excursion she had been careful to avoid over the years on the handful of occasions when duty had brought her to the cemetery.

Piers was kneeling on the grass verge to the left of the grave, rubbing away at the upper section of the tombstone which, as Mel could now see, had been defaced with unsightly blood red smudges. She drew nearer and recognised that the blobs were crudely painted letters. It was very quiet. The burial ground was situated on a slope and there was activity around a grave away on the higher ground at the far side, but Tommo and his barrow were the only other signs of life. At this time of year, scavenging for an occasional stray dead flower must be one of his easier functions. Mel crept up behind Piers. He had his back to her and was absorbed in the job in hand. His neck, smooth and evenly tanned from hours of bending over plants in the St Mark's garden, could have been that of a strong young soldier. Adam's neck, lined and pitted in dark crisscross patterns could only belong to a middle-aged clergyman. For a moment she stood and watched him, sharing, unseen, in the fractious buffing of sandpaper on stone. Then, taking him by surprise, she whispered a hoarse, 'Boo!'

Startled, he turned, smiled with relief and stood up. 'Greetings Amelie. As you can see, I have turned stonemason this morning.'

Mel pointed at the graffiti. 'What is it all about?'

'Someone has considered it an amusement to go round with a paint-brush altering words by prefixing or suffixing letters and with this particular epitaph, he has had a field day.' He indicated the crude red symbols. Incongruously interspersed amongst the neatly carved words they resembled a set of pagan adornments. Mel had the uncanny sensation that she had seen something like it before and she was rapidly reaching the conclusion that it would be unwise to feign ignorance of the rhyme, in case, by some chance, Elizabeth had divulged the details of their recent tangle. So she proceeded with caution.

'Someone told me about the unusual inscription on your parents' grave. What is its history?'

'Mummy's idea,' he stated simply. 'She saw it on a tombstone in the churchyard at St David's. It made such an impression on her that she left instructions in her will for it to be inscribed on her own memorial.'

'I see,' said Mel - irritated that he still called her Mummy. It was alright in a woman of his age, but not in a man! She forced herself to read the verse - a superfluous exercise since the facsimile was housed in a showcase in her mind.

'I have removed an 's' a 've' and an 'ed' from line one,' he explained, as he picked up a rag and a bottle of white spirit, 'and I'm ready to pitch into the rest.'

'What was the effect of the additions?' she asked.

He stressed the differences. 'Remember friend**s** who'**ve** now pass**ed** by,' and teased, 'past tense, and plural! For scholars of English!'

Mel read out the next line. 'As you are now, so once was I.'

'There's no assault on that line, Amelie.'

'No, I wonder why not?'

'The words of the second half make it difficult to meddle.'

Mel thought about it, agreed, and then referred to the first line again. 'Whoever did that understands apostrophes!'

'That struck me, too,' he admitted. 'No dunce! I've a hunch that the culprit is some Queen's School upstart. An aggravating prank.'

'You may be right. Have you reported it?'

'No need Amelie,' he said, dampening the rag again, and kneeling down. 'The Council informed the Police and the matter is under investigation. They have taken photographs and made a thorough search for evidence. I received the all clear to clean up this morning.'

Mel wandered round to the other side of the grave. 'So it happened some time ago,' she reasoned.

'Three or four weeks, now,' he answered. 'Around the time I went up to see Monty.'

This was also the time that he had sent Mel roses, but she refrained from comment. Certainly it was all very weird and if the calendar factor was significant she might be forced to admit finally that a supernatural forced was at work and that Mummy had some kind of control over it. That was positively ridiculous! There must be an explanation. She waved an arm towards the surrounding area.

'What about graffiti on other graves, Piers?'

'Several instances. One or two nearby. Mostly adding an 's' at the start of 'In memory of' - not very erudite - and some more over by the far gate.' He stopped work and looked up with a twinkle:-

'There's a naughty one which turns 'Ever thoughtful, ever kind' into 'Never thoughtful, never kind', and another states that 'The seekers of the light are Done', and a third has 'Unsafe in the Farms of Jesus''.

Mel chuckled. This was better. Refreshing examples of supernatural humour! '

'A crazy game,' she pronounced. 'Scrabble in the churchyard. We don't have to clear up the others, too, do we?'

'No,' he reassured. 'I'll check on them in a week or two and do the decent thing if no-one else has coped.'

'The Council should do it,' Mel remarked petulantly, kneeling down to help. Piers muttered something about demarcation lines as she enquired, 'What's the best method?'

'I think it's oil paint' he conjectured, 'white spirit softens it and fine sandpaper seems to help; but if you've got Brillo pads there they might be just as efficacious.' He stood up and added, 'I'll fetch some water for you Amelie.'

'No! I'll go,' she said.

He handed her a bucket and she went over to the tap. The sooner this exercise was over, the better. What had compelled Piers to deal with it this morning? He could so easily have postponed it for a day and she would have known nothing of it. The damned grave had haunted her enough over the years! She carried the bucket back, bent over the top of the headstone and set to work vigorously, even angrily, on an 'm' and an 'e' tacked on to the 'so' in the third line. Piers, at a lower level, busy with the last line, was removing a 'd' from the end of 'Prepare'.

Suddenly, Mel stepped back, studied the crippled couplet while the additions were still visible and slowly enunciated it in its annotated form.

'As I am now, so**me** **y**outh shall be, Prepare**d** for death **s**andy follow me.'

She frowned. 'Does that make sense, Piers?'

He stopped rubbing, breathed hard, and admitted, 'It foxed me. But in fact, if you stop after 'death' and presume 'sandy' to be someone's name, then it does scan.'

'Surely that's a bit far-fetched,' she persisted.

He shrugged, dismissively, and remarked, 'Not worthy of analysis!'

He shook out the last drops of white spirit and found a fresh piece of sandpaper.

'A final onslaught, my Amelie. The hills are beckoning...'

Mel concentrated on the portions of granite which were still tinged with pink, ready to stop the moment Piers gave the word. The renovation was almost complete and it was a relief when he stood up, scuffed the gritty dust from his navy blue trousers and tucked his shirt back into the waistband. He stepped towards her, so that his left foot was actually on the grave and stretched out his hand; their eyes met and he gave a small, ceremonial bow. In the enactment of this private, and unlikely scene, their hands stayed clasped until their arms stretched across the tombstone in a continuous horizontal line and temporarily obliterated the name of 'Euphemia Tarrant Jones'.

'Come, Amelie,' he said quietly. 'We have done that which could not be left undone...' He crossed himself, murmured, 'Requiescat in pace', and they turned from the place.

Mel retrieved her bag and helped gather up the cleaning materials. Cleansed, and purified, the grave was once more in near pristine condition. The corpse could 'rest in peace'. Or could it? What other tricks might it perform in the name of duty? What further whims must be placated before the son, and the woman who now cherished him, were free of its dictates...?

They walked through the cemetery towards the car, and silently Mel cursed. But to Piers she said with a sickly sweetness, 'I wish I had known your mother.'

'A very powerful woman, Amelie,' he commented. 'She would have admired you!'

Mel was prepared to make a gesture towards her. The idea appealed!

'The grave looks a bit cheerless,' she said. 'I'll take some flowers along sometime.'

Affectionately, he took hold of her arm with his free hand.

'Ever thoughtful, ever kind, my little Amelie,' he said.

On a hot summer afternoon a love affair can follow any one of several courses, and if, indeed, this was a love affair, and not just a fantasy willed into existence in the imagination, then it stood as good a chance as any other of finding a way that was agreeable. Would it be all that Mel hoped it would be? What should she expect or was there to be something she had not foreseen? Neither of them spoke as they got into the car, cleaned their hands with wet wipes, and fastened the seat belts. Piers looked briefly at a map before turning the key in the ignition and adjusting his wing mirror. They were away at last!

He had planned all the details with a perfectionist's care. Chosen a place for lunch which she could never have found herself, and waited on her with coarse pate, French bread, strawberries, and a bottle of Moet & Chandon which lay swathed in a poultice of newspaper and ice packs until he was ready to propose his prepared toast. Then he had raised his glass to her and said:-

'To the continuation of our mutual devotion, my Amelie.'

He had parked within easy walking distance and they had trundled the picnic equipment along a narrow path which etched its way round a ridge and climbed nonchalantly to a small summit. There, on this swollen hillock, ringed by ancient earthworks and comforted by centuries of grass, they surveyed their midday kingdom. Manicured fields, quiescent in the shimmering heat, faded in a long diminuendo towards cadences on the purple horizon. A train whispered along the valley. It was the noon dawdler to London, yet moved with the purposefulness of a kilometre-gobbling continental express. And when Mel saw it, she was reminded of her honeymoon in France, although on this day she did not wish to think about her husband. She leant against the slope of the neolithic ridge, savoured a generous sip of champagne, closed her eyes and offered her face to the sun. This was happiness...

'Are you comfortable, Amelie?' he asked.

'In paradise, Piers,' she replied. 'What an amazing view. A perfect choice for a favourite place!'

'I'm glad you approve,' he said prosaically.

She was disappointed. She was expecting more than a mere platitude.

'What does the ambience do for you?' she said provocatively.

He thought for a moment and then replied, 'Poetry is my ally. And the miracle of existence enhanced and confirmed!'

He had gone from one extreme to another, but, in the circumstances, she would encourage him. Perhaps he was itching to recite some ardent love poem...

'Quote something,' she invited. 'That fits the scene.'

He pondered possibilities while refilling their glasses. She felt his scrutiny and smiled her encouragement as he leant back next to her. When he spoke, his voice was quiet, even reverent, and in no way over-expressive.

'I have learned,' he began:-
'To look on nature, not as in the hour
Of thoughtless youth, but hearing oftentimes
The still, sad music of humanity,
Nor harsh, nor grating, though of ample power,
To chasten or subdue. And I have felt
A presence that disturbs me with the joy
Of elevated thoughts. A sense sublime
Of something far more deeply interfused,
Whose dwelling is the light of setting suns,
And the round ocean, and the living air,
And the blue sky, and in the mind of man.'

Mel was silent.

Eventually he asked whether she considered the choice appropriate and she nodded. She was unable to speak because the *'presence that disturbs'* in the quotation had activated something inside her that had to do with God and her conscience and she was momentarily confused.

213

Also she was not at all enthusiastic about the prospect of an afternoon of religious poetry: that had never been a part of the plan!

'More Elgar?' she trifled, mocking him.

He ignored the taunt.

'William Wordsworth, my Amelie. The only man who could have written such prose.'

'Ah,' she accepted. 'One of Seb's idols.'

'Yes, Seb appreciates Wordsworth,' he said. 'He called in at the week-end. He's into the war poets now and I've looked out several volumes for him for the coming holiday.'

'He'll be pleased,'she said sleepily. If the day was to yield nothing else, it had already been an insight into the special mix of poetry and nature which Piers and Seb found so mutually enjoyable

They dozed companionably for a while and then decided to return the picnic things to the car and to go for a walk. This time they branched off to the right where the terrain was shaded by columns of pines and the silence only disturbed by the snap of a twig underfoot or the cry of a sky-borne bird. After the heat, the quivering air was refreshing, walking was pleasant, and it was easy to stroll further than they had intended. They found it agreeable to hold hands...

Suddenly, she said, 'Piers, I'm sorry, but I must pee! Can we get away from the footpath?'

'A damsel in distress must be accommodated,' he said, smiling, 'and shall be. Don't worry, I'll keep guard.'

After he had kept guard, they went deeper into the forest until they came to a clearing where a long, wide shaft of sunlight penetrated a circle in the giraffe-like tree-tops and baked the ground with a continuous melting warmth.

Mel removed the cardigan from her shoulders, smoothed it on the ground and sat down.

'Tired?' he mused, tenderly.

'Not exactly!' She patted the fern covered ground beside her. 'Join me!'

He took his wallet and car keys out of his trouser pocket, unwound the jersey from round his waist, and sat down, clumsily, before piling his possessions neatly beside him. That is what he would do in his bedroom, she thought.

'It won't get stolen, Piers,' she remarked.

'What won't, Amelie?'

'Your wallet.'

He laughed. 'Of course not, but it gets in the way when I sit down. I'm actually happier with a jacket.'

'Well, you don't need a jacket today!'

'No, Amelie,' he said meekly, leaning back on his elbows and looking at her. 'Women manage things better – with handbags!'

Her own handbag, which she had been stupid to bring on the walk, lay untidily between them. He rescued it, wrapped the shoulder strap carefully round the bag itself, and then, with affected concentration, placed it alongside his own things.

'Women manage so many things so much better,' he repeated slowly.

'Like what?'

'Like everything! Families. Friendships. Relationships...'

He paused, reached for her left hand and examined it with the intensity of a consultant, before concluding with the words 'and love.'

He had waited, before pronouncing the final diagnosis, but at last he had spoken. Now anything was possible. He continued to study her hand.

'Your rings are very beautiful, Amelie,' he appraised, 'the same two that you wore when you first came to St Marks.'

'Really,' she said, surprised that he remembered such a detail. 'I think I would have worn my engagement ring on that occasion.'

He looked disconcerted and touched the ruby.

'Isn't this your engagement ring?'

'No, it isn't, actually.' She drew her hand away, took off Alastair's ring and handed it to him with the pride of someone who wants a treasured possession to be admired.

'It was a present from Alastair Green,' she said, 'for helping him when Adam was chaplain.'

'You mean *bishop* Alastair?'

'Yes.'

He held it up to the light, as she had done so many times, and appreciated the exquisite colour of the jewel and the rare setting. He was perplexed.

'You do not want for admirers, my Amelie,' he said thoughtfully.

215

'I worked jolly hard for that, Piers,' she protested. 'Sherry parties, lunch parties, teas... dinners...' His reaction troubled her. It was as though he had discovered something unfavourable, and nothing could be further from the truth. She lay back with her hands behind her head, pretending to doze. There was no point in making life more complex by detailing the history of the ring. She would wait for him to recover. It was still only four o'clock...

After a while, she began to count slowly to herself, partly for something to do, and partly to counteract the rapid beat of her heart. She could hear his breathing and sensed that he was looking at her. But she did not open her eyes. Not even when she felt his fingers caress her hair.

'Look at me, Amelie. Look at me and tell me that you must not love me and that I may not love you. Look at me!'

His voice was persuasive, almost angry, and she opened her eyes to find him leaning over her. He was semi-recumbent, on his right side, his torso supported by his right arm. She felt his knees against her hips.

'Tell me, Amelie,' he repeated. 'Say the words!'

She trembled with distress.

'I cannot tell you that, Piers, ever since that evening, nothing can be the same again. You know it too... Goodness knows, I've tried to control myself, but it isn't any good. Don't ask me to say such things...'

She lifted her head and tried to put her hands behind his neck in an attempt to pull him closer to her. 'Please, please. I ache to show you...'

But he wrenched away, violently, and she fell back, colliding with the ground. Wincing, she stemmed the stinging reflex tears with clenched fingers. He had not noticed the impact. He had turned away and buried his face in his hands.

Soon, licking his lips, his face glistening with sweat, he confronted her again. He was calmer.

'Amelie, listen to me! What happened on that evening was my fault. An error of judgement; an aberration; a brainstorm. Call it what you will. I was not master of myself. I prayed that what I told you and Adam later would help you to understand... Spare me from adding to the tragic devastation of my own life by destroying yours...'

Mel interrupted him:-

'You talk of devastation and destruction. If I am destroyed it will be because of my love for you. It wasn't just the other evening. You have

216

become a part of me - of the family. Look how we have encouraged your friendship with Seb. You're a substitute parent. He thinks more of you than of Adam...' She ran out of words. She sensed him slipping from her. He continued as though her interruption had not occurred.

'Where you are concerned, Amelie, I have known for too long that my inclination might overcome my conscience. The balance between the two is a finely drawn boundary line which may not be violated. I yearn to take you in my arms, and to be close to you. However, it is an incontrovertible fact that had I not forgotten myself the situation with which we are wrestling now, would never have arisen. And you, Amelie, would not have been caused pain... Because I love and admire you I am desperately concerned for your happiness. I will do almost anything to put it right...' The phrases which she had heard him utter at last reverberated in the stillness. His sincerity was unmistakeable.

'You love me. You yearn for me. If you will do anything, my darling, then kiss me,' she begged.

He waved aside her plea.

'Can we restore the status quo, my Amelie? To the marvellous, tranquil, friendship which has belonged to us for so many happy years. I ask you to try for this - for both our sakes.' He moved towards her again, and she allowed him to take hold of her hands, but a blur of tears prevented her from seeing anything.

'Beloved Amelie,' he said passionately. 'Everything forbids. We cannot hurt those closest to us. I cannot make myself an adulterer and you an adulteress...'

'We do not have to hurt anyone,' she sobbed. 'We don't even have to commit adultery as you so grandly put it. Just offer me the chance again - the one that I threw away so foolishly - the chance to show you...'

She was clutching at his hands and scratching his arms in a desperate attempt to mould him to her. 'Piers, my love. Please.'

He broke from her again and during the long black silence that followed, he averted his gaze from her distressed features and stared into the wooded depths beyond the clearing, while his hands toyed with a tattered fern.

'Adam,' he moaned, when he spoke again, 'think of what it would do to him. Charity forbids us even to contemplate actions which would spell out the ruination of his career. Headlines in newspapers, Amelie.

That is what it would mean. Everything that you and he have built together - shattered! You have told me how hard you have worked, ever since those days at Amsworth. Treasure the years of happiness and think of your family. A family whose life I have been so privileged to share. My family! I love you all, my Amelie!'

Anger was beginning to smoulder inside her. Piers the holy, Piers the preacher! Her tears evaporated. She would not allow him the pleasure of witnessing any more - sadistic beast! She dragged at him, forcing him to look at her. There was heat in her voice and her eyes blazed.

'You talk of Adam. My husband! What do you know of his neglect of me? When did I last come first in his life, ahead of his endless committees, confirmations, carols, and God knows bloody what! How often does he make love to me? Ask him! Look at him with fresh eyes and see him for what he is - a sanctimonious prig! His dreary career bores me! Why has Seb turned to you? Because, for the past ten years he has looked for a father and found a list of engagements. And now I've turned to you, God help me, because I want someone to care for me, laugh with me, and to see me for what I am - not just great Adam's charming wife. You have said 'my Amelie' so often. I am yours. You may take possession, don't you see. It has to be...'

He was listening to her now. She was showing him a new Amelie, a woman who swore and discredited her husband. Not quite the woman whom he had worshipped for so long. Up on a pedestal, the epitome of all that an accomplished wife and mother should be. This angry Amelie was more like his mother! And what about the association with Alastair Green? What had that meant to her? No doubt if he had thought of her sexually he had been too courteous to allow his imagination to run riot, and anyway, he was untutored in sexual matters, as they both knew. Now she was alone with him in this place. No longer the goddess: his for the asking - an attractive married woman awaiting her destruction...!

A silver-edged cloud sealed the gap above the tops of the pines and the air around cooled perceptibly. What was he thinking? Were the main events of his life unwinding in his mind as though from a fast-moving video tape? Was he in mental turmoil, and challenged, too, by the enforced celibacy from which his body had never escaped? Was it a mental as well as a physical release that he needed? If he did not make

218

it now, for the second time in his life, the chance might never again come his way...Could such an act be contained into an afternoon? Perhaps it could. Once. Not to be repeated. No offence to Adam. A gift from her, and a gift to her... Perhaps he would not need to be shown. Not anything at all.

He took her face between his hands...At first she assisted him, but the horror of the reality of the situation dawned upon her very quickly. His tongue and teeth lashed her mouth and neck and his powerful hands tore at her clothes.

'Stop, Piers. Stop! Let me show you,' she pleaded. But, straddled on the ground as she was, with Piers fumbling and forcing his way like some brutish beast, there was nothing that she could do. She struggled to breathe as she endured the humiliation of his crude assault, until she heard him gasp, triumphantly, 'No, I can't stop! I've waited over twenty years. Too many of them for you!'... And when the eye-shade became dislodged during the affray and he snatched it off, she found herself face to face with a monster and tasted the gruesome aspect of his dreadful disfigurement now saturated by her tears.

He rolled away from her. One arm lay across his face, and the other hand groped blindly with his trousers as he tried to neaten himself. Crumpled, flattened, and hysterical, she sobbed uncontrollably. He waited until she was quiet and then said simply,

''I thought that was what you wanted...'

'I did,' she moaned, in a voice bereft of animation. 'I did. But not like that...'

Eventually his chivalry returned, and he reached out to touch her.

'I am truly sorry, Amelie,' he said gently. 'Can you forget! It is over. It did not happen to you. Only to me. I shall always be grateful...'

The illusion was over. Ravaged, she sat up, dried her face on her skirt, and surveyed him with contempt.

'Find your eye patch,' she said coldly.

****

The shadows lengthened. It was time to return to the car.

'We must get back to our ordinary world,' he said. 'Back to the Festival! We shall have forgotten by then, Amelie.'

Miserably, she shook her head, asking herself as she dragged her feet along the forest path, why, when everything had been so perfect, it had to end like this? She was no longer angry. She was glad now that she had not spat invective at him, indeed she realised that she had probably overstepped the mark in shouting at him about Adam. She would have preferred to hide this side of herself from him. It could not have helped. It might have hindered! She began to see that her persuasive behaviour might have upset him. How else could she account for his incomprehensible insensitivity, and the cruel castration of their tender relationship. Laboriously, as they drew nearer to the car, she began to see that all might not be lost, and, tentatively, but with a rebirth of excitement, she began to formulate a plan. This time, there would be no mistake.

When they reached the 'Public Footpath' notice, a stone's throw from the car, he put his hand on her shoulder, and tilted her face upwards, so that he looked into her eyes for the first time since leaving the copse. His expression was the one she had come to know through her love for him, and she managed a thin, wan smile.

'You will not remember, Amelie!' he ordered.

'I shall remember,' she said.

'But how will you remember?'

'I shall remember it as an interlude,' she said almost briskly.

They opened the doors of the car, brushed the dried humus and dust from each others' backs, tidied their appearances, and drove off.

Being behind the steering wheel had the effect of loosening his tongue. He was like someone after an accident, who, when the initial shock is past, anxiously mulls over every tiny detail. Mel, busy with her own thoughts, played out the role of listener. He was not heading for home, so there was still time to salvage something from the evening, and despite what had happened, she was beginning to understand certain things more clearly. For example, his rough behaviour on this afternoon had been perfectly in keeping with the brute force which had excited her on that fateful evening, and once she realised this she began to be able to regard the whole terrible episode as more of a disappointment than a desecration. She began to think about the future and to plan for another time, and another place. The score was even now, one game all, and in the next encounter she would teach him to subdue that frenzied animal passion and to substitute for it the strange delights of a slow caressing love. Only then would today's 'interlude' be replaced by a beautiful consummation worthy of their devotion!

He was solicitous, and anxious to ascertain that she was not 'damaged' as he put it. He realised how thoughtless he had been. Indeed, deep down, he had a nagging suspicion that what he had done could be interpreted as rape. He had read about such things, of course, but never allowed himself to dwell on the details. He had to satisfy himself, too, that in his mad moment of frolic, he had not fathered anther child! She reassured him and taunted him for not knowing about something called a 'coil'. He had missed out on too much in his life. Sometimes, latterly, it had seemed like a huge empty house in which only a couple of rooms and the bathroom were ever used. His feelings for her had been pure affection. He hoped he had not misled her. He had never meant to. He loved Adam, Sebastian, and Ruth, too, he reiterated. Each in a different way.

She questioned whether he hadn't, in fact, misled her, and asked,

'What was I meant to read into your bunch of roses?'

'Exactly what I wrote, Amelie,' he replied.

'Then I read aright,' she murmured.

He sandwiched her hand on the gear lever again, partly to reassure her, and partly to show her that things had not changed all that much since yesterday. She was not averse to the contact. She was biding her time. It was not, after all, that he did not love her. He loved them all!

He took her to a little restaurant, where outsize pepper mills stood on blue and white checked tablecloths. The whitebait and lobster were 'out of this world' so he said, and the piquancy of the home-made lemon sorbet refreshed her mouth and made her feel clean again. Before they left they stood and watched the bright red-orange sphere that was the sun sink beneath a backdrop of vivid, purple-capped, cloud mountains. He drove back at speed until they saw the lights of the town twinkling in the valley below and the abbey, transformed by floodlights, a shining architectural monarch of the night. Then he pulled into a lay-by, undid his seat belt, and turned towards her.

'It has been a long day, Amelie.'

'Yes,' she said.

'We have learned things about each other that we did not know before.'

'Yes,' she repeated.

221

'We have broken the seventh commandment!'

'The seventh is it?' she said.

'Where do we go from here, Amelie?' he asked, seeking some response from her.

'Take me to see Monty,' she ventured.

The suggestion surprised him, although he had known earlier that she wanted him to take her ... If it would help then he must humour her. Above all, as he explained, he felt that he needed some respite. Maybe he could postpone seeing Monty for a few weeks and thus give himself time to come to terms with the fix in which he had landed.

'If you take me one day soon,' she continued, 'then I can take Adam later on when we go to Scotland. We both want to see him. After all, he is a part of the family, too...'

He winced. This was not to his liking, this full exposure of Monty, but perhaps he owed her something in the way of commitment, however tenuous, or temporary.

'Sometime after the Festival, then,' he agreed. 'I'll arrange it, and let you know.'

'It will be easy to square with Adam,' she said, 'but what about Ruth and Seb; they will be home for the holidays after the Festival and Ruth's music course?'

He did not reply immediately but finally said, 'If it's unavoidable you will have to explain. It is the price I must pay - but with a heavy heart. I treasure the especial regard which Sebastian has for me and I fear it may colour his view.'

'He is seventeen,' she said, drily. 'What if he were to learn the truth about today?'

In the darkness his face contorted with grief.

'Amelie,' he said, horrified, 'that is a price beyond payment! He must be protected from this knowledge for ever. And will be. Always. I promise you.'

The emotion in his voice was unmistakeable and Mel realised, with an ice-cold insight, that Ruth could after all, be right. It seemed that he might love Sebastian with a love more passionate than anything he had ever felt for her...

'Don't fret, Piers,' she said. 'I shall never tell him... unless,' and she realised the power of her hold over him as she spoke, 'unless you forget to take me to see Monty.'

'I won't forget,' he said quickly. 'I promise.'

He began to switch on the ignition and the lights, but she restrained him, undid her own seat belt, and drew his face towards her as she had tried to do earlier in the day. And at last she kissed him as she had longed to do, secretly, for so many weeks. And although it was pleasurable, and he appreciated being initiated into the way in which lips and tongues could behave, there was something a little stale about it for both of them, which tasted of old wine.

He drove through the archway and up to the front door. They got out of the car. She had the door key ready in her hand and hurried up the steps. He stood on the paving below her.

'Love which ends in tears is madness, my Amelie,' he offered. 'Love must have laughter.' She shrugged, indifferently, and thanked him for the day. By the time he had turned the car, the front door was shut. She went straight upstairs, drew the curtains, undressed mechanically, and sank into a warm bath. Her mind was a void. She was like someone who has suffered a long, unpredictable illness; barely strong enough to face the convalescence. Once she was in bed, and able to relax, she might summon the energy to consider the feverish fluctuations and emotional emergencies of this long, critical day.

Clean and cool, in a favourite nightdress, she sat on the bed filing her nails. She was desperately tired, and yet she would have liked someone to talk to. She half expected to see Adam propped up by pillows, in his familiar late night pose, extracting a few last pennyworth of value from the newspaper. Momentarily she had forgotten where he was and then she recalled that he would be back tomorrow. She switched off the lights, opened the curtains, and slipped between the sheets. It seemed more like fourteen weeks than fourteen hours since the morning walk to the cemetery for a tryst by a tombstone splashed with red. Now she remembered where she had seen something like it before. It had been on the day that Felix died. Blood red words on a white stone dancing in front of her eyes; and this morning blood red letters on dappled marble making nonsense out of sense. And Piers, urging that old mother of his to rest in peace. What price her peace, now, after her son's latest escapade in the heat of the afternoon?

Mel turned over, and stretched her limbs across the cool, dark emptiness that was usually Adam. She forced herself to think about the day and came to the conclusion that in the complex game that she and

Piers were playing, she had been outclassed by his sophistry and ambivalence. Restless, lonely, and frightened, she relived the violent details of his crude possession of her and tried to reconcile them with the fantasies of the past weeks. Where had it gone wrong? So much was good, and yet the day had misfired. Had they tried too hard and expected too much? Why was he not still with her? It would have been so easy, providing he had crept out early enough to avoid bumping into the milkman! She racked her brains. After their escape from that dreadful grave they had been so happy. The picnic was perfect! So when did it start to crumble?

Suddenly, in a frenzied, agonising, panic which sent fluxions of blood racing into every vein and artery, she sat up, switched on the bed side light and staggered to the dressing table. The ring. Alastair's ring. It was then! After she had given it to Piers! Where was it now? Like a demonic burglar, she rifled her handbag, tore open drawers, spilt jewellery on to the bed, rushed to the bathroom, and crawled all over the floor in case she had inadvertently dropped it. She could not recall replacing it on her finger after removing it, and now, unless he had absent-mindedly pocketed it, then the ring must still be lying somewhere in that place, tumbled away, and maybe lost forever. She was distraught. Sobbing bitterly, and clutching the small sad blue velvet box, she fell on to the bed. Desperately she tried to summon the well-mannered prayer voice, but since this morning, the voices had gone strangely quiet. So she was driven to shout the words aloud, between her sobs, over and over again, and she cried out many times, pleading that they would find the ring, when they looked for it, on the morrow...

After a sleepless night, Mel telephoned Piers early the following morning and hung on anxiously while he emptied his trouser pockets, pulled out each lining, and detailed the contents as though to emphasise their neutrality. There was a small hole in one of them, he said. Her heart sank. He supposed the ring might just have fallen through. Certainly they couldn't dismiss the possibility, although he didn't think he had put it in his pocket. He was sure he gave it back to her! He offered to drive her back to the place to hunt for it, but she had already calculated that it would not be possible to cover the two journeys, negotiate the forest walk both ways, make a thorough search, and be back in time for her to open the Christian Aid lunch. So he agreed to go on his own, straight after breakfast, and would let her know the outcome as soon as he got back. She begged him to keep his eye open - to scour all likely places, and to leave no blade of grass undisturbed. If, by chance, he had put it with his jersey and the other things, and it had fallen, unnoticed, to the ground, then there was every hope that it was still there, cosseted by a friendly fern. Unless it had been found by a forest prowler, or plucked away by a pecking magpie! He tried to reassure her. He was confident that he would find it. He would even phone the restaurant! But in her heart, she believed she knew the worst already. She had faced it since that agonising moment of realisation the previous night.

When he came to tell her, late in the afternoon, having let himself in, she was in the garden. He walked slowly across the grass, every gesture registering sympathy. Unable to speak, now that all hope had faded, she collapsed on to him. Lovingly he took her into Backs View and sat with her on the sofa endeavouring to console her. Through her grief, she saw that his eye, and cheek, were wet with his own tears, and she pulled herself together because she remembered, from his description on that fateful evening, what terrible things this would do to him.

'My dear,' she choked, 'please don't.'

'But my Amelie... If we had not gone there, yesterday... this would never have happened...'

'No recriminations, Piers. There is nothing that anyone can do.'

'It is very special to you, Amelie, this ring, is it not?' He was becoming visibly more distressed.

'Very special. But please don't blame yourself. I should never have taken it off.'

Mel offered him her handkerchief, but suddenly, he was trembling so violently, that he was unable to help himself. As she dried his tears, she had the extraordinary feeling that the perspective of their relationship had shifted, and that, for the first time, they were seeing each other stripped bare of extraneous extravagance, artifice, or stilted emotion. He, too, sensed this change and they stayed together on the sofa, close enough to be aware of the warmth of each others' bodies. It was some time before either of them spoke. Then he murmured:-

'You could show me now, my beloved Amelie. I am ready to learn...'

She stroked his hair, as a mother might stroke that of her young son.

'I could! But I am not going to,' she said quietly. 'We will wait until we go to see Monty!'

'I love you all so much, Amelie,' he said, wearily. 'I cannot bear to see you unhappy.'

'I believe you,' she whispered.

Over a cup of tea they discussed the ring objectively. He pressed her to tell Adam that she had lost it somewhere and to claim on the relevant insurance policy. But there was no way of doing this without resorting to lies about the circumstances, and when he suggested she could say that she had gone for a walk in the country, she pointed out that it was very unlikely that she would have removed it in that situation, let alone lose it! They debated going to the police. Here again, it would be difficult to report the details without eyebrows being raised and embarrassing questions asked. Piers did offer to make enquiries to see whether it had been handed in, but neither of them held out much hope.

'I don't know what I shall say, ultimately,' she admitted, 'to Adam - or Alastair!'

The thought of telling either of them appalled her ''I will just have to keep it to myself and let things take their course...'

'Surely Adam will notice, Amelie,' exclaimed Piers.

'How little you know about husbands, my dearest,' she said as she looked at her watch and he took the hint that it was time for him to go.

'Yours is on his way back, eh, Amelie,' he surmised.

She nodded.

'And will he want to know what you have been up to during his absence?'

'I doubt it,' she said.

At the front door Piers asked whether Sebastian would be home for the concert. When he knew that he wouldn't, he said that he would be in touch with him about holiday walks and poetry when he broke up. Mel opened the door and reminded him to remember their trip too. He took her hands and kissed them, tenderly, one after the other. Then he pushed the half- open door to, with a foot, took her in his arms, and kissed her in the way that she had demonstrated the previous evening; a long, lingering, passionate embrace which left her, once more, totally under his spell.

'I always keep my promises,' he said. He opened the door again and disappeared.

An hour later, Mel walked to the station. Members of the town band, on their way to a sweaty rehearsal in the Memorial Hall acknowledged her as she dodged out of the way of euphoniums and trombones. 'Evenin', Mrs Ellis, ma'am!' She responded to each of them with her serene episcopal smile and a comment about the lovely weather. It would be a bore if Adam had missed the early train. She would have to turn out again later, or order him a taxi. Piers would have fetched him! Why hadn't she suggested it? She chatted up the ticket collector, admired his tubs of lobelia-encircled geraniums, crossed the bridge and sat, waiting on the platform. Her thoughts sifted themselves into two heaps. The first contained permitted elements from the past three days; ones that she would share with Adam later. These included an account of the lunch, which had been a success (and at which she had been pleased to see Ellen), the problems over the cars, and the fact that she had asked Piers to chauffeur her to the Centre. The second heap was taboo! It was already fetid inside her, a fermenting compost of guilt, activated, no doubt, by the prospect of Adam's imminent arrival. The loss of the ring had filled her with heaviness and this particular ingredient was creating maximum turmoil. The ring was her talisman. It protected her. She feared that the irreplaceable bonus points which it represented may have been forfeited alongside it, at the very moment of its loss, and that the rest of her life would be counterfeit.

Like a giant caterpillar the train curved into the station. Adam was waiting by a door, ready to jump out.

'Hello darling,' he said cheerfully. 'I hope you didn't need the big car. I went off with the keys in my pocket!'

'I know,' she said, kissing him on the cheek. 'It has caused complications! Do you want to walk or get a taxi?'

Chapter XIII

FESTIVAL

They had been discussing it and planning for so long that, when the Festival finally took place, Mel half expected it to be an anti-climax. After balmy weeks of dependable sunshine, a question mark hung over the weather. Charts indicated increasing frontal disturbance and ominous, muffled, rolls of thunder sounded in the distance, like rumbles from a battlefield. However, fey floral groups arrived in estate cars filled with flowers and foliage, a consignment of uncomfortable slatted chairs was unfolded and disciplined into neat rows across the Abbey floor spaces, strong mallet-swinging roisterers assembled the tea marquee and bolted together swing boats and a helter skelter, ready for the Fete on Saturday afternoon, and policemen brought notices, flashing lights, and deterrent cones which they were prepared to place almost anywhere providing someone asked them.

Piers, who had established a Festival HQ in the vicarage, strode resolutely around directing operations, and occasionally popped into the Tower House to report progress, leave a message, or cadge a cup of coffee. More than a week had passed since the breaking of the seventh commandment, and no further opportunity had presented itself for him and Mel to spend more than a few minutes together. But she did have a chance to tell him that Adam had been perfectly amenable when she had broached the idea of her and Piers going to see Monty, and had, indeed, seemed enthusiastic!

The shadow of the lost ring never left her. Like a crippled limb, it was there when she went to sleep at night, and when she woke up in the morning. She dreaded the day when an explanation would become

228

imperative. Ruth was bound to notice, eventually, and then the questions would begin until the time came when she could prevaricate no longer. The irony of the tragedy was the near miraculous way in which it had brought her and Piers to such affinity and understanding on the Thursday afternoon before Adam returned. Suspended in a state of calm, they could wait, patiently, for whatever was to come. In her own mind Mel was certain that they were now committed in a way that they had never been before. She behaved with enthusiastic cheerfulness as she prepared for the rigours of the weekend. Everything must be done to guarantee the houseful of guests an enjoyable stay and she also had to ensure that Ruth would be adequately protected, fed on a diet of grapefruit and glucose, and excused from social commitments until after the concert. Then she would let her hair down and have a real ball!

Hester was the first to arrive on the Friday afternoon. She chugged into the courtyard in her wheezy old Triumph after four hours on the road, and, scatty as ever, did not draw breath until Ruth, Vivien and Diana turned up in the evening. Ever since Adam's time as bishop's chaplain, she had worshipped Alastair and she was as excited as a teenage pop fan at the prospect of seeing him again over the weekend. She had knitted him a pullover, baked a batch of mince pies, and brewed some sloe gin.

'Don't I get one of those, Hester?' teased Adam, surveying the bottle covetously.

Hester was always definite. 'Not this time, Adam. But Mel, there, could do with some of the mince pies. She's too thin. What's wrong with her?'

Sucking his pipe, Adam studied his wife. 'Nothing so far as I know,' he said, 'apart from a headache a while ago.'

'I'm fine,' said Mel.

'You're not,' persisted Hester. 'You men are all alike, Adam. A woman's got to grow green fungus or come out in stripes before you notice!'

She eyed her niece closely.

'Are you prescribing Sanatogen again?' Mel queried, with the submission of a dutiful relation.

'Stout will do you more good at your age. You can't be too careful. Your mother wilted around fifty.'

Adam rallied to Mel's defence. 'Come, come, Hester. Mel's barely past forty!'

'White around the gills,' she said. 'Something's amiss. But I can't put my finger on it.'

'If midsummer mince pies will revitalise Alastair, I'll eat a few with pleasure,' Mel capitulated. 'Does he really like them that much?'

'Surely you remember that time I spent Christmas with you in The Close and he ate seven on Boxing Day!'

They all laughed. Whenever Mel laughed now, she remembered that 'love must have laughter!'.

As soon as Ruth and Vivien arrived, they disappeared to run through the cadenzas and get the feel of the abbey acoustics. Fortunately Diana and Hester seemed to get on well together. Hester's bluff good humour resembled Hannah's, although she was quicker to impose limits. They were both equally good with strangers and had the capacity to draw them out and make them feel wanted. Diana was very appreciative of this second dose of Tower House hospitality, and Mel (having rejected Hannah's offer of a 'bunk' for her) was grateful to have her there to help with Vivien whom she obviously knew well. Nothing about Vivien mattered except her face. The rest of her was frugal and nondescript. If one was asked to describe her hair, or clothes, it would be impossible. She cared about neither, and lived on a diet of milk, raw apple, cheese, and grated carrot. But her face, with its craggy bone structure and deep set fanatical eyes was like an animated sculpture, purpose built to monitor the emotional response to every phrase of music. Ruth recognised her fortune in having a mentor who made a habit of attending either a rehearsal, or the performance, of any concert at which one of her pupils was playing a particular concerto for the first time. It was immensely supportive and kept students on their toes.

On Festival Saturday morning the weather was stickily oppressive and the town steeped in a thundery mist. When the phone rang, soon after eight, Adam answered. It was Piers with messages for Ruth. Could she be in the abbey sharp at two thirty because the concerto would be rehearsed first, and if she wanted to practice meanwhile it would have to be before ten. He hoped she would not mind a couple of 'flower ladies' wandering round to check the displays and replenish water levels.

'Let me speak to him,' Mel signalled. Adam mentioned that he would have a word with The Almighty about the weather – and then handed her the receiver.

'Piers?'

'Amelie.'

'Just to say we hope to see you at the party here this evening. After the concert.'

'Delighted, Amelie. I shall look forward to it.'

'Good luck with everything. I'm sure the day will go well.'

'My compliments to Ruth. The concert will be splendid.'

'We hope so!'

'Until this evening, Amelie.'

'Yes. Goodbye.' It wasn't easy to talk to Piers with Adam in the room. Mel wanted to tell him that she loved him.

She went upstairs to wake Ruth, taking her a cup of coffee and half a grapefruit. Ruth groaned when Mel said she would have to get up now if she wanted to practise before crowds poured into the abbey to view the flowers.

'I'll go and play some scales,' she yawned. 'Viv won't approve. One has to conserve one's energy for the performance.'

Mel told her that no one else was up yet and asked when her friends would be putting in an appearance. Six o'clock, she hoped. They were coming in a minibus.

'How many of them?'

'Eight! Is there enough food?'

'Stacks,' her mother assured her.

Ruth wanted to know who was coming to the party afterwards.

'Everyone here, including Alastair whom Daddy will fetch this afternoon. All the obvious people connected with the Festival - plus James Adler, Hannah and Giles, the Davidsons, Ellen, maybe Elizabeth, curates John and Edward, and anyone James decides to bring from the orchestra.'

She sat up in bed and started to eat the grapefruit. 'That man isn't coming is he?' she said.

'Which man?'

'Your boyfriend!'

'Oh Ruth,' Mel protested, 'don't call him that! Of course he's coming. He's run the Festival since Felix died.'

'Sending you roses,' she said scornfully. 'He'd like to be your boyfriend, you know.'

'Don't be so silly.'

Ruth shrugged and drank her coffee. 'Thanks for the breakfast. I'd better get up if I'm going to the abbey.

Mel got up from the edge of the bed and stood looking at her. Why did she so dislike Piers? It vexed her!

'He sent his compliments to you,' she said.

'He can keep them,' retorted Ruth as she tugged off her nightdress. It was some time since Mel had seen her undressed. She had a perfect figure and was stunningly attractive: she would look ravishing in her flowing apricot taffeta dress this evening. Mel wondered idly, as mothers do, whether any one of the eight supporters arriving in the minibus would turn out to be Ruth's 'boyfriend'! Her daughter's antagonism to Piers must be something to do with feminine pique. For the past few years she had distanced herself from him and was consequently on the defensive whenever they met. This had bred a tactical aloofness in Piers which probably hurt Ruth's pride. However, Mel could not have a difference of opinion with her at this moment; nothing must throw her today!

She went downstairs to sort out breakfast for her guests, thankful to discover that Maidie was already laying the table and brewing a large pot of coffee.

Mel was relieved when the morning and first part of the afternoon were over. She had imagined herself trailing round the sideshows with a party of retainers, like a courier with a group of tourists, but when it came to it she and Adam were able to go round early, and quickly, and escape after a minimal appearance. Hester gave them a 'sub' for raffle tickets and opted for an early afternoon nap so that she would be fresh for the drive with Adam to fetch Alastair. Viv and Ruth relaxed and prepared themselves mentally, after the rehearsal, and Diana, who had spent the morning assisting with the preparations for the late evening fork supper, decided to do her own thing in the town. Although it was very sultry the rain held off, but it was a day when headaches threatened and Mel was glad of the respite which the middle of the afternoon afforded.

The Green thronged with people. The band played, away in the western corner, and the coconut shy and lucky dip did big business.

Colourful balloons floated obligingly up into the grey heat and headed for some unspecified destination. Someone would win a prize for the distance drifted, providing the label was posted back! Boys from Queens won bottles of wine and sherry on the bottle stall and hid them under their blazers, and small children queued excitedly for rides on equable donkeys. Everyone was pleased, and no one more so than Piers. Adam and Mel congratulated him when they met by the balloon stand.

'It's the least we can do for Felix,' he had said, modestly. 'People have rallied round magnificently.' Then he had rushed away to cope with a crisis in the tea tent.

'See you later,' Mel called after him and he acknowledged them with a backward wave.

Mel was nervous that Alastair might notice that she was not wearing the ring, because, over the years, she had made a point of doing so whenever she saw him. Not that he had ever referred to it, and she did not really expect him to comment this weekend. Even so, she knew that she was going to feel uncomfortable in his presence. If only she hadn't lost it...

They were sitting round the kitchen table having tea when he came in on Hester's arm.

'Mel,' he said, warmly, 'how lovely to see you, and Ruth,' he held out his arms, 'my adopted granddaughter, how are you?'

He kissed them affectionately. They introduced him to Vivien and plied him with tea and scones.

'This is a real treat,' he said. 'I have so looked forward to it.'

He meant every word, too. He was an old man now. The years of distinction had been discarded like a well-worn overcoat. Yet goodness and dignity still emanated from him, and even Ruth's friends, when they drifted in later, realised that he was somebody very special.

'We've put you in Seb's room, Alastair,' said Mel, 'I hope you'll be comfortable.'

'You'll find some goodies waiting for you,' prattled Hester.

Ruth would be embarrassed by this! Hester treating Alastair as though he was a little boy! But Alastair was delighted at the prospect of 'goodies'!

'You spoil me, Hester,' he protested. 'Like the rest of this marvellous family.'

'Where's Diana?' enquired Adam, noticing that she was not with them.

'She wanted to look round the town,' answered Mel, 'she'll be back soon.'

'The shops will be shut by now.'

'She's probably gone for a walk, or into the abbey to look at the flowers. I expect the rest of the rehearsal is over.'

'Not if they're competing with your town band,' said Vivien blandly.

Diana came in soon afterwards. She looked flushed, as though she had been hurrying.

'I'm so sorry to be late,' she apologised, after being introduced to Alastair. 'I'm afraid I've been completely carried away by this historic town. I've walked miles! How fortunate you are to live in such a beautiful place!'

'You raved about it when you came before,' said Vivien drily.

Ruth was looking pale. She needed to be alone, but Mel suspected that she was waiting around to welcome her college friends and was glad for her sake when they arrived. Suddenly the normally sedate Tower House was bustling with cheerful young people, and the ground floor took on the aspect of a camp site as they heaped their gear into the front hall.

'Ruth will sort you all out after the concert,' Mel explained, 'meanwhile, come and have a cup of tea. Or would you prefer coffee?'

Most of them preferred coffee.

On the rare occasions when the Abbey became a concert hall, it was surprisingly easy to forget its true function, unless you happened to be unfortunate enough to find yourself stuck behind a pillar. On this evening the rows of festive dresses, alternating with dinner jackets and dark suits, the loud hum of conversation, and the magnificent flower arrangements, strategically placed wherever one cared to look, all helped to create effective camouflage. Boys from the school, smart in their suits, showed ticket holders to their seats. There was a generous sprinkling of the middle-aged and elderly from the county, many of whose homes Adam and Mel had visited socially, although she could remember very few names; and a chain-bedecked mayor and party were formally escorted to a reserved pew at the front. The Ellis family and guests, too, had a row of reserved seats and in so prominent a position that the ethnic/scruffy aspect of some of Ruth's friends doubtless caused a number of unchristian comments! Piers was here, there and everywhere. Sorting out seating problems, checking lights, talking to out-of-town folk who recognised him, and tidying the seats and stands for the orchestra. His dinner jacket had seen better days, but he still looked distinguished. When he paused for a brief word with Adam, Mel indicated that there was room for him in the pew, alongside Alastair, Hester, Vivien and Diana, but he shook his head and frowned slightly and Mel realised that she had been stupid. He seemed a little distraught. He had a lot on his mind. He was anxious that the evening should go without a hitch.

The members of the orchestra filed in, and the quiet reverence of the building reasserted itself. Piers came to the pew for a second time and escorted Adam to the lectern. He announced that 'applause will be welcome' and then asked the audience to stand for the Right Reverend Bishop Ellis to lead them in prayer. Mercifully Adam had a suitable offering about 'God's gift of music' tucked away in his memory. Mel saw them standing there together, the two men in her life. The one that she had once loved, and the one that she loved now. She felt Alastair's benevolent presence at her side - and she was aghast at the enormity of what she had done...!

****

There were no hitches. It was an unforgettable evening. Ruth's playing, especially in the haunting slow movement where the lyrical, ghost-like quality of her tone captured the audience, held them spellbound. She looked right and she sounded right. They were justly proud of her. Even Vivien shouted 'bravo' at the end! As she explained later, you can be a top teacher, and coach top talent, but that does not ensure that your pupils will measure up under pressure and here, on her home ground, Ruth was under immense pressure. No one had ever suggested that she was a prodigy; she was a sensitive, accomplished performer who had complimented a one-tenth quota of genius with the necessary nine-tenths of dedication. Adam was as thrilled as Mel was. He even tried to squeeze her hand at one point. Maybe he had forgotten that he was in the abbey!

They came out humming the themes from the New World Symphony, the only other item in the programme. The rain, which had threatened all day, was beginning to fall and litter left on The Green after the fete fluttered restlessly. They hurried back to the Tower House where Maidie, who had laid out the food during their absence, was waiting to hand round the wine – a ritual Seb would have undertaken had he been there. Ruth, reasonably happy with her performance, was able to relax quickly and enjoy being the centre of attention. People piled their plates with cold curried chicken and appetising salads and wandered from room to room before settling down to eat next to a congenial neighbour. Mel pushed the curates into Backs View where the young musicians were congregating, and made sure that Vivien had found something that she could eat. Remembering Ellen, and hoping that she wasn't stranded, she found her in the drawing room, balancing a plate self-consciously on her knees and attempting to converse with Diana between polite mouthfuls. They did not seem to be on the same wavelength. Either Diana had not explained that her father and Felix had known each other, and that she had been at the funeral, or Ellen, flustered by this total stranger, simply had not listened. Mel rescued them from a somewhat angular conversation by asking Ellen whether she had decided what to do with the cottage and was surprised to learn that she had made up her mind to live in it. She encouraged her to elaborate. 'Do you know Wales?' Ellen was saying to Diana, as Mel moved on just in time to hear Diana reply, with a laugh which would hurt Ellen, 'It's rather a big place to know, Mrs Hughes...' Poor Ellen! Mel wanted to protect her. She was safe with most of them because they knew her limitations, but a woman like Diana was far too clever. As Mel passed Adam she intimated that it would be a good idea to retrieve Diana, and send Mary or Hannah to talk to Ellen. He glanced across the room, surprised. He, too, would have expected them to be talking earnestly about Felix.

Hannah pushed her way through to Mel.

'Great evening, ducky. Ruth was terrific!'

'It went well, Hannah, didn't it.'

'Bloody well. She's a smart girl! Nice to see Diana here again,' she continued, 'who's the one that looks like Dracula?'

'Ssh, Hannah,' cautioned Mel. 'That's Vivien Green, Ruth's professor!'

'Oh Gawd!' she said. 'By the way, message for you from old Piers. He's missing out on this 'jolly'.'

Mel was dumbfounded! 'Why? He said he was coming!'

'Don't know, ducky. Didn't say. Caught me on the way out. Said he couldn't make it and sent his apologies! Probably too tired!'

Hester interrupted, fussing. 'Alastair wants to make a speech,' she said. 'Is that alright?'

'I expect so,' Mel said abstractedly. She was completely thrown. She had been looking forward to talking to him, albeit in public, and now he wasn't coming. She could not bear it. What had happened?

Adam brought her a glass of wine. 'Alastair's going to propose a toast to Ruth, darling,' he announced.

'Fine,' she said automatically, 'sweet of him.'

Alastair made a lovely speech. All about the girl who liked Mars bars! How he had given her a cello and how her brother had said that it sounded like a sick cat. And he eulogised, as an old man, whose life is nearly over, can, and drooled over a fresh young woman whose life is just beginning: and he said flattering things about them, her parents, and recounted what outstanding, wonderful people they were. Everybody drank to Ruth, and to 'Mel and Adam', and Ruth hugged and kissed Alastair because she loved him dearly!

When they all resumed their noisy carousing Mel crept up to the telephone in the bedroom, and dialled St Marks. Piers sounded strained and exhausted. He had a splitting headache. Probably the weather, and the worries of the day! He begged forgiveness and said he was going to bed.

'I'm missing you,' she said.

'I know.'

'I love you.'

'I know that, too, Amelie.'

'Take some aspirins!'

'I will,' he said.

The main party continued for an hour or so, and the smaller one, for Ruth and her friends, until three o'clock in the morning. The older generation might just as well have stayed up since the storm, when it broke overhead, prevented anyone from going to sleep.

****

Sunday was a funny day! Mel had warned Adam not to expect their guests to line up to attend a church parade and forbidden him to drop hints to Ruth and her friends. In fact, one of them, a harpist, so Ruth

237

revealed later, crept out of the house early, found the Catholic Church, made her confession and then crawled back into her sleeping bag igloo! This was chastening for Adam, but amused Alastair greatly when they told him over the roast lamb at lunch.

By then, everyone else apart from Hester and Ruth had left. Hester intended to leave soon after lunch and was going to drive Alastair home first. This meant a diversion, but she had jumped at the idea. Adam and Mel hoped Alastair would not be too puzzled by the eccentricities of her driving habits, reminding him that she treated the Triumph as though it were a pet puppy, addressing it as 'Tiggy' and chivvying constantly with, 'Come on Tiggy up this hill, there's a good girl.' Or 'Stop, Tiggy, red light!' Or 'Careful, Tiggy, nasty policeman.'

Diana and Vivien, wanting to get back to town, had left after a late breakfast. They both said how sorry they were not to have met Seb. Ruth decided to spend the rest of the weekend at home and to go back by train. The College term was almost over, but she was going on to a music course in Suffolk and would not be home again until the end of July. Her friends took the cello back, joking, as they laid it carefully in the minibus, that she would not be needing it again after last night! Probably because they knew Adam and Mel so much better than the others, Alastair and Hester had been the easiest and most appreciative of the guests and the four of them were sad when the time came to say goodbye. There was a premature ritual of hugging and kissing and sending love to Seb. After which Hester and Adam opted to check Tiggy's tyre pressures, and Ruth offered to clean the windscreen.

'There are an awful lot of squashed flies, Aunt Hester,' she said, 'in spite of the rain!' Hester, on her knees, concentrating on the pressure gauge as Adam manipulated it, declared that 'Tiggy likes flies!'

Alastair drew Mel aside. 'Mel,' he said confidentially, 'there's something I would like you to do, when the time comes...'

'Of course, Alastair. Anything! What is it?'

'That ring I gave you, my dear - when you moved here...'

Mel's heart began to knock against her ribs and the saliva in her mouth dried up.

'Yes,' she said tentatively.

'I would like Ruth to have it. One day. If you understand me.'

Mel tried to behave exactly as she would have done if she hadn't lost it.

'Of course, Alastair. Certainly she will have it. There would never be any question of anything else...'

He looked at her fondly.

'You didn't mind me mentioning it? I know I'm being a silly, sentimental, old fool!'

She squeezed his arm, and helped him back across the courtyard.

'You were quite right to mention it,' she said, 'and I know that Ruth will treasure it as I have done.'

'God bless you, Mel,' he said. 'Towards the end of life one is permitted the occasional whim.'

As they stood round Tiggy, Alastair's gaze fell upon each of them in turn.

'There is an old Nigerian proverb,' he informed, 'which says, 'hold a true friend with both your hands,' and, in the emotional moments that followed, he carried out this instruction to the letter. First with Mel, then with Adam, then with Hester, and finally with Ruth, to whom he also said, 'I am very proud of you, beloved adopted granddaughter!''

There were tears in his bloodshot eyes and, as he eased himself into the car, he bent down, awkwardly, because his arthritic joints were painful. And Hester, who had understood that he had been trying to convey something that mattered to him very much, refrained from warning Tiggy before she started the engine!

As soon as they were out of sight, Adam and Ruth demanded to know the reason for the tete-a-tete with Alastair. Mel fobbed them off by saying that it was just another string of compliments, Alastair style, and they accepted this explanation without demur. Which all went to prove how adept and cunning she had become at knotting together the ravelled ends of her tangled deceit. She began to hate herself; but still, uppermost in her mind, now that she could relax, was a nagging worry about Piers. Apparently he had not been in the abbey that morning at the service attended by Adam, Alastair and Hester, and this was so uncharacteristic that Mel feared for his physical well-being. He had looked well enough at the Fete. The headache must have come on suddenly, and headaches sometimes heralded terrible things, like tumours, or meningitis, or blood-clots. She began to feel sick with anxiety.

Chapter XIV

MISADVENTURE

Mel caught a glimpse of Piers the following morning on her way back from the station after seeing Ruth off. He was disappearing through the side gate of the vicarage with Tertia, and she concluded that he had just taken the dog out. She heaved a sigh of relief. He was cured! Now that she had seen him, up and about, there was no further need to fret. She could practise restraint and learn to be mistress of her feelings. Days would pass; each one a step nearer to the fulfilment of his promise. She did not want to have to wait too long, although she knew that it was unlikely to be for two or three weeks yet, and certainly not before Seb broke up. It would be good to have him home again; he enlivened the place and was someone to talk to. He would actually be here this time next week; Mel looked forward to it with gentle, maternal pleasure. After the trials and tribulations of the past couple of months, a short period of calm, even equilibrium, might be advantageous. Patience must prevail. Nothing must prejudice the projected visit to Shropshire.

On the following Saturday, Mel and Adam attended the Foundation Day celebrations at Seb's school and after an arduous programme of listening to speeches, applauding prize-winners, watching matches, meeting other overdressed parents and their sons, viewing exhibitions, drinking with the Housemaster, and sitting through another evening of Gilbert and Sullivan ('Ruddigore' this time) they piled his trunk and trappings into the car, strapped the bicycle on to the roof rack and drove back late at night. The majority of parents stayed somewhere near, or drove from home again the following morning, in order to be at the final end of term service in the chapel, but Seb insisted that there was no need for them to prolong the agony. He reckoned they went to enough compulsory services, and they had supported the last four!

So their poetry loving son opted to catch a train the following afternoon. He relished the prospect of a two-month idyll. Lazy days in the garden, driving lessons, quash and tennis. Walks with Piers, visits to friends. He would read masses of books, mow the lawn, and tend the houseplants. He might come to Scotland with them. He liked the idea of Scotland! Or he might go camping. There was plenty of time. He would make up his mind in due course! He had eight, blissful, precious weeks, in which to enjoy himself.

He slept for most of the first day of the holidays but was up on time on the second and drifted in late for a bite of lunch when Mel was alone in the kitchen, peeling herself an apple.

'Bread and cheese on the side, Seb,' she said, indicating the worktop.

He piled his plate with bread, cheese, tomato and pickles and collected a can of chilled lager.

'Been out?' asked Mel.

'Seeing Tim,' he replied, 'and that crazy new bike of his!'

'Motorbike?'

'Yep! Lethal! He'll kill himself on it - especially if he's got his girlfriend behind him, tickling his ribs.'

'He's too bound up with her,' Mel stated. 'Mary's very worried. He never does any work!'

He chewed, thoughtfully, and then pronounced, 'When they get it, they get it badly, Mum. You see chaps at school going potty over girls.'

'You're not one of them, then,' she teased. 'Casanova Ellis!'

He grinned.

'Not yet! Too time-consuming! Tim is going up to see this girl for a couple of days. Thinks he'll be back on Thursday evening, so we might do things on Friday. If he gets back on Thursday, he's going to let me know.'

He ambled over to the fruit bowl and selected a banana. It was a pleasure to watch the lithe, easy movements of his body and there was a film star quality about the sensitive moulding of his features. Why had she not been able to visualise that this was how he would look at seventeen when he lay, baby-bound, in his pram, under the Amsworth trees. It should have been obvious!

'I called on Piers, too,' he said suddenly. 'But he's gone away!'

This was a surprise. Certainly Piers had kept a low profile since the Festival, but once Mel had been reassured about the state of his health she had managed to control her passion. Now her thought processes accelerated. Surely he would not go away without telling her!

'I saw that bossy-boots Ma B,' he continued. 'She gave me a pile of books.'

'Where has he gone?' asked Mel. It really would be unforgivable if he was with Monty!

'Don't know. She just said he'd gone. One of his trips, I suppose. We've never known the answer, have we, about where he goes?'

Now Mel's thoughts were out of control, like marbles catapulted on to a bagatelle board, and the more uncertain she became, the more convinced she was that he had let her down. Here she was, waiting to see Monty, a passport from Adam in her hand, and he had dared to ignore her. It really was the limit. Certainly it would have been difficult for her to accompany him this week, with Seb only just back, but, even so, he could have explained. She reached the speedy conclusion that Piers had failed her. It was tantamount to infidelity! Impulsively, because Seb had brought up the subject and presented a tailor-made opening, and because she could never tell him in the future, if she did not do so now, Mel rushed into telling him the truth. It was probably stupid but Piers deserved it!

'Actually, darling,' she said slowly, 'he has told us where he goes. He has let us into the secret at last!'

She recounted the story of Monty. Not, of course, with the precise details of that original, lengthy, dramatic, confession, but, quickly, concisely, and clearly so that Seb could digest the basic facts. A childish revenge for her bruised vanity!

'So there you are,' she concluded. 'Uncle P's guilty secret exposed at last!'

He fiddled with a coffee spoon. 'Quite a tale,' he remarked. 'There must be a moral somewhere.'

'You don't need to look far for a moral, Seb.'

'Something like, 'look before you leap,'', he suggested.

'That would do!'

He took a battered packet of cigarettes from the back pocket of his jeans, and lit up. Yet again Mel hoped he wasn't inhaling!

'I'm going with Piers sometime,' she said, casually, 'to see Monty. Later in the holidays. So that I know the form and can take Dad when we go to Scotland. You, too, if you come with us.'

'But is there any point, Mum?' he asked. 'If the chap's a cabbage, what good will it do?'

'Probably it won't do Monty any good at all,' she replied, 'but it's support for Piers. It seems the least we can do. He's carried the burden single-handed for so long.'

Mel had become such an expert in the art of deception, that, for a few moments after he had left the kitchen, she was deluded into believing that her reasons for going to see Monty were entirely honourable.

****

'He's back,' Seb announced, a couple of days later. 'I've had a note from him!'

Mel was sitting at her desk dealing with invitations and bills.

'A note?' she queried. (Why on earth hadn't he called or telephoned? He didn't normally write notes to Seb.)

'Ma B. dropped it in,' he revealed. 'I saw her in the courtyard.'

'What does it say?'

He handed it over, inviting his mother to read it. She unfolded it. The last note which Miss Biddle had delivered for Piers lay hidden beneath a pile of papers in one of the desk drawers. This one, direct and to the point, lacked the eloquence of the earlier example.

'Free on Friday.' it read. 'Any good for a day out with the war poets? Hope you can make it. P.'

Mel gave it back to him. 'Aren't you going out with Tim on Friday?'

'Only if he's back. I'll ring Piers and tell him I'll go if I don't hear from Tim.'

'Isn't that leaving it a bit late?'

'It won't make any difference to Piers, Mum. We're not arranging to go to Buckingham Palace.'

He slouched off, whistling happily. 'I'll mow the lawn,' he shouted.

Mel sat at her desk and gazed into space. Piers must be avoiding her. No other interpretation was possible. If he was back, and could write a

243

note, and give it to Ma B. to bring round, then he could come himself. Or telephone. What was he playing at? She was sorely tempted to phone up and demand an explanation. Apart from that brief glimpse, over a week ago, she hadn't seen him since the Festival. Did he really have a headache on the night of the concert, or was it merely an excuse not to come to the party? Why had he suddenly started to behave as though she had some infectious disease? How could he? After what had happened...? And his promise? What about that? He always kept his promises....Since he had taken to communicating by note, she would do likewise; she would compose one now. Then it would be ready. Seb could give it to him personally on Friday, or, alternatively, deliver it to St Marks before he went out with Tim. Yes! This was her next move. Piers must be brought to account - for his absence - and his actions! No message came from Tim, and Seb came down to breakfast on the Friday morning attired for his day out with Piers. He was wearing a pair of old, patched jeans, a T-shirt advertising the National Trust, and some well-worn trainers.

'You look great, darling,' Mel teased. 'For Buckingham Palace!'

Adam raised his eyes from The Times and peered, inquisitively, over the rims of his glasses.

'Where's he going?' he asked. This was one of Adam's more aggravating habits – appealing to his wife to relay family arrangements. This morning she was prepared to overlook it. Seb was going to see Piers and, hopefully, he would bring back a reply to her rather cryptic note.

'Out with Piers,' she answered. 'And incidentally, I've told Seb about Monty.'

'Oh,' said Adam. 'Was that wise?'

Seb looked faintly amused 'Don't worry, Dad,' he reassured, 'I know about these things!'

Adam accepted the veiled rebuke with good humour.

'A profound relief,' he said. 'It is prudent to understand the ways of the birds and the bees.'

Half an hour later Mel had to stand on tiptoe to kiss Seb goodbye and wish him a happy day out. In build, compared to height, he was still more of a boy than a man. The filling out and coarsening would come later, at university. One saw it in other peoples' sons, this irreversible metamorphosis from boyhood to manhood during the post-school years.

'Have a super day,' she said reaching up to peck him on the cheek, 'and give this note to Piers for me. It's to find out when he is going to see Monty; so that I have an idea about dates.'

'OK.,' he said, stuffing it into his trouser pocket. 'Shall I tell him I know about things?'

Mel smiled.

'I've told him in the note.'

'OK. I'll only mention it if he does. It's poetry I want to discuss!'

'Got the books, darling?'

'Yep!' He patted the lumps in the duffel bag hanging nonchalantly from his shoulder. 'And a sweater. And a showerproof top!'

'Off you go then. Give my love to Piers and don't forget the note!'

'I won't,' he said. 'See you.'

He wandered off, amiably, and she blew a kiss after him. He was a peaceable lad and she loved him very much. Today, she envied him, too. She would have liked to be in his shoes, making her way round to St. Marks. She was thankful that Tim had not phoned.

An hour later the phone rang and Adam came to find her. It was Elizabeth, he said, and he couldn't make head or tail of what she was talking about. He was obviously annoyed at what he considered to be an unnecessary interruption while he was dictating to Miss Fellows. Mel hustled Maidie out of the room and lifted the extension receiver.

'Elizabeth,' she said, 'I didn't know you were home.'

'I came yesterday evening,' she explained, 'for a break from night duty and to sort things out ready for the move. Prospective vicars will be knocking on the door any day soon and there's a lot to organise.'

'Your mother told me she's keeping the cottage.'

'Yes, for the present. It makes sense to collect everything we want under one roof and for her to have a base. People have made some kind offers but any alternative solution only postpones the ultimate one and I'm sure this is right. For both of us.'

'Do you think your mother will look for a job?'

'Possibly. Later on.'

'She won't be too isolated? At the cottage?'

'Oh! there are local buses, Mel, and other inhabited cottages nearby.'

She sounded tired and Mel sensed that she was weary of the discussion particularly now that a decision was made.

'Anyway,' she continued, 'I didn't phone you for this. I have a message for Seb. Is he there?'

'I'm afraid not,' Mel replied. 'Can I help?'

'Oh dear! I should have phoned last night. I'm so sorry! The thing is that I met Tim Davidson on the late train. The poor boy had crashed his motorbike, left it at a garage and then had to walk miles across country to pick up the train. He was shaken up, dog tired, and possibly a little shocked......'

'But not hurt, I trust!' interrupted Mel.

'No! I don't think so but I did feel sorry for him and when he mentioned that he had promised to phone Seb when he got home, about some arrangement for today, I offered to do it for him. Actually, the message was that he would be able to play tennis this afternoon.'

'I'm afraid you've missed him, Elizabeth, he's out for the day.' Thank goodness she *had* forgotten, thought Mel, but Elizabeth's next remark unnerved her.

'The thing is that when I arrived home Piers was there talking to mother. I'm afraid it went clean out of my head.'

So, thought Mel, he could call at the vicarage but only post notes to the Tower House! Never mind, so far as Elizabeth was concerned, she had an ace up her sleeve!

'Actually Seb is out with Piers. They've gone on one of their poetic walks.'

'Ah!' said Elizabeth, 'that accounts for him being so keen to take Tertia for the day. I didn't realise he was going with Seb.'

'They'll like having the dog' said Mel generously.

'Piers is going to have her permanently, Mel.' (What a bore thought Mel. Would Tertia have to go with them to Shropshire?)

'Well, she'll have a good home,' offered Mel brightly.

'Yes. Lucky Tertia!' (Elizabeth's voice had gone dull and Mel knew exactly what she was thinking) 'I do apologise,' she reiterated, 'I hope no harm has been done.'

'None at all,' reassured Mel. 'Tim and Seb will have plenty of opportunities to play tennis. I'll phone him and explain.'

'Shall I do it, as I forgot?'

'No, I will.'

They said goodbye to each other and Mel dialled the Davidson's number straight away. Tim was still in bed! Mel explained to Mary what had happened and commiserated over the motorbike catastrophe. Seb would get in touch with Tim when he got back, she said, either that evening or the following day.

What a business it all was, thought Mel, as she wandered through to Backs View. However, she was not sorry that Elizabeth had forgotten because by now her beloved Piers might have read the note!

****

Late in the afternoon, Miss Fellows came to look for Mel in the garden. She was trembling, and barely coherent.

'Your husband... Mrs Ellis,' she stammered. 'Can you come to him...'

Mel dropped her weeding fork and rushed into the house. Adam appeared to have collapsed at his desk while speaking on the phone. The receiver was off the hook and the dialling tone was buzzing continuously.

'Adam,' screamed Mel. 'What is it? Adam! Adam!'

She shook him hard. Had he had a coronary? Or a stroke? What should she do?

'Adam!' He was moving. Thank God. He managed to raise his head. His face, which was the colour of the clean ivory blotting paper which Mel had slipped into the blotter only the previous day, looked crushed – as though a heavy weight had fallen on it. He was crying!

Words – terrifying words – jerked from his mouth, between great heaving sobs...

'Be brave, Mel,' he said. 'Be brave... my darling... there's been an accident...'

(Piers! No – please, no!..Please no!)

'Seb,' he whispered. 'Seb! He's fallen over a cliff...'

Everything went dark. Dark all over. She thought the world was ending.

****

When Adam, or Hannah, or Ruth, or Maidie, told her the day, or the date, she knew that time was passing. They talked about her as though she was not there. She heard their voices: 'Is she any better?' 'Has she

247

eaten anything?' 'She's losing a terrible lot of weight!' They whispered together, outside doors, these caring conspirators, because they were concerned that she should come to life again. But she hoped she was dead. If this was death, it was more dreadful than anything for which one could prepare... If there was a hell, then this was it!

Ian came. He gave her tiny pills and counted the pulse beats throbbing in her wrist., His eyes were misty...

Sometimes they sat with her, and sometimes they left her alone. But she wasn't always alone, she mumbled, because sometimes Seb came and stayed with her... and they shook their heads.

She must think of Adam and Ruth, they said. They were coming to terms with it. She looked at them, uncomprehending, and wondered what it was exactly, with which they were 'coming to terms'. And then, a strange, new voice which had taken up residence inside her head repeated the only three words in its language: 'Seb is dead.' 'Seb is dead.' Her son, her wonderful, gentle poet. Graceful as a young colt. Humorous. Friendly. No more than a boy... Misadventure, they said. Misadventure. The verdict of the coroner! Misadventure on a Dorset cliff... with an old friend of the family... and a Labrador.

Headlines in newspapers.

'Tragic Death of Bishop's Son'. 'Teenager Dies'.

The jagged story, pieced together.

'Only a little at a time,' she whispered. 'I can only bear a little at a time.'

'You must eat,' they said.

'What happened?' she gasped. 'Only a little at a time...!'

Only very slowly, a little at a time, can one come to terms with an overwhelming and lasting encounter with death. Gradually, and patiently, Adam gave her the details. They had driven further than usual that morning, seventy miles, or more, to the Dorset coast. They chose to go there because they had not been for a long time and the idea appealed to them. After a bite of lunch, they set out along the coast path with the object of finding somewhere high up, overlooking the sea, where they could lie back and enjoy their poetry books.

They had trekked about a mile when they stopped to have a game with Tertia, a dog's game, played with a stick, which one threw... the dog went mad with excitement and they had a great time. Until, suddenly, Seb saw Piers veering towards the edge of the cliff on his blind side, oblivious of the danger as he threw the stick… and Seb called out, and rushed towards him from behind to steer him away, and Tertia ran full tilt at them both, and somehow Piers swung round and Seb lost his balance, and the heels of his trainers slipped over the edge…

A combination of circumstances as close to being impossible as to be incredible – but that was how it had happened.

Piers ran the mile back to the coastguard station. But other people had seen, and the cliff rescue team brought ropes and a Land Rover quickly, and the lifeboat arrived and sent a dinghy ashore. But in the end it was Air Sea Rescue that coped with him because of his injuries. A helicopter arrived, and winched him tightly and tenderly on board to rush him to hospital, because there was life in him still. But it ebbed away before anyone could do anything more – although there was nothing that they could ever have done.

There was a drive to a hospital, somewhere near the place where it happened. It was necessary for them to go there… but the drive was a part of the darkness.

Piers, too. He was there, somewhere, and Adam was strong enough to stand and talk to him, but Mel was shut up in the darkness. She could not look at him or speak to him. She heard their murmuring, sorrowing voices, as they exchanged words, sometime after that fearful day. She sat there, mute with misery. She hoped that she would wake up soon, that it would be morning, and that the sun would be shining. And she saw Seb, a lovely little boy, standing with Ruth in the study doorway, asking, uncertainly, whether he could ride his bicycle…

And Piers… She thought she heard Piers say something about the bicycle. Now, her son would never ride a bicycle, or anything else, again. Her grief overcame her and she groped her way around the house to be caught by Hannah as she came, stricken and shaking, through another door. Why was she there? Hannah held Mel in her arms and Mel felt Piers brush past them and in a voice, desperate with anguish, she heard him say, 'Oh my Amelie… Forgive me!'

Ruth was there. She should have been on the music course, but she was at home. Hester had brought her, in Tiggy. And Hester's voice came and went with the others. Ruth screamed. She was demented. No one could stop her for a while, until Ian came again. The screams were piercing, and horrifying, and the frenzied phrases, grotesque. It would have been better not to hear them…

'He pushed him!' 'He killed him!' 'Murderer!' 'I hate him, I hate him…'

Adam made her understand, amid this convulsive grief, that she was wrong and that it had been an accident. Her shrieks died away into sobs, and then she was quiet. But her words had torn into Mel's mind and lodged there, along with everything else.

There was a service. The abbey was full of people, many of them from Zeb's school. It was a farewell to Seb. But Seb was there! She saw him standing, smiling, near the pew. He didn't know where to sit. They weren't in their usual seats. No one believed her when she said that he was there. They couldn't see him. But she could.

Letters came. Hundreds of letters. There were too many hours in each day, but she could not answer them. People were very patient with her. They went on trying to help, but she was solitary, and inconsolable. A prisoner of guilt. Hester took Mel home with her for a time, and Hannah drove her to a cottage in Devon for a week, which the parents of a Queens boy had kindly lent. The state of numbness persisted. Heavily sedated at night, she woke weary every morning, crushed by an energy-sapping heaviness. It was the same, wherever she stayed.

They brought Alastair to talk to her and he said all the gentle, good things that Adam had said already… things to do with the love of God…!

Occasionally, Elizabeth wrote sad, stilted letters. She wanted to keep up the pretence that some kind of friendship existed between them. Mel asked herself what part Elizabeth had played in the devastation. She had forgotten to pass on Tim's message, but would Seb have stayed to play tennis? And when, eventually, he had gone with Piers, would not something terrible have happened anyway? Then there was Tertia. What part did she play? She was only there because Felix had died…!

The Davidsons were distraught because they felt that Tim had been too casual about his arrangements, and poor Tim was devastated for a while. But boys of that age have too much going for them to grieve for long, and one day, when Mel met him, she exonerated him. Seb would never have wanted him to be unhappy.

Adam blamed himself for foisting Seb on to Piers when he should have taken a more paternal interest in his hobbies. It was never Adam's fault, in the way that it happened, although there were contributory factors. And in the end, he had the strength to sustain Mel. In the ten days after Seb died, he aged ten years, but his faith kept him strong. It was, for him, the ultimate test, and he had to be seen to have the ability to accept and survive.

They resumed a kind of living.

Ruth recovered. Her nervous energy drove her towards new horizons. She did not spare herself. It was as though she had to avenge her brother's death. She did not speak of him often. She would always believe that Piers destroyed him... Perhaps it was easier for her to accept that way. Slowly and painfully, Mel began to understand it all. The people, events, and warnings fell into a sequence – and once it had all started, at that first dinner at St Marks, there was no stopping it. She remembered the dream, and the dance around that beast; the chain, and the key made of clinker. She recalled the haunting tombstone rhyme and its persecution of her culminating on that day when those grim new letters sat beside the old. She realised that old Mrs Tarrant Jones was issuing her final warning on that day when Mel helped her son to scrub up the memorial. Why had she not understood? Because, however it had come to be written, she now saw that it was a last dire prediction.

'Remember friends, who've now passed by,
As you are now, so once was I.
As I am now, some youth shall be,
Prepared for death. Sandy. Follow me.'

It had only needed another full stop. The youth was Mel's son. He died because he fell from a great height on to a beach. He lay and breathed his last, on the sand. And it was his mother's fault.

For many months Mel refused to see Piers, or to speak his name. In the end, when the spring came, Adam insisted that she must allow him to come. He had something to tell her!

She could not bear to look at him when he came into Backs View.

'I wanted you to be the first to know, Amelie,' he said, gently. 'Diana and I are going to be married in a month's time.'

'Congratulations,' she said.

He leant forward and tried to take her hands, but she drew them away, frightened to touch him.

'You don't quite understand, Amelie. Diana is – was – the girl I knew. Before Monty!'

Mel was speechless.

'It isn't possible,' she said eventually.

'I know. But it's true!'

''A chance in a million. In twenty-five million.'

'Not entirely chance, Amelie. Diana knew that first time she came that she might find me.'

'But she came because her father knew Felix.'

'No Amelie. He didn't! She took the chance to come, when it presented itself, because she knew that I lived here. She was curious to discover my present circumstances. She had never been able to understand why I had jilted her. She pretended about her father.'

'It's unbelievable,' said Mel. 'Presumably you have told her the story of your life.' She was scathing.

'Almost the whole story. Not quite all.'

At last she met his gaze.

'So she came to find *you*,' she said slowly. 'Not because Felix had died.'

He nodded, signifying that she was correct.

'She would have had no excuse to come - if Felix hadn't died!'

'Probably not.'

'And then she would not have found out about you and plotted to come again. For the Festival!'

He was silent.

'Well?' she queried.

'That is when she came to see me,' he said, 'late that afternoon. Before the concert. And that is why I couldn't come to the party. I ran away from facing you...'

'And then you went to see Monty!'

'No, Amelie. I didn't go to see Monty. I went to London to see Diana. To explain. To tell her the truth after all this time. I had made up my mind that I must do so.'

'And then, conveniently, you fell in love with her all over again.' Mel's voice betrayed her bitterness as she made eye contact again.

'Only because you had shown me how to do so,' he said humbly.

There was an arid silence. Finally Mel was the one to break it.

'Between us we murdered Seb,' she said.

'Amelie! Stop! No one murdered Sebastian. It was an accident. My blindness....' He buried his face in his hands.

252

'Then I murdered him,' she said. 'I had enough warnings about what I was doing...'

'That cannot be true, Amelie. You must not look back at paths you should or should not have taken. It is a futile exercise.'

'I have been judged,' she said.

There was another, longer silence. Then he said, 'Can we remain friends, Amelie?'

She had little more to say to him. Her heart was empty of love.

'You are going to marry Diana,' she snapped. 'Make her your friend. Take her to see Monty!'

He stood up. He had tried, and now he was leaving. Mel hoped she would never have to speak to him again.

'The note,' he said, 'I'm sorry you told Sebastian. I would have kept my promise... But in case you are still interested, Monty died at Christmas. Of kidney failure. It was always likely!'

Mel shrugged her shoulders and looked out through the conservatory window.

'I didn't know, she said. 'I'm sorry.'

'I told Adam,' he said, as he went quietly out of the room. 'I told Adam.'

EPILOGUE

One day, several months later, Adam and Mel went to see for themselves where it had happened. They parked the car and walked together, silently, for a mile or so, dipping down gently rolling hillsides and crossing neat, grassy, rivers of green which ended not in waterfalls, but in ribbons of chalk which climbed higher and higher until they were above the seagulls. The landscape bore no resemblance to Mel's preconceived image of menacing cliffs and a sea screaming for blood. She drew closer to Adam who could not bear to lift his head.

'Adam,' she whispered. 'This is a beautiful place... and it was his love of beauty that brought him here.'

He raised his eyes as they stood there together absorbing every detail of Seb's last view of this earth. Away towards Portland, several ships were silhouetted. Behind them, the hills tumbled into each other and, in the distance, hundreds of sheep basked in the sun. Far below, narrow beaches edged a sea studded with sparkling diamonds, and clear, clean, chalk faces rose upwards like giant cuts of cheese. Above and beneath them gulls staged a display of chattering, wheeling prowess which seemed to be for their especial benefit.

He would have looked, and marvelled, as they did now. She could see exactly how it had happened. The blindness; the shouting; the rushing. In her imagination she heard Seb's last petrified cry as he fell, that great fall, knowing, for an instant, that nothing would save him. The seagulls would have seen it all. And afterwards, Tertia would have barked into the silence.

There was a power and serenity in the vista of beauty in that place which seemed to bring them together again.

And because their life had to continue, Mel wanted, finally, to unburden herself.

She plucked up the courage.

'Darling,' she said. 'There is something you should know. I should have told you a long time ago…'

'Then tell me,' Adam quietly encouraged.

'Something happened… when you were in London last summer, before Seb died… I lost something… It was very precious. More precious than I knew… I should not have lost it!'

His face filled with compassion.

'I know Mel,' he said quickly. 'You do not have to tell me. Piers confessed. I know **all** about the day you lost Alastair's ring.'

He gripped her arm with a strength that indicated where she belonged, forever, and they turned to go home.

****

Printed in Great Britain
by Amazon